Praise for The Joy of Funerals

"As Ms. Strauss brings characters into more than one story, she creates an interconnected world of people who sometimes do outlandish things, but they are recognizably human. And despite the book's fascination with that final leap into the great beyond, *The Joy of Funerals* is decidedly about the here and now."

—*The Wall Street Journal*

"Darkly humorous. . . . Reading *The Joy of Funerals* is almost like going through the five stages of grief. You start off in denial because you can't believe these characters are actually doing these things. You progress to horror but then begin to understand and empathize with what these people are going through. Finally . . . you come to some kind of catharsis and acceptance and move on."

—*Los Angeles Times Book Review*

"Alix Strauss provides an intense (and sometimes bizarre) look at how women cope with grief and loss. A collection of short stories that will both captivate and disturb you."

—*Marie Claire*

"The desire for human connection runs throughout Alix Strauss's dark and spirited novel, *The Joy of Funerals*."

—*Vanity Fair*

"Die-hard fans of *Six Feet Under* will go crazy for this kooky collection of short stories about nine women dealing with love and death . . . each tale is so strange and twisted, you can't help but keep turning the pages."

—John Searles, *Cosmopolitan*

"Strauss is a sharp-eyed accountant of the fleeting moments that wound us."

—*Elle*

"A sort of literary *Six Feet Under*, this collection of dark and sometimes surprisingly buoyant stories examines the fascination some people have with death as a way to find love and connection."

—*Glamour*

"This is chick-lit for the melancholy—the dark humor throughout does little to blunt the aching sadness of these women struggling to find their places in the world."

—*Booklist*

"A truly unique, compelling and strangely life-affirming work of literary investigation. The perfect book to get you through the night."

—Rona Jaffe, author of *The Room-Mating Season*

"Don't miss this darkly comic novel about funerals, sex, and loss. Throughout these cleverly interwoven stories, Strauss navigates a taboo subject with wit and style. *The Joy of Funerals* is original and moving."

—Libby Schmais, author of *The Perfect Elizabeth*

"Alix Strauss is a truly gifted writer. *The Joy of Funerals* is a moving, funny, and painfully honest book!"

—Molly Jong-Fast, author of *Normal Girl*

"Death has never been so sexy—or so funny, entertaining, surprising, and, yes, occasionally even sad. Alix Strauss has an enormous talent for bringing characters to life, and for finding the heart and light in even the darkest tale . . . a rollicking read that will make you glad you're alive."

—Pamela Redmond Satran, author of *How Not to Act Old*

"Alix Strauss dares us to admit to ourselves that there is a peculiar kind of comfort born in the wake of a death, a universal communion that serves to remind us that we, in fact, are still alive."

—Cynthia Kaplan, author of *Why I'm Like This*

Thaddeus Watkins

ALIX STRAUSS has been a featured lifestyle and trend writer on national morning and talk shows including ABC, CBS, CNN, and Today. Her articles, which have appeared in the *New York Times, New York Post, Time, Marie Claire, Entertainment Weekly, and Self,* among others, cover a range of topics from trends in beauty, travel, and food to celebrity interviews. She is the author of the award-winning short story collection *The Joy of Funerals* and *Death Becomes Them: Unearthing the Suicides of the Brilliant, the Famous, and the Notorious.* She is also the editor of *Have I Got a Guy for You,* an anthology of mother-coordinated dating horror stories. Her short story, "Shrinking Away," won the David Dornstein Creative Writing Award. She is the recipient of several awards and fellowships. Strauss lectures extensively and has spoken at over 100 events and symposiums. For more information on upcoming projects, recent articles, past events, and book reviews or to view clips of her television appearances, please visit www.alixstrauss.com.

Also by Alix Strauss

Based

Upon

Availability

Alix Strauss

HARPER

NEW YORK • LONDON • TORONTO • SYDNEY

This novel is a work of fiction. Any references to real people, events, establishments, organizations, or locales are intended only to give the fiction a sense of reality and authenticity, and are used fictitiously.

A note from the author: Though I adore the Four Seasons, I have no idea what happens behind closed doors. I would, however, love to live there someday.

FIRST EDITION

Designed by Joy O'Meara

Library of Congress Cataloging-in-Publication data is available upon request.

ISBN 978-0-06-184526-0

10 11 12 13 14   OV/RRD   10 9 8 7 6 5 4 3 2

To M. E.

For being the smartest person I know.

For being right about everything.

And for always being there.

You continuously amaze me.

To Lisa Rosenstein

A better friend would be hard to find.

*The great advantage of a hotel is that
it's a refuge from home life.*

GEORGE BERNARD SHAW

Chapter 1

Morgan

The Four Seasons Hotel

Today is my dead sister's birthday. She would have been thirty-five.

I eye the clock, 11:20 a.m., and phone my mother with the intention of asking if she'd like to have lunch at the hotel so she won't be alone. I barely got through Thanksgiving dinner at their house, and feel as though I've OD'd on my parents rather than turkey and stuffing, but I'm desperate for her to share a Dale story, a memorable moment I've forgotten. I wish we had the type of relationship where we could do that, console each other like war buddies, reach for a hand from across the table, while carefully maneuvering past our wineglasses. I could give her my napkin, watch her dry her eyes. She would pass it back, smile lightly, tell me how much she misses her first child, then add how thankful she is to have another. Just once I'd like her to phone and say, "Your father and I are going to synagogue, and then we'll light a candle at home in memory. I'll make a roast chicken and we can grieve together. If you'd like, we'll pick you up in a cab in a few minutes."

When she answers on the third ring, she sounds irritated. She tells me she's late for a hair appointment, that the cleaners have lost her good dress shirt, which she intended to wear today to some luncheon.

"Women for Women's Rights or women who care about . . . I don't know. I can't recall," she says.

I search for something in her voice, an indication that she remembers, but when I get nothing, reply with silence.

"Morgan, are you still there?"

I am, but I can't find my voice. Can't gulp down enough air into my lungs to say anything.

"Are you smoking?" she asks.

"No."

"Why do you sound so breathless?"

"I was exercising." One lie on my sister's birthday, what's the harm?

"In the apartment? You've got a beautiful gym at the hotel, it's such a perk."

"You and Dad could use it if you wanted," I push out. Even though I'm already at work I don't correct her.

"I couldn't get your father to go down there if you offered a free buffet. Just blocks from his office, you'd think he'd be able to work out once a week . . ." Her voice trails off.

I visualize my parents at the gym, confused by the equipment, scared to take a class. My mother assumes spinning is a cycle on the washing machine, and my father thinks it's when you've had too much to drink. There's a clacking sound coming from her end as she digs around in her makeup drawer, probably looking for a lipstick, Crimson or Dusty Velvet.

As a child, I loved to watch my mother dress for a party or a dinner date. I have vague memories of Dale and I sitting on her bed, studying her reflection in a huge oval mirror that hung above a black lacquered vanity table. Dale had just had her first operation. They'd found a tiny tumor on her spine and after they removed it she had to wear a back brace for six months. Watching my mother change for a party was one of the only activities she could do.

My father, a hand, arm, and shoulder specialist, would often work late, performing surgical procedures, and meet her at the agreed spot: theater, restaurant, supper club. My mother would get dressed with an audience of two. We'd sit with her as she made herself up, watching her apply makeup, aching to blot our lips on tissues, take long, delicate strokes of mascara to make our lashes bold just like hers. Dale would pretend to rub blush onto my cheeks and blend it into my skin. Within minutes, our mother would metamorphose into a beautiful woman. Dark hair cupped her face, dewy skin was clean and lightly dusted with matte powder, her big brown eyes added a youthful appearance. And her lips were full and smudge-proof. She was perfect.

I peer at my reflection now, wondering if my mother and I are sharing this moment, if we're both staring at ourselves at the same time—and if we are, what she sees. Traces of a dead daughter? Cruelty of time? Lasting, positive work from a plastic surgeon or two? I'm about to ask her a question that would require her to look at a calendar, but her line beeps.

"Morgan, I've got another call. I'll talk with you later." She clicks over to someone else leaving me looking at the phone like one of those actors on a soap who's just found out their identical twin sister has slept with their husband. I'm still holding the receiver when a staticky recording of an operator comes on. "If you'd like to make a call, please hang up and dial your number." I want to make another call. I'm just not sure to who.

Instead I hang up the receiver, push back my chair, reach for my navy blazer, my cell phone, my employee card, which I stick into the back pocket of my slacks, do a quick check in the mirror, and pass though the sales office, saying a friendly hello to my co-workers.

Rather than wait for the elevator, I take the stairs. Instead of thinking about Dale, I focus on the clicking of my heels against the shiny stone, the heaviness of my breathing as I strain for air, the idea that a nuclear war could happen and I'm so far underground that I'd be safe—all things that usually calm me, but don't.

Upstairs on the main floor of the Four Seasons Hotel I survey the clean, crisp lobby, take stock of the efficiency of my staff, of the attractive patrons who stay with us, sometimes for a night, others for days.

I walk to the front desk and slide over to the side that's momentarily not in use.

The turnover of our hotel is tremendous. According to the computers, every three minutes and forty-nine seconds someone is either checking in or out. There are three small boxes responsible for imprinting room assignments and security codes to the key cards. Upon checking out, the information is erased and a new number and code is given. When I select the room cards I never glance at the computer, let alone the guest's profile that automatically pops up on the screen when the room key is activated. I like to do this without help.

I close my eyes, run my fingers over the duplicate guest's keys. Like a deck of cards waiting to be fanned out by a magician, I remove one and stick it in the box. 1709 lights up in green. In the six years I've worked here, I've never gotten this room, until today. I've been in 70 percent of the quarters, and I'm as familiar with each line as I am with my own apartment. I know which has the best layout, the grandest view, the largest bathroom, the nicest closets. That the corner rooms are twenty-five square feet larger than the regular ones. That the water pressure in suite 2510 will never be as powerful as the others, no matter how many times we try to fix it. That Oprah will only stay in the Presidential Suite, and that the housekeeping once found a wad of cum on the wall in room 615.

I take the elevator up with an attractive Japanese couple who are decked out in Gucci. I bow my head as I exit, then utter good-bye in Japanese. They smile politely, returning the bow as the closing doors disconnect us.

The floor is quiet, deserted. Not surprising since 11:40 a.m. isn't a heavily trafficked time. Three or four hours earlier, the hallway was active with men in crisp white shirts and expensive ties, newspapers tucked under their arms, cell phones already attached to their ears. The women dress in smart pantsuits or good-girl skirts and pull boxy, black suitcases on wheels. Then there are the young, pretty ones who wear jeans and V-neck sweaters. Sunglasses hide their faces, baseball hats cover their heads, underwear is tucked in a pocket of their coats or hidden safely away in their Prada handbags. Those who want to sleep in never can because the slamming of doors pulled harshly by the fire-friendly hinges is endless. But now, all is quiet.

I knock on door 1709 and wait for an answer. When another knock produces no response I slide my passkey easily, professionally, into the opening. I announce myself, hand on the door, body half in, half still in the hall. "Housekeeping," I say. Lie two—okay, two fibs on Dale's birthday.

Nothing.

I glide in and stand in the entranceway, close my eyes, tilt my head slightly to the right and catch the light aroma of . . . lily. A woman is staying here. The fragrance is mature, yet fresh.

I scan the area. Some people leave their room in a disgraceful mess. Liquor bottles and half-eaten eight-dollar candy bars or potato chip bags sit open, haphazardly placed wherever the guest felt like leaving them. Some abandon empty soda cans overnight so that the sticky rims have left marks on the leather blotters or glass tables. Leftovers from dinner reside on the floor by the door, uncovered and picked over. Towels are discarded on the bathroom tile or tossed carelessly on the beds, the wetness seeping through the sheets. Not this woman. Though housekeeping hasn't been here yet, you can tell by the way she's left the room that she's respectfully tidy. Even her shopping bags from Bergdorf, Dior, and Ferragamo are stacked neatly on the chair by the couch.

In the closet closest to the door is a stylish duffel bag, which is free of flight check-in tickets or stickers. It's too large to fit under the seat of an airplane, but small enough to carry without struggling, and would fit comfortably on a train or in the back of a car.

I check the mini refrigerator and bar to see what's been consumed. Everything is untouched. I don't need to look at the price card and, like a game show contestant on an upscale version of *Lifestyles of the Rich and Unhappy*, can announce the cost of each child-size item. I close the bar door and inspect the desk area. The leather-bound directory, blot board, notepad, stationery, in-room service listing, and menu all seem undisturbed.

I enter the bedroom, noticing that the pillows have been aligned and placed up against the headboard, the comforter and sheet pulled up and smoothed out.

The bathroom is clean, used towels folded neatly over the tub. On the vanity table sit three small LV bags. The first is filled with enough Chanel makeup to impress the salespeople at Barneys. I apply some blush, Warm Mocha, with the enclosed brush, then spray some of her Jessica McClintock perfume on my wrist.

Another bag holds a set of Chanel travel-size bottles: toner, face cleanser, eye cream, moisturizer, and anti-aging serum. I save the best part for last. The third bag is filled with personal items: toothbrush, toothpaste, eyedrops, and a bottle of pills. I love the sight of a punched-out *V* or *K*. A few small tablets of lavender or yellow or white pills—mood enhancers, elevators and downers, painkillers and relaxants—all in similar small see-through rusty-colored plastic bottles with white tops. *Valley of the Dolls* anyone? I read the recommended dose, then see if I know the name of the doctor or patient. Her medication selection is disappointing. There's only one type of pill inside, and the bottle of Xanax belongs to Ben Theron. Her husband?

Lover? I reach for a glass, fill it with water, wash down one of Mr. Theron's pills, which I'm hoping will help me relax, then wipe the glass clean and replace it in its original spot.

Back in the bedroom, I open another closet, several pairs of pants hang motionless next to a navy jacket. The first dresser drawer has a sweatshirt and matching pants, control top underwear, and T-shirts. The next drawer reveals three silk shirts. I touch the cream-colored one, then remove it from its resting spot. It smells like her perfume. I twirl in front of the mirror, the silk shirt held up to my chest, until I feel dizzy. I fall back onto on the bed, her shirt draped over me like a shadow.

I tally up the information: Chanel products are too mature for most women in their thirties. The shopping bags are from sophisticated, high-end neighborhood stores. The clothing has a mature feel, too. On the nightstand is this month's *Town & Country* and *Vogue* along with a Discman and several CDs. Anyone in their twenties or thirties would own an iPod or MP3 player. People who bring their own music selections are usually seasoned travelers who spend more time in hotels, airports, and train stations than at the office. There's no laptop, so this might be a pleasure trip. She didn't fly here, and she's too chic and product-oriented to live in a small rural place, so my guess is she lives in a large urban city like DC or Boston.

I close my eyes and listen: to the buzz of the florescent light above me, the low murmur from the TV escaping from the next room, the hum of the refrigerator, the annoying ticking of the clock on the desk, the distant zooming noise from the cars outside, the deep, hollow sound of my breathing as I wait for the Xanax to take effect.

Fifteen minutes later I fold the shirt, return it to the drawer, fix the bedspread, and slip out unnoticed.

I watch the ladies parade into the bar of the Four Seasons Hotel, their muffled, yet distinctive voices getting louder. They look like a pack of tourists following a guide, who, unfortunately, in this instance, is my mother, Rose Tierney.

"Morgan, we're here!" Acting as if she's Norma Desmond descending the staircase, my mother signals to me from across the room.

She's both breathtaking and distancing. A-list in the looks department, Wicked Witch in the nurturing arena. I want to run to her, open armed, ready for her embrace, and I want to run away as the reality sets in that she will never be the person I'd hoped she'd become.

Within seconds I'm accosted by the smell of several flowery and sweet fragrances making me think I've entered a stale perfumery. I glance at my mother's friends, their faces already embroidered in my memory. They're as familiar to me as the conversations that take place in the hotel's lounge every Wednesday either before or after they've played bridge at the club next door. Somehow Midtown Manhattan's Four Seasons has become a halfway house for wayward Upper East Siders.

I smile like a good daughter and fall, rather slip, easily into the role I'm expected to play. I excel at this. My whole family does. By thirty-two, I had assumed a curtain would have dropped, followed by several adoring minutes of applause, and an award would have arrived on my doorstep: Best Acting in a Family Drama. But it didn't, and the ovation hasn't started, and from what I can tell, intermission isn't coming for years.

Usually I can find a way to escape, a reason to be MIA. It's a large hotel with over 368 rooms. I could be anywhere: in a budget meeting, speaking with housekeeping, planning a corporate event, showing a room, dealing with a celebrity in crisis. The list of excuses for a general manager of a hotel is endless. But today I've been caught. Today I've been inducted, or abducted, into my mother's ritual tea hour.

It takes several minutes for them to settle in. Shopping bags are stacked noisily on the unoccupied banquette, recently completed bridge scorecards are removed from pockets and purses, fur coats, hats, and wool scarves are draped over the backs of the mahogany chairs. The sound of the wooden legs scraping against marble floor, the snap of white cloth napkins, of water being poured into glasses, of bangle bracelets clinking and scratching against the fine china plates all seem to converge. It's a musical ballet, rhythmic and smooth. Dramatic and entertaining.

The only way to tell my mother's friends apart is by their drink orders: White or Red Wine, Cosmo, Martini, Gin & Tonic.

"The food is good here," White Wine says.

"Yes, the food *is* good here," agrees Martini.

"Marvelous," announces Cosmo.

"I just love it," my mother contributes, winking at me before taking a swig of watered-down scotch. "And having a child who runs the show doesn't hurt either."

"I tell Robert he can't take me anywhere else for my birthday, it's always here."

"I know," says Red Wine, slapping the top of the table. "I love high tea. It's absolutely charming."

"Best in New York."

"And there's so much food."

I watch them eye the traditional three-tier holders. Two have been set in the middle of the table, each filled with warm berry scones and mini lemon poppy seed muffins, egg, tuna, and cucumber finger sandwiches, quarter-size salmon and cream cheese on toasted brioche, cookies, and coconut macaroons. As they reach for the snacks, rings on appropriate fingers, a rainbow of nail colors flashes. What the hell am I doing here?

"I wouldn't dare eat this by myself," continues Gin & Tonic.

"Nor I."

It's bad Mamet no matter how you look at it.

"You know, honey"—my mother says, leaning forward, her hand shooting toward my head—"you could really use a shaping. And perhaps some fresh highlights. You're looking a tad dull."

As I attempt to dodge the oncoming fingers, they somehow arrive at my ear and push thick, blondish-brown strands of hair behind it. My quick head jerk surprises her, and I can't tell if she's embarrassed or hurt. She pulls her hand back, and as she does, her ring gets caught. There's a slight tug, the momentary throb of pain, the holding still while she tries to untangle her wedding band. White Wine and Cosmo attempt to help, but only make things worse.

If I don't break free, if I don't get myself out of here, I swear to God my head will explode.

A sharp yank releases both of us, and I excuse myself from the table stating I need to check tonight's reservations. The *New York Times* food editor is supposed to be having dinner here. This causes a collective "Ohhhh" from the group, which fades as I head deeper into the restaurant and push through the swinging doors that open into the kitchen. Moist heat hits me like a humid summer day. The banging of pots, the steam from the scorching water, and the wet heat from the dishwashers is overwhelming. The chef is yelling while slamming down a bowl. There's the clanking of plates and glassware. Everything sounds extra loud, and the light is ultrablinding as the bustling culinary area moves to its own rhythm.

My eyes eventually rest on Renaldo, the busboy. He's cute and young and innocent, and he likes me. I know this because he blushes whenever I'm around and always asks if I'd like a muffin or coffee or one of the freshly squeezed juices when I pick up my morning paper and fruit cup.

I slide up to him, whisper into his ear that I need help reaching a jar of jam kept in the dry pantry. Would he lift it down? I pull him by the untied strings of his apron, the universal sign for the end of a shift, and lead him into the back room where the economy-size bottles of condiments and baking ingredients are stored.

He flips on the light and walks directly to the oversize bottle of raspberry preserves. The room is small but well organized. Large plastic containers, bottles, and packages of spices are stacked high on a shelf above a sink and cutting table. On the opposite side are racks and racks of cooking paraphernalia: soy sauce, salad dressings, oil, and vinegar. Cans of teas and jams. On the floor are the supersize boxes of flour, sugar, rice, and wheat.

He's in midreach when I shut the door behind me. He spins around and smiles sheepishly. His skin is tan, his face smooth. His lips look soft, eyelashes full. His cropped black hair has too much gel in it, giving off a bristled appearance. When I dim the light, his face almost glows. I glide over to him, lean in close, and rest a hand on his right shoulder blade. It feels strong and narrow, and I wonder what's going through his mind at this very minute as I do something I've never done before. I don't have one-night stands. I don't have interhotel relationships. I slide my hand down until I reach the belt loops of his pants, place myself up against the cutting board, and kiss him. He tastes salty and smells of olive oil and sweat and a hint of Old Spice, which reminds me of the commercial with the kid and the father who's dressed in a blue turtleneck at Christmas time. A wife and golden retriever are at his side, a sailboat is in the background, and everyone seems enormously happy in a fake sort of way.

At first, Renaldo doesn't return the kiss. He is uncomfortably quiet. Seems frozen and confused, and I must lead him though this, find a place to put his hands on my body.

"It's okay. I want to do this," I whisper into his ear, breathy and warm, like on TV, like in a porn video.

His light brown skin is darker in here, and I can barely make out his facial features. I close my eyes and breathe deeply. I undo my belt, unbutton my slacks, search for his small, calloused hands and place them on my hips, help him feel in the dark for my underwear. I reach for his belt and remember he isn't wearing one. Instead I undo his pants, push them down, hear them drop to the floor, feel the elastic band of his briefs, no, boxers. Renaldo's fingers are lingering at my waist. They seem lost in the lacy fabric and I shove his hands away and take off my underwear for him. Frustration is building inside my chest, like a balloon filling with air, the inner pressure pushing on my ribs.

"Please, it's fine. Really."

There's a stillness, followed by the breathing through nostrils. Then something takes over inside him. Male hormones?

Perhaps it's the understanding that this is actually happening and he becomes all man. He hurriedly undoes my shirt, pulling at the buttons and lifting it up over my head. Then he reaches for my breasts, cups his hands over my bra while brushing his face up against mine.

Yes, I think. *Keep going*, I mentally encourage him. I grasp his face, hold his chin, feel for his cheeks and lips to see if he is smiling. He twists his face to the left and kisses my hand on the palm side. His lips are damp and soft, like moist cotton. He is so gentle, so kind I want to cry.

His body is narrow and slight and it almost feels as if I'm fucking a child. "I swear," I murmur into his ear, "I will never be one of them." He pauses for a moment, tightens his grip, and brings me close to his body. I would rather spend a lifetime alone than become one of those ladies at the table having tea and wearing rings and spending their husbands' money.

When I return to the table, my damp face has been patted dry, hair restyled, makeup reapplied.

"Morgan, what took so long?" my mother asks.

Sweat is running down my back. I'm slightly winded and a little disoriented. I can feel my face contort into a smile. As hard as I try, I can't remove the grin, and I must restrain myself from leaping onto the table shouting, *I just fucked the busboy. I fucked the busboy while you all sat on your asses and ate.*

I take my seat. "I was following up on some reservations. We have a divisions dinner next week . . ."

"There must be a lot of them, you were gone for twenty-five minutes."

"Was I?" I say, head tilted to one side, an innocent expression on my face. "There was a small crisis in the kitchen." I reach for a salmon tea sandwich and a raspberry scone.

My mother turns to Cosmo and Martini. "Who would have thought," she beams.

My mother extends her hand from across the table, rests it on mine. This time I stay still, remind myself not to pull away. "At thirty-two, she's the youngest divisions manager the hotel has ever had. Such responsibility."

"Not too shabby," Martini adds.

The women nod, their recently Botoxed eyebrows not arching, their collagen lips full and pressed into closed smiles.

"I barely see Lindsay. Sony works her like a dog," states Gin & Tonic. "You really have no idea. And James stays at the office sometimes till ten or eleven at night, can you imagine?"

I look at my watch and calculate in my head how long it will take for people to remember my sister. How long until they switch subjects.

It only takes a few moments for the acknowledgment to happen, for memory to register. Red Wine shoots a look to Cosmo who, in turn, nudges Martini, who is quick to add, "Anyway, it's really wonderful. Your mother is very proud."

Everyone nods as a check is placed close to me. My mother starts to reach for the leather billfold, but I arrive at it first. "I got it, Mom."

"Nonsense," the women say at once.

"Really, ladies. Please. My hotel, my pleasure."

"You'll be able to write it off?" Cosmo asks.

"Yes, we don't want you paying for it," White Wine adds. And with that, an outpour of wallets surface: LV and Prada and

Gucci all make an appearance, their accoutrements as signature as their liquor choices. "Really, I'm happy to do it."

My mother is radiant. Now they won't pity her. Sure one of her daughters is dead, but the living one has clearly made up for the loss.

Finally free from my mother and her bridge friends I swing by the party room at 5:10 p.m. to meet with Trish Hemingway, who is already waiting for me.

"I'm sorry, am I late?" I ask, my right hand already extended as I walk over to an attractive, well-dressed woman with long dark hair and soft brown eyes. "I'm Morgan. I'm guessing you're Trish?"

She nods, her brown locks dancing as her head moves up and down. She's pretty in an earthy way. Her tan wool turtleneck, jeans, turquoise ring, and thick silver cuff bracelet remind me of a Ralph Lauren ad.

"So this is the room I was thinking about for you. It holds fiftyish people, and we would handle the catering and . . ."

"It's perfect. Really perfect," she says. "Do you mind if I take a picture or two?"

"No. Go right ahead."

As she snaps away with her camera, the old manual kind, the clicking and fast-forwarding sounds reverberate off the tan, linen-lined walls. And suddenly, something inside me feels both hollow and heavy. I look at Trish, her face partially hidden by the camera and realize there's something strikingly familiar about her.

"I checked over the price sheet you faxed me, and I hate to ask this, but is there any chance in getting a discount or anything, even if I paid in cash?"

She brings the camera down to chest level and looks at me. "Or perhaps you have a neighborhood price? I just bought a gallery space two blocks away from here and if you did have some sort of . . . never mind." She rolls her eyes and shakes her head, her lips curling up in embarrassment. "It was stupid of me to ask. It's just that my life savings is invested in the space, and I took out a loan, and my best friend, well she used to be my best friend, but she's marrying this awful guy and she's lost all this weight and I just wanted to do something nice for her—" She stops short and glances at me, then at the floor. "Really. It was ridiculous for me to ask." She looks back up, her eyes are glassy. Then she snaps my picture. "Sorry. Old habit."

After Trish leaves I head down two flights of stairs, swing open the door that reads SALES AND ADMINISTRATION and take solace in my office. I wonder what Renaldo is doing. I think about sticking a note in his box that says, "Please don't worry. Everything is fine," while trying to see if I'm wearing his scent. It's not on my shirt or in my hair.

I knock on my boss's door, get no answer, and proceed back into my office where I check messages, plan out Tuesday's sales event with the chef, and before I know it it's almost 7:00 p.m.

Before Trish left, she handed me an invitation to her gallery opening. It's a black-and-white photo of an eighth-story window taken from street level. One can just make out a silhouette of a woman pressing her body up against the glass, as if trying to escape. I wonder if it's a self-portrait. Underneath, in bold red letters, it reads FRESH ART GALLERY.

Trish blames her camera obsession on her parents, who are both famous in the art and writing worlds. I've read most of her mother's books, and one of her father's sculptures resides in my parent's home. I trace the figure with the tip of my index finger, and wonder what I'd do if I weren't in the hotel business, if I had star-status parents rather than the Jewish, neurotic, anal-retentive ones I've got. I lean forward and stick the card on my bulletin board. As my eye catches the picture of my sister that sits on my desk, it hits me why Trish looks so familiar.

My parents have only one photo of Dale: a small black-and-white kept in the den among a flock of others. In it, candy is strewn everywhere and plastic pumpkins rest on their sides, haphazardly tossed, their services no longer required until next year. I'm four and dressed as a mouse. Dale, six, is a cat. Our arms are wrapped around each other, and large, toothy smiles spread across our faces. It's a hokey shot, one that exudes happiness. The photo is like a magnet; people are somehow drawn to it. When company comes over to my parents' home for dinner or a night of cards and if they're new friends and don't know about Dale, they often ask who the children are. They pick it up, examine it like it was a report card. They smile, say how sweet. They usually guess I'm the mouse, but look up, perplexed, faces waiting for information on the other child. A cousin? Next-door neighbor? Now my mother hides it. Sticks it in a drawer and takes it out when they leave.

I own the same photo, had it blown it up to fourteen by sixteen. It hangs on my wall in a silver frame and is one of the first objects people see when they enter the apartment. I say hello to it everyday. Living with a ghost is easier than living alone. Other belongings and photos of hers reside in a fireproof box hidden in my hall closet: her first shoes, a stuffed monkey purchased at FAO Schwarz, a T-shirt, a handful of Smurfs, and hair ribbon. My mother doesn't know I have them, and if she does, has blocked it out. The night before the Salvation Army was to come and remove her possessions I went into the back hallway, opened the boxes, rummaged through the large, durable black garbage bags, and, like a burglar, stole them. Each year on the anniversary of her death I rifle through these items. My mother, on the other hand, writes a check to Sloan-Kettering's children's ward and another to the Ronald McDonald House. Though the box smells of metal, it cannot erase the scent of baby powder, gummy bears, Mr. Bubbles, and rubbing alcohol. To this day, I can't touch a drop of liquor that smells medicinal. Can't forget the feel of my sister in my bed during story time, her arm draped over me, my cold feet trying to get warm by touching her calves. The way we would giggle with the lights out. Make shadows and silly finger figures on the wall with our flashlights. The sound of her voice as she uttered "Peanut," the nickname she'd given me.

The last photo taken of Dale is at Disney World. We're standing on either side of Goofy wearing matching mouse-ear hats with our names written on them. Hers covers her bald head. When we came back to New York, she refused to take it off, insisting on wearing it to bed. We'd wake up and find it on the floor, having fallen off sometime during the night. In the photo, she is pale and thin, fragile, but smiling. Though her wheelchair is missing, we still don special bright purple VIP badges that hang down from our chests. In Disney World, no one waits on lines when you have cancer.

Once outside, like magic, a cigarette appears at my lips, and for the first time all day I feel my body let go. It gives in as I listen to the paper burn, as I watch smoke leave my mouth. My mother's been demanding I quit for years.

"Isn't it enough I lost one child?" she routinely asks.

"Lung cancer is completely different than leukemia." Though every headache I have makes me think *brain tumor* in blinking neon. Every yearly checkup brings about waves of anxiety. Every gynecologist appointment where my doctor feels my breasts, I pray silently to God or whoever decides the fate of young women in their early thirties, that I'm too young to die, that the doctor should find nothing. That the soft pads of his fingers should move effortlessly over the mounds on my chest without hesitation or focusing on a small area.

I loathe filling out the contact sheets. Hate the heading FAMILY HISTORY that appears in bold black type. "Cancer, older sister died at eleven from leukemia" are the words that follow in messy blue penmanship. It's a CliffsNotes version. An abbreviation of a life taken too soon. When doctors skim my chart, or ask me to refresh their memory, as soon as I utter "leukemia" they are kinder; their faces become more serious and reserved. Their actions are slower and they linger at my throat, spend more time on my lymph nodes. They palpate under my ears, stay at my glands longer, ask me to swallow, and draw blood.

At home, the clock on the stove reads 7:38 p.m. One hour until I'm to meet Bernard, who is waiting to discuss our moving in together, for dinner at Gobo. We met a year ago on a blind date coordinated by the hotel's chef. We've been on-again, off-again, though lately it's more off than on.

I step into the shower, steam envelops me, the hot water and pretty scented exfoliating soap removes the smell of smoke and sex. It erases my day, washes my mother away as I try to figure out how I can move in with someone named Bernard, Bernie to his friends.

Bernie sounds like a beagle that never comes when you call for him. Bernie is the name of an old man in elastic waistband pants and a golf hat who plays cards with his cronies in Florida. Bernard is not the name of my future. He is, however, a wine aficionado. He writes about it, gives talks, has published books, and works with wineries. He is doctor to the sick grape and the shriveled vine. Bernie will never cheat, doesn't take spur-of-the-moment trips, uses a money clip rather than a wallet, and knows the interest he earns from his 401k. At five foot nine he is five inches taller than I, wears a tie—always—is very corporate, and truly understands hotel and food politics, which is a major plus. My friends adore him, and love when he comes to their parties because of the wines he shares and the vast knowledge he has. He teaches a course at the New School, and young groupies call him from liquor stores in a panic requesting last-minute suggestions. They're in a bind, they want something to impress their date, or their date's parents, or their boss. "What to bring?" they squeak. Bernard never turns his cell phone off, as if he's on a transplant team waiting for a heart or kidney to arrive in a mini cooler. He is dependable, kind, sophisticated, and smart. His parents are lovely, his brother a sweetheart. But he's boring, passionless—unless we're in a museum or wine store. Bernard makes good investments and his shoes are always freshly polished, like his teeth, which he keeps as white as winter snow. He likes his dentist, who he sees every other month for a cleaning. "Wine stains, Morgan, trust me," is his mantra. The four of us have dinner often, Bernard and I, the dentist and his trophy wife. When everyone talks, their teeth glisten, like a toothpaste ad.

"I'm too young for this," I say to no one, wishing Dale were here to give sisterly advice. "He's too much man and not enough boy." In actuality, he's too much man for the woman I have yet to become.

I spot Bernard, who's already seated, as I enter the restaurant, which is tight and crowded and reminds me of the kitchen at work. Flashes of Renaldo appear in my mind and I wonder what he's doing now. I visualize him repeating the story in Spanish to his friends who hoot and clap, pat him on the back and high-five him.

Bernard hasn't caught a glimpse of me yet. He's talking to the hostess, holding a dark bottle, glowing like the proud father of a newborn. If I wanted, I could leave. Slip out unnoticed. My hand is already on the doorknob, cold brass in my grip. I twist the round handle, feel the lock release and the door push open, feel a sudden surge of guilt rise like bile in my throat. A sliver of cold air enters as I exit.

Chapter 2

Morgan

The Executive Offices

I wake to the sound of my own breathing rather than mine matched with Bernard's. There's no arm thrust over my shoulder. No one to fight for bed space. No bad breath I have to worry about masking. Knowing this bathes me in relief. I can move at my own pace, make coffee thick and dark, the way I like. There's no racing against a steam-filling bathroom as I rush to put on makeup in the mirror and Bernard takes his long hot shower. It's just me. And Dale.

The morning concierges, Julia, Cecile, and Anne, are waiting for me at the round table downstairs in the executive offices.

We girls meet once a week to go over management issues and the ever-present feeling that the hotel business is testosterone driven.

I'm running late because I thought I was having an asthma attack this morning. I was getting dressed, and as I bent down to put on my socks and boots, found myself gasping for air. Now I keep trying to yawn, hoping that will help cure the problem, but as soon as I do, I'm back to feeling breathless. Air hungry. My guess is it's suppressed guilt for standing up Bernard. I called his cell from outside the restaurant, explaining I had to work late, that I didn't know if he was already waiting for me, and would he mind if I canceled.

"No problem," he said, his voice void of disappointment or irritation. "I completely understand." He was so nice about the whole thing I found it extremely frustrating.

The sound of Julia's spoon clinking against the china cup is driving me crazy. I put my hand over hers hoping it will bring some silence. She smiles embarrassedly.

"Sorry. Terrible habit, I know. Jason's actually removed the silverware from the kitchen. I've resorted to stirring with the plastic salad tongs his mother gave us."

I watch Anne fiddle with the sugars in the glass container, watch her run her fingers back and forth along the tops, as if she were petting a shag carpet. Cecile clears her throat and Anne removes a blue packet. She hesitates, then puts it back and takes a pink one instead.

"Don't they all taste the same?" Julia asks.

"I think the pink is sweeter," I venture.

"And gives you cancer," Cecile adds, licking her spoon.

We wait while Anne rips the saccharine pouch halfway through the large red musical note, and pours the entire contents into her drink. Then she sticks the ripped piece inside the packet and folds it in half. When Anne stops shifting in her seat and settles down, I start the meeting. As I open my mouth, I see her index finger tap the table, as if she's got a twitch or something, as if she's bored and is anxious for me to start.

I lean forward, "So, with Thanksgiving four days away, I wanted to know if we're prepared. Each guest needs to be aware that a special dinner is available—housekeeping should have received an updated list with this year's holiday room amenities. We need to be concise about which rooms are blocked and which are blown. The turnover is going to be a bitch, so please have half-hourly interactions with housekeeping, catering, and room service—"

"I'm sorry to interrupt, but I was wondering if we can request vacation time," Julia says. "Last year it seemed like the guys got time off before the women. Didn't it?"

Cecile nods. "We were thinking of doing a family thing. Disney World, I guess," she shrugs and rolls her eyes. "Where else do you go when you have kids?"

The photo of Dale in the mouse hat materializes before my eyes. I barely remember the trip. Instead I have bits of memories. Tiny pieces of moments reinforced by the photos in the family album: us in a yellow teacup, our mother in the middle; us in the "it's a small world" ride; a floating ghost from the haunted house. But there are no feelings of these experiences. Just visuals of a sister I no longer have.

The meeting turns into a gabbing session with Julia talking about her problems with Jason, Cecile hating her nanny, and Anne giving us a play-by-play regarding some man named Gage, who she met on the Internet.

"He's an artist who uses objects that he's found on the street and incorporates them into his work," she explains.

"So he goes around the city collecting garbage?" Cecile asks.

"No, not exactly. These are things he finds like bottle caps or metal objects or pieces of discarded picture frames . . . He's very talented . . ."

"And you met him on the Internet?" Julie interjects, trying not to smile.

I can see Anne's face getting red, and her foot starts to tap under the table. I want to tell them about Bernard. About the breathing problem and if they think the two are linked, but talking seems too hard a task at this moment.

As we head upstairs, I hear Anne's tentative, soft voice behind me.

"Morgan, could I talk to you for a second?"

I see Cecile and Julia exchange looks with each other, then with me.

"Sure."

We park ourselves near the Fifty-seventh Street entrance. I scan the enormous lobby, marvel at how the hotel has been transformed since last night into a decorative rustic scene. Branches with moss, red berry clusters, and colored leaves hang down from the ceiling. Green vines with golden yellow and rich brown rosebuds popping out run up and down the eight columns that surround the room. Massive pumpkins rounded to perfection have been purposely placed in several popular spots on the marble floor. Near the front desk station are two baskets, one is filled with packaged chestnuts, a mini silver cracker attached to each, the other has baby-size pumpkins, fresh apples, and brown pears.

Anne is shifting from one foot to the other, antsy and fidgety. She looks like a librarian-in-training. She's what my grandmother would have called "dowdy mousy." For some reason I have a soft spot for her. It makes me want to apply some blush to her cheeks, paint her lips a soft tawny red. Add some life to her face. Help her become the person I think she aches to be. Even though she's only a few inches taller than I, I always feel short standing next to her. She's in high heels, which she doesn't need, and it accentuates her lean, lanky frame. But today she seems especially off. Tired. Her frizzy hair appears extra coarse, her pale skin extra ashen. Her lips are dry and cracking, her eyes are slightly glassy, and her pupils look small. Perhaps there's been a death in her family or someone near to her is ill.

She crosses her arms, wraps them tightly around herself. "I was wondering if anyone found my bracelet. I checked with the front desk this morning but they don't have it." She smiles nervously. "It has a lot of sentimental value. You don't think a guest might have picked it up and hasn't brought it to lost and found yet, do you?"

I try to take a deep breath. "Well, I . . ."

"Perhaps I could slide a personal note under everyone's door. I'd be happy to type a letter explaining the situation, and I'd do it during my lunch break so it wouldn't be on company time."

"I'm pretty sure that's not allowed, and to be honest, it's not my call to make." I finally get a gulp of air, and it must seem like a disinterested sigh to her. "I sent out an e-mail to the staff yesterday, and put a note up on the employee bulletin board so everyone's aware you're missing it."

I hear her mumble something, see her lips twitch ever so slightly, like she's cursing me under her breath.

"I really appreciate your help." She looks at the floor, then back to me, "I just feel really naked without it."

"Of course, I'll let you know the moment I hear something."

She nods and I watch her walk away, her head down, shaking it slightly from side to side.

I remember when Anne came to the hotel four years ago. She showed up in the same army green sweater during the entire week of training. She seemed so uncomfortable during hotel bingo and Four Seasons Jeopardy that I thought she'd never appear for her first day of work. But she did. And four years later it seems like all she cares about is finding a lost bracelet rather than preparing for her annual evaluation.

My chest still hurts from gasping for air. At work I lift my shoulders, try to breathe in like they teach in the yoga classes at the hotel. I attempt to intake air though my nose but it doesn't work. It's not enough. Frustrated I put my hand to my chest, push in, and lean forward onto the front part of my desk. I feel my heart beating fast and when I push in harder I'm finally able to get a deep breath. I make a mental note to see my internist.

In fact, I write this down. Then I play my messages while still in breathing position. I talk to the photo of Dale on my desk, tell her I miss her. Whisper it softly, like a lullaby. I trace her face with my free hand as the woman from the art gallery flashes in my mind. I suddenly need to see her. I suddenly, desperately want to have lunch with Trish Hemingway. I could lie, stating I need her to sign another form I forgot to include last week when she inspected the party room.

I take down Trish's gallery invite and dial the number listed on the back. The machine picks up. "Hi Trish, it's Morgan Tierney from the Four Seasons. I realized I forgot to have you sign one last form. If you want to come by the hotel, we could have a bite of lunch, my treat for the inconvenience. Or if you'd like I could mail you the sheet. Please give a call and let me know what's easiest for you. Many thanks." I leave my number, then spend the next forty minutes creating a phantom form regarding damages and responsibility for hotel property.

As I walk through the lobby, I catch the elevator doors opening, which reveal a well-dressed, but harried man fixing his tie. He stops fidgeting when he sees me. The agitated look is replaced by surprise, which quickly morphs into a pinched half smile.

"Well how's this for timing," he says, walking toward me.

As he leans forward to kiss my cheek, I catch a whiff of perfume, which I know doesn't belong to Faye.

"Was your stay a pleasant one, Dr. Radkin?" I tease.

"Always."

"And how's the book coming?" I ask my uncle Marty.

"Very well," he says, patting his leather briefcase. "I wouldn't be able to do it without you. You know, Faye means well, but she hovers. I can't seem to write a thing in the apartment."

"Perhaps you should see a professional about that," I say, sarcasm dripping from my voice. "Actually, I guess you could just talk to yourself and send a monthly bill to your home."

"It's amazing what you can get done when you're not distracted."

He holds my stare for a moment before looking at his watch. I wait for my uncle to mention Dale, to acknowledge the passing of her birthday. To ask how I'm doing. Offer some helpful words, the kind I suspect he snows his patients with, but realize I don't want anything from this man, a hack of a shrink who fucks his clients in my hotel. It's enough I discount his room. That I keep my mouth shut. That my mother is unaware her only sibling might be more fucked up than the women he sleeps with.

"Will you be having breakfast with us today?" You and your lovely girlfriend/patient, who, I bet, is still upstairs. Who may or may not know that you're married. That your wife is a perfectly lovely woman who I sat across from days ago at the Thanksgiving dinner my mother had catered. That she helped clear the table, brought flowers and dessert, laughed politely at my father's jokes. And how old is this one? What mental illness does she suffer from that you feel you can better cure by sticking your penis in her mouth rather than listening to what she has to say?

"Well, I've got people to see. Problems to listen to." He glances at his watch again. I wince as he kisses me good-bye, while whispering "thanks" in my ear.

Feeling dirty, I enter the employees' bathroom, desperate to wash my hands and cheek, and hear crying coming from one of the stalls. I know it's Anne because of her weirdly distinctive perfume. Clove and sandalwood. "It keeps away negative energy," she once told me. We'd laughed because I'd asked if there was one that did the same for mothers. Now I wonder if she has some to spare.

"Anne is that you?" I bend down to look at the feet and legs of whoever is inside and feel validated when I see the black loafers. There's some sniffling, the sound of a flush, followed by the opening of the stall's metal lock. When Anne appears, her eyes are red, cheeks blotchy. They match the color in her printed flower dress. She steps toward the mirror, her perfume filling the room. Mascara and eyeliner have left a dark crescent under her lower lids so that she looks like a football player.

I'm not supposed to know about her dismissal, so I ask if she's upset about her bracelet. This only causes her to sob harder. Her face becomes distorted, like she's having a stroke, and her shoulders shake. Seeing someone fall apart is frightening. It reminds me of the way my mother looked before she and my father left to go to Dale's funeral. I found her crying hysterically in her room, trying to put on her makeup. Her face was streaked with mascara, like Anne's. Her eyes were bloodshot, she had too much perfume on, her shirt collar was smeared with foundation. She looked like my mother, but not.

I wasn't allowed to attend the funeral. Instead, our neighbor came and took me to the zoo. When I came home, the apartment was too quiet. Dale's hospital bed was gone, and a new mattress and bedspring were in its place. Her belongings had been removed, too. Like Anne. Like Dale. The magician puts the lady into the box, he seals the door, and with a flick of his wrist, a swing of the wand, poof. All gone.

Toward the end of Dale's illness, when she was still at home, an oxygen tank and morphine drip kept close by, I'd place my hand over hers and sometimes sleep with her even though I wasn't supposed to. I reach for Anne's hand now, want to give it a supportive squeeze, and as I do I feel her stiffen.

"It's fine. I'm fine. I just need to get myself—" She stops and turns around. "Today's my last day."

"What?"

"Yes, it's true." She has on her librarian expression now. Everything is stoic and she's speaking matter-of-factly, like a robot trying to get humanized. "You didn't know?"

"We could have drinks or something after work if you'd like. We could invite Julia and . . ."

"That's sweet, but I think I'll just go home." I see her tap the marble slab that separates the sinks from the mirror two times with her index finger. She does it twice more.

"My fingers are always falling asleep," she says, shaking her hands like a doctor flicking off the remaining water after he's cleaned them before an operation. Even though she's closer to the door, she doesn't move toward it, and it's only when I swing it open that she passes through.

"Is there anything I can do?"

"I don't think so, but thanks."

We stand outside the bathroom in silence for a moment.

"I should have known this was coming. It's Tuesday, I forgot to wear brown, and it's the seventeenth, the most unlucky number of the month."

Is she kidding? "That's the reason you were given for being fired?" My father, an avid golfer, used to wear the same ratty old pair of socks on a tournament day. He was the only one who could touch them. They never went in the laundry. Often, we'd find him washing them in the bathroom sink.

"No. It's just, it's hard to explain." She shrugs, looks down at her feet. "It was nice working for you, Morgan."

"It sure was. You'll be missed," I add. Someone calls to me, and as I turn my attention away for a moment, I can already hear Anne walking away.

I'm at the desk station for my weekly fix. Room number 2002 pops up—a winner. This is one of our nicer, larger suites and I proceed to the elevator looking as if I'm off to somewhere very important. I realize as I ride up that I've never had drinks with Anne casually after a shift like I have with other co-workers. I've never seen a photo of her friends or family, never been to her apartment. I don't even know if she owns a dog or if she's a cat person or if she's still seeing that guy she met on the Internet. The artist who finds objects and adds them into his work.

By the time I slide the key into the electronic lock, I'm back to being breathless. I need to quit smoking. Once inside I ritualistically take a moment, scan the room. It has a messy, almost dirty feel to it. Housekeeping has yet to show and the stale odor of what? Not old food but . . . sex. Musty sex. It hangs in the air, as if locked inside. I inspect the living room closely and find two used condoms in the trash can. On the desk is a large white envelope with a hot pink lipstick mark that's been planted smack in the middle. Then, as if the lips are talking, the owner has written "Open Me." The package has not been sealed, and inside are three pamphlets and a note: "Just what the doctor ordered. No prescription necessary." Two Viagra pills tumble out into my palm. I lay them on the desk. They sit there, like large calcium tablets on the dark leather blotter.

The pamphlets are cotton candy pink and the letters *TES* are printed in fire red. Underneath reads: "Please remember that TES was founded by masochists for masochists and only later became an S/M liberation group." Further inspection leads to a list of meetings and a calendar of programs, events, and classes.

The Novice Group, who meet on the first Wednesday of each month, offers an Introduction to the Scene with Ms. Queen. Flogging 101, whatever that is, meets on Tuesdays. Mike Bond and Master Jim teach the Switchables Group on Fridays. "The Power of Spanking," and this is a nice touch, is delivered by Dee God over brunch on Sundays. My personal favorite, a treatment they don't offer at the Four Seasons' spa, and who can blame them, is the bondage class, "Mummification with Michelle." Michelle is a mummification enthusiast, and will discuss and demonstrate the fine art of wrapping. Perhaps we should offer this special service. It could follow shiatsu with Gilda or a stone massage with Troy.

I think of Bernard, at work or perhaps at home, taking a damp cloth and dusting his wine collection. I picture him bent over, pants down, ass revealed to me. A paddle in my hand as I stand behind him ready to swing.

On the other side of the second leaflet is a list of Safe S&M Guidelines, basic terminology, and definitions. The last regards information on something called a Novice Excursion. A dinner and field trip are held once a month for S&M'ers at the Chelsea Gallery Restaurant. I put everything back feeling somewhat normal.

The bedroom is grimy. Sheets are touching the floor, revealing parts of the mattress. Pillows are tossed everywhere and dirty underwear, T-shirts, skimpy red lingerie, and black spandex shorts are on the carpet by the chair.

In the bathroom, I find a bottle of K-Y Jelly and a mini blue vibrator in a travel bag along with more condoms. I run my hands under hot water in the sink, use the soap while wishing I had those plastic gloves actors wear on crime shows like *CSI*.

About to exit, I give the hall closet the once-over. It reveals a jean jacket, down coat, mink scarf, and matching hat. Shit. She's still in the hotel. I glance my watch, 2:45 p.m. Fuck. Having late lunch? High noon tea? Spa treatment? *I need to leave, now.* I'm about to close the door when something shiny catches my eye.

I bend down closer and uncover a weird-looking leather-and-metal contraption that rests on the floor. It looks like the kind of collapsible brace you'd give a person suffering from sclerosis. I pull it out, lift it up. It's solid and feels as though it weighs about a pound. There are two padded, long bars, each about an inch in width and a foot in length that are held together by three sets of black leather straps piped in white stitching. The two lower ones seem to attach via Velcro, the top one, which looks like a collar, has a snap. I take off my suit jacket and slide the contraption onto my body, like a life vest that locks on the side rather than the front. I snap the collar part closed, then seal myself with the other straps, one of which rests under my breasts and another that wraps around my pelvis. I make the middle strap tighter and suddenly feel a tremendous release in my chest. For the first time all day I let out the deepest of sighs. The cool metal bleeds through my T-shirt. I realize if I wasn't wearing any clothing, my breasts would be poking out, perfectly exposed from the design of the unit. The two bars, one pressed up against my front, the other on my back, run from my collarbone to my pelvis where leather and metal meet again. I model in the mirror and smile. I look like a freak, a car accident victim. But I don't care. I can breathe. I feel strong and invincible. I wonder if this is how cops or construction workers feel, grounded by their heavy belts and garb, weighed down by the necessary objects that define them.

I return to the pamphlets again, hoping to find some information on where I can order one of these brace things or a description to tell me what the hell I'm wearing. As I reach for the envelope, the phone rings. I jump, realizing I've been in here too long. I rip off the unit, the sound of Velcro is loud and unpleasant, and instantly I miss the locked-in feeling. I scan the room for a shopping bag, and when I come up empty reach for the extra pillow in the hall closet, take it down, remove the case, and shove the sex thing inside. I take a large towel from the bathroom, drape it over the arm holding the stolen goods, carefully put the pills back inside the envelope, snag the pamphlet with the calendar information, put my jacket back on, and slip out unnoticed.

Back in my office I hide the brace inside a Banana Republic bag and stuff it under my desk. Three more hours to go. I should leave now. Skip the meetings I have with catering and housekeeping. Perhaps I can take a personal day. Hard to Breath Day. I wonder if my boss would permit that.

At home I say hi to Dale's smiling black-and-white face on my wall and remove the brace from the bag. I Windex and Lysol the entire unit. Then I strip down to my underwear and parade around the house. I am Super Metal Girl. I dance around for a few minutes, breasts poking out, metal cold on my skin, leather slightly itching me, and only feel silly when I catch Dale's eyes, as if she's staring in judgment. I remember the brace she wore. Twins more than twenty years later. I slip on one of Bernard's old T-shirts, which he's left here. It fits over the contraption perfectly. I light a candle, dim the lights, say the blessing for the dead, then a little prayer, the brace still on my body. I remove the photo of us from the wall and place it on the faux marble floor in my kitchen.

As a baby, I'm told, whenever I couldn't sleep and would cry nonstop, the only thing that would calm me was the hum our Maytag made. My mother swears she would hold me next to it and stand patiently, waiting for me to be lulled to sleep by its shaking motion and misty heat. I do this now, run an empty cycle. I lean my body up against the metal door, the brace still fitting securely around my body. The gentle vibration feels good on my skin, my insides feel comforted by the heat penetrating through the T-shirt. Within minutes I find myself sitting on the floor. The tile is cold. I curl my legs into myself, bend my head back against the dishwasher. There's an empty plate in front of Dale's photo, a cigarette in my mouth, vodka and soda in my hand, and cold Chinese takeout in front of me.

I then eat dinner with my sister.

Chapter 3

Morgan
The Lobby Lounge

Trish Hemingway calls back and agrees to meet for lunch. The phony responsibility document I've written, which has gotten much praise from my boss after I brought to his attention that we didn't have one and probably should, sits, like me, waiting for her.

At 1:00 p.m. the restaurant is respectably crowded. Bigwigs and power players sit hunched over, inhaling their overpriced steaks and chicken, drinking martinis and highballs. Two A-list celebs are picking at chicken sandwiches, speaking animatedly with their hands. Leisure ladies eat around their salads, talking about nothing. Waiters mill about, collecting plates, distributing new ones, depositing bottles of water, removing empty stout glasses. I look for Renaldo, a glimmer of hope he'll come by the table to say hello. In the year Bernard and I have been together I had never cheated on him, or anyone else for that matter. At thirty-two I'm a good girl. Organized and hardworking. Honest and loyal. Damaged and lonely.

When I see Trish enter the restaurant, I wave, watch her stride toward me dressed in a white T, chocolate suede shirt, and perfectly colored, slightly faded blue jeans.

"Thanks for coming," I say. I wait for her to sit before taking out the form. "I feel like a complete idiot. I'm so sorry."

"Forget about it." She pulls out a silver pen from her leather messenger bag, signs the paper, and hands it back. "This is really great of you. It's been forever since I've had lunch here."

I stare at Trish looking for traces of Dale in her dark ringlets, her soft brown eyes, her cautious smile. I've brought the dilapidated copy of her mother's book *Drowning in Ambiguity*, which I read in college, with me. If lunch goes well, I thought I'd ask if her mother would sign it.

"Order anything you want. Whatever looks good to you," I say, her face slightly covered by the oversize brown menu.

"How's the fruit platter?"

"It's standard, but nice. You can get that and something else, too."

"No, that sounds perfect." She closes the menu. "I'm on this diet thing."

I lift an eyebrow. "Why?"

"I've gained some weight." She rolls her eyes.

I imagine Dale and I having a similar conversation. Maybe she'd be married by now. Her husband a TV director or a doctor, like my father, might have made a weight comment and she'd have come here, worked out at the gym after her desk job as a book editor, and I would have told her, "You're not fat," like I do now with Trish.

"I feel fat," she says, sighing.

I nod understandingly.

We talk about the gallery, artists, her friend Olive, the party she's throwing for her. The conversation is smart and real, quick and interesting, and wakes me from what feels like a thick fog.

When Renaldo bends down to set our plates in front of us, I want to touch his tan hand, remember what his skin feels like on mine. He is careful and moves hesitantly, not looking at me, but he's smiling, shyly, to himself.

"Thank you," I say.

He nods. "You're welcome."

We walk outside, a reenactment of our first meeting a few weeks ago.

I remove a cigarette from my pocket. Trish stares at me, a smirk on her face.

"I know. I know. I'm quitting on New Year's. I've got thirty-one days left." I pull out a book of matches from the hotel. "Not that I'm counting," I add, watching the light catch flame, then attach itself to the thin, white paper.

"No, I was wondering if you had another."

"Gladly."

Rather than exchange handshakes, this time we happily share a smoke, the unspoken gesture of a new friendship sealed by bad-girl behavior. I cup my hands around Trish's face, protecting her from the wind so she can light her cigarette easily. We shiver in the inlet of the hotel as I watch smoke come out of our mouths. We look like high school kids afraid of getting caught. I nudge her with my elbow, my hands in my pocket, and we walk up the block. "No one at work knows I smoke. It's unprofessional looking."

"It's an old habit for me. Not a pretty one. It's either returning to this or eating. Somehow cancer wins over fat every time."

We tap cigarettes, as if we're fencing with miniature swords. She's unaware of Dale, and I think about telling her this now not knowing how she'll react. I take a quasi-deep breath. "My sister died of leukemia when I was eight."

Trish freezes in mid-drawl.

"It's okay. I thought the cancer thing was funny. I'm not sensitive about it." I raise my cigarette to help punctuate my statement. "I'm also not terribly concerned about my health."

"How old was . . ."

"Eleven."

She does the math. "So she'd be . . ."

"Thirty-five, same as you, right?"

She nods and blows a stream of gray smoke out of the right side of her mouth, then puts a firm hand on my upper arm. She squeezes hard enough to so I can feel her fingers through my wool jacket. Her eyes are piercingly tense and focused. "That must have been awful."

For a moment, I stop breathing. I feel the cigarette drop from my hand, but I don't see it fall to the ground because I'm staring at Trish, who seems too real in this minute. So sincere that I don't know what to do. People always say the stupidest things, their voices drop an octave or two or they whisper the words, "I'm sorry." Then they change the subject.

"You must miss her terribly," she adds.

My head is pounding and something moves inside me, deep and painful. A bit of poison escaping from a sealed sack. "I do." I could stay like this all winter in the icy air, just me and Trish, a pack of cigarettes, and her hand squeezing my arm.

She lets go and we walk together in silence to the corner of Fifth Avenue and Fifty-eighth Street. I want to continue with her one more block to the gallery. See what it looks like. Learn more about Trish Hemingway who understands. Instead, I watch her get swallowed up by the after-lunch office crowd and hassled shoppers, who are all rushing to get somewhere.

I was hoping Bernard would know we were over without my having to tell him. And since he doesn't, I've decided to strike an inner deal with myself. If he goes with me to one of the sex meetings, I'll keep seeing him. Like a sheepdog, he's loyal and always at my side. If only he was more Doberman, more Boxer, things would be different. We wouldn't be sitting at Gobo— again, wine in our glass, pad thai on my plate, vegetarian duck on his. Yes, Bernard is a creature of habit.

"So," he says, bringing the burgundy-filled glass to his lips.

"So," I answer back. I'm suddenly not hungry.

"This is nice," he adds reaching for my hand, which I extend toward him. Both of us coming together, working as a team of two.

"It is." I wish I had the brace on. I wish I was home.

"You've been rather distant lately. Is it Dale?"

"No." With my free hand, I play nervously with my napkin, shredding it into tiny pieces, rolling it between my fingers under the table.

"Something I've done?"

Yes. "No." It's something you are.

"Then what? You're supposed to be moving in with me. Wasn't that the plan?" Bernard shifts in his seat, raises a hand toward his chest, and for a minute, I think he's going to reach into the breast pocket of his blazer and expose his brown leather date book and flip to January fifth, a month away, and point. "See." But instead he adjusts his tie, loosens the knot.

I'm not a business plan, I want to say. *I'm not one of your precious wines that's going to mature the longer you hold on to it.*

We sit quietly, listening to people eat, to the clinking of dishes and silverware. We hear broken bits of conversations from nearby tables.

"I need more spice," I'm finally able to articulate.

He looks up slightly concerned. "That's weird. My food is fine. Here, taste." He scoops up a forkful of vegetarian duck, and moves it in my direction. The fork is too close to my mouth not to accept, so I open obediently.

"I meant with us," I try again, mouth full of food. "I want more life in our relationship."

I reach for my water wishing I had a cosmo, something instead of the red wine Bernard brought. He looks perplexed. I'm dating Mike Brady, Richie Cunningham. I dig into my bag, feel Trish's mother's book still inside, then pull out the stolen pamphlet and slide it over to Bernard's side of the table, like a drug transaction. He inspects the folded pink paper, then breaks into a hearty laugh.

"You had me going for a moment. I really thought you were serious." He crumples up the paper into a tiny pink ball, then reaches for his wine and drinks. "Well done," he says setting it back down. "An S&M club. Very rich."

Bernard talks like a poorly written British TV show. He pours more wine into his empty glass, then goes for mine. I place my hand over the rim. He's still laughing and only stops when he notices I'm not.

"Morgan, you can't possibly be serious." He lowers his voice a little, then buttons his suit jacket.

"I need something more. I need us to be more."

"A lot of people think I'm plenty." He's sitting upright now, posture in perfect position, as if he's interviewing for a job. Fighting to keep an account.

"I'm asking you to try something new. If you hate it, at least you can say you gave it a fair chance."

"What's wrong with the things we do? We go out all the time. Why is it that's never enough for you?" A whimper has crept into his voice, followed by frustration. "I know plenty of girls who would be happy with art galleries and wine tasting and . . ."

"I don't even like wine."

Shock registers across his face. "Yes you do."

"No, you like wine. I go with you because you do. And now I'm asking you to do something for me. For us. I've tried it." The lie flows easily from my mouth, surprising even me. "It was interesting."

"You've already gone?"

"I went to a meeting last week."

"Places like that are riddled with disease and God knows

what." He's looking at me as if he doesn't know the person sitting across from him. Then he glances at his fork, the one that was in my mouth, then his. I can tell he's thinking it's now contaminated. He's wishing he had mouthwash in his briefcase, a disinfectant wipe in his pocket.

"Why did you go? Is our sex life that terrible?"

"We don't have a sex life." Sex with Bernard is like trying to build a campfire. There's lots of preparation, correct positioning of body parts—his legs are like sticks—the waiting for things to get smoking, the anticipation of a spark. But once it comes it rarely catches on or builds into something hot and roaring.

"I'd like to experience something other than fermented grapes." *Can we get the bill?* I'm done eating, clearly he is, too. As if reading my mind he pushes his plate away from him. I do the same.

"What would your parents say?"

"I'm an adult. They have no say."

He's quiet for a moment. I put my hand to my chest, lean up against the table's edge, think about breathing, about my sister, about Trish, the book in my bag, the fact that Anne has lost her job, that she's probably sitting home by herself crying and feeling lost. "I don't think we should see each other anymore." There, I've said it.

"Because of this?"

"It's more than just the sex thing."

"I'm trying to understand . . ."

"I know. I'm sorry." I toss what's left of my shredded napkin onto my plate. As I get up I hit the table, almost knocking the wine bottle over. Bernard reaches for it, rather than for me.

"I'll pack up your belongings and leave them with my doorman."

"So that's it?" he says.

I nod, choke back the tears.

"What about your stuff?"

I look at him blankly. "I don't have anything at your place." I shake my head. "Didn't you ever wonder why that was?"

"I don't know. I figured when you moved in . . ."

I bend forward, like Renaldo did when he cleared my plate earlier today, and kiss my now ex-boyfriend on the cheek. I'm not sure why I'm doing this. I don't have a desire to touch him, but I feel as though I need to leave him with something. When I stand back up I see I've left a lipstick print on his skin, like the mark from the envelope left in room 2002. I'm tempted to pull out an eyeliner and draw the bubble quote with the word "good-bye" inside. Instead I stride out of the restaurant and hail the first cab I see.

Back in my apartment I strip down naked, put on the brace, and stand in front of the mirror. I look strong and powerful. My collarbones look sharp and seem to jut out from my neck and shoulders. My breasts are firm, legs long. I look great!

Fuck him. I'll go myself.

The pamphlet says the TES-TiNG group is for adults under thirty-five who are interested in S&M and who are looking for a safe space in which to explore, discuss, and understand what we do, why we do it, and how to do it better, more safely, and more creatively. They meet at 10:00 p.m. on the first Wednesday of each month in a basement bar.

The cab drops me off at the corner of Broadway and

Bleecker Street. I stand outside and watch hard-looking people—men in tight pants, leather jackets, and black boots, women with long colored hair, tight spandex or colorful leggings, low-cut shirts, bellies hanging out—walk downstairs and disappear.

I want to go in, but my legs won't venture forward. I reach for my cell phone and think of who I can call to meet me for a drink instead. Most of my friends are married and have completely different lives now. Their area codes have changed. Their number of family members has increased. They have weddings and reunions and events. They have other friends who have children and pets and playdates and school activities. I have only me. And my parents.

More people brush past me and enter the hidden hovel, some hold hands, some enter alone. I think about calling Bernard, telling him I've made a mistake, but I can't seem to make my fingers dial his number. My body is acting on its own. At this moment, I don't exist. And before I know it, my hand flies up, a cab comes screeching over, and my body is inside, my mouth is open, and my voice is telling the driver my home address.

Chapter 4

Morgan

Amenities and Special Programs

With Thanksgiving already a memory, the first week of December flies by too, leaving me to deal with literally the busiest time at the hotel. Yesterday was spent introducing forty-nine journalists to the Ty Warner penthouse on the top floor that costs $35,000 per night. Long-lead magazines and dailies flashed in and out of the groom suite, took photos, asked questions, drank Prosecco, inhaled mini appetizers (courtesy of our new chef), and had an outstretched arm before they even got to the door in the hopes of grasping a goodie bag that contained a press kit, two drink coupons, homemade truffles, and bottle of Bvlgari Eau Parfumée—a ninety-eight dollar value that, when someone rents the suite, is free. This morning I allocated budgets for each department and approved expenditures. Over the next two weeks I'll be reorganizing the staff, doing a tasting of the new menu, reassessing room rates, and deciding which of the managers will be on twenty-four-hour call over the weekends and holidays, myself included. The last thing I want to do is cover for Julia, who's out sick, but I accept the job with the positiveness of a campaigning politician.

I coast through the lobby searching for Ellen Thompson, who has applied for a room renovation/decorating job in the hotel. There isn't one available at the moment. There's only been talk that the hotel might want to create a day care program, one that would be available to guests with children, but it's so preliminary that decisions to move forward wouldn't happen for at least another year. For some reason, Ellen Thompson, who must know someone very high up, has talked her way into a meeting.

Julia has prepped me for her visit, stating that Mrs. Thompson mentioned she was pregnant several times during the conversation. I spot her immediately. Decked out in a long knit coat, two-piece sweater set, drawstring black pants, and comfortable black flats, everything about her, even her face, reads "expecting." A velvet headband holds back her hair, and pearls are wrapped around her neck. A pink folder with her bio, resume, references, and list of offices that she's decorated is under my arm. Stepping toward her I think how perfectly the folder and her cable-knit cardigan match.

"Mrs. Thompson? Hi. I'm Morgan. Welcome."

"You can call me Ellen. I thought I was meeting with . . . what's her name . . ." She looks confused and snaps her fingers a few times as if trying to spark some information. "It's true what they say about retaining facts when you're pregnant."

"No problem. Julia, who was supposed to meet you, is out sick."

"She isn't coming?" I watch her face collapse with disappointment.

"I'm sure the last thing you want is to be around contagious people . . ."

"It's just that we've had several conversations about my decorating work . . ."

"To be honest, Julia would be passing along your information to me anyway, so it's just as well that we're getting the opportunity to meet."

"Oh. Okay. Thanks." Her face brightens again.

"So how far along are you?" I ask as we walk slowly toward the elevator.

"Six and a half months. Or a hundred ninety-three days, but who's counting."

We smile at each other. "You must be very excited."

"It's my first so the whole thing has been really amazing. I've loved every moment. Well, almost every moment. The nausea finally stopped."

The elevator comes and I wait for Ellen to enter first. I eye the large ring on her freshly manicured nails, take stock of her professionally blown hair, her cashmere outfit, and realize that her need for this job isn't financial. It's something else.

"So is creating a baby playroom a new phase for the hotel?" The doors open and Ellen leans forward, taking a large gulp of air as she exits, making me want to follow suit. "Who better to decorate than someone actually going through the experience?"

"Well, nothing is set in stone just yet. It's only an idea we've had. We've just started interviewing . . ."

"So you're looking at other people?" Fear has seeped into her voice.

"We're compiling a list. But you're the first person we've met with. I guess you know someone rather high up on the corporate end . . ."

"My in-laws worked here," she tells me. "In fact, that's how they met. And my husband and I were married here as were his two brothers, so the Four Seasons is more than a special place to us. It has a history."

I nod, push through the door, and reveal a space typically used for meetings.

Her face lights up and her smile widens. "This room is lovely."

She rests a hand on the wall, feels the paper, then knocks a few times, I guess to judge the thickness. She pulls out a tape measure, which she runs from the floor to the ceiling, and retracts it as quickly as it appeared. "I've been a decorator who specializes in redesigning offices and hotels for the past decade, so I do know a lot of people in the industry. A past client knows someone who works here, and they mentioned you might be in need of someone like myself and I guess called on my behalf."

"Oh." I look at my watch.

"I've gone ahead and scribbled some things down," she says, removing a sketchbook from her handbag. "I was thinking bright-colored walls, shelves of educational toys, music instruments, stuffed animals . . . As you can see, there's lots of room for Mommy and Me classes or one-on-ones." She flips to another page. "The room could be divided into ages and stages

. . . This section for cribs and naps, this section for a class—"
She stops, her face winces.

"Are you okay?"

"I just felt her kick."

The sketchbook falls from her hand but neither of us reach for it just yet. Instead, we're still as statues and it's only until I see her relax that I bend down, retrieve it, and hand it to her. I look into her eyes, see something angelic and hopeful, and suddenly, I want to know what it feels like. Want to know what all of my friends—the ones who have gotten married, the ones who've had a ring slipped onto a waiting finger, packed their possessions and moved away, given up the shimmery nightlife for the subdued suburbs and are no longer here, making holidays lonelier, visits scarce, and phone calls almost nonexistent—are feeling.

Before I know it, my hand is outstretched. In slow motion I see it moving toward her stomach as the words flow out of my mouth even though I know it's wrong. You don't ask a guest if you can touch them. But I feel as though we are experiencing this moment together. Witnessing something larger than ourselves.

Ellen unbuttons her coat, raises her pink sweater, and lets me place my hand on her belly, which is warm and taut and round. I wait for something to happen. I hold my breath and concentrate very hard as a moment of loss passes over me: for the husband I don't have, for the grandchild neither my sister nor I have given my mother, for this minute I'm not sharing with Dale. Anger slips in quickly as I feel cheated out of a lifetime that I'll never get with her. I want the sonogram photo on my fridge. I want to pick out baby clothing. I want be the one calling friends on the phone saying, "Both mom and the baby are doing great." I want to be the one planning the shower, holding her hand as Dale's husband says, "Push." But I've been duped out of being the favored aunt. Left behind and left out.

I force a smile at her as I wait and feel nothing. Nothing at all. No kick. No movement.

"Anything?" Her voice is eager, childlike.

"I'm not sure."

As I remove my hand, Ellen places hers over mine and presses it firmly against her. "It's fleeting and only happens for a second or so. But sometimes it comes in pairs," she adds, as if I don't believe her. Her eyes are glassy and I don't want to upset her. "My husband will die if I don't get this job. It would mean the world for me to be working here, like his parents did. It's all the memory he has of them."

I try to take a step back, but she's strong. Forceful. Eyes intense, face now covered in red patches. Her sketchbook is still in my free hand and I don't know what to do.

"Please, I've had two miscarriages. This child is all that's holding my marriage together. Please tell me I've got the job. I can make this room look beautiful. I can create anything you want. If you don't like the sketches I can start over. They're only a few thoughts I had. I'd want your input and I take direction well."

"I'm sure you do. This is really just an informal meet and greet. I'm not the final person who decides this anyway. I'm the first stage in . . ."

"I've wonderful references and if you'd want to see some of the spaces I've redecorated and the looks I've created we can do that. I can take you to all the past jobs I've had. People really like my work."

Her breathing is shallow and rushed. It matches mine. My hand is rising up and down as she spits out short puffs.

"Oh, right there. I felt something," I lie, hoping this will get me free.

"You did?" Her eyes glisten and she releases my hand as a smile returns to her face, spreading like a blossoming flower. "Thank you," she whispers.

I hand her the sketchbook. We leave the room and wait for the elevator in silence and when it finally comes I say I have a meeting and that I'm sure she'll find her way out of the hotel on her own.

"Yes, of course. And many thanks again," she calls, her words getting lost as doors begin to seal her inside.

I take to the stairs. I'm shaky and sad and late for my next appointment.

There are people in this world you expect to run into. People you are prepared to meet accidentally while crossing a certain street, eating at a restaurant you know they frequent, showing up at a wedding where the guest list is endless and the event a free-for-all. Friends from high school, co-workers from old jobs, acquaintances of your parents and ex-boyfriends all fall into these coincidental categories. Yet the predicament is usually embarrassing and you never look as good as you intended. The way you have imagined this scenario happening, playing itself out during late-night insomniac fits, is always different. In your self-created fantasy you look great, are dressed stylishly, and are running terribly late for an important, yet exciting, meeting. In real life, unfortunately, things of this nature never go as planned. This is how I felt last week when I answered the trilling phone on my desk and was asked to hold for Honor Kraus. *The* Honor Kraus. PR icon to rock stars. She can make magazine editors in chief tremble, cause concert promoters to cry.

My interaction with Ellen has left me unsettled, but I push the feelings away and make room for the ones I hope Honor will create. I was cool and calm when I agreed to lunch, to discuss a matter of great importance, which, she said, was too important to tell me on the phone. I wait for her now at our best table in the main dining room, dressed in my best power suit, nervous and uncomfortable.

When a sophisticated, high-fashion-looking woman who appears to be in her midfifties enters, I know it's Honor even though her eyes are shaded by sunglasses, her face hidden by a hat. I observe her swift, efficient movements as she talks to the host, as he escorts her to my table, and as I stand to grasp her hand, matching the strength of her grip.

When she removes her clothing paraphernalia, soft whispers escape from the mouths of guests. It's a sound I often hear when a celebrity enters or is already seated and a guest suddenly notices they're at the next table.

An Hermes belt cinches her thin waist, black high heels show off her long, lean legs. She's wonderfully stylish and ravenously funky at the same time. She could easily be a stand-in for the actress Ann Magnuson, should Ann need a stand-in, and should Honor decide to leave her reign as Queen of Rock 'n' Roll PR.

"Thank you for meeting with me, Morgan."

She sits. So do I. Before the hostess can walk away, Honor orders martinis for both of us.

"I love this hotel." I watch her eye the room, take stock of the decorating changes: the new wallpaper, recently uphol-stered seat coverings, the resurfaced bar. "See that table over there," she motions with her head. "Bowie, Mick, and I had drinks back in seventy-nine. It was an incred—" Her cell rings and as she answers, I, too, pick up my phone and pretend to dial someone. I nod and use my office voice and say good-bye just as Honor clicks her phone shut and looks at me. Mirroring her, I leave the mini unit on the table.

"Sorry. It was an incredible time in the music industry." Her hand moves up and down her thin neck as she plays with her diamond pendant while laughing and tossing her head back Katharine Hepburn style. "My career started here. Every cli-ent I signed was celebrated with drinks. I was a power player before those words meant something."

She removes a pair of tortoiseshell reading glasses from her bag, and browses the menu while telling me about the time she organized a concert for Stevie Nicks, went on a road tour with the Dolls, and when Bowie came to her in the very beginning of his career. "He was a spit of a boy, a wiry nobody with a sketch-book filled with scribble and bits of used napkins all with song lyrics written on them and asked if I would represent him." She wears success like the wash boys in the kitchen wear their cheap cologne—strong and powerful—and I want to reach over from across the table, grab onto her hand, and say, *Please, tell me ev-erything. Tell me all the stories you have. Tell me what I need to know about life and your company and how to further advance my career.*

Eventually she sets the menu down on the table and takes a swig of sparkling water before talking. "I'm sure you're won-dering why I'm here."

"It crossed my mind."

"I got your name from the guy who manages Coldplay. Said you're very professional and extremely organized. He was very impressed with the event you threw for Chris and Gwyneth last May."

I nod.

"I have a favor to ask of you." She leans forward, lowers her husky voice a bit. "I've a client I'd like to stay here for a month or so in one of your suites while she works out a few issues."

Her eyes become very intense and her facial expression turns stonelike. And I know already what she's trying to tell me but can't say. I've seen the best and the worst of it. Celebrities who come here to cheat on their wives or husbands, who use our bathrooms for drug deals, our lobby for their film and TV sets.

"Many stay with us to recoup after a tour, after some cosmetic procedures . . ." My voice trails off. I lean in closer to Honor, smell her expensive perfume. "We can certainly be discreet. We've done this," I pause. "I've done this before."

She nods. "I know."

"I'm assuming we'll remove the items from the minibar and restock it with organic juices and such."

At this Honor nods and smiles, leans back in her chair. An unofficial official deal has been struck. And by the time the waiter appears to take our lunch orders, Honor knows everything will be fine.

Once our drinks are placed in front of us, Honor gives me a CliffsNotes version of Louise, her dear friend and client, who's an old rock star trying to reinvent herself as a clothing/jewelry designer.

"She's already got name recognition and God knows all the other assholes out there are doing it so why not her." She lifts her glass, takes a dainty sip, removes a green olive, and slips it into her mouth.

Louise used to be in a band called Hit Me Harder before going solo, and is rather infamous for hanging out with New York rockers like Debbie Harry, Lou Reed, and Iggy Pop. She was briefly engaged to one of the Eagles, but Honor can't recall which one. When she broke away to cut her own album, she called herself Unlimited Lou, a name taken directly from Aleister Crowley's famous 1922 British novel, *Diary of a Drug Fiend*, which seems fitting since Lou has a nasty little habit with the devil's powders. Like all good musicians it landed her in a lovely room at Betty Ford's. This was followed by a visit to Golden Door, which was followed by a stay at Silver Hill, rehab to the rockers.

"By the time she was clean and sober nobody else was. The post-punk wave had come and gone and the grunge kids were dominating Seattle, DC, and LA, making the New York music scene almost nonexistent," Honor adds.

She spills all this to me in between ordering lunch, talking on her iPhone, checking her BlackBerry, and downing her second martini. Mine sits untouched. The only second I'm on is water.

I already know about Lou. I know about her problems, her music, her love life. Her CDs sit on my shelf, her songs already transferred into my iPod. The poorly written unauthorized biography some failed music critic wrote about her a few years back is on my nightstand. But I let Honor fill me in, let her think she's educating me.

"She doesn't know, yet, so please, until I'm able to—" Honor stops talking as a tall, frantic-looking woman rushes over.

"Sorry, sorry," she says, kissing Honor quickly on the cheek. A wave of cigarette odor mixed with stale beer washes over me. The host trails behind, trying to catch up, not sure if this woman is friend or foe. He raises an eyebrow to me.

"Lou, would dressing up for lunch be too much to ask?" Honor says, looking around the restaurant while handing her a menu. Her drink is almost drained, the two remaining olives sit in shallow liquid.

"A late evening thing last night turned into a late morning thing and I didn't know the Four Seasons was so fucking fancy."

"Well, it is," Honor says in a huff, then introduces us.

Lou arrives for my hand quickly, receptively. I feel the coarseness of her skin, the coolness of her silver rings against my fingers. Rock star quality is written all over her, from the leather jacket to the black T-shirt to the dark jeans, which are teasingly torn at her knee and fraying at the ankles, exposing just the right amount of her clunky black boots. Her lips are painted a deep purple and the color matches her chipped, painted nails. Her wild big brown eyes have a craziness to them, like spinning marbles, and I wonder if she's on something now. Her dry brown hair is long and messy, the exact opposite of Honor's, and I wonder what drew them to each other. What bond keeps them together?

Lou is surprisingly attractive, though weathered. Her voice, as scratchy as Demi Moore's, is as low and gravelly as you'd envision any rock star who's drunk too much bourbon, smoked too many cigarettes, and screeched through too many songs.

I look to Honor and can't yet see the connection. Honor in her leopard Chanel dress. Honor with the Hermes belt, the Gucci watch, the Jimmy Choo shoes. Lou's probably never had a savings account, hasn't paid her taxes in years, and still wears jeans as old as her music career.

"You drinking that?" Lou asks me, removing her jacket, revealing the T-shirt that says FLY BY NIGHT. She sports a worn-in suede bag, which she takes off and swings onto the back of her chair. She sits and reaches for a bread basket, removes a sesame-seeded cracker, and chews quickly.

"No, please, it's all yours." I steal a quick glace at Honor who seems less than pleased.

"Awesome." She goes for my drink, the glass in her hand like a magnet.

I fight the urge to excuse myself and make a call just to let someone, anyone, know I'm sitting at a table in between two icons. I think how my sister would have loved this. Loved the idea of this.

The waiter appears with the feta and beet salad appetizers, and takes Lou's order: cheddar burger, onion rings, and a second martini.

For the next ten minutes Lou talks about her new business venture, a line of liquor-and-skull-themed T-shirts and jewelry. She's so likable that I want to slip her a note jotted down on a hotel napkin like the song lyrics Bowie brought Honor, prepare her for what's in store.

"It was either start a line of clothing or jewelry"—Lou tells me, martini glass raised to her lips and half gone—"or do this coffee-table book thing I've been kicking around." I look to Honor and her expression tells me this is the first she's hearing of it.

"I want to take pictures while on my back"—visions of men's faces and body parts run across my eyes—"in a variety of places." She looks at me. "Not a sex book, a real book. Like the park, a dirty restroom, on a plane, lying on a beach in Hawaii, and then I'd pair the pictures with essays. If I can write lyrics, I sure as shit can write a few stories." She finishes my drink but has yet to put the glass down. "I just don't know what I'd call it."

"What about *Back Story*?"

They both turn to me.

"I like her," Lou says, finally resting the glass.

"She's quick, I'll give you that," Honor smirks.

I could do what you do, I think. I could leave the hotel business and work for you. Maybe that's what I need. A change of scenery. If they can erase Anne so quickly, anyone could be next.

Good-girl salads are swept away and replaced with Lou's burger and my and Honor's salmon and couscous.

"The band I was in before going solo was called Horse House because one of the girls was an attendant at a stable, which was weird because she kind of looked like a horse," Lou animatedly tells me. "I only joined because I loved the name. It was primal and angry and rhymed. Anywho, her father wanted her to be a vet or something but she just wanted to rock out. I hated her, but she was a total noodler and could play like nobody's business. And she could book a tour."

The waiter delivers Lou's second drink and reaches for her empty glass. He asks how we're enjoying the food, and we all nod politely and tell him it's very good.

Lou keeps talking in between bites of her burger. "Then I find out her job at the stable is to clean up the shit. And the horses hate her so much they kick poo at her."

I laugh so hard bits of couscous fly out of my mouth. Lou jostles me with her arm like we're old friends. Honor looks uncomfortable. Her lips become tightly pressed together, and she looks away, as if she's searching the room for someone.

"So she starts complaining and coming to practice smelling of shit, and I said, 'Let's change the name to Horse Shit,' which pissed her off and she got mad and kicked me out of the band." Lou downs her second drink, then looks for the waiter and once she has his attention, nods for another.

"Just because of one suggestion?" I ask.

"Well, there were rumors I was drunk onstage." She grips my shoulder with one hand and points at me with her other. "Rumors, Morgan. Rumors I tell you." The twinkle in her eyes and the grin on her face says differently.

Honor places a hand on top of Lou's, more to calm her down, and softly says, "Take a breath."

"Throwing me out was the best thing because I found my way to Hit Me Harder, which made me popular and famous." The third drink arrives, the second glass is removed.

"Just not with the Battered Wives Association . . ."

Honor looks up at me, her glasses are perched on her nose, her lips curling up slightly.

"You're funny," Lou tells me. "Tomorrow night the Knitting Factory is celebrating the year 1990 with a salute to rock stars who were big at that time," Lou states. "People dress up like their favorite performer and lip-synch to their songs. Some famous drag queen emcees and there are prizes. Honor and I are going. You should come." She looks at me, then to Honor, who nods noncommittally.

"Lou," she says, "we're only going for two reasons: audience recognition of you and their reaction. Once we've established that, we can make calls to the papers and TV stations."

Lou rolls her eyes. "It's my last hoorah before I do a nice little stay at a very nice little hotel." She winks at me. "Like this one?"

Silence emanates from all three of us and is only broken when Lou stands.

"I've got to pee."

Honor and I watch her walk away, her boots clonking on the marble, her hips swaying right to left, her hair swinging in sync with her body until she disappears down the steps.

"That went better than I thought." Honor takes a deep sigh. "Look, she's charming, but she's as addictive as the drugs she on. It's very likely she's doing a line in your restroom, so don't be fooled. I want progress reports. No one visits her without my approval. I want to meet the person in charge of housekeeping, and interview whoever will be cleaning her room. Is that understood? I don't want any press. No photos, no calls, take the phone out if you have to. Don't worry, you'll be compensated greatly . . ."

Is she going to slip me a check? Put some cash in an envelope? Write my boss a note on her very pretty, expensive Smythson stationery? "It's fine. It's what I do. She'll go unnoticed."

"It's decided then," she says slapping the table, pleased, like she's bought something at an auction after being caught in a bidding war. "I love her, but she can just suck you dry. At forty-four she's too old for this shit. I'm too old to deal with her shit," she adds, her words almost getting lost as she turns her head to answer the phone.

Lunch lasts longer than I anticipated and by the time I return to my office I have ninety-three e-mails, sixteen phone messages, and am late for a meeting with the woman who replaced Anne. I forgo a random room inspection and instead sit in my office listening to Bernard's long-winded message about how I've hurt him and what a terrible person I am to ruin something wonderful, and to please have his things packed by tomorrow morning so he can have his friend, who owns a car, pick them up. I return his call and am so thankful when his machine clicks on. His slow, overenunciated outgoing message confirms my decision to break up. And by the time I hear him say, "Remember, there's always something good to wine about, so leave a message and number . . ." I'm practically crawling out of my skin waiting for the beep.

At 6:00 p.m. I gather myself and head out for the night. The hotel's bar is abuzz with suits and ties, women in black tops and matching slacks or tight skirts, out-of-towners who look out of place, and a handful of bridge-and-tunnelers. Others are milling about in the lobby, waiting for friends or co-workers, a few couples are holding hands while checking in. A group of Europeans is speaking Italian loudly by the steps of the lobby restaurant as they decide where to go tonight.

I'm behind the desk closing out the day's reservations when I see Trish walking toward me. "Hey, what are you doing here?" I ask, thinking perhaps she wanted a last-minute drinking partner.

"Oh, I was . . . I was just . . ." she looks around the hotel. "I went to put the key thing in the door and it didn't light up or unlock." She hands over the plastic card.

"I'm so sorry." I reach for a new one. "What's your number?"

"Twenty-three seventeen."

"A corner room, nice." I log in the number electronically, swipe it through the computer, and hand it back. "I didn't know you were staying here. If you want, we could do breakfast tomorrow or a drink later."

"I don't know if I'm staying the night. It's my friend's room. He's in from out of town." She looks at her watch, then around the hotel again and arrives back at me.

I search for something in her eyes, as if she's trying to send a mental signal, or perhaps I am. *Please share something personal. I swear, I won't tell anyone. It would be great to bond over something.* So I divulge instead. I want to tell her about Ellen, but it hurts too much, and I want to share this with her over coffee, or drinks, something more intimate. So I tell her about Bernard instead, about packing up Anne's belongings that she left behind, only to have to go home and do the same with his things, and though she seems interested she is clearly distracted.

"I'm having drinks with an old friend and we thought, well, if one thing leads to another, perhaps we might, I don't know." She smiles embarrassedly. "I just got here a bit early."

I'm in midnod when I see my uncle push through the revolving doors. I see the way Trish's facial expression changes from shyness to shock, mirroring the way Marty looks at both of us. Suddenly I know why the room number is familiar. I raise my hand to wave and realize Trish is doing the same thing, making us look like rejects from a Miss America contest.

"There he is."

My attention snaps back to her. Her lips are pressed tightly together, her body stiff. I return to relying on my psychic powers. *Please, don't do this. Don't go into a room with him.* But as I search for my voice Marty is at an open elevator waiting for her to enter.

"If you want to do breakfast tomorrow, let me know," I say.

"Thanks. I'd introduce you but he seems anxious to . . ."

"No, it's fine. Don't worry about it."

I watch her walk toward my uncle, watch him raise an eyebrow to me, then the doors close and they're gone.

At home I pack Bernard's belongings like eggs, carefully and with kindness. I fold his WINE DRINKERS MAKE BETTER LOVERS T-shirt, aware of how soft and worn it is. How it still smells of his cologne. I'm wearing the back brace and its solidness is a welcoming pleasure. *Unlimited Lou's Greatest Hits* pours from my stereo. I let the machine pick up the calls, let the two drinks I've had start to kick in, let myself become slightly unhinged as I sing loudly, trying to match Lou's sandpaper voice. *I want this*, I tell myself as I bubble wrap the bottles of wine, lay them gently in the cardboard box I picked up at the liquor store. "I want to be with someone else," I say aloud to Dale, as I seal his toiletries—toothbrush, razor, shaving cream, dental floss, special soap for sensitive skin—into a freezer-size Ziploc bag. Only after his musical theater CDs, books on wine, clothing, cigars, and whatnot have been packed into two boxes and one duffel bag and are brought downstairs and left with the doorman, just as requested, can I go to sleep.

I lay in my dark bedroom trying to picture Marty and Trish having sex in room 2317. I wonder where Bernard is tonight. If he's sleeping. I wonder how long it will take Anne to find another job. If Lou's snorting coke at some dirty after-hours bar. If my sister is watching over me. If I can go back to being single.

Chapter 5

Morgan

An Off-Site Event

As promised, Honor e-mails me the information for the rock 'n' roll event tonight, and I find myself dressed up and giddy, standing in front of Lou's apartment on the Lower East Side, waiting for her to buzz me in. The building is old and industrial looking, a mismatch on a block outlined with trees and flowers, small specialty shops, and cozy, kitschy restaurants.

After buzzing Lou two more times, I work my way down the list, my index finger hitting a different mini black button every second. I hear a faint click and pull the colossal door open.

The entranceway is painted a dark green that matches the

insides of the elevator. I enter the creaky run-down contraption and only after fighting with the metal gate that one must manually open and close can I travel upward.

I find Lou standing in her corridor on the fifth floor tapping a mini vile of white powder onto her hand. Startled, she looks up at me. I'm still inside the elevator, the gate is closed, and I peer through it as if she's on exhibit at the zoo. She's dressed in a short, tattered snakeskin skirt, brown boots, white T-shirt, and a pink furry vest.

"Don't worry, I've got some green monster to bring down the white lady," she assures me, taking a final snort. "Hey, don't tell Honor, okay?" She steps inside, pulls the wrought iron gate shut, and we ride down in silence.

Once outside, we see Honor smoking by her car, waiting for us.

"I was pleasantly surprised my name wasn't on Page Six this morning," she says, a ream of gray cloud escaping from her flawlessly painted lips.

"That's really not my style," I state.

"That's nice to know." She takes another drag and exhales, then flicks her cigarette. Red flakes fall like specks of rain. She extends her hand, indicating I'm to get in, and when I catch her looking at Lou, she shakes her head slightly.

Fifteen minutes later we pull up in front of the Knitting Factory in Brooklyn where a line of overzealous, overdressed partygoers spills off the sidewalk, onto the street, and around the corner. I spot several Madonnas, two haggard-looking Janet Jacksons, lots of Sinéad O'Connors, some MC Hammers, a few Billy Idols, and some scary-looking Milli Vanillis as we enter into sheer madness. I feel as though I've stumbled into a bad costume party thrown by a fraternity house. It's dark and smoky and smells of wet paint mixed with hairspray and Mr. Clean. Drag queens outnumber everyone by a 3 to 1 ratio, and have clearly mastered the art of dress up. Outfits range from tastefully elaborate to white-trash ugly. Honor plows through the swarm of people and creates a spot for us at the bar.

It's wall-to-wall mock rock stars as far as the eye can see. Huge billboards with the hits of the year remind us who and what songs made the charts. Madonna's "Vogue," Billy Idol's "Cradle of Love," and Phil Collins's "Another Day in Paradise" are in the top five. Number four is Unlimited Lou's "I'll Do It Tomorrow." I think back to where I was thirteen years ago as a sharp pain of reality sets in that I'm going to be thirty-three next month. Nostalgia pulls up a heavy seat next to me and I have a huge desire to run out of the club and curl up in the fetal position at home until my life is where I want it to be.

Honor orders three Grey Goose vodka tonics. Lou clinks glasses with her, then with me. I reach for Honor's glass to touch but she's already brought the drink to her mouth. A woman dressed as Lisa Stansfield is lip-synching onstage to "Been Around the World." Her actions are perfectly mimicked, the look an exact replica of the forgotten star.

"I love this song," Lou says, downing her cocktail, slamming the empty glass on the bar, and dragging Honor and I onto the dance floor with the mob of others. It's a tight fit with little room to move.

It only takes Lou a second to feel the music. Her movements are quick and funky—a snap of the head, an outstretched hand, a flick of the wrist, a jut of the hip, a bend in the knee . . . all her, all here. She's mesmerizingly sexy.

I turn and am surprised to see Honor dancing as well. Her lips are pressed together Mick Jagger style, her eyes are slightly squinty as if she knows a secret she's not willing to share. Though her actions are more stilted, movements small, calculated, and particular, they are classically controlled, full of style, and exude an air of sophistication and hipness that belong only to her. At fifty-something, Honor is the quintessential, stylish woman of power I long to be at her age.

We spot two other surprisingly well-dressed Unlimited Lous—from her Hit Me Harder days—who are more than thrilled to pose with the real one. Digital ready, I snap several photos while a stream of cells and other mini electronic devices make an appearance. Word spreads quickly that the real Unlimited Lou is here, and before Honor can do crowd control, forceful fans run us over in the hopes of touching and talking to her. More photos are taken, more people are pointing, several are shoving slips of paper and pens in her direction. One tall man dressed as Bowie undoes his shirt and exposes his chest while pushing a black Sharpie at her.

Honor is already phoning the *Post*'s Page Six while telling me to call the *Daily News* and e-mail TMZ. Lou continues to dance and smile at fans as Honor calls more papers and TV news stations while BlackBerrying gossip Web sites.

The begging and pleading for an impromptu performance happens within seconds. Lou and I look to Honor to see if this is part of the plan, the Sharpie now in Lou's hand, the man's chest in my face.

"What do you think, Lou?" Honor says, while on hold with Page Six.

She shrugs as the chanting of her name gets louder. "Yeah,

what the fuck. I don't have my guitar or anything and I'd have to sing without music."

"I've got your CD on me," Honor adds.

The music has gotten louder, I can feel it pulsating in my chest, and I can't hear Honor. Too many people are standing too close to me. I'm having trouble breathing and would give anything to have my leather brace on right now. And I realize no one has reported it missing.

"Lou, isn't the last song on *Neon Personality* instrumental?" I yell, my mouth intolerably dry, the vodka tonic suddenly hitting me.

Honor turns to Lou for confirmation, who nods. With that, Honor extracts the CD from her bag, walks to the edge of the stage, and beckons to the emcee, a man who's dressed in an aqua feather boa, a peacock-colored robe, and a head ornament made out of fruit, to bend down and talk. Honor hands him the disc and the emcee looks over in our direction, a huge smile on his face. I look for Lou and find her by the bar, a once-filled shot glass emptying into her mouth with one hand, while her other is gripping a fresh drink. I'm standing in the middle of the dance floor, and like we're in a fun house, Lou suddenly seems very far away. I try calling to her, a lost cause, and only hurt my vocal cords. I watch a third shot disappear and then Lou does the same. I look away for only a moment in the hope of catching Honor's eye, which I fail at as well, and when I glance back at the bar, Lou is gone.

"Ladies and gentlemen, girls and boys, dragsters and stars of 1990, have we got a treat for you," the emcee is saying. The fruit halo is teetering to the left and looks dangerously close to falling off. "You never know who's going to show up at the

Knitting Factory, but tonight's a real zinger. You know her as Unlimited Lou, but I know her as music goddess to girls like me whose hearts were broken into millions of tiny pieces and the only way we got through it was listening to "Heartbreakers, Scene Suckers." The mob claps and cheers. People are whipping off their wigs and shaking them high in the air. Others are jumping up and down. "So without further ado . . . Unlimited Lou."

Lou walks out timidly. Her soft eyes seem larger, her skin paler in the blaring stage lights and she holds a hand up to her forehead in order to shield the glare. She's thin and lean and the pink fur vest and tight skirt give her a perfect shape.

"This is kind of impromptu so bear with me. It's been a few, and I've had a few, so, you know?" she says into the mike.

More cheering ensues. Within seconds the room becomes jarringly quiet. Lou looks nervous. The fresh vodka tonic in her hand is raised defiantly to the audience, then downed.

"For all of you," she says. The music starts. First the guitar chords, simple but full-bodied, followed by the richness of the piano while drums blend in effortlessly. Leaning into the mike she begins to sing, her raspy, scratchy voice sounds suddenly soft as velvet, as comforting as warm soup.

Hours later, the once slightly lubricated have been completely inebriated.

The pudgy Madonna and short Cher, who fought earlier, now appear like found soul mates, swaying back and forth, holding each other to a Wilson Phillips song. As the clock ticked by the whole room seems to have changed. Strangers have morphed into a group of close friends. The world seems less vast and more manageable. I look at my watch: 2:56 a.m. The magic hour is nearing, too late to be called night, too early to be defined as morning. Everyone is drunk and stoned, costumes are now halfheartedly worn on many a tired and makeup-smeared face. Uncomfortable heels and boots have been kicked aside and lay in a mound in the corner next to purses and handbags. Wigs and jackets have been tossed in the middle of the floor, the owners too hot and sticky to wear them. Fake eyelashes barely hang on to sweaty lids.

Almost like an unbreakable ring, devoted fans have enclosed Lou in a small circle, refusing to let their hero go. They offer up their drinks to her, liquid trophies for tonight's radiant performance. Honor and I have been sitting at the bar for the past two hours watching and sipping watered-down cocktails.

"It's time," she says. "Will you get her and let's get going."

I slide off the stool and infiltrate the swarm. I take Lou by the hand as boos and obscenities are hollered at me: "You suck." "Dude, it's still early." "Lou, man, we love you. Stay real."

The cold air from outside is sobering and once our feet hit the street, like a magic trick cigarettes appear at Honor and Lou's lips. Honor extends her pack toward me and I take one. I don't like smoking as much as I love the way a cigarette fits and feels in between my fingers, the calming effect it has as I take it out from its package, put it in my mouth, light it, and take a long, slow breath in. I love the slight burning sensation in my throat, the bitterness on my tongue, the way the smoke exits from my lips, and the way it lingers in the air as it envelops me.

Lou is all smiles as she fights with the car door, unable to get it open. Frustrated, she starts laughing and sits down on the street.

"Louise, come on. You're too old for this." Honor says, flicking her cigarette.

"I'm just taking a little rest," she slurs.

Honor knocks on the window, waking the driver, who, snapping to attention, opens his door and helps Lou up and into the back seat. Honor and I follow.

"Where to?" he asks, starting the car.

"My house, for a nightcap," Lou shouts. She's rolled down the window and her head is dangling out like a dog.

I look to Honor, assuming she'll dismiss the idea, but Lou babbles something about sketches and T-shirt samples and the next thing I know we're in front of her loft. We enter her building, enter the elevator, and try to enter her apartment.

"I thought I left it unlocked," she says, pulling at her doorknob and then emptying out much of her bag onto the floor in the hallway. Several lighters, a pack of Camels, a beat-up leather wallet, some white pills, a handful of loose change, a small vile of coke, her cell phone, some worn-looking makeup, and a sealed condom spill out.

Honor watches Lou hunt for her keys. After a few minutes, I eventually find them in a zippered pocket of her purse, and rather than watch Lou struggle with the door, unlock it for her.

She flips on a light, but is quick to dim it. The loft is massive. Huge posters of the Clash and Adam Ant hang in retro frames on the walls. A British flag covers most of the ceiling. Shag carpets, fifties-style furniture, and stained glass lamps add to the kitsch feel. A neon sign of a martini glass sits on top of her wall unit and a string of plastic colored lights shaped like guitars outline the windows. Ashtrays from restaurants and hotel rooms cover the coffee table as does an old Coca-Cola candy dish filled with chocolate Hershey's Kisses.

The California-style kitchen is painted a light purple and all of the shelves and cabinets are made out of metal. Four chairs, which resemble a zebralike motif, sit around a table of white and gray marble. On it sits a large glass bowl that holds water, black rocks, and three large goldfish. The words "You Rotten Prick" are spelled out in colored letters nailed individually to the wall.

Sprawled out on the glass dining room table, as promised, are several sketches and clothing samples. Honor and I flip through her work as Lou turns on the stereo and makes her way to the bar.

"Just one drink, Louise," Honor says, like a parent, full of warning. "It's late and I've got the trainer and a massage in the morning."

On the table are several baby T's in black, white, and gray. On the caps of the sleeves Lou's glued mini silver and red rhinestones, which create the shape of a lit cigarette. On the back of the shirts are rhinestoned ashtrays with a skull inside, or a bottle of tequila and instead of the worm a skull with a lit cigarette hanging out of its mouth. I run my finger over the beads, feel the raised roughness, then feel the softness of the shirt. The sketches are of rings that double as mini ashtrays and what seems to be a line of wearable ashtray jewelry: necklaces with glass ashtrays and charm bracelets with different mini ashtrays dangling from them.

Honor holds up a black T. "Honestly, I didn't know what the hell to expect, but I've got to give her credit. These are actually—"

"Hip and edgy in a commercial way," I say, cutting her off.

Before Honor can answer, Dusty Springfield starts cooing from Lou's speakers. "Hey," Lou shouts, motioning us to the couch. "Put those down and let's fucking relax."

The dimmed lights, soft music, and leather couch make me feel like I've left one VIP room and entered into a more exclusive one. Lou sits next to me and Honor takes a chair across from us, her makeup perfectly intact, her legs crossed.

· I close my eyes for a moment and when I open them, a lit joint has materialized in Lou's hand. I smell the familiar odor of pot, hear a soft sucking noise, see the stream of smoke exit Lou's lips. She hands the joint to Honor, who I'm sure will push her hand away, but doesn't. Instead she discreetly places the paper so that it barely touches her lips and delicately inhales. A second later smoke shoots out of her mouth. They both look to me. I take the joint realizing I haven't been stoned since '93, my last year of college. The paper is slightly wet and I pray I don't cough and make an ass out of myself. I inhale slowly, feel the smoke inhabit my chest, expand inside, filling up the emptiness. I exhale. My chest feels hot and light. All of me does. I ask where the restroom is and once there, stare into my flushed reflection. My makeup has disappeared without permission. My eyeliner is almost down to my nose, my lips look dry. I reapply everything as quickly as possible and pee. The sound of the toilet flushing gives me the opportunity to open Lou's medicine cabinet without anyone hearing. I don't know what I'm looking for. I guess I expect to find several bottles of prescription pain relievers, but none are here. Just makeup that looks past due, a box of Band-Aids, bottles of nail polish that seem older than the makeup, Lancôme moisturizer, undereye cream, toner, a bottle of aspirin, Advil, and NyQuil.

When I return, Dusty's voice is hauntingly familiar and

torch song—like. Lou has her hand around Honor's neck and the two woman are swaying to the sad, soulful music. There's something so real and raw about them it hurts to look. I can't look away either though, because I fear the very act of blinking might cause them to stop. At this moment, I almost don't exist. I'm a blanket or pillow, blending into the furniture, a support item to lean upon. Forgotten until needed.

Lou glances in my direction, slinks over to me, a hand offered, her index finger curling, beckoning. I don't want to move and break the moment; I don't want to dance with them because I feel as though I'm watching a movie, but I don't want to feel left out and alone either. Lou's hand reaches for mine. She swings it, girly-like, innocently, while pulling me toward Honor, who winks. And then I'm dancing. My hips are moving to Dusty's faraway voice and I'm in between two icons. I'm living a moment I've been dreaming of since I was ten. A lost member of Heart or Fleetwood Mac, the stereo would blast and I would air guitar on my bed, positioned perfectly in front of the large round mirror that hung on the wall in my bedroom. I'd belt out the songs, give knowing nods to my bandmates, make eye contact with the audience, flirt with the invisible roadies. Other times, I'd pretend I was accepting a Grammy. I'd look surprised when my name was called. I'd wave to the fans in the bleachers, say my rehearsed speech, and thank all the appropriate people: my acupuncturist, drug dealer, agent, and Jesus—Jewish or not, you can't forget him. But this is reality. I'm not at home reading a magazine and watching reruns of *Law & Order* with Bernard breathing heavily, sitting too close to me on the couch. And for the first time in a long time, I feel utterly alive. Part of something whole and special. My mother doesn't matter. That I've broken up with Bernard. That I'm single. That I'll never know the children my sister would have had. That I'm an only child now with parents who never mention the dead one we, as a family, never visit. That there's a stolen leather brace in my closet that I wish I was wearing now. That Anne has been fired. That I can't breathe most mornings. That I wake up crying. That I often fight the urge to crawl into the corner of my apartment with nothing but a photo of Dale to help pass the next minute, and the next, and the one after that. That I'm turning thirty-three in a month and feel as though I haven't made anything out of my life. It all disappears.

The pot and cocktails have made me feel fluffy and loopy. The music is mellow, but a felt presence in the room; and Lou's hand on my shoulder, her slow, gyrating body up against mine feels pure, her movements effortless. She and the music and Honor are all consuming. They're all I care about. Them and this moment.

The song ends and as I see Honor set down her drink, I know the evening is officially done.

Lou turns to me. "You can sleep over in the office. There's a pullout couch. I'll make you eggs and the strongest coffee you've ever had in the morning," she promises, her words still slurred, her face red.

I want to. I want to stay here because the minute I step foot outside her loft door, the second the halogen light catches my face, this moment will be gone, replaced only by memory.

"I wish I could, but I've got too much work. We're announcing our new chef on Wednesday."

Honor is one step ahead of me. She's grabbed her purse off of the coffee table and is dialing her driver, alerting him we'll be down in a minute. Then her hand is on my arm, whooshing me out the door as if she owns me. As if I already work for her. And I wonder what my life would be like if I did. If I can keep Lou clean, save her even. One soul for another. One dead sister for a not-yet-dead rock star.

Chapter 6

Morgan
Ashes, Ashes, All Fall Down

There's a terrible feeling I get as I walk into my parents' home. Growing up, whenever I turned the key and pushed open the door, I never knew what to expect: my father in a good mood, all smiles; my father upset about a patient or hospital problem, yelling; my mother singing boldly to old sock-hop songs; my mother ranting about a decorating problem with the apartment.

This time, however, my mother is a ghostly shade of white when I enter their apartment for our monthly dinner. A scotch on the rocks is in her hand and her bracelets clink against the glass. Ice knocks on the other side as she drops the arm that opened the door. Her eyes are red and I flash to Anne standing in the bathroom and think, *Where is my father. Oh, God, something's happened to him.*

"There's been an accident at the office."

I steady myself. "Is he okay?"

My mother shakes her head, and I watch tears slip into her scotch as she lifts the glass to her lips. "He's not."

"What happened?"

"He had a heart attack."

"Dad had a heart attack?"

"Not your father, your uncle Marty."

Pressure fills my head as a throbbing starts in my chest. I feel like I'm underwater and I'm having trouble hearing my mother. "Do you want me to take you to the hospital? Where's dad?" Why is my father never home?

I can only make out what she's saying by watching her lips move.

"Honey, he's not in the hospital."

I think of the last conversation I had with my uncle as I rest a deli platter on his and Faye's dining room table. It was a few days after I'd seen him and Trish together. He'd asked if we could have a quick cup of coffee. When we met up, he told me he knew I knew about the women. That he loved Faye. That he was going to stop and break it off with everyone and start over. He ended our conversation by saying, "Though you've gone beyond the call of duty, I never should have put you in that situation." He let me pay the bill, patted me on the shoulder, and told me how important I was in his life. When he got up I noticed one pant leg was caught in his sock.

Today Marty and Faye's apartment is filled with well-meaning guests, relatives I've not seen in a decade, some since Dale's funeral twenty-five years ago, and some who I guess are his patients. A few lanky women with long flowing hair look vaguely familiar, a blur of perfume and freshly done faces who have come in and out of the hotel over the past two years.

I watch Faye pace around her apartment, my mother at her heels, my father in another room. My mother and Marty's strategy for getting through death and depression is to dress up for the occasion. Faye has accepted the torch and strides nervously through her apartment, her flawless skin and shiny blond hair, the Valentino dress and black high heels all translate to the casual onlooker, "Yes, my husband is dead, but I've got my shit together. No tears from me."

The memories I have in their home are few: a holiday, a birthday, a Sunday night dinner when I was younger. I remember Marty once chased me in a lame game of tag and I banged my head on the bookcase. That they used to have nice-smelling blue soap in the shape of dolphins. That their refrigerator was always filled with food, and when I was little Faye kept animal crackers in the bread basket for Dale and me. I decide to check there now, a glimmer of hope the red box with pictures of caged animals will be inside. I know there's no reason she'd have them. I haven't visited in years, let alone eaten them, but I suddenly need something from my past to prove I was here.

This is day two of the shivah and it feels as though we've not left this apartment for weeks. Outside in the hallway the clothing rack holds countless wool and leather coats, its metal bar bending in the middle from the stress. Inside, their usually spacious living room and study have been commandeered by plastic folding chairs. Guests are filling them, filling their plates, and filling their ears full of gossip as word spreads of how Marty died: "They say he crawled on his hands and knees into the elevator." "When they pulled him out, they said his face was completely distorted." "Can you imagine? That's why they chose cremation." I catch bits of their conversation as I offer coffee or tea, sparkling water, and white wine. Rather than ask, they assume I was close with my uncle and proceed to tell me what a fine shrink he was, how they all felt listened to, appreciated, and understood. I have the urge to take a survey, like with the coffee and tea. Instead of "Who would like decaf?" I'd much prefer to ask, "Who here fucked Marty in my hotel? Show of hands, please?"

I enter the kitchen and refill the tray. Boxes of cookies and cakes sent by clients and friends litter the counter space. Two rented extra-large coffeemakers are to my left. Homemade casseroles, quiches, and kugel reside on my right next to platters of sliced ham, Swiss cheese, turkey, tongue, and roast beef. I spot the silver-plated bread basket hidden behind a brown paper bag and close my eyes as I lift open the top. *Please be there. Please be there, even if the box is decades old, the cookies moldy and inedible.* Inside is a loaf of whole wheat bread and a package of Pepperidge Farm English muffins.

Disappointed by my search, I decide to collect trash instead of handing out more liquids and I walk back into the living room and collect empty coffee cups, discarded plastic wineglasses, and paper plates with crumpled-up napkins resting on them. Marty's urn seems to watch my every move.

My mother picked out the vase that holds her brother's ashes and it resides on a mantel next to the bookshelves filled with his collection of literature: Freud, Jung, and other exceptional therapists. When I look at the brass container, I see a distorted vision of myself. I shift an inch or so and watch my eyes widen, my lips grow fuller while my forehead becomes bulbous, my cheeks sunken.

A woman steps next to me and stares at the urn as well. I catch her reflection next to mine and from my angle we look like shrunken heads.

"He was a very special man. Did you know him well?" she asks.

"He was my uncle."

"Oh, I'm so sorry." She turns to face me. Her eyes are wide. Her face lean and thin, like her frame. She's one of Marty's. I've seen them together in the hotel.

"I'm Sheila. Marty was my coffee buddy. We'd meet several times a week for our caffeine fix. Well, I drink tea, and I think Marty was always trying to convert me. He'd always say, 'Come on over to my side. Coffee drinkers are trustworthy people.'"

"That's nice." My words come out tense and she seems a bit startled.

"Anyway, I'm sure you'd like a moment to yourself."

"I would."

"Could you tell me which one is his wife, Faye? I'd like to express my condolences."

I point to my aunt, then watch her walk over to her. Skinny, lanky women, all in a row. I look for Trish wondering if she'll show. If she even knows he's dead. I've not spoken to her since I saw them together. She's not returned my phone calls, making me feel as though I've done something wrong. Lost something important.

By the time I enter the kitchen my mother is on the phone and Faye is leaning up against the door, staring off. A dishcloth is clutched in her hand and every time she twists it, her wedding ring moves in the opposite direction. I see her head start to droop, like a drunk about to pass out, and before I can set the tray down, watch her eyes roll back, her body crumble.

Someone screams as I lunge for her. I lay her on the floor while realizing a swarm of people are staring over us. Faye's sister seems to be instantly at her side. She bends over her as my mother steps in with a glass of water. I look into her face and flash to a moment when she was handing Dale a cup of apple juice, holding it up to her mouth and helping her to drink it. I want to touch my mother's face, cup her chin with my palm, and tell her I'm sorry. I'm so sorry her first child is dead. That her younger brother is no longer here, either. That no matter how much I want to, need to, I can't give her back the family we never got to have. As I lean forward to whisper this in her ear, some random guest suggests we stand Faye up and move her to a chair. I'm quickly pushed aside by the sister who is incredibly calm and gently props her up against the door, brushes hair out of Faye's eyes, and does that slow shushing thing you do with people who are coming undone. I think of how Dale would be doing this for me, or me for her should one of our husbands suddenly, inexplicably die. Or maybe it would be one of our parents.

Like the animal crackers, I want her to magically appear. Almost call out for her. My hands are shaking and an inner tingling inside my body starts. A numbness in my fingers happens as a standing vertigo washes over me. *I need air. I must get air.* Voices fade as I move toward the living room, pushing my way past the people who feel they need to watch the show, and open a window. I lean out, close my eyes, and welcome the cold air as it hits my face. Only after shutting the window do I notice the urn that held Marty's ashes, the one my mother bought a few days ago, is gone.

My mother and I arrive at the police station twenty minutes later, which, luckily, is blocks from Faye and Marty's Upper East Side apartment. Not wanting to create additional chaos my mother suggested we not say a word to anyone, leaving my father and Faye's sister to put Faye to bed and continue the shivah as if nothing has happened.

Everything inside the Twenty-third Precinct is dark and dingy. The smell of perspiration is strong and offensive. Phones are ringing, people are yelling, metal is clanking, and feet are clomping. Some cops are in street clothing: leather jackets, jeans and sneakers, baseball hats. Others don appropriate blue uniforms: guns, nightsticks, and cuffs on one hip, well balanced by walkie-talkies, whistles, and keys on the other.

A broken air conditioner that looks as if it hasn't been repaired since the Carter administration hangs shakily above my head. The floor is covered with old ceramic gray tile and the wooden benches are black from age. The walls are papered with recruiting posters that read JOIN US: IT'S A MATTER OF PRIDE and wanted posters that showcase twenty or so individuals, each sought for a variety of crimes. If they really hoped to catch people, they'd use these photos as a dating service: "Robert Meyers, 38, wanted for aiding and abetting, is looking for a class-A felon with a short record, dark hair, and college degree. You should enjoy travel, pool halls, and favor old black-and-white films from the thirties."

The main room is divided into two areas, those who've committed crimes and those who haven't. Women whose wallets have been stolen, men whose cars have been broken into, couples who've been robbed, and senior citizens who've been mugged are all waiting to file reports. These victims seem to stay within their section and my mother and I stand behind them. When it's our turn, we give a quick summary to a female cop and are told to talk to the person at the large desk to our right.

Seated there is a rugged blond man with surprisingly good looks. Two metal chairs are in front of this desk. And as he sees us approaching, he extends a hand and half gets up out of his seat, making me feel as if I'm talking to a bank executive looking for a loan rather than an officer.

"Hi, I'm Wes Bater. How can I help you?"

He appears too clean-cut in his trendy suit, his good looks, his wavy blond hair to be a cop. Even in this bad lighting, I can tell he's attractive. He has smooth, freshly shaven olive-colored skin, nice brows, and green eyes. His features are sharp, but not chiseled, and there's an exciting edginess to him.

I look to my mother—who's digging through her purse and finally extracts a mini bottle of antibacterial gel, which she douses on her hands—to see if she wants to start. She wore her fur coat, and in these seats, looks like a constipated Eskimo with the thick fur pushed into her face.

"We were sitting shivah for my brother," she says. "It's our term for paying respects to the dead . . ."

"I'm Jewish, too," he smiles, then adds more seriously, "And I'm sorry for your loss."

My mother looks relieved and unbuttons her coat while letting a sigh escape. "My brother was cremated this past Thursday, and someone took the brass urn that held his ashes at his home a few hours ago." She stops to gather herself; only I can't tell if it's for dramatic effect or an honest display of emotion. "And when my daughter went to look at it, it was gone. Can you believe that?" She smacks her hand down on her knee for emphasis, a cry in her voice. "What's the matter with people?"

Wes turns to me.

"I was by the window . . ."

"My sister-in-law was not in a good place and there was a lot of commotion . . ."

As if in a bad tennis match I continue. "It was rather emotional, and I went to get some air. I opened the window, stuck my head out, and when I came back inside, I looked for the urn and it was missing."

"Why someone would do this is beyond me." My mother shakes her head back and forth. Wes looks concerned and as he opens his mouth, is beaten by someone else's voice. We all turn our heads to the left and see a black man dressed as a woman yelling.

"I have to piss," he shouts. "I got to go now."

He's standing next to a policeman who has him cuffed, hands clamped conveniently in front of his privates. No one seems terribly impressed or even in a hurry to physically move.

"I said, I need to piss. Who the fuck is gonna let me do that?"

Now that he/she mentions it, I could pee, too, as if it's an epidemic.

"Fine. Suit your fucking lazy-ass selves."

The sound of urine hitting the floor is the next noise we

hear. The people standing behind him take large steps away, as does the cop who's holding him by the shoulder.

"Fuck this crappy job," the chubby officer utters under his breath. "You just bought yourself a night in lockup, Pretty."

My mother is mortified and though we're several feet away, rubs more antibacterial gel on her hands. "Stop looking, Morgan," she urges, her voice tight. But I can't. I cannot take my eyes off this man's enormous penis.

"I'm so sorry you had to see that, Mrs. . . . ."

"Tierney."

Wes picks up a pen and starts to fill out a form requesting our names, numbers, addresses, a description of the urn, and a list of people who were at the apartment.

"People steal all sorts of things," he says, his right hand moving back and forth over the paper. He flips the sheet over and continues scribbling notes as the sharp odor of urine permeates the already stale air.

"I work in a hotel so I see this all the time. If it's not the soap dish it's a robe, or letter opener, or minibar items, even a shoehorn. I mean who wants an elongated shoehorn?" I say, knowing full well a stolen leather sex thing resides in my closet. Hypocrisy, meet irony. Irony, hypocrisy. "They assume if they take it on their last day and sign out really quickly, we won't charge their card."

"Do you remember anyone acting unusual?" he asks.

"It's a shivah, all bets are off in terms of behavior," I say.

My mother eyes me suspiciously.

"True," he agrees. We smile at each other and I tilt my head girly-like. He has nice eyes.

"Is there any reason why someone would do this?"

I can think of many.

"My brother was a therapist so it's anyone's guess. A number of his patients came to pay their respects. I'm sure many aren't terribly stable."

"Perhaps it's an open-and-shut case of separation anxiety," I add.

"You'll have to excuse her," my mother interjects, then mouths the words "stop it" to me. I roll my eyes and Wes smirks.

"What hotel are you with?" He stops writing and starts tapping the top of the pen on the desk.

"Four Seasons."

"You're kidding me."

"Have you stayed there?"

"I'm there now." He moves from tapping his pen to tapping on the computer keys, which sit on his desk off to the left.

"Really?"

"My building had a fire and well, I needed a place to stay and the hotel is blocks from the building and insurance is taking care of lodging. Got to tell you, it's been a vacation."

I lean forward and fall into flirt mode as my mother stares at us. I can visualize her telling her friends at her weekly bridge gathering how we met. "Well, some freak stole my brother's ashes, and Morgan, leave it to her to find the officer attractive. PS, he's Jewish. He was nice and promised to find the urn."

"I have to ask this, you're not a real cop, right?" I inquire.

"No, I'm not," he says quietly, like a spy sharing secret information. "I work for the mayor. I'm an assistant criminal justice coordinator."

My mother's face eases and she unbuttons her fur all the

way this time with one hand, while fanning herself with the other in the hope of creating some circulation.

"How interesting." Take that Bernard. I bet Wes doesn't worry about which wine he's drinking when he's hobnobbing with politicians.

"This was actually his idea. It's a new program we're heading up. He wants his team to experience firsthand what kind of crimes are being committed." He takes the pen he's been fidgeting with and sticks it behind his ear before returning to the computer. "It's supposed to give us a personal look at what's happening to the city and hopefully a better way to correct the problems." He turns back to my mother. "This is a truly awful and unsettling thing to have happened. But to be honest, whoever took your brother's ashes most probably did it out of anger or grief, and the chances of recovering them are rather slim. Legally, you're dealing with doctor/patient privilege, so obtaining a list or addresses and numbers is always sketchy, especially since he's the deceased party and not the other way around."

My mother and I nod in unison, making us look like those plastic bobble heads.

"What if they signed in on their own," I ask. "We've got the funeral guestbook."

Wes looks impressed. "True. That's something we'll have to collect from you. If you'd like to leave it in the lobby I'll send an officer over. I'm sure you'd prefer us not to come up and disrupt . . ."

"We're blocks away, I can easily drop it off."

"We can leave it for them downstairs, Morgan," my mother interrupts as a cop walks over and hands Wes another file.

"We got people waiting," she tells him.

"Right." He takes the new paperwork from her and once she walks away, stands. We do the same. "If we hear anything, of course we'll let you know. And I promise to give it some special attention as well."

We shake hands again and I let mine linger in his a second longer than need be.

"Thank you, I appreciate that," my mother says.

"If it's not too forward, maybe you'd like to have a drink at the bar sometime," I offer. "It's the least I can do for your kindness."

"That would be great. Friday's my last night there so perhaps Thursday would work? I'll give you a call?"

"Sounds good. You can reach me at the hotel."

My mother is slightly horrified. I can tell by the way she grips my upper arm, tight and angrily.

As we exit, we pass many of the same people we saw when we entered two hours ago. The urine has been cleaned up, and the cross-dresser removed. Outside it's dark and cold as we head west toward Fifth Avenue. There's the feeling, like at a hospital, of hours lost. As if time has stood still inside but the world has moved on without us.

I want to say something to my mother but am not sure what. When she calls my father to inform him we're on our way back, her voice is tired and hoarse.

"I could help you clean out Marty's office if you want," I suggest, once she's off the phone. "I could take Monday off . . ."

"That's kind, but I'm sure Faye wants to handle that."

As much as I'd *like* to help, my *need* to be part of the process is far greater. I didn't get to do it for Dale and I want to watch my mother mourn because I don't yet know how. And just once, I'd love something other than tragedy to bring my family closer.

As we fight the unforgiving, raw December air, I slip my arm through my mother's, like Trish did with me. I hope to feel a piece of her, something solid and whole, but I'm lost in the fur and am only able to grip the material from her thick, hairy coat.

Chapter 7

Morgan
Suite 2410

Lou's muffled voice bellows from the hallway making me hesitate before knocking on door number 2410. "It's Morgan," I call out.

Honor opens the door, a frown on her face, dressed in a chocolate brown jacket and tweed wool skirt short enough to make men turn for a second look, yet long enough to remain classy. Her heels add height and sophistication and she looks like she's going to an awards luncheon rather than a high-end dry out suite.

"He's a two-beer queer," Lou says as I enter. A lit cigarette dangles from her lips, sunglasses hide her face. Her purple suede shirt is dirty and worn. Her jeans look ragged, like the rest of Lou. "He wouldn't know a hit if Hendrix appeared to him in a drug-induced vision and played some lost song he'd written prior to his untimely death."

One of the glasses from the bar is in her hand, ice clinking against it, clear liquid swishing back and forth. "Morgan!" she shouts, finally noticing me. She stumbles forward, the smell of her perfume and smoke arriving first, and hugs me. "Might I offer you a drink before my parole officer extinguishes the liquid gold?"

I eye the almost-empty bottle of Absolut on the table. "I just wanted to check and see how things were going."

Two men are visiting her as well. The one seated at the table looks as weathered as Lou, face leathery, skin peppered with pockmarks. He's wearing jeans and a black vest outlined in silver nail heads, an orange T-shirt underneath. His hair is matted down, covering one of his eyes, and he keeps flicking his head back in the hopes of moving the strands out of his line of vision. The younger man is slumped on the loveseat. Hipper in appearance, he dons black-and-white Vans, army green pants, and a T-shirt that reads TECHNO SUCKS.

"This isn't a goddamn party," Honor says, ignoring me. "I guess bringing her here sober would have been too much to ask?"

"What do you want from us?" the older one barks. "We bloody got her here."

"Did she even go home last night?" Honor lights a cigarette.

"I'm not her babysitter. I'm not some fucking groupie and I'm not on your payroll. So why don't you just say 'thank you' and leave it at that?"

"I'm in the room," Lou slurs.

I clear my throat. Everyone stops.

"Alright Lovey. Looks like this is good-bye." The older one gets up and walks over to Lou, who is now leaning up against the wall. "We'll see you in a week or two. This will be real good for you. You'll write some new stuff, get yourself back in the recording room . . ."

"Yeah, Trevor's right. You'll be good as new."

Each man takes a turn hugging Lou, who has a lit cigarette in one hand, the other still holding her drink.

"Why don't you guys stay for dinner?" Lou suggests.

"It's noon." Honor says.

Lou makes a face, struts like Mick Jagger, then laughs, spilling her drink on the carpet.

"Okay, lunch it is, then."

"When you're well enough for visitors, we'll have a lovely meal downstairs. Okay?" the older one promises.

As the men move past me and exit, Honor takes what's left of the vodka and pours it down the sink. I watch Lou slump to the floor as I hand her an ashtray from the table. She winks while reaching for it, the silver rings on her fingers catching the light.

We both watch Honor dump Lou's bag out on the table. The cell phone skids forward while several lipsticks roll in different directions, as if trying to make a run for it, and end up falling to the floor. A wallet and three packs of cigarettes tumble out, as do matches, lighters, keys, gum, and other paraphernalia. Last to make an appearance are the small bottles of vodka and te-quila. When Honor examines the zippered pouch, she extracts a plastic bag of powder and a few tabs of what I can only guess are acid. She inspects the Camel Lights and removes two joints from the package.

"Where're your suitcases?"

Lou ignores her and starts humming.

Frustrated, Honor walks over to the couch and opens a large duffle bag, which sits next to a sketchbook, keyboard, and guitar. On the coffee table is a Discman, pile of CDs, pens, colored pencils, and headphones. She sighs deeply and searches through Lou's collection of T-shirts, underwear, jeans, sweats, and some mismatched pairs of socks. Each CD case is opened and inspected, as is the Discman, even the place that holds the batteries, in which Honor discovers a small vial of coke. Three more joints and five hundred-dollar bills, which were taped to the inside of the guitar are added to the pile of no-no's.

"This is it?"

Lou doesn't answer but turns to me instead. "She's better than any drug dog. When she's done with PR she can work for customs."

Honor puts Lou's cell, the cash, her wallet—with the exception of her driver's license—and mini bottles of liquor in her own handbag. The joints are ripped in half and stuffed down the drain along with the other drugs.

"The phone can only dial the front desk. They have a list of names and numbers that are okay for Lou to be connected to," I tell Honor. "At this moment it's just you and myself." Then to Lou, "If you want housekeeping or room service or me, just ask them to connect you. The fridge has everything you requested."

"I know. I checked. I spoke with housekeeping and the head concierge," she tells me. "You understand there will be no visitors except for you and the nurse, who will be coming three times a day for the first three days, then twice, then once a day as needed."

"What name'd you check me in as?" Lou asks.

"Telling you would only be futile, wouldn't it?" Honor says.

"Once I was KiKi LaRue," she informs me, her head moving a little bit, as if she's listening to a song. A big, blissful smile is on her face. "I was Miss Blow Cain when I went solo." She laughs and downs what's left in her glass. "That was one of my favorites."

Honor looks at her watch as her cell rings. She glances at the mini screen and ignores the caller. A second later the Black-Berry vibrates. "Okay kids, I've got to go."

"No you don't." Lou whines. "Let's listen to some tunes, or watch a movie."

"This is the pretty part, enjoy it while it lasts," Honor tells me.

"I've spent half my life in hotels. You think this is going to change anything?" Lou sneers.

"I'm hoping it will."

"Fine," Lou screams, pulling herself off the floor. "Where's the vodka?"

"You finished it," Honor tells her.

She walks over to her bag, searches through it and when she comes up empty, angrily dumps it on the table. Her items scatter for a second time in ten minutes.

"Where's my stuff?"

"I've got it." Honor pats her Hermes bag. Her coat is now folded neatly over her arm. A fresh smoke is at her lips, sunglasses are on her face.

"What about my mini bottles?"

"I emptied them out."

"When?"

"A moment ago."

"Those were mine!" The hoarse, charmingly seductive voice is gone. In its place is betrayed frustration. "You had no right. No right."

She walks to the fridge, opens it and seeing only healthy items slams it shut. "Fuck. Fuck you and this room and your great big plan to make me over."

"I'm too old to do this, Louise. I can't do it anymore. I just can't."

"So don't. No one's asking you to."

"You want to work? You want to make jewelry or T-shirts or whatever you think you want to do with the next forty years of your life? Then you better clean up your act because I won't be around to watch it." Honor's voice cracks and she stops herself. "Now give me a hug good-bye and I'll call you later."

"No. I don't want to do this. I've changed my mind." She starts putting on her coat and can't get her arm in one of the sleeves. "It wouldn't kill someone to help me, you know."

"Lou, we talked about this." Honor's voice is stern, but even toned.

"You talked about this. I don't need you to do this. I can do it on my own. If I didn't have any fucking talent you wouldn't be here in the first place. All you see when you look at me is a fast buck. Some quick cash for an old, ugly PR person past her prime."

Unable to get her coat on, she whips it off her one arm and leaves it on the floor. She stumbles over to her clothing and starts to pack. "I can fucking leave any time I want."

"Security can be here in moments. They'll stand outside your door all day, all night if they have to," Honor informs.

"Is that true?" Lou asks me. "You didn't tell me that. When were you going to tell me that? That fucking changes everything."

"We went over all of this Louise."

"No we didn't. When? Tell me when. Tell me exactly when we had this so-called informative conversation." She stands, rocks back and forth, trying to steady herself. "I didn't agree to jail."

"I'd hardly call a five-star hotel jail."

I'm worried what other guests will say when they hear the yelling and I think this wasn't such a good idea. That if things get out of hand, I could be fired. The underwater sensation returns as does the pressure in my chest. I need a vacation. Somewhere warm and sunny.

"The nurse can give you a sedative. She'll be here soon," Honor assures her.

Make that two. I'm way overdue for a room inspection, and if Lou could wait another half hour, I'm sure I could find an array of mother's little helpers. Valium, Xanax, Klonopin, our guests aren't choosy and at this point, neither am I. I think about excusing myself now. The idea of running down to the desk, selecting a few keycards, and doing a quick examination is most alluring.

"Okay, this is where I exit," Honor says, extracting a lipstick and her phone at the same time.

Lou rushes toward her and blocks the door. "Don't go. I'm sorry. Why can't we just do this at my house? I want . . ."

"This is it!" Her voice is high-pitched and comes out in

short puffs. "I swear, this is fucking it." She pushes Lou lightly out of the way but hard enough to knock her off balance and closes the door behind her, leaving Lou to take her arm and sweep it over the table while screaming at the top of her lungs as items fly in all directions.

Chapter 8

Morgan
Suite 1512

I've not slept in days and the last few room inspections have left me feeling hollow. The pills I was able to find have helped me greatly—kept the breathing issue at bay—and I feel a slight blissful sense of calm. However, it makes it hard to focus and feel awake. My normal cup of coffee is now accompanied by a shot of espresso. A Red Bull in the afternoon becomes the snack of choice. A cigarette in the a.m. quickly turns plural. An extra fifteen minutes here, another hit of the snooze button there, but I've got a morning meeting today so I'm in the office by 8:00. I'm sipping froth from the cappuccino I'm jonesing for when a frantic Paulina plows into my office, apologizing for the abrupt entrance.

An older Polish woman who's been with the hotel for years, she's squat with a plump frame, which makes her uniform look uncomfortably tight. Her short white hair accentuates her full face. Lovable and kind, she's considered grandmotherly to the younger staffers, especially those in her division.

"I so sorry Ms. Tierney, there's a woman in room 1512 . . ." She's breathless and bends forward, her beefy hands on her knees. She looks up at me, face red, eyes bulging. "Please, we go now."

"What's happened?" I ask, taking off my earpiece and disconnecting myself from the phone.

"A woman is tied to the bed in room 1512."

I'm standing now, reaching for the walkie-talkie, the digital camera, my cell phone, and an indemnity contract. "Is she dead?" I scan the room to make sure there's nothing else I'll need.

"I don't know. I go in to clean and find her there."

"Did you try to wake her?" I'm pushing her out of the office and taking the stairs, two at a time, not sure she'll be able to follow me. I turn to look at her. Paulina shakes her head. "I too scared. In the fifteen years I work here, I never see anything like this before."

Neither have I. As far as I know, we've only had three deaths in the past five years, so it's not unheard of. One heart attack, one OD, which makes me queasy every time I think about Lou, and one child who accidentally drowned in the tub. Thankfully none have happened on my watch.

And that's when it hits me.

Once a year the hotel has Manager Gratitude Day, when the staff throws us a party. Similar to Senior Appreciation or the kind celebrated at sleep-away camp, a small party is thrown to acknowledge the hard work we do, the long hours we spend at the hotel, the twenty-four-hour on call job we accept. As refined as the hotel is, we're not above a little mockery, and I have no trouble seeing one of the staffers tied to a bed while everyone yells surprise.

Paulina is doing a fine performance. She's actually shaking and sweat has formed above her lip, which upon close inspection could use a waxing and I'm tempted to treat her to this service at the hotel later today for doing such a good job.

"She was just lying there, bloody and messy."

"I'm sure it's a terrible sight," I say, playing along. "What do you think happened?"

"I don't know." She shudders in the elevator and we ride the rest of the trip in silence. When we emerge on the fifteenth floor, Paulina hands me the key. A HOUSEKEEPING, PLEASE sign hangs on the door.

Paulina steps back, looking scared and perplexed. Perhaps she's afraid of getting in the photo or if she enters first, people will yell surprise at her instead of me. I give an authoritative tap first and say "housekeeping," but when I get no response slide the card through. The door clicks open and I prepare myself for the collective cheer, but hear nothing.

"Who's there? Robin? Is that you?" A shaky, yet angry voice travels from the next room.

Okay, they've taken this a bit too far, but I can play along. "Very clever," I say, but the surprise is on me. Upon entering, I find the shades are partly drawn, creating a dim, dreary feel. I flip on the lights and in doing so almost trip over a tray of old food—brown fruit, uneaten toast, picked-over eggs, filled cups of coffee—while sliding on the *New York Times*, which is sprawled out in sections. Clothing is tossed carelessly on the arms on the couch, the back of the desk chair, and on the floor.

"Hello?" I call out.

"Robin?"

Several bags, one from Barneys, one from Calvin Klein, and another that's nondescript are by the coffee table, which has an open birth control disc, diamond necklace, pearl bracelets, iPod, and BlackBerry on it. The smell of stale tomato and urine gets stronger as we venture forward.

"My name is Morgan. I'm one of the managers. I'm with housekeeping. May we come in?" I don't wait for a response and enter the bedroom with Paulina behind me. The lights are already on and just as she said, a woman is tied to the bed. Dried blood, brown liquid, globs of cream, and what look like smoking patches cover her face. Her robe looks doused in colored dye. Clumps of hair lay on the pillow reminding me instantly of Dale. How small she looked in her bed. How her hair fell out in fistfuls. A tiara sits upon this woman's head and I mentally, involuntarily, replace it with the Mickey Mouse ears. I don't even try to breathe because I think my heart has stopped beating. I think about the oxygen tank Dale used. Remember what the plastic felt like on my face, scratchy and cold. I used it once, to see what it was like, to feel what my sister experienced. My mother walked in just as I was taking my first breath and slapped it out of my hand.

"You are never to use that," she said, her face close to mind, her finger pointed at me. "It's not a toy and your sister could die without it."

I swallow the bile in my throat because I'm sure vomiting

would be unprofessional. I force myself to look at the dirty robe, to focus on the empty bottles from the minibar that are scattered around her. I listen to the TV and radio, which are battling each other. I take note how the newscaster's voice is deeper than the DJ's. I feel Paulina nudge me in the side.

"It's okay," I say. "Are you alone?"

"Yes," she says, lifting up her head, her neck muscles straining. The tiara glimmers from the lights above the bed.

"Are you hurt?"

"No, I'm fine."

In corporate, they train you to handle all situations as professionally and efficiently as possible. I announce everything I'm doing and try to talk slowly, soothingly, like Faye's sister did. "I'm going to untie your right leg, first. Okay?"

"Yes." Her head falls back. Tears leak from her eyes.

"I need to ask what happened."

"It's nothing. Really. It was a joke my boyfriend played."

I don't know if she's been raped, I don't know if she's okay, I only know she's lying.

"I'll pay for any damages. I'm fine."

If a guest offers to take responsibility for something, a broken item, damage to the furniture, whatever the case may be, you let them. And I'm not to offer any suggestions. For example, asking if one of our staffers did this can only give fodder if they're trying to extort money or cover up for someone.

I take hold of her foot, feel the coolness of the rope belt, notice its stark whiteness up against her reddened skin and the brown of the banister. "Paulina, could you please help me undo Mrs. . . ." I pause. "I'm sorry, what's your . . ."

"Linda."

"Linda's other leg."

Paulina moves swiftly, but I can see her hands are shaking. It only takes a second for me to untie the knot and carefully rest her foot on the bed. I then calmly move to Paulina, lay my hands over her trembling ones. "It's okay."

She looks up at me.

"It's okay," I say again, and she steps back. Stands watching.

"How about getting Linda a warm, wet towel."

Paulina disappears into the bathroom while I fight with the material holding Linda's left ankle to the bed. "This one's a bit harder because the material has been knotted rather tightly. If you can hold on another minute, I'm sure I can get this . . ." My fingers are working fast but the knot isn't budging. I scan the room and spot a knife on the nightstand. "I'm just going to use this . . ." I say, walking toward her. The knife feels cold and solid in my grasp. By the time I think about the fingerprints it's too late.

While near her hand, I untie her left one with ease since it's only held by a black leather belt. Her face is maybe a foot away from me. The smell of wine and tomato and urine is making me nauseous. I want to look at her, but know once I do, I won't be able to look away.

With two of the four appendages free, I move to her foot again. Paulina enters with a cloth and hands it to Linda, who sighs loudly, mutters "fuck" under her breath. I cut through the material. Her ankle in my hand is as cold as the silver knife, as pale as our robes and towels.

Now only her right hand is cuffed to the bed. Able to move, she clutches her robe closed, contorts her body, sits forward, her feet balanced on the floor. She takes the familiar position of *The Thinker*, her free elbow on one knee, a hand on her head.

"Are you going to be sick?" I ask, then mouth to Paulina to bring over the trash can. She shakes her head no as more memories of Dale flood my mind: Dale convulsing in her bed; Dale vomiting on the floor, crying hysterically as my mother held her and screamed for me to get the garbage can; Dale gulping for air, the oxygen tank too far away for her to grasp on her own.

"I just need a moment," Linda is saying.

"How about some water? Paulina, would you mind?" I'm shaking now, sweating too, and I think I'm going to black out.

Paulina vanishes again and returns with a glass of water, which Linda drinks, and I almost reach for it myself but remain focused.

"Is there a key somewhere?" I ask. "So we can unlock the handcuffs."

"I don't know," she says, lifting her head up. Her face, now clean from the towel, reveals a nasty black-and-blue around her nose and under her eyes, not to mention a red square on her forehead from the removed patch. Her hair is chopped in short chunks and some pieces are sticking up while others are matted down. "Try the bar, or the table in the other room."

We move into the living room, I to the bar, Paulina to the bags. The refrigerator is almost empty except for a bottle of cranberry juice and two Evian waters. The basket that usually holds batteries, sunblock, chips, cookies, and a camera has been raided as well. I turn to the trash can and after spreading several sections of the *Times* out, dump the insides onto the paper. Crumpled-up tissues, empty bags of chips, candy, and the disposable camera tumble out. I reach for it. Seventeen photos have been taken. I catch Paulina looking at me, her head shaking, her hands empty.

"I find nothing."

"Me too." But as I hand her the camera and ask her to put it in her apron, something shiny catches my eye by the iPod. It's so small, yet so powerful. Only an inch, it saves me from calling maintenance, from this woman having to be seen by a man, from wasting time for all this to happen. I give the key to Linda, whose hand shakes so badly I need to do it for her.

"Can I help you stand?" I ask, my hand already on the robe.

"Look, you've been great, but I'm fine. You can go now. My boyfriend just went too far with the joke."

"Is there someone we can call?" I'm not supposed to ask this. I'm supposed to have her sign a statement releasing the hotel of responsibility, and I should let her clean herself up and shower, but something has happened that feels wrong. "We can put you in another room right now, if you'd like. We'll have your belongings brought to you, you can shower . . ."

"No, I just want to be left alone."

"Really, it's no trouble . . ."

"Jesus Christ. I said leave me alone."

Paulina and I exchange looks.

"If I could just ask you to sign this, we'll be out of your way." I pull out the document, hand her a pen, both of which she grabs from me. She can barely grasp the pen and her body shakes as she leans over the nightstand and signs her name. She shoves it back at me.

"Are we done?"

"Of course," I say, ushering us out. "I'm terribly sorry."

The door slams loudly behind us, reverberating in my ears, making the hallway feel as though it's trembling.

"You did everything correctly," I tell Paulina. "I don't want housekeeping to bother her and if she's ordering room service, I want one of the security guards to accompany them. We'll clean her room after she leaves."

Paulina hands me the camera as we wait for the elevator. Once it arrives, we ride to the lobby in silence, leaving Paulina to travel by herself for two more floors. At the front desk I find room 1512 belongs to Vicki Seidelman, AKA Linda, who, according to our guest profile, stays here three or four times a year, and frequents our property in DC often.

Several hours later, I tell all this to my boss, Larry.

"I don't understand, how long was this woman tied up for?" he says, his hair slicked back, his large silver watch clanking on the table every time he hits it with his fist.

"We're not sure. Hours. Maybe overnight?" My arms are folded over my body. I'm cold and feel fluish. I want to go home. I want my mother to bring me hot soup with noodles and chicken. And coloring books and crayons. And red licorice and butterscotch sucking candy.

"Christ." He runs his hands over his hair, then rubs at his jaw. The room feels small and Larry seems to loom at his desk. I need a vacation. Someplace warm.

I walk over to the window. The desire to let in fresh air seems overwhelming.

"The only reason they found her is because they went to change over the room. She was supposed to have checked out."

"Did you have her sign anything before she left?"

"Of course I did."

"What's the damage?"

"Nothing." I turn back to face him.

"You seem shaken," he says.

"I'm not. I just didn't expect—I don't know."

He eyes me suspiciously.

"She paid for the robe, the minibar items, even offered to pay for the sheets. I know she left a big tip for housekeeping as well."

"We got off lucky, then."

"I guess."

I stare out the window, jealousy filling me for those who are roaming freely.

Wes is waiting for me at the hotel's bar, a welcoming sight. He's all man in his work suit and tie. Masculine and concrete. Tall and rugged. I wonder if I want to see his room. Wonder what this man would feel like on top of me. I slide into the seat he's saved and am greeted warmly, first by him, then by our bartender.

"Your friend is drinking a manhattan. Can I get the same for you?" he asks, placing a black napkin in front of me.

"Passion cosmo." I'm hoping vodka will wash away much of today. Dale, Vicki, my boss. The list is ever growing.

"Sure thing."

A compartmentalized dish containing nuts, olives, and cheese sticks materializes along with my drink.

"Thanks for meeting me," I say.

"My pleasure." Like Honor, his iPhone and cell rest on the mahogany bar.

At 6:00 p.m. the bar is busy, but not overwhelming as I fear it will become. A restless hum transcends the room as more and more tables are occupied by people waiting for their counterparts to show.

I lift my drink. "Would toasting 'to finding my uncle's ashes' be inappropriate?"

Wes shrugs. "No, just optimistic."

We clink glasses, take sips from our drinks before setting them down again. "I guess there's no word yet."

"No, I'm sorry." The phone vibrates and he checks it quickly.

"Look, you've been very honest and up front."

"How's your mother doing?" I stare into his eyes for verification of whether he actually cares. As green as they are, and as sincere as he appears, there's a deadness behind them. My father wears the same expression.

"She's holding up surprisingly well. They weren't that close, but the shock of how he died and knowing someone else has him hit her hardest."

Wes nods, then takes another swig from his drink.

"What's it like working for the mayor?"

"It's okay. I think people are more impressed by the word 'mayor' than what I actually do, which can be rather tedious." He finishes his drink, then requests a second. "I work with the police commission, write a lot of reports on policies that should be enforced, attend too many press conferences, watch a lot of things done incorrectly, see more than enough incompetence, and then watch those same people get promoted. But once in a while we do something correctly."

Two drinks turn into three, which effortlessly spill into four for Wes as he tells me about growing up in Boston, attending

St. John's, about his parents and family, and, lastly, the fire that caused him to lodge with us for the past two weeks.

"The building was evacuated, and I thought about calling in a few favors, but decided it was best to let things happen on their own." He's clearly tipsy because he's talking too close to my face and a glaze has come over his eyes. "A few neighbors and myself went across the street to a restaurant and got drunk. Then we went back upstairs, I packed a few essentials and came here."

"How civilized," I order a third cosmo, and continue to chew on the end of my straw, the sight of Vicki becoming a mental blur.

"Honestly, I thought after a night or two that would be it because we were told it was safe to return. I went home to check things out, and as I'm packing a bag, mostly stuff for the Thanksgiving weekend, the fire trucks come back and I think, 'This has got to be a joke. Or maybe they're doing a follow-up' "—he laughs—"as if. But supposedly they hadn't fixed the wiring correctly or something didn't hold, who knows. We were evacuated again, and that was enough to push everyone over the edge. I came back to the hotel after the holiday weekend and have been here since."

"That's really awful." I start to giggle. "Not staying at the hotel, the idea of being homeless." The room is moving slightly, the lights are becoming harsh, and halfway through my third cosmo I realize I've reached my drink limit.

"This second time, several floors were burned pretty badly and everyone was crying and hysterical. Tomorrow they move me and the other neighbors into temporary housing, which should be a nightmare." He sets the empty glass on the bar, looks at his dancing iPhone but ignores it. "But I think I might stay here," he shrugs. "Even if I have to pay for it myself."

Over the past hour and a half the bar has become intolerably loud, filled with people who are crowding us, leaning over Wes, reaching over me for their drinks, and invading our personal space. A woman two seats away has an ear-piercing cackle. A man behind me keeps knocking his elbow into my head. When Wes's phone rings, I'm momentarily relieved for the break in conversation.

"Excuse me, might be the mayor." He raises the phone to his ear. "This is Wes." He lets out a deep sigh of frustration. "Yes Franny. I'm in the middle of something. Look, I'm really not the best person to call about these things."

There's a pause. "I'm at the hotel one more night, maybe two. I guess they'll move us individually. I really don't know."

Another pause provides time for me to realize I'm pleasantly drunk.

"I'd like to help, but I'm really not a good person to phone. I haven't been on the board in years. I would try Lester or Mitchell. They're both in charge of the fire committee."

There's more pausing followed by Wes raising his hand and making the talking sign, fingers and thumb coming together like a duck's beak. "No, it's fine, but honestly, I've got a lot going on and just can't deal with this right now." He groans, then leans closer to me so I can just make out a muffled voice of a woman on the other end of his cell. "Sorry I couldn't be of more help." He hangs up. "I think I've got a stalker."

I raise an eyebrow. "Really? Who?"

"Some nut job that lives above me. I helped carry her bags

and things when we were first evacuated, and now she assumes I'm the go-to person for answers. I'm sure your uncle would have enjoyed working with her. She calls every few days asking for updates on the apartment, if I've heard anything, where will I be staying, is there something the mayor can do. Like what's the mayor going to do?"

There's a hungriness about him, a frat-boy-like quality in the way he drinks from his glass, in the way his hand scoops out the nuts, even in the way he chews, harshly, causing his jaw muscles to bulge each time he bites down.

Room 906 is not one of my favorites. It's a standard with a queen-size bed, desk, and chair. It tends to run smaller than most, and you can hear the constant sound of the elevator. But Wes has kept it organized and hardly has any belongings for someone who's been homeless for a week or two. There's no suitcase, no shopping bags, no clothing folded carefully on the back of the chair. Nothing. The only way you'd know someone is staying here is that the desk has a myriad of objects on it: plugs for his electronic devices, yellow legal pads, handful of markers, contracts, reading glasses folded and resting perfectly in the middle of the pad.

In all the years I've worked here, I've stayed over in the hotel twice. Once for a friend's bridal shower that turned into a slumber party, and once during a blackout when I was in charge of the hotel that night. As I take a step forward, Wes dims the lights so low I can barely see. He moves to the bar, the light from the mini refrigerator momentarily illuminating him, making him garish in appearance.

"What's your poison?"

"Nothing for me thanks, I'm good."

He shuts the door and the bottles rattle inside, as if trying to escape. He slinks over in my direction. I take a step back, my body now up against the wall. Everything feels too close.

"It's been a long time since I've been intimate with someone," he tells me. "I tend to take things slowly. I know it's not very guylike, but I'm not much of a player."

The most exciting thing Bernard ever did was drizzle some wine over my breast and lick it off, and even that was tame because he only wanted to use white. But Wes is a liar. I know it and so does he. The way his mouth lingers at my ear and then hovers near my lips while his fingers press at my breast, forcefully and confidently, betray his words. He is too savvy and smooth. His business card, which has too many words and abbreviations after his name, has gotten him through many a locked door. Has let him receive knowing winks from an inner circle of power players. My guess is a hurt trail of thinly woven women who are impressed with his job and good looks feel cheated and abandoned. I wonder what he would think of the leather brace, if he would go with me to a sex club.

I already know condoms are kept in his dopp kit. That as minimal as his hotel room is, he keeps his home the same way, the burnt one that's probably fine. But a hotel is a lot sexier than an apartment. And I'd bet my job that several women, and maybe a man or two, have seen the inside of this room in the time he's been here.

When his hands reach around my neck a wave of claustrophobia drowns me. I close my eyes, fight the urge to take a deep, cleansing breath as Vicki's face mixed with traces of Dale's enter my vision. I want to leave. I need to. I don't want the back brace thing or Wes's drunken body touching mine. Instead I want Trish, and my sister, and I want my friends, the married ones, to be single again. I want them all here at the hotel with brighter lighting and a cart of make-it-yourself ice cream sundaes that the hotel offers to parents throwing their children birthday parties. I want John Hughes movies and sleepover parties and nothing but a lifetime to grow up ahead of us.

"It's late. I should go." I keep my voice even, void of emotion, just as they taught me in management class. It calms people down and is used to deactivate a tense situation. My hand searches blindly in the dark for the doorknob. "This was my mistake. I'm not allowed to become intimate with the guests." And taking the blame is supposed to remove anger in the other person.

"I won't tell if you don't." His lips are at my mouth again, his tongue trying to make its way past my clenched teeth. Acid is churning in my stomach and moving up to my throat.

"I know, but it's wrong. This was really my fault." I try to reach for the light, but can't find it. I try to push him off of me but am finding him too heavy. "Please, I need to go." Urgency has filled my voice, and I think how weak I am for not being able to stay calm. "Please," I whisper, almost beg, "I need to go. I need to go."

Wes releases me. He babbles something about mixed signals, about calming down, about my uncle's ashes, but I can't hear him because my hand is on the doorknob, my heart and cosmos are in my throat, and I'm fighting once again for the breath I can't seem to take.

Chapter 9

Morgan
The Lobby Lounge

I exit the Fifty-eighth Street side of the hotel and walk across the street to Duane Reade anxious to see the photos from the camera found in Vicki's room. Three days ago when I dropped it off the lady behind the counter looked at the device as if it were an artifact. Sunglasses hide my face as I wait my turn on line. I surrender the slip of paper with a phony name on it and ask for a pack of Spirits—the healthy cigarette. The salesgirl whispers something to her co-worker and a manager is requested to come to the front.

"Is there a problem?" I ask.

"Just a minute," she says, smacking gum and twisting her frosted orange hair with her index finger.

I can hear muttering coming from behind me, all from people anxious to get on with their shopping. Within a minute the manager appears, a stout man with bushy hair and matching eyebrows.

"She's the one with the photos," the girl says, popping pink gum.

"Oh, yeah?" He looks me up and down. Then he flicks his head to the right and we both slide over to another register. "The photos are a bit, well, raunchy. Do you know what's on this film?" he says, a smug look on his hairy face.

I nod. "I do."

"I'm wondering if I should call the police."

"We thought the same thing," I lie, hoping my hunch is correct. "I work across the street. We found one of our guests like this. These pictures are for the insurance company and to protect the hotel."

He nods as I reach for the envelope.

"I've never been to the hotel before."

"Really?" I can't believe we're playing this game.

"I hear nice things. People come in here all the time talking about the food."

My arm is still extended, waiting. "Maybe you'd like to have a cocktail sometime. I'd be happy to drop off a drink coupon for you."

He inches the packet closer.

"I'd hate to drink alone. Maybe I could bring my wife?"

"Sure." I keep my eyes locked on his. Just give me the fucking film. "Two it is."

The girl standing next to him, who barely looks old enough to ovulate let alone drink slaps him in the arm.

"And one for Kristen. After all she was the one who . . ."

"Right. One for Kristen."

He looks at the packet before handing it over. "I'm here until eight p.m. tonight, Sally Mulligan."

"Great."

I grasp it tightly but move my arm away slowly, nonchalantly. He smiles revealing a set of yellow teeth. "That's eleven dollars for the film, eight fifty for the smokes."

I hand him a twenty dollar bill and watch him ring it up. The sound of the register seems loud and I bite down on my tongue to stop from squirming when he puts the fifty cents in my hand.

Once in my office I remove the glossy five by sevens, eager to see what happened before we got there. Each is of Vicki in slightly different positions taken from various angles: up close, far away, some slightly blurry, as if someone were doing it very quickly. The last one is of two girls whose faces are pressed up against each other: one a monster, one a victim. I stare at it looking for clues. Friends? Lovers? Sisters? Though the hair and eye color are different, there is a similarity in their expressions even though only one is smiling. Yet too much of Vicki's face is camouflaged by makeup, blood, and goo to know for sure.

I pick up the phone. The receiver feels cumbersome in my hand. I reach forward and put my finger on the hook to quiet the sound of the dial tone since I don't yet know who I want to talk to. I look at Dale's photo, wish my fingers had her number to press. And since I don't, I reach out to the one person I hope will answer.

"Fresh Art. Trish Hemingway speaking."

"Hi, it's Morgan." There's a pause so I add, "from the Four Seasons."

"Hey. How are you?"

"I thought I'd call and say hi, see how things were."

"I'm glad you called." There's a break in the conversation. "I wanted to say I was sorry to hear about your uncle."

Relief whooshes through me. "I wanted to say something to you that night, but I didn't know . . . I didn't know what to say exactly, or what your relationship was, or if it was even my place to say anything at all."

"It's okay."

I hear the sound of feet and heavy grunting in the background; then Trish tells me to hold for a second, tells someone else to put the artwork over there while an intense buzzing from a fax machine follows.

"Sorry about that," she says, returning to me.

I want to ask her how she knew. Who told that he was my uncle. If she was one of his patients. I wonder how long they've been seeing each other and if that's why she chose this hotel to have her party for Olive, and if she asked for a discount because maybe Marty said he gets one from me.

"Morgan." There's something about the way she says my name that makes me feel sad and understood at the same time. "Are you okay?"

Relief is momentary because sadness steps in and bullies it away. If I open my mouth all that will leak out is a loud moan or a sob. Tears drip quietly onto the photos in my hand ruining the perfectly glossy coating, smearing the faces and blurring them into a blob. I know she's waiting for an answer, but I don't know what to say. I want to tell her about the clock I'm desperately trying to turn back. I want someone to tell me how much longer I'm supposed to feel this alone. I want her to help me without my having to ask for it.

"Everything is fine," I say.

"Are you sure? You don't sound it."

"No, it's all good. I thought maybe we would get drinks or something. Maybe your friend Olive wants to join us. She could see the space you've reserved at the hotel, we could show her the food list for her party, or even sample the appetizers . . ."

"I'd love to but it's crazy here. The gallery event is only a few weeks away, and I'm still trying to finalize the artists I'll be repping and the whole thing is a bit overwhelming right now."

"Of course. Another time. It's an open invite so whenever you want to get together you let me know."

"Absolutely. I—" Someone calls for her, and I know it's only seconds before she'll be hanging up. "Okay, then I'll call you soon. And I'm sorry about your uncle. He was . . ."

"You don't have to say anything nice about him. I know what he was."

"Helpful. I guess." Her name is called again, this time with more urgency.

We both say good-bye and then it's over.

The magician waves his magic wand and poof—all gone.

Chapter 10

Anne

The Front Desk

These are Anne's top fears—in random order, rather than by importance.

1. *Vomiting.*
2. *Having her teeth fall out.*
3. *Getting cancer.*
4. *Falling down a flight of stairs, head first.*
5. *Roaches.*

Her biggest concern is a situation that would encompass all of the above. For example, she's at a party in a stranger's townhouse, and because of an undetected brain tumor, she loses her balance and falls down a flight of stairs and knocks her teeth on the floor—which crack and fall out. Because of the tumor, and blood from her broken teeth, she vomits. She is in mid-retch when, out of the corner of her eyes, she sees a roach approaching. All this causes her to faint. An ex-boyfriend from college, who she hasn't seen in years, would stumble across her accidentally while trying to get into his apartment. He would call for help, and only after covering her with a blanket—so that she didn't go into shock—would he do a double take and say, "Oh. My. God. Didn't we date in college?" The only reason he'd recognize the crumpled-up person was her is because it would be a reenactment of a past experience when she was drunk and actually fell down the steps of a fraternity house. When he tried to help her up she retched all over him. Luckily no roaches were involved and her teeth-fear didn't metamorphose until several years ago.

Then there are the rules—all of which change as the list becomes more extensive and complicated.

1. *Objects that have lost their glow, or upon bringing them home, have instilled some kind of unhappiness, must be thrown out or returned.*
2. *Pennies heads up must be picked off the floor or street. If not, luck is passed on to another person.*
3. *Sleeping in her nightshirt inside out insures a night of sound sleep.*
4. *No wearing black on Mondays.*
5. *Her takeout menus must be piled in size order. If not, she might get sick from eating the delivered food.*

She doesn't know how the fears and rituals started. She just knows it was there one day, sitting heavy on her chest as if something was wrong. As if she had forgotten to do a task of major importance. She checked for her reading glasses, leafed through her calendar, called her machine, and retrieved her messages. Nothing.

Anne went through a second list of possibilities. Did she take her vitamins? Had she left the keys in the door? Did she turn the coffee machine off? Her smoke alarm needed fresh batteries, the red light no longer flashed, and because it began making that ear-piercing scream she'd taken the whole contraption down. Left it sitting next to her coffeemaker. She could visualize the fire starting in her apartment, moving swiftly to the unit next to hers, traveling upward to the newly renovated floor above. Anne felt her body shutting down as she dialed her doorman. She was about to ask if he'd send the handyman up to check, when she hazily saw a picture of herself turning the device off and putting her mug in the sink. She hung up before he said hello. Then innocently, she tapped the top of her desk. A knock-on-wood kind of motion, as if to say, "There—thank goodness." Like a pill taking effect, the panic went away. All was fine.

That was five years ago.

It didn't take long for the tapping to become a thing she needed to do, like breathing. If she didn't tap, something terrible would happen for sure. Then came the touching of doorframes followed by the waiting for the digital clock to change from an odd number to an even one before she could start her day. Now she couldn't drink her coffee unless all the pink, blue, and white packets were facing upward in a straight, neat row, like dominos. On bad days, the same number of each was mandatory. But these rituals were livable. They were merely inconveniences. It's the voices in her head, the ones that force her to hold her breath in elevators, wear her nightshirt inside out, and count red cars (a sign for bad luck) that she can't stand.

She would like to blame this on her parents. Find some genetic way to prove this was their fault. She knows they have weird idiosyncrasies. Once, a matter of switching office spaces with a co-worker caused her father to break out in hives a week before the transaction took place. A mere eight feet brought on red bumps to which calamine lotion had to be applied for days. And then there's her mother. Anne has seen her count to five each time she lines her underarms with deodorant, brushes her teeth, or combs her hair.

Anne goes through a list of other people's odd behaviors to convince herself she's normal. She would ask someone about them, but is afraid they would institutionalize her like they did her brother, who resides overmedicated in a hospital with other overmedicated men who do nothing all day but watch TV and roam the hallways. Anne is the normal child. The one who cannot disappoint her parents. The one who didn't have a breakdown. The one who doesn't have a love affair with sharp objects.

She blasts *Unlimited Lou's Greatest Hits* and lets the singer's signature raspy voice and melancholy music pour through her apartment. Anne has found this particular CD is unexplainably lucky. As if Lou's lyrics are cleansing the air and inviting only good into her dwelling. She lights sandalwood incense to ensure negative energies are removed. She opens the window, walks counterclockwise around the room reciting a little prayer, just as the *Good Luck* book instructs.

She waits for the clock to read 10:00 a.m. and walks out the door. She's meeting a man whose name is Gage, which sounds like an automotive part rather than a thirty-seven-year-old whom she discovered last week, thanks to an Internet dating service. Gage's bio states he's an artist who works with paint and "found objects." "Random things discovered on the street," he told her in an e-mail. She likes that he works with his hands, that he's tall, six foot two, that he has hazel eyes and a full head of hair. That he has a master's in anthropology but doesn't use it and claims to speak to both his parents, who are divorced, and his younger sister, who is married to a politician. Her favorite trait is the found objects. The ability to collect what others have lost or discarded.

Gage was the sixteenth person to respond to her personal ad. And sixteen feels lucky. She has a good vibe as she shuts her door, taps three times on the frame, and waits for the elevator, which comes immediately, another positive sign.

They meet for coffee at Chester's, a small, secluded, artsy hangout in the East Village. Gage's suggestion. She's a Murray Hiller, East Thirties, and according to her grandmother, the only bonus to living in her area is that it's near several hospitals. Useless since she never gets sick and her brother's hospital is in Westchester.

She walks the thirty or so blocks, counting the red cars that pass her, and enjoys the fall foliage. It's her favorite time of year. The air is crisp and moist. Leaves are everywhere: on the sidewalk, on top of cars, caught in sewage drains, and collecting in garbage cans. The *Good Luck* book says if she can catch a descending leaf, it will bring her fortune. She must look ridiculous reaching for the falling leaves, but she'd rather look stupid than be luckless.

Gage is already waiting outside the café, smoking a cigarette and looking like a softer version of the Marlboro man. He's exactly what she expected, right down to the leather bomber jacket and worn-in jeans. All that's missing is his motorcycle, but that would be too much of a cliche. His body is meaty, but fit. His hands are cracked and rough, large and chapped. His grip is firm and his two day's growth of beard gives him a manly appearance. His skin is tanned, like leather.

Even on a Sunday the shop is a buzz of morning action. She eyes the other customers, takes mental notes of their body language, their outfits. No one looks especially artistic. The men have wet hair, paint-smattered oxford shirts, their feet in sandals. Some women are in sweats and sneakers, their hair pulled back in high ponytails. Newspapers are strewn everywhere, tossed carelessly on stout wooden tables while loose sections cover the floor. Sketchbooks lay open revealing charcoal drawings and portraits, the creators aching to be asked about them. Random art fills every available wall space. The artist's name, title of the piece, number in the series, and the price is placed to the right of each creation, typed neatly on white index cards.

Anne's job is to secure two seats, which she snags by the window, while Gage orders the drinks. This plan allows her to prearrange the sweeteners according to color before he returns. When he does, both his hands are filled with identical-looking paper cups.

"Aren't artists supposed to sleep late, especially on Sundays?" she jokes as he slides into the rickety wooden chair.

"These guys are more Mark Kostabi than Jackson Pollock. They like to talk about their art rather than actually produce any."

She nods and smiles as Gage leans forward with his right arm outstretched, a cup within reach. As she comes to meet his hand, he recoils and extends his other one instead.

"Which do you think is yours?" he asks.

This game reminds Anne of her boss—a slick, twice-divorced Italian whom she dislikes.

"Several envelopes have your checks," he said two months ago. "One has a weekend getaway, and one is empty. Who wants to play?" He was sucking on a fat cigar and leaning back in his chair looking like a character from the *Godfather* sagas. She was tempted to kiss his hand and reach for any of the similar-looking envelopes. The other girls, all hotel concierges from her department, were amused. They had husbands and boyfriends, looked forward to last-minute escapes to balmy islands and frosted drinks with plastic animals that hung off the edges of the glasses. She just wanted her check. She was never late, did her work, covered for co-workers. This was dumb. Even though Anne knew he wouldn't really withhold anyone's pay, she didn't want to play. She was buying time by appearing as if she was *really* trying to choose, when she caught her reflection in the small mirror that sat on his leather padded desk. This vision made her wince. She could color her mousy hair or add rich blond highlights like the other women. Get her frizzy, wavy locks professionally straightened, wax her eyebrows, whiten her already-ivory teeth, wear color contacts instead of clear, get a makeover, but what would that change?

The Four Seasons had insisted grooming was a must. After all, she was a guest's first introduction. "Who wants to book a room from an unkempt person with smeared makeup, dirty fingernails, and a hairy upper lip?" her boss said during training week four years ago. She was just starting out as a front desk agent, taking reservations and organizing room cards. Her mother encouraged her to accept the free treatments the hotel offered. But when the day was over, and people were clocking out, it would still be her. A different, slightly more polished version of herself. She'd still tap the glass on the revolving doors upon exiting, carry her paraphernalia of lucky charms, and count red cars in the street. She'd still need to attend anti-anxiety classes in dreary hospitals or old church basements.

That day in her boss's office she was third to guess, and muttered the words "*Katta Katta*" before pointing to the envelope on the far right. She didn't know what the word meant or why it emerged from her mouth except that inside was her check, plus a $500 bonus. Now she utters *Katta Katta* only for extremely important events or in times of crisis.

Gage is still waiting for her decision. She feels foolish and he looks stupid with outstretched arms and two cups of whatever's inside. His hands are now equal distance, left rising up as the right drops down, the right ascending as left declines. He looks like he's milking a cow. If she chooses correctly, she bargains with herself, they'll have a second date. He's cute and charming, and Anne wills herself to relax, to play along and look like she's a good sport. She chooses left, and Gage's smile widens. He waits for her to pop the lid off and as she does he says, "They're both the same. I ordered a cappuccino, too."

She reaches for a Sweet'N Low, rips it exactly halfway through the large red musical note, and pours the entire contents into her drink. Then she sticks the ripped piece inside the packet and folds it in half. She stirs and lays the tiny plastic straw on top of the packet. She looks up at her date, watches his rough hand move toward the packets, fingering them absentmindedly. She contains her impulse to knock his hand away. The packets are in perfect order. Doesn't he realize messing them up will ruin their date? Gage removes a sugar. Now there's an uneven number. She would add a sugar to her coffee but then it would be too sweet, undrinkable, and he would ask what was wrong. He would mistake her not drinking the cappuccino as her not liking him, or her being difficult. Either way the date is ruined, the odd number will certainly make it so, and she likes this guy. Likes the way he sips his froth. The way he leans on his elbow, his thumb holding up his chin. She opts to take the extra packet and will choke down the sweet drink if it kills her. What if he judges her two-packet choice? She can hear him recapping the evening at some random bar with his artist friends making sure to highlight her sweet tooth. Someone will crack a joke about her putting on weight later on in life; maybe his mother would point out this flaw. She sits on her hands to stop the tapping, bites down on her lower lip to prevent the muttering, tells her head to stop listening to the voices.

Once as a child, she became hysterical at the Delta terminal at the airport. She had a pressing sensation that if she got on the plane it would crash. Her parents had to physically carry her onto the flight. She screamed during takeoff, during the movie, even through dinner. The steward tried to bribe her with crayons and a deck of cards, her brother poked her, and people seated in the vicinity begged her parents to do something. They never took another family vacation and Anne never took another flight.

"So"—Gage says, leaning forward—"am I your first Internet date?" He says this like he's a pro. Like no matter how many dates Anne has had, he will have more.

"Sort of. You're the second one I've gone on, but you were sixteenth to reply."

Gage seems pleased with this and smiles warmly, widely, causing the crow's-feet near his eyes to crinkle. "Not bad odds."

"You?"

"A few." He shrugs. "I'm not much for the personals, but I figured, what the hell. The women I've met have been okay."

An hour later, Gage holds the door open for her, and as she passes through she taps the frame twice and twists, as if she wants to steal one last look of the room.

"Oh, I thought I forgot my glasses." As she watches him look at their table, she catches the faint scent of turpentine.

"Looks clear," he states, turning to face her.

They walk a few blocks and end up standing in front of the number six subway.

"You think we could do this again?" he asks. A leaf sails by and she restrains her urge to snatch it.

"Sure," she says, realizing she wants him to phone, wants to see what her hand feels like in his. She thinks about this as the train cradles her uptown.

At work, she takes her place beside the other two concierges, Julia, a model-in-training, and Cecile, a mother of three who works part-time, mostly, she says, to get away from her children. Anne surveys her to-do list while feeling powerful in her black suit, crisp white shirt, and headset. The three look like stand-ins for Charlie's Angels—each dressed exactly alike.

Though she came to hotel management late in life—most of the girls she worked with were in their early twenties and still living at home—she loves her job. Things at the Four Seasons are orderly and organized. Structured. She likes the idea that everything is replaceable. Disposable. Right down to the shampoo and conditioner bottles. Use a soap once and a fresh bar is presented to you daily. Rooms are stripped clean and given another chance, the air shifting slightly with each new occupant. The early morning buzz that a new day awaits, the slick clean marble floors, the plush ribbed lounge chairs somehow calm her. She loves making reservations at trendy restaurants where most people can't book a dinner three months in advance, let alone that evening. Loves obtaining house seats for a sold-out, must-see show. Once, she was asked to locate a miniature dachshund for Madonna. She spent all day tracking down the pedigree and finally unearthed a breeder in Vermont who had just one pup left. Madonna stopped by to thank Anne personally. Gave her free tickets to her Farewell Tour. These were good days. Days when she felt connected to something other than the tapping.

At night she surfs the Web for obsessive-compulsive disorder treatments. There are over 2 million and she makes mental notes of conference dates, behavior therapy institutes, foundations, and support groups. She reads message boards and enters chat rooms with a phony name and e-mail address. Before logging off, she takes a quiz given by the Florida Obsessive-Compulsive Foundation. Last week she scored a 73. Until she gets a 90 or higher, she refuses to seek real help. This is her barometer. An alcoholic in the making. A coke user not ready for rehab.

To keep the test fresh she clicks the random button and eight questions from a list of fifty are revealed.

1. *Do you have mental images of death or other horrible events? Yes.*

2. *Do you worry about fire, burglary, or flooding in your house? Yes.*

3. *Do you worry about accidentally hitting a pedestrian with your car or letting it roll down the hill? No.*

4. *Do you perform excessive or ritualized washing, cleaning, or grooming rituals? No.*

5. *Do you check light switches, water faucets, the stove, door locks, or your car's emergency brake? Yes.*

6. *Do you perform counting, arranging, "evening-up" behaviors (making sure socks are at same height)? Yes.*

7. *Do you need to touch objects or people? Yes.*

8. *Do you think about poisoning dinner guests or injuring children? No.*

This last one puts her mind at ease. She doesn't even bother to take part two, Repeated Thoughts, Images, Urges, and Behaviors, because this last question is so off base. She shuts down the computer and taps the top twice. As she reaches for the light, her eyes catch the free box of Paxil she received in the mail last month—the medication of choice to all OCD'ers. "Magic pills" they're called in the chat rooms. She picks up the box, wonders what they taste like. Wonders if they can save her.

Anne has signed up for an anti-anxiety class given at the Red Cross, free to all New York residents. This is her first one. A step in trying to gain control over her life. She found the group accidentally. A guest needed a nearby AA meeting and while scanning the net, she stumbled upon the class.

Orthodox Jews are seated next to her. A group of black men talk about Eminem. An actor rehearses a scene by himself, his sides marked in yellow highlighter, while another woman, dressed in a bright orange sweatshirt and jogging pants, reads *Getting Over Your Ex*. Across from her, a man with a Walkman sings as if he's in the shower, lost in a world of music that no one else can hear. She doesn't know the song or she'd happily sing along, anything to stop her jabbering inner voice, the smaller version of herself that makes her second-guess every single decision she makes. A few seats away is a homeless couple. The woman's teeth are crooked and one tooth hangs over her lip. The man is fat and unshaven and they hold hands like teenagers drooling over each other. This sickens and comforts Anne all at once. Perhaps there really is someone for everyone. Perhaps Gage is her soul mate. At thirty-four she's not going to bump into her future husband at an OCD class, or find him in the hallway of some dingy hospital corridor as she heads to her group meeting and he to his Living with Tourette's class. She envisions their wedding. He could shout "Fuck me!" sporadically throughout the ceremony and she would constantly need to tap the priest's Bible. Her brother would be sedated and though he'd be best man, a ward of the state would stand behind him ready to embrace him with a padded coat. Anne's parents would need sedating too, the liquid kind, like scotch or gin. It would be a freak show no matter how you looked at it.

Then something terrible happens that takes Anne's breath away. A woman dressed in a long black coat, carrying a beat-up leather purse sits down. Mirroring an old librarian, she has dry gray hair, which hangs down past her shoulders, and wears trailer-park red lipstick that accentuates her mouth and long drawn face. Anne is about to turn away when the woman's expression becomes distorted. Her jaw juts out, her eyes widen, her mouth opens, and a horrible sobbing/choking sound escapes. It manifests into a half laugh, half ear-piercing moan, "I can't take it any more. I just can't." It sounds like a war cry and Anne expects to see tears, but nothing.

A moment passes.

The air stands still.

Anne doesn't know what to do and looks to others to see if maybe she imagined it. People are turning to counter partners, to seat mates, all with an inquisitive, horrified gaze.

"She does this every week," the actor tells Anne. "We're used to it."

The woman looks straight ahead, as if it never happened. Anne cannot take her eyes off her. Her chest aches, her heart pounds. She yearns to ask what's wrong, why those words. But before Anne can lean over and say, "Are you alright?" the wailing starts again, this time more painful.

"I can't take it any more. I just can't."

Bile rises in Anne's throat as a vision of the woman standing up and running toward the plate glass window then hurling herself through it overtakes her thought process. She wants to cover her ears and sing along with the man in the corner. This is too much for her to deal with. She asks where the bathroom is and while the actor is pointing and telling her to turn left down the hallway, she's already up and heading toward the exit. She runs down the stairs of the old church, clinging to the brass handle, careful not to fall while praying she won't throw up.

Gage's voice is a pleasant surprise on her machine, and she approximates that forty hours have passed since he walked her to the train.

"I was hoping you'd be up for pool," he says, when she phones him back. "I want you to like me and the places I go to. It's a large part of who I am." All Anne has is work, home, and the occasional get-together with friends. What would she introduce him to, the Presidential suite at the hotel that costs thirty-five thousand dollars per night?

Gage takes her to Fool's Pool, on Hudson and Thompson, and shows her how to strike the ball. The room is dank and dark. An underground lodging for late-night crawlers. A baseball game is on one TV, VH1 flashes on another, Comedy Central on a third. Eighties music blares over the roar of pool balls clinking against each other. The sound reminds Anne of her good luck bracelet. Bought at a new age shop in Soho, it has the word "happiness" inscribed on a leather band held together by a silver clasp. Attached to the clip is a thin velvet rope where two round stone-colored beads, the size of large peas, hang. Whenever Anne moves, the balls meet and make a clinking noise. Like Chinese brass gongs used to cleanse the air and remove negative energy, her bracelet does the same. Though the clicking irritates co-workers—who often ask her to take the damn thing off—the sound soothes her greatly.

Anne watches ladies flirt with men who slap hands with other men after difficult shots are made. She enjoys seeing the colorful balls spiral across the felted field of green, likes the blue chalky powder, the way Gage's body feels up against hers, warm and strong, as he tries to correct her posture.

Three weeks later, Anne finds Gage waiting for her at the end of her shift. It's freezing out, but Gage is still sporting his leather bomber jacket and jeans. Tonight, however, he's replaced his slightly paint-stained T-shirt with a black ribbed wool turtle-neck sweater, a look that Anne loves. Like her sandalwood incense, she's gotten used to the stench of acrylic paint, his dirty fingernails, even his smoking. When he sees her, Gage takes one more drag and drops the unfinished cigarette to the ground. He steps on the butt, then bends down and sticks it in his pocket. This is his most endearing quality. Anne wonders how many Parliament pieces are in there, and if that's why his fingers always reek of smoke. He seems older in the dark, more manly. More weathered. They kiss hello. His mouth is warm and tastes of smoke. She wonders if she turned off her computer and if she put her to-do list in her desk drawer. She'd ask him to wait for her while she goes to check, but doesn't want to break their moment, doesn't want to add to the teasing that takes place at work from the other women in her department.

This is their seventh date, and in honor of the occasion, he has a surprise at his apartment. He lives at the Union Square Hotel in the West Village, a once hot spot for icons like Andy Warhol and his factory misfits, Keith Haring and Kenny Scharf. As they walk up the five flights to his studio, Gage points out which celebrities stayed in the various rooms. "The year is 1979. Refugees from the School of Visual Arts flood the area," he says, imitating a PBS documentary. "The streets are rich with excitement. Painters mingle with poets; underground filmmakers prey on would-be actors. Rents are cheap and drugs are abundant."

She laughs at his cleverness. Kisses him in the poorly lit, wallpaper-peeling hallway to let him know she thinks he's smart.

They stop in front of room twenty-four, an even number. Good.

He blindfolds her with a red bandanna he pulls out from his pants pocket before he opens the door. She doesn't trust him well enough to do this. Takes deep breaths of stale air as she gulps down the anxiety. She strains to see through the cloth, which is soft and smells of smoke and hair gel. "Stupid girl," she can already hear TV watchers say as her body is flashed on the ten o'clock news. "She let him blindfold her, tie her up somewhere in his apartment, and then is surprised that he raped her. What was she thinking?" She might as well run through Central Park at 4:00 a.m. naked, wearing only the diamond necklace her grandmother gave her for her thirtieth birthday while shouting, "Sex anyone? Anyone want free sex?" She taps on the frame as Gage's rough hands lead her into what she guesses is his hallway.

The room feels small and smells of day-old paint. It's hot and musty. She takes baby steps while her right hand gropes for something solid.

"You're doing great," Gage whispers. His voice is hauntingly deep and smooth. She wants to do this. Feels this will help her lose her need to tap.

"There's a canvas on the floor," he continues. "It's a perfect square, six feet by six feet. Right now you're standing at the far right. Basins of different color paint are at each corner."

"What do you want me to do?" she asks.

"Whatever you feel like. Make me something pretty."

She feels his hands at her feet removing her shoes and socks while thinking how lucky it was she wore a skirt today. She hears him place them on the floor somewhere to her left. She can feel him staring at her and she doesn't want to disappoint him so she dips her feet in the paint, which is cold and squishes between her toes, then steps on the unrolled canvas. She's giddy and laughs nervously while asking what colors he's chosen for her.

"Guess," he responds.

The room is quiet and she listens to her breathing, then to his. The clicking of the fan over her head gives her brain something to focus on rather than the fear of the unknown.

"Red? Maybe white? And black." She pretends to tap dance, waits to hear a laugh from Gage and when all is silent, stops. She steps in another color and lets the paint drip off her heel. She brushes her toes lightly in a half circle. Then again. And again. She goes for more paint and moves thoughtfully, slowly. She's dizzy and off balance. Feels drunk. She wants to see what she's created, wants to take the blindfold off.

When she's finished he lifts her up, as if she were a newly-wed and places her on something soft. A couch? A thick cushion? Her hand travels hurriedly over the fabric until she finds the edge, then moves down to finger the frame. He removes the bandanna, her eyes focus as she searches the room. It's dark and bare. The only light is from the dozen or so candles Gage has lit. He kneels in front of her, looking like Prince Charming with his broad shoulders, thick hair, and massive hands.

He submerges her feet in a large bucket of warm water,

rose petals float on top. He exfoliates her skin up to her calves, towels them dry, leans her back on the futon, which squeaks as he climbs on top of her. She laughs, thinking this is like a badly written Harlequin Romance novel or sappy movie of the week starring Shannon Doherty. But it's happening to her, so it feels silly and surreal and she plays along, forces herself to let go. She wants to tap her thumb and index together for luck but Gage extends his hands on top of hers. Fans her fingers out like a deck of cards. His are coarse, like the canvas, like the futon. He presses them down hard so she can't tap. She wants to mutter her *Katta Katta* but his lips are over hers before she has a chance. She screams inside her head, wonders what to do, calms herself by counting to ten, by listening to the clicking of the fan above.

Anne notices her bracelet is missing at 1:09 p.m.

As if she's broken up with a lover, a deep sadness sits in her heart. She carries it with her all day. A cold she can't shake, a heavy malaise that covers her like a thick wool blanket. She looks everywhere, retraces her steps at home and at work. Even phones Gage to see if she left it at his place.

To rectify the problem, she scans novelty shops and browses department stores in the hopes of finding a substitute. She holds an array of possible replacements tightly in her hands, waiting for a positive sensation. "If my cell phone rings within the next minute, that will be a sign that the object is good luck," she tells herself. But her phone remains silent when she holds the sapphire silver necklace or charm bracelet at Urban Outfitters. No tingling occurs at the gift shops at the American Craft Museum or MoMA, even though she holds on to twenty-two different objects.

At home, Anne puts on a pair of bright yellow plastic cleaning gloves and tosses the plant she purchased last week down the compactor. Perhaps this is the culprit that brought bad luck into her home and shifted the peaceful balance. She goes around the house bagging items, sealing in the sour luck to see if that will work. If that will make her bracelet appear.

On Wednesday at 6:30 p.m. Anne tries to make a reservation for a frequent guest at Tao, but is unable to pull any strings. She breaks a heel, her computer crashes, and she loses a week's worth of work, including her recently updated calendar of hotel events. Worse, Gage hasn't called since the painting incident.

Anne finds Darjeeling's name wedged in between an ad for a religious advisor and a holistic nurse in the classified section of *Cosmic Times*, an alternative and spiritual magazine new age stores distribute. A proclaimed psychic and spiritual cleanser, Darjeeling has named herself after the tea because she is both soothing and has healing powers. "I'm a harmonious blend of calm and balance," she tells Anne on the phone. Even though $150 seems like a lot of money to find a strap of leather, Anne is desperate.

Darjeeling, who shows promptly at 7:00 p.m. as promised, makes an unpleasant face as she enters Anne's apartment. She's dressed in a colorful kimono with a large eye stitched on the back. Her tights are blood red and match her high heel shoes. Her dangling earrings are so long they practically touch her shoulders. Her short auburn hair sticks straight out in sharp points, making her resemble Cyndi Lauper on crack.

"When you moved in, did you bring a broom with you?"

"No."

"How about a loaf of bread?"

Anne shakes her head from side to side. She can feel her throat closing. Can see the room growing darker.

"Well, you definitely have negative energies here." She drops her bag, a large clothlike sack, onto the floor and removes a huge green candle. "Tell me again what happened and why you want it back."

Anne relays the bracelet story while Darjeeling pours essential oils onto the candle before lighting it. She asks Anne to kneel beside her and the two chant—Darjeeling first, then Anne. Next, Darjeeling tosses fistfuls of crystallized sea salt in every corner of the apartment. "The windows and front door are to remain open for at least six hours. If the candle does not burn out during that time, you will find your jewelry within two days," she claims before exiting. At 11:00 p.m. the candle still glows. Anne remains hopeful.

While Anne is standing next to the new girl who is checking a couple into the hotel, she answers the phone hoping Morgan is on the other end. Morgan who makes everything look easy. Morgan who is thin and pretty and efficient and smart. Morgan who can hopefully help her find her bracelet. Instead she finds her boss on the line. He wants to see her now.

He's on the phone when she enters his office and with his hand beckons her to sit.

"I'm sorry," he says, hanging up and leaning back in his chair. "We're doing some restructuring, and, well—" He looks at down at his tie, notices a stain, dabs his finger with some spit, and tries to remove the mark. He looks back up as if he's forgotten she's sitting in his cigar-smelling office. Her ears are buzzing. She mumbles *Katta Katta* under her breath, adding, *Please, please don't do this...*

"Anyway, I know you've been with the company for a number of years, but I think you've gone as far as you can here. The next step is assistant general director, and I just don't feel that's a position you'd be happy in."

"No, I would. That's been my goal from the beginning." She eyes the clock on his desk, waits for it to change from 11:59 to 12:00 and continues. "I know I can—"

"Let me rephrase this. We wouldn't be promoting you to a higher position, so it's unfair to keep you here. I'm saying this as your friend. Really." He leans forward. "We'll write you a lovely recommendation and give you a generous severance package."

Anne knows she should leave the office, but the clock reads 12:01. The *Katta Katta* isn't working and if she can just wait until the minute passes, then perhaps he will change his mind. Perhaps this is all a joke.

Her boss stands and extends his hand to her. "It's been lovely working with you. This is coming from upstairs, it's not my decision."

The only thing upstairs was the third floor, the less expensive rooms. As far as Anne knew, corporate was two floors down.

Hours later, in a fit of panic, Anne rushes through the hardware store and purchases several brooms, the kind you'd imagine a witch using for flight. She hits the new age store to retrieve a fresh box of sandalwood incense before stopping at the bakery for bread.

At home she collects all of her "lucky" objects: her *Good*

Luck book, a silver coin with the word "fortune" printed on one side, an angel on the other, a ladybug pencil sharpener, and a piece of black string given to her by a palm reader at a party her friend had. She gathers them up, like a mother with a newborn, and builds a small shrine on top of her glass coffee table next to Darjeeling's green candle—which is still glowing. She lights incense. A broom is in each room and a loaf of sourdough bread sits open on her kitchen counter. She begs for luck to come back as she mutters the *Katta Katta* mantra while chanting in a circle. She wishes she owned a small silver cross like her mother wears. If she did, she'd add it to the mix. Pray over it while rubbing the sacred entity. She wants to call someone, but there are no sponsors, no twenty-four-hour hotline numbers that she knows of. She's crying and shaking and chokes down the free Paxil. Chews them until they're like powder in her mouth and swallows. She knows it can take anywhere from two to four weeks for them to work, but the chewing makes her think it will travel through her system quicker.

She wakes on her living room floor.

Her mouth feels stuck together. Remnants of the four chewed pills are caked in the crevices of her back teeth. She's nauseous and hungry and dizzy and disoriented. She can barely stand up. Still she tries to dress for work, before remembering she no longer has a job. She tries to piece together last night as she phones Gage, a professional finder of objects. He will help her look. He will find her missing item. This is why they met online. It will all come full circle.

She meets Gage on the corner of Prince and Greene and practically breaks into tears. She babbles on about her bracelet, the tapping, the counting. Vomits up her life so he can help, so he can understand why this is everything to her. He looks confused but wraps his arms around her, squeezing her tightly. Anne is surprised by how good it feels to be held, how her cheek rests easily, cozily on his broad shoulder, how strong and sturdy his chin feels on the top of her head.

Gage promises to help, but insists on showing her something first. "It'll only take a minute," he swears. "Trust me."

He takes her shaking hand and the two walk silently for several blocks until Gage stops in front of a rickety-looking building on Fourth Avenue.

He tells her to close her eyes, which she does. According to the psychic, she has five hours left to find her bracelet and because of the time factor, she lets Gage guide her through the massive doors without protesting. He helps her into the elevator and she tries to count the floors but loses track after what she thinks is four. She feels the elevator stop, hears the doors open, and is lead out carefully.

"You're doing so well. Just a few more steps and we'll be there." His voice is a comfort to her, and she squeezes his hand, leans her body into his arm.

She hears a door open, and her eyelids tell her she's entered a room with more light. She thinks about peeking, but doesn't want Gage to get mad.

"Okay, open your eyes."

She does and finds herself in a run down studio. The room is drab and cold and smells of paint.

"I'm sorry I haven't had a chance to phone. I've been so busy. But now you can see it before anyone else."

Six collages, each of women, lean up against the white walls. A phone rings but after the third trill a machine picks up. Gage moves her swiftly from one canvas to the next. Each is a mix of odd objects—those that Gage has probably found on the street, she thinks—and photos, cutouts from pop culture name brands like cereal boxes or detergents and paint. The work is impressive and Anne squeezes his hand to show her approval and excitement.

The last picture is covered by black fabric. Anne thinks perhaps Gage has done a painting of her. Maybe something with her feet, and is about to ask when Gage puts his hand on the top corner. "This one's my favorite," he says, pulling at the cloth. "It came out the best."

It takes a minute for Anne's eyes to settle on the image. A minute for her to grasp what's going on. He has seen her so clearly—captured her and bottled up the ugliness of who she is, of everything she hates about herself. She is both nauseated and in awe. She steps forward.

A distorted photo of her face is front and center. Her eyes look extra large, her mouth is open, and she's out of focus. It reminds Anne of the moaning woman from the Red Cross. Her Sweet'N Low packet and straw, personal ad, and bottle top from the beer she had at the pool hall, even a meeting schedule is smattered throughout the painting. The leprechaun from the Lucky Charms cereal box and the letters from the word "lucky" cut up in pieces have been glued to the canvas, adding a dimensional look. "A charmed life" is written in green while gold painted horseshoes outline the frame. A large squiggly smear of blue chalk and a pink penny mirroring a sun appear in the upper right-hand corner. Her bracelet is there, too. The word "tap" is printed three times in bold. The last item she eyes is her footprint. Written underneath is "Anne's Achilles' heel," with a four-leaf clover painted on her big toe.

If it wasn't her up there—if it wasn't her life, if she didn't tap—the painting, the collage, would be beautiful. She wants suddenly, desperately, to jump into the picture, retrieve her life, lose herself.

"I thought you work with found art. This is stolen." Anne is unexplainably calm.

"This *is* found art. I found you, didn't I?"

She remains still.

"Smell it," he urges. "Go ahead. I've sprayed it with sandalwood." He's almost gleaming and despite her hesitancy, she obeys, leans in, and sniffs. She smiles at the familiar scent, which she's grown to appreciate, finds it comforting. She closes her eyes and puts her hands on the tightly stretched fabric, fingers the objects, runs her hands over the texture. She hears a click of something and flicks her eyes open. Gage is standing in front of her, a camera in his hands. He smiles and takes another photo, as if he is trying to steal something else from her.

"I always offer my ladies first crack. It's only fair." He shrugs.

The pieces come together, forming like a night of heavy drinking, slow and foggy. She eyes the other women hanging on the walls, and even though she's never seen them before, feels as if she knows them. They are her, only different. Each portrait bares a small piece of someone's soul. She wonders who they are. If he met them online, like her, or did he merely collect them, like the pieces of found art he supposedly finds in the street. She looks from wall to wall, making quick, swift movements until the gallery becomes a dizzying blur of Gage's so-called art. She rests her eyes on him, then looks at herself on the wall. And then she understands the words uttered by the crazy woman at the Red Cross. They are the same ones that emerge wretchedly, quietly, from Anne's own lips. "I can't take it anymore. I just can't." It's a small moan. Like bone breaking from the inside. "How much?" she asks, her voice cracking. She wants to know what he's charging for taking her life and how much he wants for her to reclaim it.

His eyes glow, a wolf hungry for his Red Riding Hood. "Five thousand."

He's picked the perfect amount, an even, whole number. Not impossible to get, not too much to ask for. She has most of it in the bank. It's taken her forever to save and now that she's jobless she'll need it to live. She could break her CD or ask her parents for help, tell them her rent increased tremendously, could they lend her some money. It wouldn't kill them to buy the painting. They pay for her brother's health care and this is imperative to her mental health. She thinks about her brother. Perhaps she should take the five thousand dollars and move in with him. Surely the hospital has room for her. She could inquire about receiving a discounted rate for relatives. A half-off for additional family members, maybe.

"After today, the price goes up. It becomes part of the exhibit. Part of my show."

Anne can visualize herself hanging in some swanky apartment surmised and dissected by art wannabes swilling expensive wine and nibbling on cheese and foie gras. She sees them picking her apart, awed and amazed by Gage's fine eye for detail and cleverness.

She touches the painting again, gives it one last tap, and it's done.

She's done.

"Keep it." The words fall out. She almost looks around to see who has spoken.

"What?" His voice is an irritated disbelief.

"Keep it."

"You're kidding, right?" His eyes are squinty, his lip becomes a snarl. "You could have the bracelet now. It's Velcroed to the painting." He pulls it off, then reattaches it. "See?"

Anne almost reaches for it, then stops herself. She doesn't know what to do.

"Okay. Four thousand dollars, cash," he barks. "Tomorrow it goes for eight."

She doesn't want it. She doesn't want him, or her OCD or her life, even. She just wants everything to be gone.

Anne has no memory of walking toward the door of his studio. No memory of twisting free from Gage's grip, no canvas with her face on it under her arm, no handbag on her shoulder. She just remembers her hand, the way her fingers looked midtap on the door. She recalls pausing, letting her hand linger on the frame for a split second, and then releasing her grip.

Chapter 11

Trish

The Party Room

"This is perfect," you say as you stand in the middle of the party room at the Four Seasons Hotel.

The space is modern and warm. Sophisticated and classy, much like Morgan, the pretty, petite sales director who is helping you plan the event.

"You see my best friend's lost all this weight, and I wanted to do something special for her."

Morgan is nodding understandingly.

Feel stupid for having trouble encapsulating the most important friendship you've ever had into a few sentences. "We met in college. We were photography majors."

It was you who saw Olive walking through the massive metal doors of the photo department eighteen years ago. She had long thick hair that ventured beyond her shoulders. A lit cigarette dangled from her burgundy-painted lips, she sported cat-style reading glasses, was dressed in all black. Her skin was pale and smooth and reminded you of a porcelain doll, the heavyset Russian kind. You remember how heavy she was. That her large body, which could have easily been 280 pounds, filled the room. Consumed it.

Feel even dumber for trying to persuade Morgan to give you a discount on the food and space in order to celebrate Olive's weight-loss. After all, you've invested everything you had to purchase an art gallery. You figured if you couldn't make it as a professional photographer, you could at least nurture and represent those that can. This comes at the great disappointment of your parents, the people you've learned to call Mom and Dad. At least your lack of accomplishment answers the nature vs. nurture question. You are sure your adoptive parents tell people you're adopted so they don't blame you, or even themselves, for your lack of success.

You don't dislike the people who raised you, but you've never felt especially close to them. Fame is hard to compete with. Your mother is a best-selling feminist author, responsible for changing the lives of thousands, while your father is a renowned sculptor.

You never asked if you were adopted, you just knew. Realized one day around your seventh birthday as you flipped through family albums that there wasn't one shot of your mother pregnant.

"Why is that?" you had asked her.

She was writing in her study and looked up at you, horrified and pale. She picked up the phone and called your father, who was in his studio downstairs.

"She wants to know why there are no photos of me pregnant," she told him when he entered the room, his shirt smattered with clay, his hands wet and dripping.

They sat you down on the couch, and your mother put a hand on your arm. You remember it feeling cold and uncomfortable.

"We wanted to wait until you were older, but the shrink said you'd ask when you were ready," she said. "I guess you are."

"Your mother couldn't have children. Do you know what the means?" your father inquired.

Your mother sighed and shook her head at your father. "Trish, you were chosen. It was very important to us to have a child and since we couldn't have one naturally, since I had trouble conceiving, we went to a doctor . . ."

"And then a lawyer," your father added, "helped us pick you out."

"We were very excited to have you."

It wasn't until your father used the word adoption and took out the dictionary that you started to understand. They swore they didn't know who your real parents were. "Your mother picked you out instantly," your father said, snapping the dictionary shut and smiling. "You were beautiful. Everyone said so."

Sometimes you think you were brought into their lives for creative purpose, divine inspiration. You love them the way you loved rock stars or soap actors as a child. They're unobtainable, untouchable gods, worshipped by others, strangers who aren't related to you. For the next two years, once a week, you talked to a shrink about how this news made you feel.

Years later, while helping your father hang his artwork at a gallery in SoHo, you announced you wanted to be a photographer. Your parents looked at each other in surprise.

"You know, you don't have to be that for us," your mother had said, unwrapping one of your father's paintings.

"Yes, two artists in one family is plenty," your father added.

You swore right then and there that you'd show them. That you'd be as famous as they were. That your real parents would have hugged and kissed you and told you could be anything you wanted.

Morgan appears interested, almost captivated by your "Olive" story.

Tell her that you snapped Olive's photo without her noticing. The classroom was filled with other eager Penn freshmen. You had a zoom lens and she was far enough away not to hear the click of the camera. Later in the darkroom you watched her massive figure emerge on glossy paper. It was blurry at first as it floated in the developer, but, in a few minutes, it became something tangible.

As she neared, you extended your hand and introduced yourself. "Hi. I'm Trish."

"Olive," she said, short and crisp, like her handshake. She took the seat across from you and you could tell from her glare, then from the way she positioned her back, facing away from you, that she hated you on sight. This became a running joke shared with others, strangers you met at downtown bars, trendy restaurants, or charity events as each of you searched for possible future husbands.

"She's my oldest friend, my longest relationship," you'd say. It's been eighteen years of fights, trips, family emergencies, two photography shows, one abortion (hers), and one broken engagement (yours). Now of course, all that is over. Olive is just months from having a ring slipped onto her finger, you guess, by a man you can't stand, and who you know can't stand you.

A month later you are at Olive's parents' home in Connecticut. They're away so she's having a party. Look at your best friend lying in the water doing the dead man's float in an enormous pool enclosed by rocks and shrubbery. Her eyes are closed. Strands of dark hair sway with the ripples. Her blue bathing suit masks most of her body so all you see are pale appendages and a bobbing head. There are seventy-five pounds less of her than last year. It has taken over thirteen months for her to shed them and although she has an additional forty to go, she looks amazing.

Wonder if she feels lighter in the heated water, lighter when she walks, when she breathes. For more than a decade, you've been the encouraging one, the instigator of activities, the cheerleader of new projects. Though you offered to join a gym in her neighborhood so she could have someone to go with, choked down sandy-tasting protein bars, picked out smaller-size clothing at heavyset women's stores as incentives, nothing has worked until now. His name is Ray. She met him at a bar. Suddenly the word "baby" has formed on her lips. Now there's a ticking clock. The world is getting married and she, too, wants to be part of that. A worried look from her doctor during a recent checkup when he took her blood pressure and she refused to get on the scale probably helped, too.

Glance around and mentally tally up the guests you don't know—eighteen. Outsiders. Friends of Ray's, some of Olive's who she met online, or at the park or God knows where.

It used to be these parties were filled with both your contemporaries: business associates, art directors, sculptors and artists, co-workers from MoMA, where Olive works. Now, instead of being surrounded by friends, you are surrounded by photography magazines, portfolios belonging to wannabe artists, resumes, show proposals, slides, and contact sheets from eager publicists who represent today's new artists, all of whom want to exhibit their work in your new space.

Ray's friends are hefty, burly, and unkempt. They wear Hawaiian shirts or ones that have rock bands you've never heard of printed on their chests. Their swim trunks are faded and pilly. There's too much hair on their backs and arms, and on their faces. Beer cans and bottles are in their hands instead of the martinis or cosmos you used to serve. They talk about alternative music and independent films as if they were authorities or part of the business. Words like "dude" or "right-on" start or end every sentence.

The stereo changes CDs, the White Stripes invades the air. Long for Ella Fitzgerald or Sarah McLachlan. Wonder if you'd feel this badly if you and Ed were still together. If he hadn't broken off your engagement last year. You have nothing on your finger to prove someone loves you. But you do own a gallery and that means something.

When you met Ed, you had liked him immediately. He was intense and sexy. Shaggy yet polished. He wore faded jeans and a camel blazer with a white shirt and tie. You had just turned thirty-one and had celebrated with a small photo exhibit in

SoHo. He was a friend of a friend's and he kept looking up at you, smiling boyishly during introductions. He bought one of your photographs. Hung it on his bedroom wall. When you had sex at his place, it always caught your eye. Five months later he had a drawer in your apartment, you commandeered closet space in his. A respected journalist, he would read you his work in bed: travel essays, articles, celebrity interviews of Prince, Julia, your mother. You took photo after photo of him, memorized his features in your head.

Then one Monday, two and half years later, you entered your home and found it half-empty. At first you thought you'd been robbed. You went to your jewelry box, checked your camera equipment, and when you looked for Ed's computer, realized his belongings were the ones missing. Ed himself was gone, too. A last-minute press trip to an exotic place was a reasonable explanation. But he phoned from some bar hours later, mumbling incoherently that he needed space, he wasn't ready, he didn't have the feelings he once thought he had for you. It only added to your bewilderment. You waited for a letter explaining, an e-mail or last-minute invite to your favorite restaurant so he could tell you face-to-face what was going on. Tell you what went wrong—a midlife crisis, cold feet, anything would have been better than sheer confusion. You phoned his cell for days, but he never answered. You phoned his friends, but they avoided your questions. You prayed to God in your bathroom, in full kneeling position, naked and wet from the shower, to send him back, but he never materialized.

For weeks you used his shampoo and conditioner, shaved with his razor, drank his pomegranate-flavored vodka, anything to feel closer to him. For the first month, doped up on

Ambien, you'd wake from thick, groggy sleep, and for a moment, forget he wasn't next to you. Almost call out for him, half expecting to hear his muffled voice coming from another room in your apartment.

You'd already written thank-you notes for the thoughtful engagement gifts bought off your registry. The boxes and packages sat neatly stacked by the front door along with the belongings Ed had left behind: ski equipment, a spare computer, dumbbells. You'd booked a loft for the after party, investigated honeymoon trips, listened together to CDs from bands recommended by your friends.

It was Olive who filled your apartment with flowers, took you for long car trips to picturesque places, made you spa appointments. She insisted you get out of your funk, helped you clean your usually spotless apartment, stood in your hallway, vacuum in one hand, scrub bucket in the other. Empty pizza boxes, sour cartons of skim milk, half-eaten pints of ice cream, dirty clothing, used tissues, unread newspapers, and stacks of old *ARTnews* and *Focus* magazines carpeted your floor. She begged you to shower, to do the laundry, to take a walk around the block. She finally called your parents and asked them to come see for themselves what had happened to their only child. Your father was in Europe creating sculptures while your mother was at Yaddo, a writing residency. Unable to leave, she phoned and suggested you document the process. "You need to use your suffering better, Trish. All great artists are in constant pain. Put that in your work," she had said.

Until Olive's recent meeting of Ray, it was you two who were like a married couple. You joked that if she were a man, you'd propose, flaws and all, because you love her so, like no one else ever will. She gets the jokes without having to give additional explanation. You've had more holiday dinners with her family than your own. She taught you how to drive, to blow smoke rings, to make apple crumb pie from scratch. Some of your most creative times are due to her. When you broke your foot five years ago, she drove you out to her parents' home, turned the basement into a darkroom, and gave you full use of the guest room.

Get up from the pool area and enter into the kitchen, walking directly past the basket of bread and sticky buns, and the apple pie someone brought, and into the bathroom. When you close the door you catch your reflection in the mirror. At five foot five and 120 pounds, you are fit and athletic, lean without having to try too hard. It's only recently at thirty-five that your body has failed you. Switched sides in the middle of the night without your consent, like Ed—one minute he loved you, then not. You've noticed over the past several months as Olive loses part of her, you are gaining some of it. Now your jeans, which once fit perfectly, showing off your svelte body and cupping your ass just so, are hard to button and though you'd like to blame it on the dryer, you know in your heart, and the scale confirms this, that it's you who's gotten bigger, not your jeans that have become smaller. In fact, everything is tight. You could almost be what people call pudgy.

Recall your thirty-fifth birthday party, which was a few months ago. A sugary frozen margarita was to your left, a piece of chocolate cake with vanilla buttercream frosting in front of you, where someone commented, "From this point forward Trish, it's all downhill. You'll see, everything changes and drops." You laughed the comment away. Took a forkful of cake, shoved it defiantly in your mouth as if to say, "Oh yeah, try me." And now, of course, it has. As you stare at yourself, notice how stretched out your bikini looks, that your hand can pinch more than an inch of belly fat, that sideways, if you push all the air from your lungs into your stomach, you look pregnant. Consider telling people you are, should they ask or comment that you've put on weight. You could lie and tell them you're working on a series of distorted self-portraits and you've purposely packed on a few pounds in the name of art. Consider this seriously. Your mother would finally be impressed, say you were really throwing yourself into your work, and encourage you to gain more weight so your whole body could be distorted. Slide your hands down to your hips and admit they, too, appear wider, your ass has expanded, your thighs rub together, your neck looks thicker, your face fatter. Even your breasts, though this could be the only positive place to get bigger, seem fuller. Jump up and down and watch everything jiggle.

Return to the deck area. No one has even noticed your absence. Slip on a T-shirt and pair of sweats to hide your body, then reach for your 35 mm Nikon, your hand fitting comfortably, familiarly around the base, the cool metal feeling nice against your skin. Look into the lens, zoom in, like you did that first day in photography class and snap away, searching for who Olive has become.

The weight isn't the only thing different about her. She does things now that make you uneasy. There are late-night rendezvous with older married men she's met at weird parties, in hotel lobbies, or online. Ray is unaware of this and she swears she'll stop once a ring is on her finger. You cry inside when she insists she doesn't want to know their names, that she likes sex rough, that she wants it like this. Enjoys it. You ache to hold her in your arms and ask her to be honest with herself. To be more safe. You don't want to sit in another abortion clinic with her, filling out forms and not talking. You don't want to celebrate a negative blood test. You don't want her to die early from AIDS or a massive heart attack, which was how you foresaw her future if she didn't lose weight. And though it upsets you to hear these stories, you'd rather her share them with you than not.

Olive's look has changed, too. Her clothing, once worn conservatively, seems skimpy and tight, as if she trying to squeeze into her new frame before her body is ready. There's also the buying of expensive items—small blue boxes from Tiffany's, orange bags from Hermes, leather high-heel shoes that feel like butter—you know she can't afford from her curating job, and when you ask her how much something cost, she shrugs her shoulders and changes the subject. There are no slips or receipts, no price tags on any of the unworn clothing that hangs in her closet.

Watch her emerge from the pool. She still hurries to cover herself with a towel. Notice that everyone is staring. You don't know whether to start clapping or distract people by dropping your glass. What you really want to do is toss the camera into the pool, sit next to her, and make her swear she'll dump Ray. That she won't leave you.

The following week you are standing in your gallery on Fifty-seventh and Fifth Avenue, watching traffic merge from your eighth-story window. After nine months of searching for a space, negotiating price per square foot, and haggling over rent, the gallery space is finally yours. The walls, painted eggshell white, are smooth and crack-free, the doors lock, the phones ring, the computer connects to the Internet, the lights work, even your windows have been cleaned and the name Fresh Art etched in large red letters. You've purchased a message pad and notebook. You have an unblemished calendar, which hangs on the wall next to your desk/reception area. Your name is spelled correctly on the business cards and stationery. The community bathroom, shared by others on your floor—another gallery that specializes in fine art and three established designers—is clean and private.

Your space is ready.

You are ready.

Today you are interviewing gallery assistants and artists whose work you are considering to show.

Meet with several students, each from FIT, all of whom are young and eager and wear too much makeup and not enough clothing and talk about their boyfriends and their degrees and what a great location the gallery is in because Bergdorf Goodman, Abercrombie & Fitch, and the Louis Vuitton flagship store are just a block away.

How can you give a job to girls who are so young? Why on earth is everyone suddenly so fucking young?

The first artist appears without his rep. He's thin and fair and girly. His fingers, which are long and feminine, remind you of spider legs. He tells you about his vision before he hands over his bio. The black-and-white photos he has spread out on your floor are of people, buildings, everyday objects, each taken purposely, he tells you, out of focus.

"People are always watching the world incorrectly. My goal is to show them what they're missing—and what they really see."

Strain to decipher one large print. You think it's of a woman, but you can't be sure, maybe it's a child or a man with a lot of hair.

Think about your own work. For years you carried around a camera snapping away at random people you saw in the street. You wanted to steal a bit of their soul to dissect later. You would stand for hours staring at their faces, a nose, a smile, the shape of a forehead, desperate to find yourself. Slight resemblances that could connect you to them. This was the basis of your work, your manifesto. An exhibit of strangers who look similar to you, even in the minutest of details. The woman on the bus with the sad blue eyes had your hands. A woman waiting for a cab in front of Saks had your full lips. A third, your large eyes. Click. Snap. Last year you were convinced that you were related to the man sitting next to you in an all-night diner when he ordered his tuna melt exactly like you. He apologized for the special changes, but he was allergic to tomatoes, as are you. Only 3 percent of Americans have this allergy. You've spent hours researching it on the Internet—tracking anything that could help solve the puzzle of your life.

Your mother and father swear they have no concrete knowledge of who your real parents were. You've been to the National Adoption Center in New York, driven out to the United States National Adoption Department in Albany, searched through files at the police department for missing children. Unbeknownst to your family, you've hired two different private detectives each who specialize in searching for birthparents. Both came up empty. According to them, you have no past.

The out-of-focus artist is still talking.

"People need to look harder in order to really see the world they live in," he says. "The quick glances they take are not sufficient anymore. We need to slow down, and well, smell the flowers," which of course, is the last photo in his collection. The only piece taken in color. It's a less-out-of-focus shot of pink roses.

"I'm what you call an environmental/cultural artist," he adds, smiling.

Stare at him blankly, thank him for coming after he asks if the paint you've used in your gallery is "ecofriendly."

The next hopeful, a woman in her forties from Georgia, is dressed in red. Red cords, red shirt, red boots, even a red portfolio case. She has taken photos of toilet seats, bathtubs, soap dishes, sinks—and anything else she's deemed as "restroom art." From the rest stops on freeways to restaurants from around the world to McMansions, she shares all the dirty, personal, and telling moments of life. Her Southern accent is jarring. Wonder what drove her to New York. The art is interesting and something to consider, it just doesn't move you, though looking at it makes you need to pee, which you're sure is not the intent of the artist, or the reaction a buyer is looking for.

The third is a meaty-looking man with tan skin and thick, dark hair.

"Gage, this is Trish, Trish meet Gage," the rep says.

He's tall and broad and when he shakes your hand, you feel how calloused and coarse his skin is.

"We brought you three completed pieces to see. The others were too large or fragile to get on the subway," the rep continues, as he leans his client's work against your wall.

Even though the artist is smiling at you, something feels off with him. He's creepy and stands too close to you when he talks. You can smell his breath, a mix of beer and ham and cigarettes.

"As you can see, Gage uses several textures and materials in the work," the rep says.

"Real objects, oil paint, and photographs I've taken." He winks at you. This makes you cringe inside.

"He then brings the three components together to create disturbing, yet character-like versions of people. Or he makes statements on societal trends."

In one of the pieces, a screaming woman's face is in the center of the canvas. Outlining her are objects of desire: a ring, money, a miniature groom—the kind you imagined on your and Ed's wedding cake—and a house made of Legos, all of which have been attached to the painting. "I want" is spelled out using pennies.

Another is of two brothers, you guess, who face each other. Medals from swim, track, and wrestling meets have been purposely placed around their faces along with badges from camp or Boy Scouts, college acceptance letters from Yale and Harvard, a report card or two, and CPR certificates. Underneath, the words "Mother's Favorite?" have been spelled out using stickers in the shape of newborns.

The last is the real deal. Instead of canvas, the artist has used large pieces of mirror, which stand about your height. Framing the mirrors are syringes, a medical bracelet from a hospital, a surgical mask, a birth certificate, a passport. A woman's disfigured post-face-lift photo is stapled to the top of the structure. The words "Age Before Beauty" have been spelled out using mini birthday candles. Two large candles, shaped in the numbers five and zero, have been glued to the bottom of the piece. Most of the mirror has been left untouched so that if you stood close enough, your face would be replaced with the woman's, and your body would be the only part reflecting back.

The work is upsetting, yet captivating.

"Your gallery is great," the artist says, his voice raspy and deep. He stares at you strangely, as if he's trying to uncover something you're purposely not showing him. You realize he's the kind of man, who, if you met him in a bar, you wouldn't accept a drink from. In fact, you would thank him for his kind offer and then switch seats or pretend you see someone you know. You watch his mouth move because you don't want to look him in the eyes. He sees too much of you already.

"Thanks," you reply. "Your work is really . . ."

"Disturbing?" he suggests, a hint of glee in his voice.

"Unusual," you correct. "They're fascinatingly rich and raw."

"An accident you can't look away from," the rep interjects.

You nod, listen to the sound of the room, of the passing cars outside, the way Gage breathes.

"I'm a big fan of your father's," he says. "What's he working on now?"

The rep shoots him a look, as if to say, "You said you weren't going to mention that." But you are professional and answer the question kindly.

"He's in Paris, working on a retrospective of his early sculptures."

The two men nod.

"Are there other pieces in your collection?"

"Yeah. I've got eight more."

"It would be great if you would drop them off tomorrow,

and perhaps leave them here over the weekend. I'd like a little time with them. See how much room the work might need."

"Of course," the rep says, not waiting for his client's response.

Gage is smiling at you, his eyes like slits, his expression smug.

"I'll have them delivered later today," the rep says. "Give me a call on Monday when you can." He extends a hand, which you shake. The artist's right hand appears within seconds, and you reach for that too, though the feel of his skin makes you queasy. You inconspicuously wipe your palm on your jeans as you walk them to the door.

"Thanks again for coming," you say, then lock the door as you watch them head toward the elevator.

Hours later, in the privacy of your gallery, you lay your own photography over your newly buffed floor, while you ache to be related to someone. Think of the book *Are You My Mother?* as you peer into strangers' faces. As a child you loved this story. Clutched it at night, hoping to find your real mother sitting beside you in the morning. You used to run up to people in the street to see if one was, indeed, your mother.

When you look up at Gage's mirror creation propped up against the wall, see yourself sitting on the floor. As much as you hate to showcase him, his work is exceptional.

Crawl toward it.

Your face is tired-looking, your body fat.

Peel off your shirt and drop it next to you. Do the same with your bra, followed by your jeans. You have never been model thin. Nor have you ever wanted to be. But you are also single and if you had trouble meeting men when you were ten or twelve pounds lighter, think how much harder it will be now. Wonder if men still find you attractive. To gain some control and make yourself feel better, schedule an eyebrow waxing, a hair highlighting session and cut, a manicure, the works. On your new memo pad, compose a list of products you want to buy tomorrow at Sephora, the cosmetics emporium, a crack house for makeup junkies. You might not be able to lose the weight overnight, but you can sure as shit look good while doing it.

Meet Olive for dinner at BLT Steak. You're here first and feel small and childlike sitting alone in the mammoth leather booth. The restaurant is dark and loud. The bar is filled with men in stiff-collared shirts and ties that hang loosely around their necks. These are moneymaking men who work hard and play harder. The smell of butter and steak sauce is overwhelming. You spot Olive and wave. She looks magnificent. Radiant. Though you always thought her attractive, the weight loss has only made her more so. Her double chin is gone. In its place is an angularness you've never seen. Her skin is clear and blemish-free, color contacts make her eyes shine, her hair is silky, makeup flawless. You hated when people would whisper, "She's got such an attractive face, if only she could lose the weight," as if it weren't enough that she had the pretty face. That she's smart and funny, charming when she wants to be, clever and artistic. But now her pretty face is more beautiful, not to mention smaller. Less of her spills into your seat at the movie theater or on an airplane. You no longer need to sit in the banquette, she in the chair, because she couldn't slide in and out like you could. Though you used to say you preferred this seat because of your bad back, you did it so she wouldn't have to.

"Okay, what's wrong?" she asks, finally seated across from you. Her voice is eager. Concerned.

Stare down at the menu, mumble, "Nothing. I'm fine." Maybe you should go on antidepressants. Everyone else is.

Her eyes and expression say she doesn't believe you. "Trish, what is it?"

Hear the history you share in her inflection. In the way she pronounces your name, the *Tr* accentuated, the *ish* drawn out just a hair, just enough to prove she knows you best. You want to tell her everything. Want to start from the beginning, explain how you spotted her first, eighteen years ago. You want to jump back and reclaim your late teens/early twenties. You want to blast Seal or U2 while you sit in a parking lot as Olive teaches you to drive in her candy-apple-red Toyota.

Feel her slipping away, even at this moment. You are struggling, drowning in the desire to hold onto her, and to your friendship. Even to yourself. But you can't say this because you don't know how.

Olive puts down her menu and extends her hand in your direction. Her brows furrow, and she leans forward. Look at her waiting palm. You know it's soft and warm, like socks that have just emerged from a dryer. You want to reach toward her. Have her hold not just your hand, but all of you. Rest your head in her lap and have her stroke your hair while she insists things will be fine. You are about to meet her halfway when something sparkly catches your eye.

Look from the diamond to her face.

"We wanted to tell you together, but Ray had a meeting he couldn't get out of."

Watch her eyes shift momentarily away from you, a habit she has when she's lying.

The ring is beautiful, like Olive, and even though it looks odd on her hand, it suits her.

Last on your list of appointments today is a shrink. Your mother recommended him. She'd seen him a few years ago when she was stuck creatively and said he was a master at tapping into her subconscious.

You sit in Dr. Marty Radkin's office, the ubiquitous box of tissues to your left, the ubiquitous-looking man sitting in a just-as-ubiquitous brown leather chair four feet away from you as you sit in an exact replica. You want to tell him about your mother, about the real one you don't know, about your best friend, about how fat you feel, about Ed. That you can't let go of the fact he's not here to love you anymore. That you absolutely hate every single moment of your life.

Marty is handsome and alluring, and there's something magnetic about him. His office smells of pipe and the room is filled with books and art and you wonder if he's married. If the way he's looking at you is normal for a shrink. Because to you, he seems to be flirting. And though you can't explain it, something makes you smile. And you stop crying and study the man sitting across from you.

He leans forward, reaches for your hand, which you let him hold. His is solid and warm. His eyes sympathetic. And in his voice, which is low and steady, he tells you everything will be fine. For a moment, you believe him, because you need to believe in something. And he feels like all you have right now.

You and Olive are speeding up Madison Avenue, late for Carol's—another close friend from college—baby shower.

Olive's perfume wafts over in your direction thanks to her open window, sending instant comfort, cocooning you in familiarity. You smile at her, drunk on memory, and pull on the sleeve of her jacket. You want to mumble softly, *Dump Ray. Dump Ray.* A subliminal mantra. A deep wish.

"You're still coming by after the party, right?" You ask her.

Olive's cell phone is open, her hand already dialing as she nods her head yes, then turns her attention to her call. "It's me. No, we're running late," she tells Ray. She pauses, and you can hear his muffled voice coming through the phone. "I was thinking about going back to the gallery with her. I haven't seen it yet . . ." Olive trails off as Ray talks over her. "Oh, what time? I didn't know you already bought them."

Roll your eyes, stare out the window.

"Okay," she adds. "Why don't you pick me up from Carol's at five p.m."

More silence on her end.

"Love you too. Bye." She snaps her cell closed. "He got us tickets to a concert. I didn't know it was for tonight."

"Oh."

"I'll see the gallery another time. We'll have lunch, make a day of it."

"Sure."

You and Olive talked about opening this gallery together years ago. You devised business plans, created a list of artists you wanted to represent. You saw yourselves traveling to exhibits and art expos to find fresh faces, budding talent. You were going to swill expensive wine at cocktail receptions, meet with other gallery reps, go out every night until buzz was generated about the new hot duo who had an incredible eye for talent. But now it's just you. Just you and your gallery.

Arrive at Carol's mother's apartment. Though it's lovely, classy, and spacious, it could be an array of people's homes, and this could be any event: a wedding, a good-bye party, a bridal gala with lots of people and food and happiness—they all seem to bleed together. But this one is coed. Good-looking men in suits are mingling with other good-looking women in designer outfits. Everyone looks alike. You joyfully kiss old chums hello, shake hands with their significant others, comment on how well everyone looks, how excited you are to own a gallery when everyone else seems to have moved up the corporate ladder.

You and Olive take the customary lap, searching for Carol, who you find by the dining table, plate in one hand, sparkling cider in the other. Her face brightens when she sees you. She hugs you first, awkwardly, because of her large belly, which lightly presses up against you. How can your friend have a child? You used to get drunk with her. Crashed fraternity parties. Crawled out of your second-floor freshmen dorm to buy pot and wait for the cookie guy at the front of the building. She can't be someone's mother. You can't be thirty-five. When you look in the mirror, on a good day, you still see a twenty-three-year-old. An age when it was okay to be single. Okay to not have the best job in the world.

Lunch is an odd mix of high-calorie food—meatloaf and lasagna—and girly, dainty salads—chicken and tuna. Pick at your food, move it around with your fork, look like you're having a good time.

When several desserts make a much-anticipated appearance, circle the table like a hungry hawk. The caterer has done a magnificent job of making you salivate. You have been disciplined for the past thirty days, depriving yourself of your favorite treats and sweets and still there's been no real weight loss. Walk away only to return a moment or two later. Have you no willpower? Watch other people inhale the chocolate pecan pie, party-pink petits fours, the lemon mousse tart, the cheesecake brownies while taking pleasure as you sip coffee with skim milk. You are strong. You are better.

Enter the kitchen and offer to help. This will give you something to do, keep your thoughts focused, your hands busy. Carol's mother looks at you, comments how wonderful and odd it is to have her baby have a baby. See her glance at your hand, searching for something sparkly on your appropriate finger. Hate how empty your hand feels without the engagement ring. How empty you feel without Ed.

Long for him now. For his body and the space he used to take up in your bed. For the softness of his sleep shirts. The way his hand fit in yours. When he got travel assignments from magazines to cover new hotels and resorts, and was allowed to bring a guest, he would hold your hand during takeoff, without your having to reach for his first. You have visited the Grand Canyon on donkey, parachuted over volcanoes in Hawaii, tasted wine in South Beach. He proposed to you in Charleston while you were taking a tour of historic homes of the nineteenth century.

Every now and then you get a letter or magazine addressed to Ed, which you promptly rip into tiny pieces. On several occasions you've come across random checks, back money owed for articles that finally got published. You signed his name and cashed them. You sold your engagement ring on eBay to pay for Olive's event at the Four Seasons and several months' rent at the gallery. Realize you've not been on a plane since he left you seven months ago. Realize the date of your opening night party, which is in sixty days, is on the same day that you would have said "I do."

Wonder what he's doing right now. You heard he was seeing someone. What could she offer him that you couldn't? Decide you will diet and clean up your act, and prove to yourself this was not your fault. Ed is the one with the problems.

Carol's mother has been talking to you but you have no idea what she's said. So you nod and smile and tell her how terrific her daughter looks. That she's carrying well. The mother agrees, then carts a tray of clean coffee cups and a plate of fancy sweets out to the dining area. She's left you alone with an open box of cookies that catch your eyes, leftovers from the tray that just went out to the table. Lean in to smell, only to smell. Smelling doesn't count and doesn't contain calories. Touch one, just to prove to yourself that it's loaded with fat. There, see, it is. They even glisten in the light, and as you get closer, observe that the box has several grease stains on the cardboard.

The next thing you know, one is in your mouth. It's only a cookie and you are celebrating a happy occasion even if you, yourself, are not happy. Finish the cookie, walk away, and join the others. Look for Olive.

As you refill your coffee cup, Carol asks if you've tried the pecan pie. She knows it's one of your favorites.

"We thought of you when we ordered this." She cuts you a slice while holding an outstretched fork. Comply because a slice of pie is different than a piece of cookie and nuts are healthy and you feel it would be rude to turn her down.

One cookie, one slice. Done. But somehow you are drawn back to the box of cookies in the kitchen where no one is because they are toasting Carol and you are missing it because you have a date with a box of pastries.

The kitchen is warm and quiet. No one is here to ask what you're doing with your life, if you're dating anyone, give their opinion on Ed, or tell you how great Olive looks.

Eat a cookie.

Then another.

And another.

You barely taste them in your mouth, hardly enjoy the crunch or texture or sweetness. Feel the scraping as it descends in your throat, pieces of unchewed pastry forced hurriedly down your esophagus. And then there's only one left in the box. You can't leave it alone because you need to throw out the box, remove the evidence. You've eaten nine or ten of them, one for each pound you're to lose and what's one more when you've eaten enough for four people. Toss the box in the garbage, not on top, but underneath the other trash just like you've seen Olive do with Ben & Jerry's, Pepperidge Farm, and Kathleen's cookies.

Hate yourself.

Drink water.

Wish you were dead.

In twenty minutes a pain in your stomach starts. You've been betting it would and are not surprised when the dull ache begins. Ten minutes later it's more like a throbbing, and though you're standing in a pretty mocha-colored bathroom staring into Carol's mom's medicine cabinet, the box of chewable Pepto-Bismol in your hand, refuse to take them. This is your punishment.

Remember how, as a child, you would shadow your mother's friends. Follow them around their homes, hoping to melt into the furniture, into the very fabric of their lives. You used to go into their libraries to see if they kept your mother's books on their shelves or their nightstands. You'd look on the walls for your father's paintings or the corners for his statues, each purposely placed in their dens or studies. Decide to do that now.

Proceed into the family room, which is "off-limits" to the party, and see if your mother's books are here. You know they are, they're always here. It's just a matter of where. The room is still and smells of cedar. Eye the spines that stand upright, look for the signature green. Spot it and remove it from its place. *Love, Loss, Lust,* your mother's first book. Open to the dedication page: "To the mavericks, leaders, and forward thinkers: Gloria Steinem, Betty Friedan, and Erica Jong. Women who changed the world."

My Temporary Life is here, too. This one is dedicated to her parents, grandparents you barely got to know, who died two years apart when you were four and six. The third book in the trilogy, *Sit with Me,* is also part of Carol's collection. "For my brilliant husband who creates more than art." This was written while you were in high school. The famous book everyone raves about, *Drowning in Ambiguity,* the book you read in college, is dedicated to no one. Your mother was going through her "angry" stage, and supposedly didn't want to acknowledge a soul. Read several pages. Like the photos you took, strain to find your mother in the thick, coarse paper. In the black ink look for a secret message to you that she would have sneaked in, a code that says, *I love you no matter whose genes you have. No matter who you look like. You were chosen, not given up.* No book has been written for you, yet. Hope the one she's working on now will be yours. This would almost make up for her absence in your life.

Your eyes are heavy and your stomach hurts. You are no longer drunk on sugar, instead you are crashing. Coming down hard from your cookie rush. Sit on the leather couch, unbutton your tight pants, lean back on a pillow, your mother's book in your hand, a blanket draped over you, and close your eyes. Just for a minute.

Wake unsure of the time. Fuck, how long have you been asleep? Fix yourself, return the books, fold the blanket, and rush back to the party.

When you re-enter the living room, Carol is opening the last of the gifts, a hat made of brightly colored ribbon is perched on her head. See Olive on the couch laughing and flirting with one of Carol's male cousins. Suddenly long to be stoned and tipsy, like the late nights you pulled in college, and rest your head on her shoulder. Realize it's been an eternity since someone took care of you. Scraped you off the floor and held you while you sobbed uncontrollably like they do in the movies when the main character is having a cathartic breakdown, or breakthrough, like *Good Will Hunting* or *The Prince of Tides*.

Look at Carol's mother. Watch her dote on your pregnant friend, one hand resting on her shoulder, the other rubbing small circles over her large belly. Wish someone were resting a nurturing hand around your bloated middle. Consider getting pregnant so people will touch you.

Another month goes by. December finds you at the Four Seasons' party room, filled with friends, co-workers from the museum, and family. At least fifty people are raising a glass of low-cal champagne and listening to you toast your once-best friend. Yesterday she reached her hundred-pound mark. This is monumental. "To my wonderfully terrific, gorgeous friend and her equally wonderful fiancé." The words flow easily out of your mouth at Olive's weight-loss-engagement-party-turned-you-don't-know-what.

You look at your friend glowing in the praise, wearing clothing purchased in regular stores. Search for familiar gestures: a smirk, the tilt of her head, the way she caresses a glass when she talks. Find none. Now when you develop photos they're of a stranger. When you look through the lens of your camera, you have trouble locating her, trouble understanding where she's gone.

Ray has barely said hello to you, and though you tried to strike up a conversation with him, he seemed uninterested in talking. He drank from his beer, rubbed at his goatee, and looked off to the side. Eventually he said he was going out for a smoke.

Find Olive's parents talking with their friends, and when her mother's eye catches yours, she smiles, nods her head, and raises a glass in your direction. Then she mouths the words "thank you." Wish your parents were here. Look around the room hoping to spot them, or Ed. You want that magic moment where he shows up, dressed in a suit, red roses in his hands, and begs for forgiveness. You even find yourself looking for Morgan, thinking perhaps she cares enough to show. That she'll want to make sure this event runs smoothly, too. So what if she's a little younger than you. Maybe it's time to make new friends. Unite with someone over something other than a college connection. She's clearly reached out to you. So you scan the room again. When you spot no one, feel utterly alone.

Go into the bathroom. It's tranquil in here. Sleek and slick with its marble floors, long row of sinks, basket of fluffy hand towels, bowl of wrapped mints. Look at yourself in the mirror. Three months of dieting and you look the same. You might possibly look worse. Though you're wearing your best suit, you still appear pudgy. Your makeup seems to have disappeared, somehow slipped off your face. At closer glance you appear tired, pale, and ghostly.

"Olive looks wonderful, don't you think?" someone says to you, Laura or Betty or Sally. You can't remember her name even though you were just introduced. Nod and agree. Watch her reapply lipstick, fix her hair, and leave.

Wait for the bathroom to empty out.

When you are the only person left, go into a stall, preferably one with a sink in it, the one used for wheelchair-bound people. Remove your jacket, make sure your shirt is tucked into your pants, tightly. That your hair is pulled back, is secured by a rubber band. Lift the seat up, inspect the rim. So clean. This is why you like hotels. The anonymity of it all, the traceless marks people don't leave because someone is always cleaning up after you.

Take a deep breath, lean forward, and stick your index finger down your throat. Gag. The third try produces a gross amount of vomit that floods out of your mouth. Do not stop until you see a brownish yellow. The omelet you ate for lunch. The first bite of food that entered your mouth. Flush and take deep breaths. Listen to see if anyone has entered. It is silent, calm, and you are lucky. Thank God for this favor as you spit the last bit of puke into the fresh bowl of water. Sit on the floor until the shaking stops. Until the throbbing in your head eases. Wish you had water. Next time you'll remember to bring a glass in with you, or some iced tea. Iced tea would be so nice right now. Talk yourself into believing you can get used to this. It isn't so hard. You have other friends who have done it. You've watched them, held their hair back.

Cheer yourself up by thinking how successful your gallery will be. You could be the next Mary Boone. Fuck Ed. Fuck the family you don't have, or the one who gave you up, even the one you would have started with Ed if he weren't such a moronic, scared piece of shit. Fuck them all. You are a wonderful person. You are strong and stable and resourceful. You may not have a mother, but you have a gallery. You have your photographs if not your best friend. You may not have a husband, but you have something better. When everyone has left you, at least you'll be thin.

Chapter 12

Sheila
Room 1608

They met randomly, by accident really, as New Yorkers often do.

Sheila noticed him first standing on line at the Starbucks on Ninety-sixth and Madison Avenue, his face crunched up, impatient from the wait, frustrated by the slow service. He noticed her, too. She could tell. She caught him glancing at her while they stood with the others, all of whom ordered frappuccinos and other overly sweet drinks that took forever to make.

During those first few weeks she'd turn her head toward the crowd behind her, appear as if she were searching for something outside, and see him staring at her. She'd blush, he'd nod slightly. Once she could swear he was sniffing her. Another time she caught him looking at her hands and wondered if he'd made a mental note that they were clean, finely manicured, and wedding band–free, just a simple ruby ring on her pinky. Often they displayed signs of recognition to each other; a raised eyebrow, a flick of the chin, a small half wave.

She liked hearing him order, his voice smooth and confident, like a voiceover actor. Liked the way he'd dig into the breast pocket of his trench coat and pull out a thin brown lizard billfold.

If he was sitting in the back of the coffeehouse, which he usually did, she'd pretend she was interested in the wall of useless items on sale: aluminum thermoses for the car, mugs that were microwavable, coffee machines, boxes of candy. She'd spot his hands and head partly hidden behind his *New York Times*, and if a seat were available at his table, she would ask if she could sit there. He always seemed happy to oblige.

He was clean-cut, freshly shaven, and smelled of something woodsy. His dark hair was thick and wavy and he had a boyish charm for a man who appeared to be in his forties. And there was something smart and worldly about him. She could see it in his hazel eyes, which seemed to take everything in at once. Even the small scar that ran over his left brow added a level of sophistication and edginess to him.

Eventually they started a dialogue.

"I'm Marty," he offered first, his hand extended.

"Sheila," she replied.

On these occasions when they sat together, they exchanged passing comments about the weather, about current events, about their jobs. He was a therapist. "I specialize in compulsive behavior," he told her. "Gambling, smoking, OCD . . ."

"How do you know the difference between a vice and a compulsion?"

He smiled, exposing two dimples. "Well, that's a rather complicated question. Is the vice ruining your life?"

"No, I just like tea. Though I have over thirty-eight different kinds at home."

"That sounds like more of a collection than a compulsion." He took off his wire-rimmed reading glasses and set them on the table. "I don't think anyone ever died from too much tea."

"And it doesn't seem to be affecting my life choices."

"Good to know." He raised his coffee cup for emphasis, then took a large gulp. She watched his Adam's apple click up and down as he swallowed. "I'm all about coffee. In fact, I think it's both my vice and my compulsion. But that doesn't mean we can't be friends."

"Absolutely."

They clinked cups. Then she watched him rub the tip of his finger over the rim of his mug. "You didn't tell me what you do."

"I'm a teacher, fourth grade. I'm at Nightingale-Bamford, just a few blocks away." She took a sip of her Earl Grey. Was it possible for grown women to get schoolgirl crushes?

"Ah, short days, summers off."

"So that means both of us are free during the month of August?"

They laughed at this, their voices melding together, his deep and rich with texture, hers light and bubbly, something she hadn't heard released from her throat in years.

And that's how it started. Perhaps that's how all affairs begin, she didn't know, she'd never had one before.

———

Soon their accidental encounters became planned. They progressed from Starbucks in the morning to lunch—Mondays and Thursdays at Sarabeth's, one block from her school and two from his Park Avenue office.

He had made the first move, innocently brushing his knee against her thigh. And they had touched hands when both reached for the small metal container of milk. She had giggled, he had smiled while their eyes held a long, intense stare.

Weeks later they sipped wine in her living room. Then they'd move shyly into her bedroom, his thumb caressing the outside of her hand as they walked through her narrow hallway.

When they ate Chinese takeout in bed, she'd watch in great dismay as his wedding ring would catch her bedroom light, the glare reflecting off of the simple gold band. She had tried shifting the colorful faux Tiffany lamp from one side of her dresser to the other, but it was useless. It was almost as if an eye was watching from above.

"Do you think this means we're bad people?" she asked him. "Do you think we'll be punished later on in life?"

"I think I'm more to blame than you are," he said. "We're both adults, and I'm making a choice." He sighed, she moved closer to him. "And you? Well, you've just fallen for a guy who happens to be married. Unhappily, unexcitedly, married."

She's dreamed of Marty leaving his wife and marrying her. They were so good together. Their bodies meshing the way first-time lovers did, raw and organic. They would hold hands and listen to each other breathe, and walk naked around her apartment unashamed. Sometimes she'd put on a CD and make him dance with her, closely, so that their bodies, still warm and slightly sweaty, could stick together, like conjoined twins.

But she wasn't in it for the sex. She'd told this to him on that first day in her apartment when everything was new and unshared. She loved him more than she'd loved any man. More than her college boyfriend, Leo, who she had been close to marrying. Even more than her father. She loved the way he lit his cigarettes, the way his lips fit over hers, the way his clothes hung on him, but mostly it was how he listened to her, as if she were the most important person in the world. And she wondered if this was why people adored their therapists.

She'd always been the good girl. No one-night stands, no drugs, no need for an AIDS test. She was respectful, did well at college, led a quiet, uncomplicated life. But with Marty, there was something exciting yet soothing about him. Often they'd hold each other, their bodies feeling the coolness of the sheets while they listened to the lull of the traffic outside. During these moments, her mind would wander as she conjured up countless images of what their life could be like. She envisioned vacations and long holiday weekends spent at their cottage home in Maine or Cape Cod. Saw their children—he didn't have any with his wife, Faye—having his eyes and soft full lips with her laugh and kind disposition. During the month of August, since neither would be working, they would travel abroad, leaving the children with his parents.

Sheila never had playful, carefree summers or family vacations. Her father, an overseas radio communications operator, was never home. Every year or two she and her mother followed him to whichever air force base he was assigned to: Texas, Nevada, Ohio, North Carolina, and Arizona. Husbands and fathers were always being called away from their families. Worried wives would talk with other worried wives who lived on the base, their voices becoming hushed when Sheila walked by. And there was the ever-present feeling that at any given moment a knock would come at the door. That they'd open it to reveal a somber man wearing an officer's uniform who'd tell them that her father was dead.

A man of great presence, her dad was broad and tall. Dashingly handsome and charming. When he was home, they'd read together, play cards, do crossword puzzles found in the backs of newspapers, take long walks around the base camp, and he would tell her about his job, how he hated to be away, about the adventure he was having. With him home, she felt complete. She and her mother and her father. A threesome. A perfect unit.

Marty made her feel complete, too. Even though he was twelve years older, she could see her future forming in front of her. She had tried the support groups the government offered for children who grew up in a military world. But the men she met were hardened by what they'd seen and ruined by the wars they fought in. There were very few male teachers at her all-girl school and most of her friends, neighbors, and co-workers were married, living a different life than the one she was trying to get through. At thirty-five there was still plenty of time for her to get pregnant. To start a family. And though she loved taking care of other people's children, was honestly good at what she did, that's what they were. At the end of the day, she handed them back to their parents, and she went home to nothing. The cost of guilt she felt being with a married man was overridden each time by the safety and love she experienced when she was next to him.

Sheila wanted to write Faye a letter of apology each time she slept with Marty. *I'm so sorry.* Or *Please forgive my poor behavior, but he makes be feel whole.* There were no cards at the Hallmark store that echoed her sorry-I-slept-with-your-spouse sentiments that she was aware of. She ached to tell Faye about the two of them as much as she ached for Marty to leave Faye. Sometimes she would dial him at home from the pay phone on the corner, the words already in her throat busting to come out, and hope Faye would answer. But she was never home. She only heard Faye's earnest, wistful voice on the answering machine telling her that she and Marty were not available, and if she would leave her name and number, they would gladly call her back.

She tried to picture what Marty and Faye did at home. Saw them in their predictable lives, he paying bills, maybe smoking a pipe, talking about his patients. She might be on the phone, gabbing with her friends, or showing him her recent purchases: pair of shoes bought on sale, a tie for him, maybe a vase or new towels. At night they might watch a foreign film, the lights turned down, bowl of microwave popcorn and plate of freshly cut fruit situated between them. She would gladly take that life, a life not unlike the one her parents had. And as humdrum as Marty claimed his life to be, she would give anything to exist with him in it. She needed him more than Faye did, couldn't he see that?

This is the question she still asks herself, even though it's seven months later and they have moved their lovemaking to Fifty-seventh Street, to a hotel room on the sixteenth floor. The Four Seasons was Marty's suggestion. And though Sheila liked being in her own bed, Marty mentioned how her apartment was too similar to the one he lived in, and how lovely it would be to have sex in a bed that belonged to no one in particular. To make love on a floor where hundreds of people had stepped. To take a bath in an enormous tub where no one claimed ownership.

"Everything in a hotel is common property," he said last month, as he reached for his glasses and kissed her above the bridge of her nose. "Here, you and I are equals. Nothing in this room is yours, nothing is mine. We're just two people sharing universal things."

She hated the room for the very reason he insisted on liking it. Nothing *was* hers. The familiar objects that brought her comfort, that she spent a lifetime amassing were gone. And though the Four Seasons was a lovely hotel, it wasn't her home. She had moved around enough as a child. The constant packing, the minimalist living, the simple fact that one moved into a furnished home and stayed there for only a year or two made her feel terribly unstable, as though she were living with roommates she never met. Nice as the Four Seasons was, the sheets weren't as soft as hers, the pillows too puffy, the comforter too crisp and white. She longed for her teas, for the smell of the freshly baked chocolate chip cookies she'd make for her students. For the simple, yet specific objects that defined who she was: her collection of ceramic teapots, her shelves of children's books, an old cuckoo clock given to her by her mother that was broken—the little bird only shot out at two and five o'clock.

She'd also heard reports on TV and read them in magazines regarding how hotels weren't as clean as they insisted. Where sheets weren't changed and soaps not replaced and carpeting went unvacuumed, especially in hard-to-reach places like under the bed or by the curtains. The sheets felt dirty. She felt dirty.

Every time Marty would get ready to leave she thought of her father. The way he'd reach for his watch or his wallet made her see quick flashes of her dad in his uniform. She'd see him reach for his military hat, see him take the receiver from her mother's hand and nod solemnly to whoever was on the other line. Her mother's face would drop and fill with a defeated sadness.

Over the past several months, Sheila has brought up the possibility of Marty leaving Faye, a woman he says he married by mistake, and now can't leave.

He was tracing his fingers over her stomach and chest, explaining the floor plan of his office, the setup of furniture and where his patients sat or laid down depending upon the work they were doing. His finger was at her right nipple, which at that moment doubled as the light stand in his office.

"Maybe we could go away for a long weekend?" she suggested, as his finger inched toward her other breast. "Take the train out to Connecticut or Boston?"

"You know weekends are impossible." He leaned over and sucked on her nipple.

"Okay, how about the theater and dinner, or a jazz club at an after-hours piano bar?"

"Honey," he said laughing, "I can't just come home at three in the morning."

"Please. I want us to do something other than stare at four walls."

"You know that's not possible." He was sitting up now, the floor plan temporarily on hold.

"Why? You're not happy with her. You said you don't love her anymore. Why are you staying with her?"

"Because . . ." he stopped, seemed to be searching for something to say that would appease her and sound honest at the same time. "I'm not ready for that kind of change right now."

"Does that mean you will be in the future? In a few months? A year?" She was sitting up now, too.

"You're projecting," he said.

"And you're avoiding."

He smiled at her, impressed she was using his jargon.

A month ago she began looking at apartments, something that wouldn't remind Marty of the one he lived in. Her broker, Robin, is a young woman with an eagerness to please and an eye for detail. She's always waiting for Sheila with a cold bottle of water and a folder filled with glossy photos of the future. Of the twenty dwellings they've seen, only three meet Sheila's requirements: that it's affordable on her teacher's salary, and that it doesn't look like the one she lives in now.

"The further east you go, the more space you'll get for your money," Robin tells her as they stand in a cookie-cutter one bedroom off of First Avenue.

The floors are overly shellacked and the fire escape has three locks on the large grate that covers the window. She tries to picture Marty walking up four flights of stairs after he's already walked several long blocks east from his office.

"The rent isn't terrible, and there's a lot you can do with the space," she says looking at her notes. "I know it's not much now, but when furnished, it might be very charming."

Robin is too honest. Her voice and lack of eye contact betray her, causing Sheila to feel even worse for wasting her time. Truth be told, Sheila has the best deal in town. The building she lives in now is rent-controlled and specifically caters to low-income people: teachers, hospital interns, residents, and graduate students.

She's told Robin very little except that she and her doctor boyfriend are looking for something a bit larger than what they live in now. Robin has been an angel, easy to work with, doesn't ask a lot of questions, and uses the term "we," which makes Sheila feel less alone. And hopeful, as if she and Marty really could be together.

"Perhaps it would help to bring your boyfriend with us next time," Robin suggests as they exit the building. "Maybe a new set of eyes is just the thing we need."

On Tuesday a miracle happens. Marty concedes to look at apartments. Sheila has only said she needs a change, and the idea of moving might help her feel unstuck. Then she stroked his ego adding, "You've got such a great eye and logical mind that it would be extremely helpful."

At 7:50 p.m. the three stand in a living room in a high-rise off of Lexington Avenue in a doorman building that everyone knows Sheila can't afford. Still, Shelia has talked both Robin and Marty into looking at something seductive. The two bedroom, two bath is truly stunning. And the second room could be a study for Marty. The closets are spacious, the living room massive, the kitchen is newly renovated. She reaches for Marty's hand as they look out the window that overlooks Park Avenue. The night is crisp and sharp. The city sparkles with possibility.

"How much is it?" Marty asks Robin.

"Four thousand per month. Or forty-eight thousand for the year. That includes electrical and there's a storage unit and garage. Both are extra but available to residents. There's also a roof deck. All things considered, though it sounds like a lot, it's actually a very good price."

"It certainly is," he says, dropping Sheila's hand. He walks over to Robin, who hands him a spec sheet of the building. The two stand inches apart.

"What's most interesting and unusual about this apartment is that the owners are willing to sublet it for a year with an option to buy. If, after six months, you decide to purchase the apartment, your maintenance is only two thousand dollars a month. Of course the apartment is 1.8 million, but again, given the location and everything the building has to offer, it's an amazing deal."

Sheila watches Marty take another step closer to the realtor. She watches the way he puts his hand on her shoulder as he tells her how informative she is. How well she does her job. That a few more moments here with both of them, and he'd be ready to take out his checkbook, and perhaps they should leave before he is overcome with a case of "real estate envy." And though he's a talented shrink, he might not be able to cure a New Yorker's need for a larger apartment.

And then it hits. She wonders for the first time if she's the only woman he sees. A line of faceless women appear, some his patients, others random women he might meet in the elevator here, or at a bar, or in the park, even at their Starbucks. If her apartment really mirrors his or if that's just a line he uses.

Today, Marty is midsentence, something about not being able to see her on Thursday, when Sheila realizes he's ending their relationship. Though he hasn't said it, she just knows. She can tell by the stiff way he clenches his fedora hat, by the coat draped over his arm, even in his posture as he leans against the hotel's bedroom door, his body half in, half out, that he isn't coming back. No more weekly dinners, no more sex in expensive hotel rooms, no more Marty. What kind of therapist is he to be so easily readable? His intention is so specific and clear to her, a novice, someone who had never been in therapy. He won't look her in the eyes. He does this sometimes when they're in bed, their fingers intertwined as she looks at him and he stares out the window.

It's in this hotel room, tangled up in what she hopes are clean sheets, that the idea of killing him seeps into her mind. She could offer to make him dinner, a last encounter, a fine food farewell she would tell him.

She pictures him standing in her hallway mirroring the position he encompassed minutes ago. His coat draped over his arm, fingers gripping his hat, eyes not really looking at her, rather focusing somewhere just above her brows and yet not over her forehead. She bets he does this with his patients when he's bored. And only after he had eaten, and they had said their good-byes, and she lingered in her hallway waiting for something to happen, giving him one last chance to change his mind, leave his wife, be with her instead, would she reach for the metal vase on her mantel. She pictures him leaning in for one last kiss, or maybe she would ask, say she needed it for closure. Conceding to her request, he would bend forward and then she would grasp the metal piece and smack him in the back of his head. He would stagger, stumble at first, look confused, raise a hand to the sore area, maybe the same hand that held his hat, and when he brought it back down that hand would be bloody. Maybe his eyes would roll back, maybe he'd drop to the floor, first on his knees, then on his face, like in the movies.

Sheila takes her fantasy one step further, envisioning Marty lying on her floor, blood oozing from his head. She can see herself kneeling down next to him, turning his body over, pulling back the left side of her hair, wrapping it around her ear and bending close to his mouth to see if he's breathing. If hot air is pushing out from his nostrils. She conjures up a mental image of how surprisingly peaceful he would look: a relaxed calmness on his face, his skin warm and slightly pale.

She sees herself as a Lucille Ball waiting for her Ethel Mertz to come barreling through the door, trying to move Ricky's boss, who's fainted, out of her apartment before Ricky comes home. Sheila can almost hear the Cuban accent, "Lucy, you got some splaining to do."

All of this ridiculousness and the dark thoughts are dismissed as she showers, dresses, and leaves the hotel. She's being paranoid and silly and rather than kill him, she decides to confront him instead. En route to his office she pictures the padded chairs and matching couch, the layout of his belongings and his waiting room. The plants, the photos, the framed diplomas, even the way his officemates have their work space configured. If she closes her eyes, she can see Marty mapping it out on her that time they were lying naked and both were in love with each other. If she tries hard enough, she can visualize his patients. God knows she's heard enough about them: faint-looking women who hang on his every word and drink too much, married women who long to leave their husbands and have sex with strangers, others who wished they didn't have children, men with addiction problems who hate their bosses, don't love their wives, feel misunderstood by the women in their offices—and on and on. Even the shopaholic who buys Marty monthly gifts he couldn't care less about.

Years of hurt and abandonment, first by her father, then by Leo, and now by Marty have led her to this very moment, standing in the lobby of his office building looking at the large board that lists the names of the firms and the people who reside in the building.

She will not be left. If need be, she'll leave him first.

Marty, who shares his office with three other shrinks, is on the sixteenth floor. She thinks this is funny since their hotel room is also on the sixteenth floor and wonders if Marty does this specifically so he won't forget where he's going. She wonders if he lives on the sixteenth floor in the apartment he shares with Faye. Beautiful, wistful Faye, who may or may not know about Marty's infidelity.

She gets in the elevator with others and as they ascend higher and higher, Sheila has second thoughts. Rather than confront him, perhaps she should just take the elevator back down. Maybe she's pushing too hard. Maybe if she acted more distant, that would make him want her. Want her back.

But it's too late. The doors open and as she steps onto Marty's floor, he's already standing there. A hat is in his hand, a coat draped over his arm, a waiting-to-be-smoked cigarette held in between his index finger and thumb. Caught off guard, she's as shocked as he appears to be.

"What are you doing here?" He looks around the deserted hallway, seems momentarily relieved. "Did we have plans? Did something happen?" He takes a step closer. "Are you okay?" It's not concern that registers in his eyes. It's panic. "You're not pregnant are you?"

She could lie right now. Tell him she is, give him a reason to leave Faye.

"I'm not. I just wanted to talk. I wanted to know why you seem so distant. Why you're going to leave me." The words are hard for her to say, even now, almost twenty-six years since the man dressed in the dark navy suit knocked on her door. She was only nine, home alone, her mother at a weekly support group the air force base provided. He asked where her mother was and after she told him, the two walked to the meeting in silence. She was standing in the room filled with ten or so women, whose eyes were red and tissues were in their hands. They turned around at the interruption, all with the same look of horror on their faces. Her mother was the one to stand up before she was asked or her name called.

Leaving the air force base was hard, but living with her grandmother was worse. Only after two years of sharing a room with her mother in the very house her mother had grown up in were they able to move out and get a place of their own. Two years later, when her mother remarried, she was sent away to boarding school. Her new father was nothing like the first. He was mean and cranky, didn't have time to talk to her, or play cards or do the crosswords. He merely shoved some money into her hand when she came home from school, or wrote her checks after college so she could afford to live in Manhattan while searching for a teaching job. Even now, years after her mother has died, she still gets a check for one hundred dollars each month with a note that reads, "Hoping you are well."

"How did you know it was over?" Marty asks, his hand on the elevator button, which he presses.

She watches it light up in yellow and shrugs. "I just did."

"I think you went into the wrong line of work. You'd have made a great shrink."

He starts to pace.

"So I'm right?"

He nods, "I've been trying to tell you for weeks. I know you want more but I can't." He stops moving and faces her. "I never meant to hurt you."

"But you did," she says. "I guess I'm just a vice? I've not made it to compulsion status."

"Don't do this. Please. You're not either. You were"—he corrects himself quickly—"are very important to me. I just need a break. I need to figure things out."

"What's to figure out? I love you. You feel the same about me. You're not happy at home . . ."

"Christ, people think shrinks know how to handle everything, but we don't."

She stares at him. "I just expected some honesty."

"I *am* being honest. I'm honestly confused. I'm honestly fucked-up. I'm honestly sorry we did this and I'm sure as hell honestly sorry you came to my office. How's that for honesty?" He's shouting now. His face red and his teeth clenched. "Jesus, everyone wants a piece of me."

And then Marty is on his knees. His tan coat cleaning the dirty floor. For a moment she thinks he's going to apologize. Maybe beg her to forgive him. She bends down to meet his face, wants to share this moment with him, and notices his face is wet with perspiration. Upon further inspection, Sheila can see all the color has drained out of him.

"Are you alright?" Panic floods her voice.

The elevator finally comes. The doors open harshly, the sound filling the small hallway.

"Go on," he barks. "Get in."

The elevator is empty. She doesn't want to leave her once lover, who seems crumpled up in a ball on the floor. She reaches for his hand to hold in hers. It's warm and soft. She stares into his pale, terror-stricken face. His eyes are intense, his lips pressed together. The rustic smell of his aftershave engulfs her. Even in this position, Marty is handsome. She could almost love him all over again.

She turns and moves toward the elevator, hoping to catch the closing doors, hoping to bring Marty with her. Drag him in and get him the help he clearly needs. But he refuses to budge.

"Just go. I'm fine. I'll be fine."

Her lower body is in the elevator, her upper half leaning far forward, still gripping him. Her hand is wet with sweat and it slips as she tries to hold on. Slips more as he pulls away.

The elevator starts making a horrible ringing sound and the doors are opening and closing on her arm, which is still extended, grasping Marty's hand as if he's the most important thing. They stay like this, their fingers intertwined, until she feels him slip away. Until the elevator swallows her whole.

Chapter 13

Robin

Suite 1512

It's twoish on Friday as I wait for my sister's plane to arrive. LaGuardia is unusually, eerily calm. The morning traffic, the people racing to catch their flights, the red-eye victims have all scattered. Only a handful of layover people and anal travelers who adhered to the two-hour early arrival rule remain.

And me.

Fifteen minutes later a clutch of people have formed a small circle and we wait for flight number 8756 to land safely. Within minutes, a fistful of first-class passengers make their way down the long corridor looking like returnees from an alien abduction. I would have bet Vicki had finagled her way into a first-class seat, but nothing. After a momentary break in the swarm, the next series of faces emerge. I think perhaps she's taken a later flight and forgotten to call. A number of scenarios play in my mind until I catch her, see her from afar. Her hair is surprisingly long and colored a rich brown, a new shade for her. She's dressed in tan pants, a sleeveless black mock turtleneck that makes her shoulders look lean and her breasts perky, and a matching jacket, which is folded over her arm. She's carrying a Coach briefcase and looks like the political lawyer she is rather than a person who's here to celebrate our cousin's shower. A weekend in New York, her hometown that she never visits and rarely calls home. The town she's from now is Washington, DC.

Our older brother fled to Israel. My parents sent Michael there for his twentieth birthday. Six weeks later he returned as Scholmo, an orthodox Jew. He married a virgin just like the Bible commanded, and the two reside in the Promised Land on a kibbutz. They have several children and seldom see us.

Last time I saw Vicki was two years ago. I'd just turned twenty-four. It was a brutal time to be in DC in terms of the weather and because it was an election year. She was working for a senator, hating her job, and depressed with life in general. I thought spending a few days together might give us a chance to connect. I took the Acela Express and when I got to the station waited for twenty minutes before phoning.

"Not to worry. The hotel's just a few blocks away," she said, still in her office. "Take a cab there and I'll leave work early and meet you. We'll have dinner someplace nice."

"I thought I was staying with you?"

"Robin, you're the only one I know who'd be unappreciative they were staying in one of the best hotels in DC. If it's about the money"—her voice became softer—"I'm not paying for it, so don't worry."

Then I heard someone call for her. It sounded distant and planned. I could visualize my sister cuing a co-worker to beckon her into a nonexistent meeting. "I gotta go. See you tonight."

I checked into the Four Seasons, a nice man escorted me to the room that my sister had reserved. A fruit basket greeted me when I entered, the note, scribbled in someone else's hand-writing, read: "Welcome to Washington. See you at 6:30 for drinks in the lounge. V." The clock on the table said noon. I remember this as I wait for her now when I could be showing prospective buyers apartments in the better part of Manhattan. I could be telling a lovely, recently married couple that the sun gleams brightly in the morning. That the co-op board is flexible and both a washer/dryer, not to mention a half bathroom, are allowed. Or reconnecting with the schoolteacher and therapist who looked at the two bedroom last week, and gently suggest they reconsider buying, that they would be a board's dream team.

I offered to share my apartment with Vicki, but she pre-ferred staying at the Four Seasons' sister hotel in Manhattan.

I watch my sister talk to a handsome man who's carrying a boxy purple bag, which I know is hers because we have the same luggage, a well-meaning holiday gift from our aunt. If I don't rush up to her, I wonder if she'd even recognize me; my straw-berry blond hair is newly cropped, my heels add a good three inches, my skin's cleared up, contacts have replaced my glasses. But my sister walks directly over to where I'm standing.

"I'm missing underwear," she announces when she gets close enough for me to hear.

I look at her blankly, think about hugging her hello.

"Someone went through my bag at the airport and took out my good panties."

"Why would anyone want your underwear?"

"Forget it, Robin. I wouldn't expect you to understand."

The man clears his throat. For a moment I think she's going to invite him to dinner—or state that she's already done so and this guy, David or Mark or John, and Vicki will end up sitting close to each other in a padded booth at an expensive restaurant with me on the other side. He'd pay for her. I'd have to pay for myself. After dinner, if I was lucky, they'd drop me off in a cab and then they'd go back to her hotel so he can get lucky.

"James, this is my kid sister."

James extends his hand. It's firm and solid, the way I hope my husband's hand will feel in mine someday.

"Kid sister? I thought maybe you guys were twins," he says, flashing a broad, toothy smile.

That's original. "Yes, it's true. I'm only twenty-six. Vicki's four years older."

She eyes me coldly and mouths, "Thanks."

James is on my sister's left side, still carrying her bag as we exit the airport.

We wait on the cab line with men in trench coats, women wrapped in wool capes or Burberryesque quilted jackets. Small patches of two-day-old snow now turned black from fumes and soot are all that's left from the storm we had a few days ago.

She looks older than I remember, tired too, yet she's still

beautiful in that Banana Republic catalog way. Everyone in Washington looks older than they are. Frown lines, crow's-feet, bags under their eyes, weighted down leather bags on their shoulders filled with briefs, legislation, secret documents, listings of who's who in the White House.

"You lost weight," she jabs as she digs angrily around in her handbag.

"I thought you gave them up?" I say.

"I did. I'm looking for the gum."

"What about the patch?"

"What the fuck do you think I'm wearing?"

I look at James who arches his eyebrows, then shrugs.

We move up the cab line and when it's our turn, James hands Vicki back her bag. "So, I'll give you a call later," he states as our ride approaches. I watch my sister's eyes narrow as she mentally tries to send him a signal. Now she can't claim exhaustion or sudden headache.

"I'll call you," she says, pushing me into the car. I watch her lean forward and kiss him on the cheek, watch her lips move ever so slightly by his ear. I watch him smile and nod, then watch him get smaller as we drive away.

"You made dinner plans with some guy?" I ask, facing her.

"No. He was just being friendly. He works at the *New Republic*. It's good business." White Chiclets-shaped gum appears and Vicki pops two pieces into her mouth. She chews feverishly. "I told him I'd try to meet him for drinks or something. It's just what people say."

My sister is a terrific liar. It's a gift, like knitting or cooking.

———

As we pull up to the Fifty-seventh Street entrance of the hotel, a doorman rushes to help us out. Vicki loves hotels. The mini soaps and products in the bathroom, the mini olives at the bar, even the mini bottles of overpriced liquors found in the fridge. She loves the strange men who wear simple, shiny gold bands on their fingers, have condoms in their pockets, and large bills in their wallets. She loves the room service, housekeeping, and the thin credit card key that goes undetected in the pocket of tightly worn jeans.

In Washington, you can be easily erased. In New York, you can be anyone you want, change your name, create a phony job, or blend effortlessly into the sea of shoppers on Fifth Avenue. I think about all this as I flip through channels in room 1512 while my sister unpacks.

For the past ten minutes I've been waiting for her to notice the blue shopping bag sitting on the desk I dropped off earlier, and she only becomes aware of the present because I point to it.

"That's for you." I raise my hand in the direction of the gift.

"Oh, look what Abby sent. That was sweet."

"Actually, it's from me."

She doesn't bother with the card that's written in my penmanship rather than some random assistant or hotel worker. Instead she rips it off the bag, places it on the table and, taking a handle in each fist, pulls the stapled bag open. Fingers dart in and reemerge grasping a book.

"I already read this," she tells me, dropping the novel on the desk with a thud. "And I have an iPod," she informs me, holding up the cases that contain the books on CD.

"I thought you could listen to them in the car." A rerun of

Friends is on and I wonder what makes Monica and Ross have such a good relationship. Why the sisters in *Charmed* always seem to get along. Even Mary and Laura Ingalls had each other's back.

"Who would listen to books in a car?"

"Lots of people. Kevin says they sell really well. You could burn them and then load them onto your iPod. That's what I do."

"I don't take long trips." She sighs. "Why don't you give them to Mom, or Dad. He's always taking what's-her-name away somewhere."

"Sharon."

"Whatever."

When the T-shirt makes an appearance, I don't even bother asking if she likes it.

"This looks too small." She holds it out in front of her, the words "Killer Instincts" are printed on the back.

"I thought you could keep it at the gym. You know, as an extra." I flip through the channels, flip through the magazines on the table, try to appear nonchalant.

"It's really not my thing." She tosses the unfolded shirt into the bag.

"So you don't want them?"

"Not really."

I walk over to the table and collect the discarded belongings, my head shaking from side to side in frustration.

"Don't be like that, Robin." She's facing me, her hands running through her hair, pulling it into a ponytail, then releasing it.

"Would it have killed you to have just said *thanks?*" I match her glare, a showdown.

"You want me to be honest, don't you? It's not like you paid for them, right?"

"No, but I went to Kevin's office and picked them out myself and . . . I just thought it would be nice to have something to do on the train ride back."

"So you're still seeing him?"

"I am." I continue staring at her, wonder what she's really thinking.

"Why?" She sneers, breaking eye contact. She reaches for the menu on the table and looks through it.

"And you're dating whom?" I ask.

She laughs, a snicker, sharp and quick. "Don't take everything so personally. It's not like I asked you to get me something." Her cell rings and in one fell swoop she scoops it up and walks into the bedroom leaving me standing by the unwanted gift bag.

"No, I thought it might be nice," I call to her, my words heard only by me.

Within seconds a deep, rich laugh comes pouring out of the bedroom, spilling onto me like a fresh spray of perfume. It's infectious, contagious. I hate hearing it because I don't possess this quality. I hate hearing it because I can't make her do it for me no matter how witty or sassy I am.

"I can't believe he said that." Her voice is now edgy and harsh. "His dick is the size of my pinky and that's being generous." There's a long pause, and a ringing in my ears. "Hey, it's a boy's game, got to play like one."

The hotel phone rings next and Vicki emerges, snaps her fingers at me, then points, indicating I'm to answer the call.

"Hello. Seidelman's room."

Vicki mouths, "Who is it?" To which I respond silently, "Mom." She rolls her eyes, then motions to me that she doesn't want the phone, snaps her cell closed, and goes back to her open travel bag and continues to unpack.

"I'm not sure. I can ask." I look at Vicki. "Mom wants to know if you want to have dinner tonight. She was hoping to see you."

Sighing, she removes the phone from my hand. "Hi," she says, sounding suddenly cheery. "I guess mine's not getting reception in the room." She eyes me and winks. "I think Robin and I are going to do a girl's thing. She said she had something she wanted to talk to me about." There's a pause. "Okay, I will. You too. See you tomorrow night at the shower." She hangs up.

"Why did you tell her that?"

"What does it matter? You didn't want to eat with her either."

I stop flipping channels when I get to CNN. I let the anchors' voices take up the dead space, filling the room with heavy banter so we don't have to.

At home I slide one of the discarded CDs into the stereo and wear the T-shirt Vicki didn't want. I think about phoning Kevin when I remember he's in Frankfurt for a publisher's convention. He's not met Vicki, but he's heard enough about her. He's heard the demanding messages she's left on my answering machine when she wants me to look into renting her an apartment, or when she can't get in touch with our father and wants to know where he is, or is having a fight with Mom and wants someone to spew at. I wish he were here now. He'd take me out to a movie, we'd sit in the back, bucket of buttery popcorn, bag of Peanut M&M's and a large Diet Coke to keep us company.

I rummage through my old camp trunk, which doubles as a coffee table and locate my childhood photo album, which resides next to yearbooks from high school, Valentine's Day cards, and love notes from ex-boyfriends. The album cover is weathered and has Wacky Pack stickers all over it. The pages are brown and have lost most of their stickiness. The pictures, however, are in decent shape. There's one of Michael, Vicki, and I dressed up for his Bar Mitzvah. Another showcasing the three of us playing in the sand. Gangly arms are wrapped around each other's shoulders. Comrades in battle, we are skinny and tan and our faces beam with brightness, with optimism for the future. In another Vicki and I are in flowered bathing suits, lying on towels with cartoon characters on them. Last is a picture of us dressed like Indian chiefs. We have patches of rouge on our cheeks, feathered headpieces on our foreheads. I'm six. Vicki is ten. It was a snow day. Bored and antsy, Vicki snuck into our mother's room, retrieved her makeup bag, and applied round circles of blush to my cheeks. Then she smeared thick streaks of eye shadow on my nose, and chin. When it was my turn to do her face, I was so nervous my hands shook with a desperate desire to perform this task perfectly. We gave each other Indian names. She called me Little-One-With-Big-Mouth. She was Older-One-Who-Runs-Fast. We took the belts from our robes and tied our dolls to our backs hoping they would look like papooses. What doesn't show in this photo is the rope burn I got when Vicki ripped the belt from my hands. I'd wrapped it around my wrist, and four years stronger not to mention taller than me, she tugged so hard I fell forward, banging my knees and head on the floor. As I gasped for air, she tore the belt from my hand, burning the skin on my wrist. I looked up at her, caught her laughing, caught something dark in her eyes, and in that instant knew she didn't love me. That something was missing. My mother put ice on the grape-size welt on my forehead, while Neosporin promised the scar on my wrist would fade. It didn't. It was raw and blistered and every winter the scar becomes brighter. When all was calm, my mother took this picture.

Vicki and I saunter up Madison Avenue the following morning peering into store windows. When we hit the corner of Fifty-eighth Street, she pulls on my arm and we enter Calvin Klein—or a bad Robert Palmer video. Four painfully thin and pale girls are standing in a straight line, moving their boyish bodies left to right, nodding to us as we pass them. The store is gray and elongated and I run my hand over the racks of expensive clothing, satin brown this, sheer black that, something gauzy, something see-through, that all look alike.

The only dress Vicki wants to try on is being worn by the mannequin, and after finding out that's the last one, we wait for a saleswoman to dismantle the outfit. Once Vicki has possession, I follow her into the dressing room.

"What are you doing?" she sneers, pushing me out the door so that I hit my elbow on the frame.

"I was . . ." I shrug, ignoring the momentary throb of my funny bone. "I thought you might want me in here for an opinion or something."

"God, you're so weird. Can't you just sit on the couch like a normal person?"

I take a seat, and after a minute Vicki materializes in the black satin dress looking like a model ready to hit the runway. The garment clings to her body as if the designer stitched the fabric on her.

She lets the salesperson adjust it as we all look in the mirror.

"You can wear it like so," the salesperson says, fussing over her. "Or if you want it hanging off one shoulder, just adjust the back here. This belt is optional. You can wear it low so it accentuates your hips, or not at all."

I reach for the price tag, see the perfectly printed number $1,500, and raise an eyebrow.

"Do you know how many formals I need to go to for work?" she says, ripping the tag from my hand.

Only after Vicki is rung up, the bag meticulously packed, do we soldier onward.

Two blocks later, Vicki drags me into Barneys and we head down a flight of stairs onto the cosmetic floor where an over-zealous makeup artist paints her already attractive face with perfectly packaged products from Nars and Dior. She dusts browns and tans over Vicki's lids, smears creamy blush on her cheeks, applies a glossy rose to her full lips. With no one to assist me, I reach for one of the eye brushes and attempt to do myself.

"I'll be with you in a minute," the saleswoman informs me without losing concentration on Vicki's face. "These colors are so neutral"—she sweeps her hand over the shadows, like Vanna White showing off an uncompleted puzzle—"that anyone can wear them. Besides, you both have similar coloring so why don't you just copy the colors I'm using."

As I dust my face with powder, a lost-looking woman comes up behind us and stands silently still waiting to be noticed.

I clear my throat and the makeup artist turns around.

"I was wondering if you had cream to combat or prevent stretch marks," she says. "My sister-in-law said you carry a line of baby creams and such?"

The saleswoman takes an annoyed breath. "Yes, I can assist you but I'm with a client. If you can give me a few moments, I'll be happy to help, or if you want, the line you're speaking about is right over there." She points with the blush brush off to the right and my eyes follow the silver wand and black mink.

"Oh, thank you, I'm sorry to have interrupted," the woman says. "Just one last thing . . ."

My sister shifts in her seat.

"I hear some women can have acne breakouts when they're pregnant. Do you have something that prevents that?"

Another irritated sigh escapes from the makeup artist. "Yes, Kiehl's has one as does Bobbi Brown. "It's right over there if you want to look at it."

"Thank you. Sorry to have interrupted."

She smiles at me. Her curly chestnut hair is covering one eye slightly, and she takes her fingers and pushes it behind her ears, while blowing a few strands off of her face.

"After today, this is all getting chopped off," she says. "If I have to do the hatchet job myself." She runs her hands through her locks once more, then takes the pink band from her wrist and twists her hair into a ponytail. "Who knew being pregnant would make your hair grow so fast. Plus it's so hot. I sweat all the time."

I look to Vicki, who rolls her eyes.

Absentmindedly, I run my hand through my own hair, remembering when mine was her length. I look at Vicki's long layers and momentarily regret getting it cut.

"You wouldn't happen to have a suggestion where to go?" the woman asks. "I'm not from Manhattan."

"Neither are we," Vicki is quick to say. I look at my sister and arch my eyebrows.

"Oh. Well, thanks anyway."

And then she's gone.

"What a freak," Vicki says, once the woman is out of earshot.

The makeup artist is at my sister's eyes, applying mascara, and I watch the two snicker.

"That's nothing, they're all freaks," the saleswoman says.

I attempt to duplicate the dramatic strokes, highlighting my cheekbones as she's doing to Vicki, using the gooseneck mirror on the glass counter to see what I'm doing. But when I'm done I emerge all wrong. The colors too heavy, the mirror too small. Before I have a chance to wipe my face with a tissue, Vicki looks at me and starts to laugh.

"If you rub it in a bit Rob, it will look really pretty. You should get them." There's a softness, an authenticity in her voice I haven't heard in years. It's one she uses with friends and occasionally with our parents when she wants something.

The salesperson hands her a mirror and waits for a response.

"Nice. I'll take whatever you used." She slides off the chair and reaches into her bag, fishing out both the nicotine gum and her wallet. The gum is popped into her mouth and a gold card removed from the LV case. I reach into my jeans to remove my credit card but my sister beats me to it.

"I got it." She looks to the saleswoman. "Just duplicate what you've used on me and put it all on my card."

"Are you sure?"

"Forget it," she says, waving away my thank you while signing the slip. "Just blend the makeup in a bit more. You look like . . ."

"Aunt Ella," we both say, our words in perfect sync. We laugh at this and I am so thankful, so very thankful for this moment only she and I can share.

We clutch our purchases like buried treasure, silent promises to make us prettier. My sister grasps hers so tightly—as if she thinks I'm going to snatch it from her hands—that her knuckles are white, her fingers red. It swings in straight, short movements as we continue our shopping adventure. With a skip to our step, smiles on our faces, we take the elevator to the ninth floor, the dining room and gift shop.

Once seated, we peruse the menu, pick at the focaccia, sip mango lemonade, and pretend we are on vacation somewhere exotic.

"I'm glad you're here," I say, reaching for her hand. "It's been forever since we've spent time together. And I know going to Abby's thing tonight might be hard for you, but I just wanted to say"—I try to find my breath, find the words I want to utter—"I'm just really glad you're here." I can feel my face getting hot. A prickly sensation emerges inside me.

She pulls her hand away, looks around the restaurant to see if people are staring. "What the fuck Robin? You act like we're dating."

"That's not what I meant." I sigh and try again. "I know weddings are a touchy subject and that . . ."

"I wouldn't marry the guy Abby's marrying if his penis

shot out gold coins instead of urine. I'm fucking *over* Toby, anyway."

Vicki was once engaged to a man she'd met at work. Fourteen years older than she, he'd already had two divorces, three children, and when he found out my sister was pregnant, called off the wedding and told her the relationship was over. Worried about her, my mother and I took her out for lunch and calmly, softly said it was for the best. That we'd go with her to the hospital or doctor's office if that's what she wanted. She sat there, her foot tapping the floor, fingers tapping the table to a rhythmic beat neither my mother nor I could decipher. She was smoking a pack a day back then, and though we'd only been at the outdoor restaurant for fifteen minutes, six butts were already in the ashtray, deep red marks perfectly outlined on the pristine white tops. When the waitress finally came over to take our order, Vicki got up, told us she was no longer hungry, and had already had the "problem" taken care of on her own. We watched her walk away wondering what else we could have done. Though we phoned her, left long, nervously wordy messages, made apologies, she didn't return one call. It took her over eight months to speak to either one of us and she only did so when my father phoned telling her to get off her high horse, grow up, and apologize to her mother. My parents had been divorced for over a decade by then, and he was still the only one she ever really listened to. She phoned my mother the next day, talking to her as if nothing ever happened.

Vicki is still staring at me, her fingers tapping the table, the beat somehow sounding like an old camp song, *The ants go marching one-by-one hurrah, hurrah*. I sing it in my head hoping it will make the room stop spinning, quiet the ringing in my ears, which, sadly, has gotten louder. I'm treading on familiar territory now: the quick rise of anger in her voice that comes out in short, hot puffs; the sharp, jerky body movements; the exasperation that shows in her face all seem to happen at once. I want to pedal back, reclaim the moment. Return to a time when we were friends. Only I'm not sure when that was.

"What? What did I do? What are you always so fucking mad about?" I reach for the mango lemonade and accidentally knock it over. I watch it crash to the floor, the glass shattering. I see the orangey yellow liquid bleed out onto the marble. See the waiter walk over with a mop. See my sister start to laugh.

"Are you okay, Miss?" The waiter says, bending down to scoop up the shards.

"I'm so sorry. I'm fine. I just . . ." I look at Vicki, who's smirking, observing me coolly from behind the menu. "I'll be right back."

I shove my chair out from under me, hear it slide on the floor, glass crunching beneath it, hear the sound of my shoes, the winded huff of my breath.

I push open the bathroom door, which reveals a small, simply decorated room, walls painted a soft cocoa color. Of the three empty stalls I go for the middle. I lock the door, lean my forehead against it, extend my arms out to either side so that they press up against the metal walls of the stall as I will myself not to cry. I take a few deep breaths, close my eyes, hear the small whimper in my throat escape. I want—am owed—the basic nurturing and consoling that everyone longs for. It's part of the job. An unwritten, unspoken rule of siblings.

As a child, when I couldn't sleep, I used to fantasize about getting some rare disease just to see if Vicki would be nicer to me. If she'd take care of me. I'd visualize her sitting by my hospital bed, a hand on my forehead, another on my arm as she relays stories about our childhood.

The ringing in my ears is gone and the few moments I've allowed myself have calmed me down a bit. As I exit, I tell myself it won't matter if I come back to an empty chair, some cash on the table, her place setting cleared while mine contains the burger and fries, a new mango lemonade by its side. To my surprise, she's still there, waiting for me, a cell phone pressed to her ear, her fingers twirling the straw in her drink.

Hours later Vicki has bought a navy cashmere V-neck sweater, a pair of jeans, and a Prada satin clutch, which miraculously matches her new black dress. Our last stop is a sex shop on Fifty-third off of Second Avenue. We walk down metal stairs, past the neon lips and winking eye. The smell of incense hits us hard as an overweight woman in her sixties wearing a pushup leather bra and a tight, short leather skirt greets us just as strongly. She sells us gag gifts Vicki insists Abby should have: a pair of handcuffs, a pink vibrator, a red garter belt, and a sparkly tiara.

"Mom's going to have a small coronary," I say, as Vicki surrenders her credit card to the sex-shop lady.

"Every party needs a little excitement," she comments, pushing it through the machine.

Vicki signs the slip, hands the bag off to me, and looks at the receipt. "Mini vibrator, thirty-four dollars. Handcuffs, twenty-three. Embarrassing Mom, priceless."

We both laugh, friends once again.

———

A DO NOT DISTURB sign hangs on Vicki's hotel door, and she slides in her key without any effort. The suite is a mess. Clothing is sprawled all over the place. Her birth control disc lies open on the table. Only small green ones are left. My mother's good jewelry case, which contains the diamonds my mother once wore, is out in the open, almost a dare for a staff member to steal. I wonder why it is I've not been handed down any of her good jewelry. Why Vicki gets everything she wants. Her iPod, BlackBerry, and this morning's *Times* lie haphazardly on the coffee table. Evian water, two cups of coffee, a bowl of half-eaten fruit, another that contains some yogurt and granola, uneaten toast, and picked-over eggs and hash browns reside on a tray placed on the floor. It's a lot of food even for my sister.

I reach for the black jewelry box, feel the worn velvet, the solidness of the case. I push in the tiny gold button and the top flips open revealing a gold chain with diamonds interspersed between the links. Two pearl bracelets are here, too. I've not seen them before, but they are lovely. Expensive and ornate.

"Do you have to look through all my stuff? Can't you just leave things as they are?"

"I didn't know you were getting so dressed up. I mean it's just a dinner, right? Maybe I'm underdressing for the shower."

Vicki is about to answer when her cell rings. She looks at the number and ignores the call. As she struggles out of her jeans I catch something on her lower back. A bruise? A scrape? No, a tattoo. I take a step closer, my hand outstretched hoping to touch it, see if it's raised, how it feels. The words are already spilling out of my mouth, "When did you get this?" when she pulls her T-shirt down, causing it to vanish instantly.

"I'm jumping in the shower," she says, shutting the bathroom door. "Be out in ten."

The box is still in my hand and I set it down, think about cleaning up, taking the tray outside, and calling for housekeeping, but as I reach for the phone, it buzzes.

"Hello?"

"Vic?"

"No, this is her sister."

"Oh hey, it's James."

"Hi James . . ." my mouth forms the words as my mind searches for something recognizable in his voice or his name, and finally remember the man from the airport.

"I've been trying your sister all day. I just wanted to know what time she was meeting me and if she still wanted the car?"

"I'm not sure. Our cousin is having . . ."

"Yeah, the party thing. She's only staying a few minutes because the wedding's at the same time."

As James talks I eye the day's purchases, which my sister has left by the couch. The bag from the sex shop is red and raunchy looking, and stands out among the conservative, almost nondescript black and gray bags that have become signatures for Barneys, Calvin, and Prada. And then it hits me. The dress, the good jewelry, the glitzy purse, the birth control pills, the new makeup, the large breakfast. I feel my chest tighten as my breath quickens. *What a bitch*, I think. *She's got to be fucking kidding.*

"Actually, I'm glad I got you on the phone. I wanted to know if you had any suggestions for your sister's birthday. You'd think after a year I'd be able to pick something out myself, but she's so hard to shop for, you know?"

Anger is swimming through me, filling the cavity in my chest like a tub whose bathwater is ready to spill over onto the floor. She was never coming here for my cousin, or my mother, or even me. Like everything else, this weekend, this time with my sister has been a lie.

"Yeah, she's a tough one."

"You're telling me. Anyway, have her call okay? I really don't want to be late."

"Sure will," I muster, chipper like Vicki would. I'm in mid—hang up as she emerges from the shower, dressed in a plush ter-rycloth hotel robe, looking fresh and clean. She eyes me funny.

"What? Why are you looking at me like that?"

"Like what?" Disgust escapes from my voice.

"Forget it."

I walk over to the unmade bed, unsure of whether to make it, sit down, or what.

"Was that the phone?"

"Yeah. Mom wanted to know what time we were getting to the restaurant."

"What'd you tell her?"

I shrug. "I told her we would be late."

Vicki looks like she's about to say something, but disappears into the living room instead. When she comes back a moment later, gum is in her mouth, the handcuffs are swinging around one finger. "Let's see if these actually work," she announces. I see the gray blur, hear a light swishing.

"Not a chance." I reach for them but she snaps them away, hides them behind her back. "I'll put them on you."

"Hold out your wrists," she commands.

"No." I take a step away but my sister grabs hold of me and

pushes me. Losing my balance, I fall backward, my neck snapping slightly as I hit the mattress.

"Come on, Vicki. I don't want to." But before I can get up, she leaps onto the bed, bringing her legs up, straddles me, like she did as a kid.

When I was little she would wrestle me to the ground, sit on my stomach, pin my arms down, and spit on me, sometimes forcing my mouth open, dropping her wad into it.

There has always been more of her than me. As far back as I can remember, she has always reveled in being born before me. She used to say she saw the womb first. She lived there, made it hers. Like an apartment you inherit, the faint smell of the perfume or cooking from the past tenant hangs in the air so that you never really feel it's yours. For years she told me the reason our parents got divorced was because they had only wanted two children, and that neither could put up with me. She'd even gotten Michael to play along and when I sobbed this information to my parents, they seemed unsure of how to deal with her and asked me to be more tolerant.

I try to squirm away but she's too powerful. I'm laughing, but it's fake. I know it and she does, too. I can't get James's voice out of my head. All I can think about is how long they've been dating, how much my sister has kept from me, and how stupid she thinks I am.

Vicki takes hold of my wrists and squeezes hard. Then harder.

"Come on. I'm serious."

"This is the best you can do? You're pathetic." There's anger in her voice, a frustrated disappointment. She takes her thumb and index finger and flicks me in the forehead. Not hard at first, but by the fifth time, it starts to hurt. I watch her smile as I struggle, her eyes gleaming as she squints. I look into her face searching for something familiar. Something that proves she's related to me.

My sister is beautiful. Even in this state—her rich brown hair is long and soft and silky. Her makeup, even though she's showered, is somehow still perfectly preserved from earlier. Her eyes are a wild blue and if I were a man I'd want to kiss her. Take my palms, move them up to her face, cup her chin in my hand, and bring her toward me. I'd push her hair behind her ears. Let her dangling earrings that shimmer and shine move freely. Instead I lift the top of my head and smack it right into her nose. We both hear the tiny crack, both see the blood as it drops from her nostrils onto my face. For a moment she's surprised. She smiles for a second before it morphs into anger and slaps me across the face. My cheek stings and is damp from my sister's blood. I close my eyes, will myself not to cry, but there's a wetness on my face and I know it's too late and I'm ashamed to be sobbing in front of her. I feel tears run down the sides of my cheeks and as I open my eyes, realize they aren't mine.

"You're useless," she says, rolling off of me, trying to hide her face. "I fucking hate you." She puts a hand under her nose to see how much she's bleeding and as she shifts her weight, twisting away, I reach out to pull myself up and feel the coolness of metal on the pads of my fingers. I grasp for the handcuffs that are lying next to me and without thinking, clamp one side to her wrist, the other to the bedpost. She shoots an arm out to grab me, her hand stained with blood, but I'm too fast and leap off the bed.

"Stop fucking around, Robin. I don't have time for this. I've got to get ready."

"Oh, it's okay for you to fuck around with me. To pin me down . . ."

"Shut up and get the key, will you?"

I do what I'm told, walk into the living room, reach into the bag, extract the key, walk back over to her, take hold of her wrist, feel the smoothness of her skin, like expensive leather, and as I bend forward, she spits in my face. It feels thick and wet. Warm and cold at the same time.

My heart is beating too fast, my hands are shaking, and my face is still burning from where she slapped me. My palm wipes away her saliva and I slip the key into my pocket and calmly back away and go into the bathroom. She wants a fight? Fuck it, a fight she'll get.

"I'm sorry, Robin. Come on." He voice fades as I close the door, locking it though I'm not sure why. For the moment, she isn't going anywhere.

I stare into the mirror. My face is red and sweaty, my eyes glassy. Lipstick is smeared, mascara is smudged. I see the red mark on my cheek, see the remains of blood, of spit, or her tears. I turn on the faucet, reach for a perfectly white wash-cloth, reach for the free egg-shaped Bvlgari soap and submerge both under the warm water. The smell from the soap is fragrant and soothing. I wash my face, wash my sister's remains away.

As I search for a hand towel, my eye catches another robe on the floor. It lays limp and lifeless. I grasp it, pulling the belt out of the loops. I open the bathroom door and find Vicki knocking the metal up against the wooden pole.

"Look, I'm sorry, just undo me and we'll forget about it."

The belt is in my hand, hidden behind my back. I sit on the side of the bed closest to the bathroom, close to her free hand. As I guessed, Vicki reaches for my shirt, up by my neck and tries to pull me close. But this time I'm ready for her. I grab her wrist and with my other hand take the belt and tie it tightly against the second bedpost. I watch the skin bunch up as the photo of us dressed as Indian chiefs materializes in front of me. I look at my wrist, see the red mark from years ago almost glow.

"You've got to be kidding me," she says, looking like the character from *The Exorcist*, each arm attached to the bed, my sister flat on her back, a position I'm sure she's been in a number of times. Her legs are flaring and her foot keeps kicking me. I look at her waist, am tempted to remove the belt from the robe she's wearing, but undo my own instead and strap her ankle to another post. Not taking any chances, I want another accessory to restrain the last limb. I remember the sash from the new dress—the wedding dress, the I've-lied-about-why-I'm-here-this-weekend dress—trot back into the living room, and remove the black satin strap. When I return, I take her other leg and tie that too, rendering her completely incapacitated.

"Robbi, come on." It's the honest voice. "I've been a total bitch. I'm really, really sorry."

I remain frozen. Then like a seductive lover who whispers warmly, softly into your ear how much they adore you, she says, "I swear to God, I'm sorry. This whole weekend was for you and I to bond. I don't care about seeing Abby. Or even Mom. I just wanted to see you. I miss you. I miss the time we could have had together if I wasn't such an ass."

Vicki is the ever-alluring sun, the perfectly baked chocolate chip cookie too hot to eat.

I enter the bathroom again, find her cigarette patches, and return. I slap a patch onto her forehead. Another on her chest. I'm about to put a third and forth on her right leg but think better of it. Instead, I reach under her nose, collect some remaining blood and with my index finger smear two lines across her cheek. I then retrieve the tiara we bought for Abby. It's so lovely, heavy in my hand, childlike and playful. The knife on the food tray catches my eye and I think of the weird pregnant woman at Barneys, the one with the lovely hair, which according to her will all be cut off. I think how much my sister loves her hair. How hard it will be to go to a wedding bald. I return to Vicki, put the knife on the night table, the tiara on her head, a modern-day replacement for the feathered headband from years ago. "How do you feel about a new Indian name," I say. "Maybe Selfish-Bitch-With-No-Feelings?"

As if in a trance, I find myself standing by the refrigerator. "You said the company was paying, right?" I call to her. With the door open, the cool air feels good on my hot face, my sweaty shirt. The little bottles jingle as I tap the top of the door. *The ants go marching one-by-one hurrah, hurrah.* My finger sweeps left to right over the mini bottles looking for the perfect one, something sweet and sticky. Something that will stain and trigger unpleasant sense memories later on in life, perhaps as she relays the incident to a therapist on a leather couch. I unscrew the seven-dollar bottle of Kahlúa. Take a deep whiff, smell memories of a family vacation in the Bahamas. I close my eyes and picture the beach, the sand, the way the three of us once got along, when my parents were still together. I think about Michael and his children whom I don't know, about his wife whom I've only met once, about my father and his new wife and how lonely my mother was after they got divorced. How Vicki and Michael were gone and only I was home to watch her cry.

I take a small sip. It's thick and syrupy and overly sweet. I wish there was a container of milk and a shot of espresso at my disposal. But there isn't. And then my hand is reaching for the Beefeater, the Baileys, the red wine, the tomato juice. Holding all the overpriced mini bottles of liquid I jog back into the bedroom, the bottles clinking in my arms. I climb over her, sit on her as she did to me minutes ago, decades ago, feel her twist underneath me, feel her bones and the warmth of her skin. I drizzle the Kahlúa first, slowly, purposely over her face, making a star on her cheek. The liquid is cold and she presses her lips closed.

I pour all the liquor on her. Watch the red wine soak into her hair, run down her face and into the robe. Smell the salty, unpleasant scent of tomato sauce. As a special sacrifice, I take the knife and cut her long, beautiful brown hair. A modern-day scalping. I almost shout out a war cry as clumps of hair are in my hand, on the bed, the floor. I wonder if the pregnant lady's hair will be this short. If we should have invited her back with us and talked her into having only one child. "See," I could have told her, "not all siblings get along. Some are mean and hurtful and kill every good relationship they ever had."

I take a step back and look at what I've created.

"This deserves a photo. Don't you think?" My cell doesn't have a camera in it, and my digital, which I normally carry around in order to take pictures of people's apartments, is at home, along with the outfit I'm supposed to wear tonight to Abby's shower—where my mother, my aunt, my cousins, and friends will all be. I remember a camera is in the basket on the refrigerator that holds the overpriced sunblock and extended cell battery. I run back and return with the flash indicator already glowing.

"How do you feel your boss will take this? Perhaps you could say you were merely entertaining in your room?" I hold up the camera and take a photo.

I take a step forward, lean in further. Click. Another shot. Then another.

Vicki tries to look away, but I get in closer, not letting her escape.

"Okay, show me anger. That should be an easy one."

Click.

"Okay, now show me horror."

Click.

"How about love. Can you show me that?"

Her expression remains unchanged.

"Hmmm. I guess not." I put my face up close to hers, snap another as I think about the picture of us as kids and once I get these developed the two can sit side by side.

"One more for your boss. Oh, and one for James. You can't forget him. Or the wedding I guess you'll be missing." Hearing this, she looks at me hard, almost a glee in her eyes. I wink.

"Fuck you!" she screams. "You'll fucking pay for this, Robin."

Back in the bathroom I make one last trip to the sink, turn on the faucet, try to warm myself by running hot water over my hands and face. I sneak a peek at my reflection, hoping I look liberated. Like a teen after she's lost her virginity and expects to see something different, a hint that her former self, the girl she once was has been left behind and now looks for something to prove she's changed, that this incident has meant something. I fix my hair, reapply makeup with what Vicki's left in here—a lipstick, some blush—then take a photo of myself and exit.

"It was great seeing you," I say, emerging from the bathroom, my face freshly painted. But when I see Vicki, I stop short. Her complexion is pale, making the blood across her cheeks stand out even more. Her face, sticky from the liquor, seems slightly distorted and instead of looking at me, her head is turned away slightly. Embarrassed. The once perfectly applied makeup is gone. Mascara and lipstick have smeared. She looks grimy and tarnished. Long clumps of brown hair are scattered everywhere. The white robe is soaked with wine and tomato juice. The tiara is crooked and I think about fixing it, think about rubbing a hand across her forehead soothingly and tell her I'm sorry.

"Just go," she barks. "Just fucking leave."

I think about James, realize when Vicki doesn't show at the wedding he'll phone and after getting no answer eventually come back to see what's happened. If not, housekeeping is bound to enter at some point.

I walk into the main room and collect my belongings: cell phone, purse, the black Barneys shopping bag that holds the Nars and Dior makeup. I look through Vicki's new purchases as well to see if I want any of them. Pretty things she bought, mine now. All mine. What doesn't fit I'll exchange for something else or get a store credit to use later. The navy cashmere sweater feels soft and lovely. I put it up against my face and smell the faint fragrance of my sister. I'm about to add it to my stash when I realize I don't want anything of hers. Not the sweater, not the new makeup, not even Vicki's makeup, which I've just applied. I reach for the cloth napkin, which rests on the food tray that has yet to be cleared away. I wipe my lips harshly, do the same with my eyes and cheeks. I toss the throwaway camera into the trash, return the bags to their places, and leave the handcuff key on the desk. I then slip on my sunglasses and try to catch my breath, which seems lost.

I reach for the door and pull it open.

"Come the fuck back, you fucking bitch!" Vicki screams.

I don't answer her. Instead, I step out into the hallway and realize I'm shaking and crying.

The DO NOT DISTURB sign is still hanging on the shiny doorknob when I close the door slowly, quietly behind me. I watch it swing back and forth. Back and forth. I reach out to stop it from dancing as I listen to Vicki's muffled rants. At the far end of the hallway I can see the housekeeping cart and realize it's already passed this side of the hallway. Hear it rattle as the plump woman pushes it further and further away from me.

Then, unable to help myself, I switch the plastic marker over so that the black words read HOUSEKEEPING PLEASE. Because someone needs to clean her up. Because she needs fixing. Because at a hotel, that's what they do.

I walk away, my sister's voice barely audible in the background.

Chapter 14

Ellen

Conference Room

Ellen is at the Baby Gap in Connecticut's Milford Mall holding up a cotton onesie with a duck on it. Everyone here is very nice. The salespeople talk in bubbly, vivacious sound bites and the customers are all smiles, happy to share information. Happy to be a partner in kiddy-clothing crime.

Ellen isn't sure what she'll need, so she turns to the woman standing next to her. "Could I trouble you for a second?"

The woman is petite with cropped, pixielike hair. She's seven, maybe eight months pregnant and her wool sweater is rising up on her stomach, exposing her stretch marks.

"Sure." She smiles at Ellen, who holds a bright blue jump-suit in her hands.

"I wanted to get a few items for a newborn, but I'm not sure what one needs during that first month." Ellen takes a deep breath, blows a few unruly strands of hair away from her face.

"Well, you'll need booties, a swaddling blanket, countless cotton tops . . ."

Ellen starts reaching for the items the woman has mentioned. They are so tiny, so beautiful. "How far along are you?"

"Eight months."

"Your first?" Ellen asks, her arms now laden with miniature items.

"Second. You?"

Ellen is so happy to have been asked this. "Two and a half months."

"I wasn't going to say anything, because you barely show, but you've got this look about you. My friends call it pregnancy glow."

This makes Ellen ecstatic.

At Dreamtime Baby she inquires about a crib, even though this is incredibly premature. And though she's not superstitious, she thinks perhaps she should wait. But she can't and orders a bassinette, rocking chair, and changing table.

Back in her car, she sits in the garage at the mall going through a mental list of names, people she hasn't talked to in years, some even as far back as her wedding. The iPhone is in her hand and she flips through her address book and settles on her old college roommate. The answering machine clicks on and she hears a child's voice informing her the Reinhearts aren't home.

She leaves a greeting.

"Hi all, Ellen Simon-Thompson here. A blast from the past, you must be thinking. Been forever since we've talked. I was changing over my address book and when I got to your name thought I'd give a call and say hi." Then, almost as an afterthought, "Oh, by the way, Harry and I are expecting, so hopefully you'll have some tips to share. Love to everyone." She hangs up and makes another call. Then another.

She wants to phone her good friends and share the news but she knows they're tired of listening. They were so excited the first time she told them. Then they were wonderful when she relayed the sad information.

She was at ABC Carpet with clients when it happened. She was going over decorating suggestions when the cramping started. She was two months along when she felt what can only be described as a tiny, internal snap. Like a cord being released. She excused herself. Left the two partners of the accounting firm surmising the leather couches and hurriedly entered the bathroom. By then the cramping had turned into a stabbing pain and there was a wetness in her crotch. Inside the stall, she sat on the toilet, vaguely aware she hadn't put down the protective sheet or lined the seat with toilet paper. As she doubled over she felt slimy clumps of something ooze out of her—which she was later informed was fetal tissue and placenta. She called her sisters-in-law to come and get her. Catherine arrived first, followed by Gail, who had to explain to her clients what was happening. She bled for days, had cramps like she was back in high school, and stayed in bed with the blinds drawn, the phone off while wondering what she could have done differently. She'd had a drink or two before she knew she was pregnant with clients one time, champagne with Harry one night at dinner. She didn't smoke but many of her clients did, especially the older men who loved to have a cigar and go over floor plans and drink port and whiskey late at night at expensive hotel lounges.

The second time she disclosed the news, her friends' responses were filled with cautious congratulations. They were happy but tried to stay realistic. That miscarriage hit her even harder. She didn't emerge for weeks. And still everyone was understanding. Everyone had a friend of a friend to talk to, a doctor to see, a fertility clinic to investigate. And she did. There were blood tests for chromosome abnormalities, an ultrasound of her pelvis, a hysteroscopy—a viewing of the uterus through a special scope—even a hysterosalpingography, an X-ray of the uterus.

She met with specialists, researched her options and possibilities on the Web, even joined a group for women like herself. The group was nice—the women were gracious, though bitter, but mostly sad. Incomplete.

She stopped going to the biweekly meetings when she discovered she was pregnant. In that last group, a woman had broken down, telling them how useless she felt. That after all this time, she still couldn't attend children's birthday parties, that her friends had stopped inviting her over to their homes, that she and her husband were going to adopt, because that's got to be better than not having anything.

Ellen wanted to talk about those rare moments that come after the crying. A rainstorm ends and a blissful floating feeling takes over when for five or ten minutes, sometimes an hour, she doesn't ache. She dreams of waking in the morning to find the emptiness gone. She wanted to share this with the others because she knows they'll understand. But all she was able to say when it was her turn to speak was "I hurt all the time." And they nodded and dabbed at their eyes.

But now she's pregnant. Now nothing else matters.

That night Ellen is standing on the scale, again. It reads 161 pounds. Three pounds more than two weeks ago. Which is okay, because her five foot eight frame can support it. And though she's a little plump or chunky, she can see that her belly is swollen. Her breasts are sore. And she can't get rid of the nausea, not that she wants to. She's been begging for these feelings, these very symptoms for years.

Two new pregnancy tests lie face up on her bathroom counter, one reads negative, the other positive.

Harry looks at them sadly, like broken eggs, chicks that were supposed to have hatched but didn't. He sighs, takes her hand, and leads her away from the scale.

"We'll keep trying."

"Keep trying? What are you talking about? Didn't you see the scale?"

He's already tossing the tests into the trash. "Please. I can't do this." He sits at the edge of the tub and looks at her, his eyes almost glassy.

"But one is positive. Two weeks ago, they all read negative. Can't you see this is progress? We might have been too early."

They'd been dating for three years when she said, "I do." And at the wedding, surrounded by her family and friends, Harry's two brothers, then both single, glasses raised in their honor, she squeezed her husband's hand and thought, *Yes. Yes, you really can have it all.* Now it's ten years and two miscarriages later. Harry is a partner at a law firm. Ellen sees the boy who cuts their lawn more than she sees her husband. Maybe this is too hard for him. Perhaps he doesn't believe her because he wants this baby as much as she does and the disappointment would be all consuming.

They get into bed.

Harry has his reading glasses on, briefs and contracts by his side.

She wants him to look at her. Wants him to comment that her breasts do seem larger, her belly more distended. She wants him to believe in her the way she believes in this baby. She tries moving closer to him, hoping he will set aside his paperwork, put his arm around her, and hold her, like he used to. Like before they started trying to have children. Instead, he puts the papers down, rolls over, and turns off the light.

"Have you thought about calling the shrink Dr. Tepler suggested? I really think it's a good idea. I'll go with you if you want." His head is on the pillow, the sheets pulled up close to his ear.

Her gynecologist, a short thick man with eyebrows that remind her of Groucho Marx, suggested the next doctor she should see be a psychiatrist and wouldn't let her make another appointment with him. His assistant sent back her chart with a note that perhaps another gyno would be more suitable.

She remembers the first time she and Harry were sitting in his office. The warm rose—painted walls were a comfort, the chairs and space inviting. Dr. Tepler was kind and supportive. Offered her up the box of tissues, told them couples often have miscarriages the first time around. That they could try again. She sat holding Harry's hand, her other wrapped around her stomach.

The second time was similar, only other tests were suggested.

"The good news is that everything is where it should be. You have no signs of tearing or tumors or cysts," Dr. Tepler said, closing her file and leaning forward. "It takes some couples a few tries to get it right. I'm not concerned, and you shouldn't be either, but just in case I'm happy to send you for a few tests."

But last time was different.

Three weeks ago Ellen was waiting for him when he entered the exam room, her body cold, the paper gown uncomfortable and too big. She remembered thinking how much better it would fit in four or five months when she'd be able to fill it out. And that maybe they should have colored gowns. Visual indicators to show what trimester you were at. Light pink for first, darker pink for second, and purple for third. Her feet were in the stirrups and her ass was squatted forward in perfect position. The words were out of her mouth before Dr. Tepler had a chance to walk into the room and close the door behind him.

"I haven't had my period in forty-five days."

"Really?" His voice was cool and even toned as he fought with the latex gloves. "Where's Harry? I was hoping he'd be here, too."

"He couldn't come. But you know how regular I am. And I've been nauseous and had morning sickness four days in a row."

Her chart was in his hand, filled with papers, and he looked a few things over before approaching. "Okay, let's see what we've got." He sat on the padded stool with the wheels and put her chart down.

"My stomach's distended, too."

"First I'm going to press on your abdomen, and then we'll look inside. Let me know if this hurts," he said, his thick hand at her belly.

"You can see how bloated I am, right? All of my pants are tight."

Dr. Tepler didn't respond. He moved to her vaginal area instead, his head disappearing between her legs, his brows looking like a furry animal from her point of view. The clamp was cold and a sharp pain occurred when he inserted the instrument inside her. She winced.

"You're doing great, Ellen."

"Do you see anything?"

"Just give me a few moments."

She stopped talking so he could do his job.

"Okay, if you'll come down to me just a hair more."

She did.

"Perfect. Now I'm going to put some pressure here, and I'm using one more instrument so I can see better . . ."

"Everything's okay, right?"

"Just relax and take a deep breath for me."

As she inhaled she felt him pull out, quick and painful, like Harry did sometimes after sex.

"Okay. Why don't you get dressed and come into my office." Before she could say anything, his gloves were off and he was out the door.

Dressed once again in her clothes, she knocked lightly on his open door before entering, found him seated at his desk, a phone to his ear, scribbling notes. He looked up as she entered. She eyed the box of tissues, already placed at the edge of his desk, a glass of water, too, as if the room had been prepped for her visit.

"So how far along am I?" She took a seat as he hung up. The room felt less comfortable.

"I wish Harry was here with you," he said. "I know how much you want a baby, but I'm sorry to tell you . . ."

Her heart stopped and she held her breath while thinking, *Not again*.

"You're not pregnant." His eyes were soft but intense, and filled with pity.

"I am."

"You're not. And I know how hard this has been . . ."

"I am. I have every symptom. I'm three pounds heavier. The scale says so. I've thrown up for the past four mornings. I've even had weird cravings for bananas and I don't even like bananas. Please," she begged, voice cracking, "check again." Perhaps the doctor was playing a joke. Perhaps he blamed himself for her miscarriages and didn't want to admit to being incompetent.

"Harry phoned yesterday and told me the home pregnancy tests came up negative."

"They're not very accurate. And he shouldn't have called without telling me."

"I think he's just concerned. We all are. You know, if your body thinks it's pregnant it can produce too much progesterone and estrogen."

"That's not the case here." She was adamant. Why was he doing this to her?

"Hormones are a funny thing. They can stay in the body three or four months after you've miscarried, they can trick you into thinking you're pregnant when you're not . . ." His voice trailed off and he took a deep breath. "What you're feeling, the symptoms you have are called pseudocyesis, or for the layman, phantom pregnancy." He handed her a crisp white sheet of paper with too many words on it. She didn't reach for it. Instead she left him hanging there until he set it down next to the box of tissues.

"Please, take this."

"You're wrong, Dr. Tepler. I know I'm feeling something."

"I don't doubt that. But it's not because you're pregnant. I wish you were, honestly."

Tears streamed down her cheeks, saliva leaked from her side of her mouth. "My breasts are sore, I've not gotten my period, you can't just make this stuff happen."

"Actually, you can. Some women even secrete milk."

"What about an amnio? The doctor said . . ."

"I think the next doctor you see should be Dr. Benton. She's a terrific lady and a specialist in this field." Dr. Tepler scribbled something down on his prescription pad and handed that to her as well. After a moment of her not reaching for it, he left it next to the other items, pushed himself away from his desk, stood up, and suggested she leave. "I'm sorry, there's nothing more I can do."

Because she didn't know how to spell the clinical term, she looked up phantom pregnancy at home on the Web, and instantly found over twelve thousand sites. Ellen was a walking, bloated poster child for what was called imaginary pregnancy or hysterical pregnancy or her favorite, wind in the bowels syndrome, which sounded like something you caught in Mexico. She fit every single demographic from being in her late thirties, married, having suffered two miscarriages, and was still child-less. Each site talked about depression, but who wasn't depressed these days and who wouldn't be depressed if they were thirty-eight, childless, and couldn't conceive? Besides, everyone knew being pregnant plays havoc with your hormone levels. Even Tepler had admitted to that, and many pregnant women were incredibly depressed during their first and second trimesters.

After the second miscarriage she cried all the time, at the bakery when they told her they sold out of carrot muffins, at the dry cleaner when Harry's pants were lost, at the park when she spotted a woman breast-feeding. So they put her on Wellbutrin, an antidepressant with few side effects, except it lowered the chance of being able to conceive. Once she read that, she got off the drug. Other mood stabilizers could cause birth defects so that was no longer an option.

She pushes all of these old memories out of her mind now as she stares at Harry, the bed sheets around his neck, his table light turned off, his hand not touching hers. "If one test is positive, and one is negative at least be honest and say it's possible."

She waits a moment for him to respond, but Ellen doesn't get an answer.

Harry is up and out the door just as Ellen's alarm clock turns to 7:00 a.m. It's Friday morning and she moves slowly, waves of nausea rocking her from the inside.

She makes some decaffeinated tea and tries to eat a piece of toast. Her fridge is now stocked with organic items and she's stopped eating raw fish. Not an ounce of coffee has been ingested in weeks and she's upped her folic acid intake, just as the books suggest.

She talks to the baby as she gets on the scale: 166 ½. A half pound more since yesterday. Her ring is tight and she swears her nails are growing faster. She gazes into the mirror and smiles. Her cheeks are rosy and there's no acne as of yet. She looks pretty pregnant. And though her curly chestnut hair frames her face nicely, long locks falling over her shoulders, she thinks about cutting it all off, like the woman at The Gap. Once the baby comes she won't have time for hair maintenance anyway. She takes her hands and lifts the hair off her neck and face to see what she'd look like with a short style.

At 9:30 a.m. she calls Dr. Tepler and gets the assistant, who is hesitant on the phone.

"Hi Brenda, it's Ellen Thompson."

There's a long pause.

"I was hoping to make an appointment with the doctor. You know it's been a month since he's seen me, and my condition hasn't changed."

"I'm sorry, Ellen. Dr. Tepler feels he's done what he can for you. I have to go; that's my other line."

Ellen hears the buzz, then the sound of dead air, which leaves her at this moment hanging on the phone listening to the sound of her own hurried breathing, her breasts still sore and swollen, her stomach still full and bloated, three-and-a-half-months pregnant. She smiles as she thinks how foolish Dr. Tepler will feel when she shows up at his office in five months, or better yet, with her healthy, beautiful child in her arms.

She dresses, moving slowly, but when the nausea feels so overwhelming that she must sit and wait it out, she cancels her meetings with clients and decides not to push herself. She will not make the same mistakes as before. She misses Harry and as she phones him, starts to cry. She hangs up before he or his assistant answers because she knows he can't hear her sob anymore. When her phone rings, and she finds Harry on the other line asking if she just called, if everything is okay, she suddenly feels so much love and joy that she's back to crying.

"Hormones," she tries to explain.

"You up to seeing a movie?" he asks. "Maybe that will take your mind off things. How about I meet you at the theater in front of that statue thing at five? I'll leave work early. Okay?" This makes her so happy she cries harder.

At 5:17 Harry is still a no-show, and though he often runs late, something feels off. All around her, couples are doing coupley things. They are dining at restaurants, window shopping, holding hands while waiting on line to purchase movie tickets. But Harry isn't here and she's not feeling couplish. And she thinks when she lost the babies, she lost him, too.

Harry was an associate at the law firm when they met. A lean, freckle-faced, curly-haired redhead who looked like a thinner version of Donny Most, the actor who played Ralph on the TV show *Happy Days*. A job promotion got them together. When his boss handed Harry the keys to his new office, he also gave him Ellen's business card. She was in charge of decorating the firm. His office was the last to be completed. They fell in love over paint chips, fabric swatches, and carpet samples.

It took him two months to decide on a couch and carpet. Took him another month to ask her out, and another to tell her he knew what couch he wanted that first day, but liked having her come by to show him samples. The more Ellen thinks about this, the surer she becomes that Harry is getting preparenting jitters. If it took him months to tell her about the couch, telling her he's scared of losing her or becoming a father will take years. Their child will be in middle school when he finally comes clean and admits his heart was broken after the miscarriages. That hope hurts too much and that's why he didn't believe her.

She worries something has happened and pictures a car crash on the Hutch. Maybe he's forgotten. Or something came up at work. These days he's distant and tired. Disappointed in her, rather than their situation. After all, none of his brothers' wives had this problem—one of them had twin girls. His mother was able to conceive a month after she got married. Even Ellen's own mother feels she must be doing something wrong. "Really, honey, he'll leave you if you can't get it together." Her mother is on her third husband, so what does she know? One reason Ellen never sees her is the lack of nurturing skills. This has only heightened Ellen's need to have children. Fix the past. Break a cycle. And she knows she will. She's utterly desperate to share her love with someone other than Harry.

She's in mid-dial to his cell when she sees him get off the escalator. Though he's had a full day of work, he somehow looks perfectly held together. Shirt still crisp, tie in a taut knot, his suit is wrinkle-free making her feel dumpy in her unbuttoned jeans, baggy sweater, frumpy slicker. The tears she hasn't been able to control all day start again.

Tonight Ellen is watching her husband reach for a tie, the one she gave him for Valentine's Day three years ago, wondering if he still loves her. If he'll be jealous of the baby. Maybe this is why he's grown cold.

When she asks him to zip her up, her black dress is so taut over her middle and snug at her breasts even Harry admits to having trouble. That there isn't enough fabric or his wife is too heavy to seal the dress. She turns to him. "Just stop fighting it. Put your hand on my stomach, feel my breasts. Do I look like I'm making this up? You can't even close the damn thing."

He's at a loss for words because he knows she's right.

She reaches for his face, cups her hand at his chin and cheek. "A baby will only bring us closer together. And I have enough love for both of you."

He looks away, but takes her hand and holds it gently. "Is there something else you can wear? We're going to be late."

Ellen changes into a black turtleneck and matching skirt, which she retrieves from the Salvation Army pile. Two sizes too big, she was going to donate it to charity, but it fits perfectly now. To save time, she takes her makeup bag, hairbrushes, and accessories and will put herself together in the car.

Once they hit the highway, Harry turns on CD101, cool jazz, and though she hates this station, let's him have it because it makes him happy. Because she knows seeing his two younger brothers makes him nervous. Because he's the only one with no children. She already knows he'll pick up the bill for dinner. That the Four Seasons holds special memories for the Thompson boys. Each has married there, each has celebrated their anniversaries there. It's where Harry's parents met decades ago. His mom was an office assistant, his dad waited tables. Harry was the first to get married. His younger brothers called Ellen often regarding shopping questions when it came to buying gifts for their girlfriends. She helped them pick out the wedding rings when their girlfriends became fiancées, threw them bridal showers, and became a surrogate mother when their parents died that first year she and Harry got engaged. A car accident on a snowy bank in Colorado killed them instantly. Ellen liked them tremendously. More so than her own parents.

The Thompson boys are rather inseparable and every vacation the six adults travel together: Ellen and Harry; David and Catherine, and their twin girls; Mark and Gail, and their son. She never minded. It gave her the family she'd always wanted but never had. Her mother's many marriages only produced several moves to new cities and a handful of stepsiblings Ellen has never known. And even though his parents are deceased, each event they celebrate at the hotel is like a toast to them. But tonight is special, an adults-only evening to celebrate David's birthday.

"Please, do me one favor," Harry says as they pull up at the hotel. He doesn't need to ask, she already knows what it is. He wants her not to say anything about the baby. He wants to keep it a secret until he's convinced. "Please don't say anything about your being pregnant. Okay? It's David's night . . ."

"Sure." She rests a hand on his and feels him stiffen at her touch.

Harry's two brothers and their wives are already at the bar waiting. There's hugging and kisses and the smells of perfume and cologne and giddy chatter. Tonight feels like an exact replica of a dinner they had three years ago when Harry turned thirty-eight. Ellen was thirty-five and pregnant for the first time, the baby still alive inside her. When the bar bill is paid, they move to a table in the main dining room. And as the waiter takes the drink order and David's wife, Catherine, asks for a club soda, everyone looks at her.

"Well, it's not like we could have kept this in much longer. Sooner or later you all would have noticed." She reaches for David's hand and he winks.

"What can I say, my boys are good swimmers," he shrugs.

Everyone laughs until Catherine remembers. Catches herself and lowers her voice. "El, I'm sorry. I didn't mean to . . . I thought . . ." she looks to David who looks at Harry.

"It's fine. I'm happy for you. Besides, Harry and I have some news as well." She can't help herself. Before she's even aware, the words have left her mouth. Harry shoots her a glance that starts off as anger and quickly morphs into pleading. "We're expecting, too," she says, gripping her menu.

David's right hand shoots up and hangs in the air, waiting to be high-fived, but Harry doesn't move.

"Dude, that's great," says the youngest Thompson boy. "We'll keep it on the low down."

The women nod, smile sweetly. "It's all good. No more talking about it until you're comfortable, El."

"We all have our superstitions," Catherine continues. "I've not announced it to any of our friends yet. Just you guys, and my mom."

Hours later the six wait for the valet to appear with their cars.

"I thought you looked heavier, but I didn't want to say anything," Catherine says. She squeezes Ellen's hand. "If I went through the hell you did, I wouldn't say anything to anyone until I was pushing the child out of my vagina."

The women chuckle but several feet away the men do not,

and Ellen sees Harry has on his serious face: jaw clenched, brows furrowed. His head is shaking side to side, his hands are in his pockets. Both brothers are frowning too, looking at her, then away. David rests an arm around Harry's shoulder. All Ellen can think is how stupid they'll feel when the baby comes in five months, five days, and four hours. When she pushes out the small, pink head. What would they say then? That they were sorry for doubting her? And she would understand and forgive them once the umbilical cord was cut and the baby had taken its first breath, cried, and was placed in her arms. She would forgive everyone.

A month goes by. Then another. There's still no period. Her bras no longer fit. Her shoes are snug and she must purchase new ones half a size bigger. Her stomach seems enormous to her and the scale shows she's maintaining a healthy weight for someone in her condition. Having successfully entered her second trimester, she picks up baby books and anti–stretch mark cream at Barneys, orders a stroller, and purchases maternity clothing. She's not made it this far along before. Both babies died during her first trimester. She doesn't want an amnio for fear of risking the baby's health. She's heard and read horror stories about this. No sonogram either. The medical industry has done nothing but disappoint her. Now that she's entering her sixth month Ellen starts investigating Lamaze, looks into birthing doulas as well as hospitals she'd like to deliver at.

While getting a tour at the clinic in New Haven she spies on a Lamaze class where several couples are working together. Each man is sitting behind a woman, laughing, smelling her hair, rubbing a large belly, whispering encouraging words like,

"Stay focused Hon" or "You're so brave. You can do this." She wonders if Harry ever loved her the way these men seem to love their wives. All she can picture is her husband telling people his wife's a liar. "It's all smoke and mirrors. Even her gyno won't see her."

Tonight, while rubbing lavender-scented oil over her round stomach she feels a slight, almost imperceptible movement inside her, like a swishing or fluttering. She's desperate to share this with Harry. Wishes he were here massaging her swollen feet, resting the heating pad on her lower back. Or just holding her until the fears she has, which are growing like the baby inside her, subside. She's tired all the time now. She naps during the day. Her weird cravings continue. Yesterday it was chopped apples and peanut butter in vanilla ice cream.

She's dozing on the bed—the *Baby Mozart* she downloaded onto her iPod playing, the headphones resting on her belly— when Harry walks in and finds her like this. He shakes his head, crosses his arms over his chest, and stares at her. He won't look at Web sites, won't walk through Baby Gap, refuses to make lists of things they need to buy, and ignores the congratulatory messages people have left on their answering machine. He won't tour hospitals, won't read books, and doesn't come home until she's close to sleep.

On Tuesday, six-and-a-half-months pregnant and drained, she finds herself at the Four Seasons. It was Catherine who told her about the decorating job. She'd found out through a friend of hers who works in their corporate office that they might be adding a day care room where guests could leave their children with nannies hired by the hotel or that a Mommy and Me program might be offered. If she can get this job, Harry will be ecstatic. He'll have to realize that everything—the baby, the job, their life—has come full circle.

She spent the last two weeks lying in bed, her feet slightly elevated, surfing the Web for ideas, making sketches, and putting a price proposal together. Usually these were offerings she spent time doing once she was hired. Once half her decorating fee was received. But this job is different.

Catherine was supposed to come with her today, but canceled last minute saying she was dealing with morning sickness. Ellen knows Harry asked David not to have Catherine encourage her. So she drove in alone, and after dropping off samples and paint chips, floor plans and architectural suggestions at another client's office, is standing in the hotel's lobby, waiting for Julia.

In her fantasy, she and the baby are taking a Friday class, held in the very room she has created. Harry, already in the city, meets them after a half day of work, and the three spend the rest of the afternoon and evening together. Too late to drive home, they stay over at the hotel, and this becomes their special time together. Their own tradition.

Ellen spots a stylish woman with a confident gait walking toward her. A pink folder is under her arm.

"Hi. I'm Morgan," she says approaching, a hand extended. "Welcome."

"Oh, hi. I thought I was meeting with, um . . ." for a moment her mind goes blank. "Sorry, it's that forgetful pregnancy thing everyone is always talking about."

"That's okay. Julia's out sick today."

"She isn't coming?"

Ellen watches Morgan's mouth move, but her thoughts are

on rescheduling. She's talked to Julia a handful of times over the past month, each phone call ending with Ellen stressing how important it is she gets this job.

She forges ahead, overlooking the setback, and follows Morgan through the lobby, past the second restaurant, past the desk clerks, the magazine and gift stands, and as they wait for the elevator, tells her what a fan she is of the hotel.

The elevator comes and the two enter. When Morgan tells her they're compiling a list of other decorators, Ellen's heart stops and she flashes to sitting in Dr. Tepler's office that last time when he told her she wasn't pregnant. The doors finally open and she's so happy to get out. To take a large gulp of air. They enter the room, which is filled with a huge oval table and glossy blond wooden chairs. To mask her nervousness she knocks on the wall, pulls out her tape measure, and, finally, shows Morgan her sketches.

"I was thinking bright-colored walls, shelves of educational toys, music instruments, stuffed animals . . . As you can see, there's lots of room for Mommy and Me classes or one-on-ones." She flips to another page, reminds herself to take a breath. To not be such a hard sell. But she can't help it. "The room could be divided into ages and stages . . . This section for cribs and naps, this section for a class . . ." She has to think of something else. She has to make Morgan choose her. The next thing she knows, she's relaying the story of how her in-laws met, how talented she is, how pleased her past clients have been, how smart it would be to have a pregnant woman creating a baby room. As she speaks, her eyes getting glassy, she feels something flutter inside her causing her to wince.

"Are you okay?"

"I think I just felt her kick." She freezes, waiting to see if more will come.

"Really?"

"Yeah."

"Would it be okay to feel? If not, in fact, I can't even believe I've just asked you that." Morgan cuts herself off. Then starts again. "I'm sorry that was very unprofessional. I just . . ."

Morgan is one of the few people to ask this. Even Harry hasn't touched her there yet. Hasn't tried to make any contact with the baby. "Of course."

Ellen unbuttons her coat, raises her sweater so Morgan can place her hand right on her skin, which is taut and stretched. The hand feels warm on her belly and Ellen remembers how nice it feels to be touched by someone other than a doctor or herself.

"Do you feel anything?" Her voice comes out eager, child-like.

"I'm not sure."

She feels Morgan start to pull away, but Ellen puts her hand over Morgan's, keeps it there for a moment longer as if challenging her to feel something.

"It's fleeting and only happens for a second or so. But sometimes it comes in pairs." Ellen is so desperate she tells Morgan about her miscarriages, about Harry and their wedding and that of her in-laws, and her brothers-in-law, and how important the Four Seasons is to her. How crucial this job is. How it's holding her marriage together. She watches Morgan, whose hand is still pressed to her stomach, listening to her. How Ellen won't let her go until she sees Morgan's eyes soften. And when they do, she knows the job is hers.

At home, she adds more items to the baby's room, a stuffed

bear, a diaper dispenser, a mobile. She thinks about how she'll decorate it. When she and Harry were house hunting, this room was one of the selling points. Not too far away from the master bedroom, and with a view that faced the backyard and drew in the morning sun, they had nodded and smiled at each other, afraid to show their glee to the sellers. Though this room has been decorated and stripped twice, she still loves it. Still feels as though her child will be happy here. And once the baby is born, she'll stay at home and work from here. Really all she needs to design these corporate offices are floor plans, talks with the client, and a few high-tech computer programs.

Next, she enters the den and puts Harry's mail on the desk. He didn't bother to make up the pullout couch where he's slept during these past weeks. Not because his snoring is keeping her up, and a woman in her condition needs as much rest as possible, but because he doesn't know what else to do.

She hears the front door open and Harry on the phone. "Hold on a sec," he tells the caller. "Ellen," he shouts out. "El?" She remains quiet. "El, you home?" She doesn't answer, stays frozen in his new bedroom. "I'll stick it out for the next three months. I'll either be a proud father and perhaps the worst husband in the world, and she'd have every right to leave me for being such an asshole, or she'll realize what everyone else knows—that there's no baby and she needs to get herself some help."

There's silence and the other person, who Ellen bets is one of the brothers, is talking. She thinks back to the night when Harry and she made love. After the miscarriages, she became obsessed with trying again. She didn't want to wait like the women in the chat rooms suggested. She did everything she could think of to seem sexy: lit candles, made meals that were known aphrodisiacs—linguine and mussels in clam sauce, chocolate cake, cherries—bought expensive wine, wore revealing lingerie, even ordered a porn tape. One night they'd come back from dinner with his boss and his wife, who, during dessert had shown them a pile of photos of her children. Frisky and slightly drunk, they'd had sex on the very couch he was now sleeping on.

"I don't know. I honestly don't," Harry continues. "She was so good to me when Mom and Dad died, I don't know if I can leave her. But I can't live like this anymore. It's been three years of crying, of mood swings and depression . . ."

She stifles the tears, holds her breath, and swallows. Lets it out slowly like the women in the Lamaze class did. If he leaves her she'll be fine. She'll be a terrific parent no matter what. She had three fathers growing up. None of them made a difference in her life and she turned out great.

In one last attempt to show Harry how wrong he is, she quickly takes off her clothing. Tosses her elastic black pants, her white maternity shirt, bra, and underwear and socks onto Harry's unmade bed.

He enters, face startled when he sees his wife standing naked in front of him, her belly extended and round, her breasts large and full. She begs him to touch her like Morgan did. To feel the baby, his baby, move inside her. She tells him about the Four Seasons and the possible Daddy and Me class. She waits for his face to become illuminated with excitement. But Harry says nothing. Does nothing. She reaches for his hand to place on her stomach and once it's there, she watches a sadness wash over him.

A few days later Harry's bags have been packed and wait

by the front door to be loaded into his black SUV. His eyes are red and he doesn't bother to hide the tears that streak his face. Ellen doesn't try either. Though she's been told all this emotion isn't good for the baby, there's no sense in keeping it inside. Ingested rage and swallowed hurt can't be good for her. She's done begging Harry to stay. He's done begging her to see another therapist. So she lets him leave. Lets him feel the baby inside her when he goes to hug her good-bye. Lets him walk out the door.

He'll be back, she thinks. When the baby is born he'll come back.

Seventy days later Ellen is looking at a line of newborns, each wearing a pink or blue cap, each dressed in a tiny white cotton onesie, just as she said she would. Just as her calendar indicated. She is worn and tired but happy. Triumphant. She peers at the row of children behind the glass window and is able to pick her child out instantly. Hers is one of the few not crying. Wendy, who is gurgling, has ten perfect toes and ten just-as-perfect fingers. She is perfect in every single way. Ellen's stunning long hair is gone. Like the woman in The Gap, it's now cropped short, shaped pixie style, just like she told the women at Barneys it would be. It's not as becoming as she'd hoped but certainly more convenient and manageable. She presses her forehead up against the glass and waves while smiling. "Hi baby Wendy. Mommy's here. Mommy's right here." A woman a few years younger than Ellen is standing next to her. She's dressed in the same gown and robe. Both have hospital bands around their wrists.

"Which is yours?" Ellen asks.

"That one right there," the woman says, pointing to a red-faced, crying boy whose hat has fallen off. "Sixteen hours, not so bad, I guess. I don't know, this was my first. You?"

"The little one there, second on the left."

"Oh, she's beautiful."

"Thank you." Ellen turns to look at the woman and smiles widely. "My first, too. Twenty hours. Worth every moment."

"Let's hope so."

They laugh like old friends.

Ellen's nurse, a pale, milky-skinned woman with a faint mustache, clears her throat. Dressed in white, she's been waiting quietly off to the side. "Ellen, we've been here enough today. It's time to go back to your room," the nurse informs her.

Ellen says good-bye to the new mom, then blows a kiss to her baby.

She and the nurse wait by the elevator. "Isn't she gorgeous?" Ellen asks.

"Yes," says the nurse.

"Isn't she just adorable?"

"Yes," she answers.

The elevator arrives and the two ride in silence. Both keep their eyes on the light just above the doors to let them know which floor they're passing. Ellen watches the light move from the fifth floor, maternity, to the seventh, the children's ward. Eight is oncology. The last light to blink is the eleventh floor, psychiatric. The doors open and another nurse greets her. The first nurse guides Ellen gently out of the elevator by her arm and hands her off to the second nurse, like a child being deposited at school, delivered from one adult to another.

Some type of Muzak is playing softly in the background. It's familiar, but she can't place the tune. Can't think of the title and blames this on the medication. Patients are aimlessly milling about. Some are dressed like Ellen, others are in sweats and T-shirts.

"Did she go down to see the newborns?" the second nurse asks.

"Of course. Been here a month and that's all she'll do."

"Which child did she pick out today?"

"Another girl."

She looks for Harry and remembers he's not coming, which is fine. She'll make it work. She had a life before him, and now that she's got Wendy, has even more to live for. "When can I take her home?" Ellen asks the pasty-skinned woman who is holding the elevator door open. Her facial expression tells Ellen she's anxious to go back downstairs.

"Soon, Mrs. Thompson. Very soon."

This makes Ellen smile as she's lead into the main room. *See*, she thinks, *everyone was wrong*.

Chapter 15

Franny

Suite 2011

They stood outside in a muddled mass, watching. Waiting.

The men were off to the side, securing hotel rooms, calling insurance companies, talking claims and estimating damages. The women, a bit more hysterical, dialed up relatives and friends, relaying the horror over and over. They talked to the people on the phone and to the neighbors standing next to them, sustaining several conversations at once. And the children. They clung to their mothers' legs, shivering in the cold November air, begging to be hoisted into arms, or were comforted by their nannies. Franny Jamison stood there, too, chilled and coatless, opened mouthed, slightly horrified, slightly titillated. Sure, fires happened in the South, but not like this. She laughed for a moment thinking, *Only in New York could a fire be glamorous.*

It was like watching a movie on the world's largest flat screen. Attractive, rugged men dressed in bumblebee fireproof suits scurried around, securing the area, axes in one hand, walkie-talkies in the other. Red and yellow lights swirled, bouncing off of windows and resurfacing onto rubberneckers' faces. As policemen ran into the building, which was consumed by thick gray clouds of smoke billowing from the lobby and pouring out into the street, neighbors ran out like rats, scampering off in different directions. Some went to get their cars, others fled to nearby friends' homes. A few took their kids to restaurants or a movie or to Borders bookstore. Others, like Franny, lingered in the dreary early afternoon and observed.

An electrical fire had spread underneath the building, damaging the circuit breakers, eating away at the cement like a cancer, causing several manholes to explode from the pressure. Any appliance on at the time was totaled. TVs and stereos smoldered, computers sizzled from the inside, and bulbs grew Stephen King bright before cracking and bursting. Though the interiors of most apartments were still intact, the building had to be evacuated, the avenue sealed off.

An hour later five neighbors from 210 East Fifty-ninth Street were seated at a table with a window view of their building and drank until it became blurry. Franny was sitting next to Joy, whose husband, Chuck, and three-year-old son were staked out at her aunt's apartment two blocks away with another couple and their twin daughters. On her other side was Wes, a lawyer who worked for the mayor and lived directly below her in 7E. He was lean and fit with thick blond hair and chiseled good looks. A rugged Ken doll. Manhattan Ken, she had dubbed him. She often caught him coming home from work, briefcase in tow, iPhone attached to his ear. On the weekends, she looked forward to him rolling past her on his blades, his muscular body decked out in black spandex shorts or shiny runner's outfit, headphones hung around his neck. She'd get all dolled up, as if she were going to a swanky restaurant, and strategize her excuse for being downstairs: no heat, clogged sink, stuck window.

As far as she could tell, Wes had three standard expressions. The left-eye wink, the nod and smile, and the half-wave walk-by. On rare occasions he'd stop and chat, ask what she'd been up to, how her day was, if she'd seen any new movies. Across from her was Netta, an artsy elderly woman whose husband, an old army colonel, had died last year, and Randel, a gay gynecologist, who lived with his lover on the fourth floor.

"What a waste," her doorman once said to her when Randel entered the building and Franny was picking up a package. "Here's a man with the best job in town and he can't appreciate a woman's pussy."

They ordered another round and toasted the building, then each other. She loved being out with them as they bonded, blended together over this catastrophe.

"I was on the john when a fireman knocked at my door," Netta admitted sheepishly, her glass still raised in the air. "I barely had time to flush."

They laughed as a group, their voices melding to create a pleasurable, harmonious sound. Franny turned from Netta to look at Wes, to see if he, too, was appreciating the humor. His face was bright, his eyes seemed extra green against his olive skin. As if someone was taking their photo, she held her face near to his, trying desperately to capture the moment: Wes's laugh, Netta's voice, Joy's strong perfume. To onlookers they must have appeared like this was a weekly gathering.

It was after her third or fourth glass of wine that Wes's fingers slid like mini snakes over to her thigh. The warmth of his palm seeped through her skirt and she dropped her hand from the tabletop and searched for his until she found it. She smiled to herself, then looked up at him as he stroked her thumb.

"Fire good," he whispered to her, imitating Frankenstein.

Something moved inside of her, and she suddenly thought herself very lucky.

Nothing like this ever happened in Mississippi. Sure someone's cousin's father might get drunk and bring a loaded gun to the nearest bar and threaten to shoot someone's daddy for doing him wrong, but it usually got smoothed over by treating the already-intoxicated man to another shot of whiskey. Random fights over Elvis often took place, or a crazy relative would be found late at night, walking down the road in nothing but their pajamas. Franny remembered a fight that broke out years ago over a corn crop, but that was pretty much it. Incidents like this were why she came to New York. The idea that something huge could happen at any moment that could change your life instantly was the reason she'd come to live here at twenty-two, fifteen years ago.

They migrated back to the building, met up with other tenants, and were informed they'd have ten minutes to collect belongings if they wished. After being advised they'd be entering at their own risk, each was given a mask and flashlight, and asked to sign a waiver. A fireman would escort them up the stairs and the group would reconvene across the street afterward.

They carefully made their way up the stairs, laughing nervously at the situation, at the poor timing for a fire to happen. With Thanksgiving two days away, half of Manhattan was gearing down while the other half was moving at high speed.

Fireman Jack ordered them to hug the right side of the stairwell while he patted the walls, feeling for heat. From above, they heard feet scuffing against steps, voices becoming louder, bags thumping, four-legged creatures making light scratching sounds. They passed neighbors who were making their way down: older tenants, pregnant women with young children, men carrying suitcases, strollers banging behind them. They looked ghostly in the barely lit stairwell. People were eerily quiet as if they were expecting complicated directions or to see a burst of red flames run through the cable wires. A few firemen made momentary appearances, dodging in and out of the doorframes, like adults playing peek-a-boo.

By the fourth floor Franny was sweaty and dizzy, from the liquor and the smoke, the plastic face mask, maybe from Wes's touch. She could feel him from behind, his hand placed at the small of her back helping to steady her.

When they got to Franny's floor, they waited for her to enter her apartment and say "I'm okay" before moving on. Even in her tipsy state, she could hear her Southern twang escape from her mouth. Thanks to improvisation classes and diction coaches, she could turn her drawl on and off when she wanted, except when she was drunk—then she was powerless.

Once inside, she absentmindedly reached for the light, momentarily forgetting, and dropped the face mask on the dining room table. She scanned the apartment with the flashlight like a cat burglar. Broken bits of bulb sprinkled her floor like confetti. The TV seemed intact, as did her computer.

Packing came second nature, like making coffee in the morning or brushing her teeth before bed as she recalled with clarity the invisible list she'd created for situations such as these during late-night insomniac fits. In the dark of her closet she felt for her good suits and gowns, knowing them like children, each with a different texture and fabric. The rhinestones, the sequins, the beaded crystals all sent out shocks of memories: her at the Grammys, the Tonys, the VH1 Awards.

Like a game of celebrity musical chairs, it was her job to occupy an empty seat while a star was temporarily MIA. When they returned, either from the restroom or bar, or from backstage with a statue in tow, they reclaimed their seat while she looked for another opening. Everyone thought Franny led the glamorous life, holding spots for others. Sitting next to the likes of Julia or Tom, or being caught by a panning camera was all some of her colleagues—bored women whose husbands worked, college kids, retired ladies, men who wanted to get laid—needed. For her, it was being part of a momentous occasion. Participating in something epic.

"Everyone wants a cushy seat to the kingdom, but only a handful of people know how to open the door," the casting director, who was responsible for hiring seat fillers, told her. "I got twelve hundred applications for the MTV Awards, but can only use twenty-five people."

Before moving here, Franny's biggest opportunity came

from her cousin, who was going to be a historic tour director.

"I'm moving to Georgia and getting a job with the Southern Historical Preservation Society," she'd said. "They need lots of girls to explain about the famous homes and talk about the history behind them."

Aside from her mother's sister, who married an artist and moved to Philadelphia, no one had ventured east or west. And though she missed her family, they never quite understood why Franny had felt smothered.

"Smothered on forty acres of land?" Her father had said in disbelief when she told him she was planning on leaving. "That's impossible, young lady. God didn't make family so we'd be split from them."

Ironically, it was her Southern, generic looks that earned her entrance to the Promised Land. Allowed her to blend in. She could be anyone's wife or girlfriend. Her ashy auburn hair and green eyes made her pretty to look at. Her nonthreatening, cheery personality made her easy to forget. The twangy, endearing accent was an icebreaker for nosy New Yorkers who inquired, "Where are you from?" While it was her transplant qualities that got her work, all she really wanted was to be mistaken for a New Yorker. But the more she repressed her middle American qualities, the less bookable she became.

There were exciting moments. She'd sat next to Cher once at the Grammys, shared an armrest with Michael Douglas, even rubbed shoulders with Sigourney Weaver, but she was whisked away before Franny could congratulate her or feel the heaviness of the trophy everyone was always commenting on. She participated silently at game shows, asked questions to guests on morning talk shows, and laughed on command at sitcoms. She contributed in focus groups, helped paper the house of previewing musicals, and ate at an array of new restaurants. These were great stories to tell at parties or on dates, sitting on wooden stools drinking white wine. But at the end of the night, getting on a bus or sitting alone in the back seat of a cab dressed in other people's gowns she'd purchased at consignment shops and on eBay, with no one's hand to grasp, was devastatingly lonely. At home, though she could sit anywhere she wanted, she never found a comfortable spot, a place where her body could just relax. These were the moments when she longed for home. For her mother's cheese biscuits and creamy grits. Her soapy smell and sweet cherub face.

She took three pairs of evening shoes and crammed them into the stuffed garment bag. In a large LeSportsac she packed two sweaters, underwear, jeans, and a toiletry kit. Extra cash, checks, her passport, jewelry, makeup, plug for her cell phone, and a mini binder of contact numbers for her jobs got shoved into a knapsack.

She was in the middle of reaching for her date book when the knock came at her door, which she'd left open as instructed.

"I thought you might need help." He stepped inside and shined his flashlight around her apartment, finally resting on her. Franny squinted and brought her hand up to her eyes, shadowing them. At first she thought it was fireman Jack informing her time was up, but Wes's silhouette filled the frame of her entranceway instead.

"It's me." He flicked the light to just under his chin so that his angular face was instantly illuminated. His baseball hat caught the light and framed his face, making him appear slightly demonic. He, too, was maskless.

The smell of smoke wafted into the apartment as he walked over to her. She returned the gesture, and thought of the light beams from the *Star Wars* movies. And popcorn. The smoke reminded her of severely burnt kernels.

"You okay?" He had only one large duffel bag and a bike helmet, which scraped on her floor.

"Where's all your stuff?" she asked.

He shrugged. "I don't think this is as serious as everyone's making it. My apartment's fine. Besides, everything important is at my office."

She nodded, feeling silly for packing.

"So, you need some help?"

"Sure."

As he leaned forward she caught the scent of his citrus cologne, followed by the smell of hair gel. She thought he was reaching for her bag, but when he went for her lips instead she assumed he was drunker than he thought. His breath was toothpaste minty, but still had the lingering taste of scotch. She wished she had some mints in her pocket. He put a hand on her shoulder, his other cupped her chin, and his tongue slipped into her mouth before she had time to steal a breath. *Nice Southern girls don't do this*, she could hear her mother scolding. She pushed away the voice by concentrating on the softness of Wes's skin and his firm muscles. She ran her hands under his sweater as he pressed up against her, pushing her to the floor. He was heavy on her, as if he was struggling. A wave of nausea returned. She shut her eyes, willing herself onto a soft, warm beach, the scent of sea air replacing the smoke and her coarse, sharp carpet, which was scratching her back, arms, and thighs. He kissed her hurriedly, hungrily. She considered searching through her travel bag for the emergency condom she always packed but never had an opportunity to use. Fearing it would take too long, she waved the idea away. The building could still explode, and the fear of getting pregnant or VD became, somehow, less important.

Before she knew it, his jeans were unbuttoned, her skirt bunched up, her underwear pulled down. She sucked in her stomach trying to match his firm body. When he was inside her, she winced for a second, let out a muffled cry as she talked herself into enjoying this. After all, this was risky and exhilarating. A naughty, raunchy story to share with others as she waited to fill a seat or stood on a movie line. "Death made me do it," she imagined herself proclaiming over sushi with girlfriends. They'd be shocked, a little mortified, but they'd have new respect for her. A badge of courage, a medal of sexual honor. "We will all go down together" she'd say, "and I did." She visualized her burnt skeleton wrapped around Wes's. They would find her, a mess of melted skin stuck to another just-as-scorched body, the bones indecipherable, as if they had been entwined on her Pottery Barn carpet. She pictured fireman Jack breaking down the door with the intention of pulling a rescue, only to find them on the floor. At first he would be alarmed, perhaps they had fallen, passed out from smoke inhalation, then he'd discover the truth. At least her friends would think she'd had one good fuck before she died. At least they could say she wasn't alone.

She felt feverish and itchy and cold as she followed Wes slowly down the dark stairs, forcing herself to concentrate on the weak ray from his flashlight. It was too quiet. All she could hear was their breathing and footsteps, and his bike helmet bouncing lightly off his knapsack.

When they arrived at the meeting place everyone was waiting for them. Her hair was a mess and she was wearing the scent of burnt clothing and sex, and just a hint of Wes's cologne. She wasn't even sure if she had buttoned her shirt correctly in the dark. People would assume it was the dangerous situation or the burst of adrenaline that was to blame for her discombobulated state. But when no one said a word, she felt a little disappointed.

After much deliberation, cell phone numbers were exchanged and promises made to keep each other informed with updates. Joy offered the apartment of her aunt, who was away promoting a music tour, to those who had nowhere else to go. Randel was meeting his partner at the Four Seasons, where they would be staying.

"Though it's ghastly expensive," he said, his hand waving in the air, "it's one of the only hotels that wasn't sold-out. Besides, fires are depressing. We deserve a little reward for this."

Wes announced he, too, was checking himself into the same hotel. Franny glanced at her feet. *Don't look at him. Do. Not. Look at him*, she thought, waiting to see if he would ask her to join. But when Netta opened her mouth to say a friend was picking her up and the two would be starting their holiday weekend early, Franny knew Wes wouldn't ask. The minute, the opportunity, was gone.

Joy had brought Simon's stroller and she and Franny took turns pushing the piled-high contraption up Sixtieth Street. Neither packed winter coats, so Franny pulled out two of her sequined gowns and they wrapped them around their shoulders. They looked like well-dressed homeless people huddling together.

By the time they arrived at Joy's aunt's apartment, the others had sent the nannies home and made themselves comfortable, commandeering the kitchen and den. Crayons were sprawled over the mini plastic table in the kitchen, the TV played a cartoon, a tape one of the adults had packed. Diaper bags, toys, pacifiers, and books were scattered everywhere. Joy's aunt, Honor Kraus, was a famous publicist to rock stars and her home was magazine-spread beautiful—sleek and modern—and smelled like fresh roses. Ornate molding along the floor accentuated the high ceilings in the entrance and hallway. Glossy chrome dominated the living room, offsetting the white couch, matching chairs, and vanilla-cream shag carpet. A zebra throw covered most of the floor in the den, which was decorated in hunter style—butter leather couches, warm, rich mahogany wall units, even an antique gun collection that she had won in her divorce settlement. The dining room had an elongated table, the kind that easily sat ten people and Franny could almost hear the laughter coming from past dinner parties Joy's aunt threw. She pictured celebrities and rock stars laughing, heads falling back, hair spilling over faces, men slapping the table with the palms of their hands as they drank expensive wine and ate quail or escargot. The living room was her favorite, art deco with a black baby grand piano residing in the corner, which, she bet, was never played. The shelves were filled with photos that showed Joy's aunt with celebrities of all sorts—some of which Franny had sat next to for work: Bowie, Sting, Cher.

Her other neighbors, David and Catherine Thompson, were

an attractive couple with twin girls who lived on Franny's floor. She was blonde, he wasn't. Both had substantial jobs, though she worked from home part-time. The kids seemed well-adjusted. They owned three apartments that had been constructed into one large home and ruled the eighth floor. An American dream all around. Chuck, Joy's squat and chubby husband, owned a hedge fund company and had the personality of flat seltzer.

Simon ran to his mother before she could park the stroller.

"Thanks for helping," Chuck said to Franny after she'd gotten the full tour. He stood by the front door holding it open. Everyone stared at her until Joy announced she'd be joining them for dinner. Chuck pulled his wife aside, and Franny could see his mouth moving, his hand gripping Joy's upper arm, see her wiggle free and walk away. Maybe she should leave, take her belongings, and just go. She glanced at the Thompsons who smiled uneasily.

They convened in the kitchen, the children at work coloring, Cheerios on a paper plate, sippy cups in a rainbow of pale colors. The adults mulled over a Szechuan Palace menu, a second bottle of champagne was already opened and nearly gone. She watched the two couples scamper around the kitchen, each with a list of tasks to accomplish, doing the shorthand speaking husbands and wives perform.

It was an odd feeling standing in someone's aunt's kitchen surrounded by individuals who would normally have nothing to do with her. It wasn't a snow day, though it felt like one. "Natural disaster day" Franny wanted to call it, almost suggested it to the gang. But these people here tonight weren't friends. And they weren't family. Still, she knew intimate details about them:

how they lived, where they shopped, what they ate, who they got food deliveries from. She knew their routine, what type of music they favored. She'd seen them dressed up, waiting for the elevator, off to attend some glamorous event. Saw the aftereffects the next day—hungover, unshowered, still smelling of sleep—as they picked up their newspapers from outside their front doors. She'd borrowed ice, sugar, milk, lent them pots, glasses, chairs. She knew their friends, heard arguments with spouses, and saw them lose control with their kids. For many, she'd been a witness when the women first began to show, and when those children celebrated their first birthdays. She'd received respectful hellos, cordial courtesies from people who had earned a peculiar kind of status. They'd bonded over the simple fact that they lived several feet away, shared a wall or ceiling.

"How about orange beef?" Chuck suggested, relinquishing the menu to his guests.

"Oh, Catherine doesn't eat red meat, remember?" David answered for his wife.

"Right," he said, a hand placed on Joy's shoulder.

"We like garlic chicken. Anyone else?" Catherine chirped, leaning over her husband to see her options better. "And shrimp. We're big shrimp people."

"Us too." Joy, who had finished the champagne Chuck poured her, sat down next to David, who refilled her glass without having to be asked.

"To new friends," Joy sang.

"To new friends," they all repeated.

Without Wes at the house, Franny felt unexplainably lonely. She wanted to make a toast also, to their gracious hosts and to herself for being able to get through the evening.

"Franny, any requests?" Catherine asked.

If she were dating someone he'd have known what to choose. If she were closer to these people they'd be able to order for her. She hated this, the simple arrangement of things, the common understanding of jobs. The team of two. It was a Noah's Ark hierarchy, man and woman. Even if she and Wes weren't a couple, she could have pretended they were in this situation together. He would have paid for her portion of Chinese food. The men would have reached for their wallets simultaneously and pulled out crisp green bills. Even without kids, they could have been a team. She wondered if he'd call to check in, wanted, somehow needed, to hear his voice. She flashed to them on the floor, tried to remember how she felt. Wished he were here now.

She had spent a lifetime looking for her husband, a partner to walk up the wooden plank into the foreboding ark. This was why people married, she thought, so they'd have company, a partner in crime to go through trauma with. Good times were just a bonus.

At thirty-seven she was tempted to marry just so she could be included in group activities that couples did together: weekend trips to Connecticut and the Hamptons, vacations to Florence or Spain. She wanted dinners with friends who ate as couples, dined as a group of married professionals. She contemplated adopting a child so she could fit in with the rest of the world, go to classes, chat with other mommies in Central Park, carry bite-size food in Ziploc bags, share toys and books. But it was just her.

It was always just her. She needed a program or group therapy meeting for normal people who wanted to connect with others. But those didn't exist. And if they did, they were called mixers or events for single professionals with a cutoff age that Franny always seemed to just miss. She'd entered the dot-com dating movement with the rest of the world, read the personals in the back of *New York Magazine*, even joined the Ninety-second Street Y in the hopes of finding someone through educational evenings. All that came from her hard efforts was bad banter from men who weren't really ready to meet women, didn't share her goals or interests, or were divorced with kids and an ex-wife or two.

The line of distinction ended with her single, childless state. Her independence. "The problem is, Franny, you're too self-sufficient," her sister had told her once. "Appear too put together and no one thinks you need help."

Dinner was surprisingly enjoyable, with comfortable conversation, tasty food, dishes Franny wouldn't ordinarily have ordered: bean curd soup, chicken chop suey, rainbow pork, and prawns in garlic sauce. The kids ran around the table, grabbing fortune cookies and breaking them open, thrusting the tiny papers at the adults to read. Everyone made up sayings so the kids would understand them. When Simon gave his to Franny, she switched "A change in scenery will open more than just your heart" to "Cookie Monster says you love cookies." Simon jumped up and down. "I do. I do." And everyone laughed. Franny tucked the paper into her skirt pocket, she wanted to hold onto something. And this, if anything, besides her sex-soiled underwear, was at least a souvenir of the evening.

An hour later, Catherine and Franny stood in the kitchen. As Catherine leaned forward to place a plate in the dishwasher,

her diamond earrings reflected off the fluorescent light, momentarily blinding Franny. She caught her staring at them.

"A present from David," Catherine shared, her hand clasping each ear to make sure they were both still in the appointed spots. "An anniversary gift. He thinks I don't know that his sister-in-law bought them, but to be honest, Ellen's got better taste than he does. Sometimes I phone her and drop hints on what I want around holidays. They live in Connecticut. We were thinking of staying with them. They have a lovely house."

Franny nodded.

"I think part of me married David because he had brothers. When you're an only child, anyone with siblings looks attractive."

She nodded and thought of her sister who she suddenly missed intensely.

"So, where are you going to stay?" Catherine continued, as they scraped plates, removing remnants of pancake and Peking sauce. Everyone had asked this question at different intervals throughout the evening. On autopilot she replied, "I'm not sure. Joy said I could stay in the housekeeper's room. I've been trying to get in touch with my aunt, but they might be away for a few days. They live in Pennsylvania and they weren't expecting me until Thanksgiving. And it's kind of late to take a train." She took another dish from Catherine. "I might stay with friends." Though most had left for the long holiday weekend to see in-laws and family members. She could have gone home, but flying to Mississippi was costly. The train to Philly was much cheaper.

The clock on the microwave blinked 11:30 p.m. Wes hadn't called. She was tempted to prank phone him at 2:00 a.m. "Could you ring Mr. Bater's room please?" Once he answered she'd say, "Dick Hurts?" If Joy was still up, and if they were closer, she could have told her about this afternoon, and she would have gone next, asking for Jenna Talia.

She was still thinking about pranking him as Joy and Catherine made breakfast plans.

"EJ's?" Catherine suggested. "The girls enjoy it."

"First one there grabs the table . . ."

"In the back," Catherine finished.

Both mothers smiled. They were like two people sharing one brain.

"Nine a.m.?" Joy said, walking everyone to the door. One of the twins was asleep in Catherine's arms, the other, wide awake and whimpering, thumb in her mouth. David juggled the bags, luggage, and kid paraphernalia.

"Let's just order in room service," he added, trying to organize the bundles. "The kids will love it. Come over whenever and we'll have a pajama party."

Everyone seemed to nod at the same time, like robots obeying a command.

Franny could already visualize them talking about her as they lulled around in the hotel's thick terrycloth robes, the kids emptying out the minibar, pretending it was a supermarket.

"I don't think I've ever seen her go on a date or have a man over," Catherine would say, her earrings catching the light from the chandelier.

"Does she have friends? I never see her with anyone," Chuck would add.

"I feel sorry for her," Joy would comment, cutting up Simon's food and calling him back to the makeshift picnic area they had created on the floor.

She watched them hover in the doorway waiting for the elevator. There were kisses and good-byes, the sound of a door opening, the twins' cranky voices growing fainter.

Now Joy and Chuck were staring at her, waiting for a decision.

"I think time snuck up on me," Franny said, looking from their faces to the floor. "It's kind of late to call friends. Would it be okay to stay?"

Chuck's upper lip twitched ever so slightly, but he somehow managed a smile.

"Of course." Joy was already moving swiftly toward the housekeeper's quarters.

The room was small, dreary, and reeked of lemon Pledge. The mocha-colored blanket matched the carpet so well that it looked as if it was floating. The walls were a dull brown and the wooden dresser could have been from her college dorm.

She stacked her belongings in the corner, trying to take up as little space as possible. She wanted to be invaluable, but invisible, like her seat-filling job.

"Sorry if it seems, I don't know, uncomfortable," Joy said, getting Franny a fresh towel. "My aunt's been saying she'll redecorate for years now. It's just that Simon's set up in the guest room . . ."

"No. It's fine. I'm just glad to be here." She sounded like an idiot. "I mean, this is really decent of you."

"Nonsense. What are neighbors for? See you in the morning." And then she was gone.

She changed into a T-shirt and jeans since she hadn't packed any sleepwear. She opened a window, got into bed, worried that too much dust or dirt would come in, and not wanting to disrupt anything more than she already had, closed it. There was nothing to stare out at since the room faced the back, nothing that seemed familiar.

She was still tossing and turning at 2:43 a.m. She was going to watch TV, but thought the set might be up against the wall to Joy's aunt's bedroom and was fearful of waking them. Frustrated, she sat in one of Simon's tiny chairs in the kitchen, a white sheet of paper staring blankly in front of her. Finally, she wrote the words "Future Plans" at the top. The writing looked foreign to her at this hour. The words did too, as if they were misspelled, even though she knew they weren't. The pen wasn't hers, the paper didn't have her name on it, even the kitchen seemed somehow dizzying. She added "Join a book club." Then "Find a movie group. See more off-Broadway plays. Fill house with fresh flowers. Eat better—only organic. Learn to cook a new dish each month." She ended with "Meet men. Have children. Make a better life."

She was up before anyone and by 8:00 a.m. had stripped the bed, emptied out the dishwasher, and made coffee and tea. She hoped she'd be invited to join the morning's outing at the Thompson's hotel suite in the Four Seasons. She tried calling the building but got a busy signal, and it was too early to phone the other homeless tenants.

She heard Simon's padded feet before he leaped into the kitchen. He was happy to see her and outstretched his arms in order to be lifted up.

"You're still here," he proclaimed. "Cookie Monster says I like cookies."

"Me too," she said, kissing his cheek.

"Who doesn't?" Chuck added. She handed him a filled coffee mug. "I didn't know how you take it." She pointed to the milk and sugar she'd laid out on the table. "And juice or milk for Simon?"

"Juice, juice," he said.

She had prepared one of each, waiting in freshly washed sippy cups. She was midreach to Simon when Chuck intervened. "Milk in the morning."

"Juice, juice," Simon screamed, stamping his foot. She could see Chuck's annoyance.

"Joy's showering," he said, handing Simon his drink.

"Great." There was a long pause. "So, any stock tips?" The words fell out of her mouth. She could tell Chuck hated small talk.

"Not really."

She waited for him to say something else, and when he didn't, they both stirred their coffee, spoons clanking loudly against the ceramic.

"So, what are your plans?" he finally spit out.

"I've left a message for my parents and my aunt, whose home I'm supposed to go to, but I don't know if they've tried to phone back. I'm not getting reception on my cell and there's still no power at the apartment so I don't know if they've left a message. They thought I was coming tomorrow."

Tomorrow she would pack another bag, take the Metroliner, and wait to see if her uncle would arrive on time, or if he would make her wait in the station on Thanksgiving while he waited for halftime or one more tackle before leaving the house. She almost couldn't bear to see herself sitting next to her aunt's widowed friend, or her uncle's bachelor fishing buddy who'd put his hand on her knee during Christmas one year.

Chuck nodded. Both sipped coffee.

Joy appeared, her hair still wet. Franny handed her a cup of tea. "Peppermint, right? That's what you had last night, so I figured that's what you drink."

Joy smiled and they clinked glasses. Everything would be fine.

It was almost 9:00 a.m. when Franny emerged from the shower. She had a moment of panic, a thought that maybe they had left without her and she'd be stuck, unsure of what to do. She'd find a note on the kitchen counter, next to the list she had made regarding her life. "Great having you here. Leave the room as it is, the housekeeper will clean it when my aunt gets back. Just close the front door behind you when you're ready to go. Best, Joy." She dressed hurriedly and found everyone in the den, Chuck on the landline phone, Joy on her cell, Simon hypnotized by the TV screen. She almost cried when she saw them.

Franny had eaten in the Four Seasons' restaurant once, but had never stayed in any of the rooms. If she closed her eyes she could picture the hotel's matches, which sat in a bowl on her coffee table. She always took two sets of fancy matchbooks or pretty magnets, one for her collection, the others to be mailed home in a monthly package to her parents, which contained postcards, pens, key rings, and other extras from the goodie bags she got from her award shows.

Open and inviting, the hotel was all marble: marble floors, columns, archways, stairs. A swirl of browns and whites and

grays making Franny instantly long to live here. She hoisted
Simon up so he could press the twentieth floor button. Once
the doors opened he ran down the hall calling for the twins,
the adults trailing behind. Hello kisses were given, and though
David seemed slightly surprised to find her in his hotel doorway, holding a diaper bag and standing next to Joy and Chuck,
he sweetly invited her in.

Randel had stopped by earlier for an apartment update and
had already left to be with friends in the Village. She felt bad,
as if she had missed out on something. Wes was still here too
she bet. She thought of this as she sank into the room, getting
high from seeing the same people in such a short time while
taking in the comfortable, modern suite. Large bay windows
made the room feel airy, and the high floor overlooked much of
Manhattan. The couch, where the twins must have slept, was
in pullout-bed formation. There was a desk, a pair of swivel
chairs, and a glass coffee table. The main bedroom was sealed
off by wood-and-glass-paneled doors.

"The tub fills up in sixty seconds," one of the twins
shrieked, pulling Franny into the bathroom.

"We take a bath this morning," the other stated. "Put us
in!"

"Put me in, too. I want to go in," Simon echoed.

She lifted each child into the huge tub, arranged them in the
traditional "hear, speak, and see no evil" formation, and called
the adults to come and look. Within seconds, everyone was in
the bathroom.

"You know we got married here," Catherine told her as
someone pulled out a digital camera. "Both my brothers-in-law
did, too."

"And my parents," said David. "They met here. Well not here in this room, but at the hotel."

She loved hearing personal information from these people. It built a sense of history. At work, Franny could spend hours getting to know a total stranger intimately while waiting for seating arrangements or just going through a technical rehearsal. Now she felt this way with her neighbors. They had been through something together, survived a crisis. No matter what, they'd always have this.

"Hey remember when . . ." Franny could say years later. By then her child would be a year or two. Her husband would be by her side. Simon and the twins would be starting nursery school or first grade. This time, they could order dinner for her, she would be the one David would call for gift suggestions for Catherine. She'd already know what Catherine wanted, have a little cheat sheet she made from times she commented on what she liked as the two went window shopping. Maybe one of them would introduce her to a friend of theirs, making the courtship even sweeter. She'd be easily accepted, welcomed in with open arms. They could hang out at each other's apartments, like her old dorm days, no locks on doors, each apartment an extension of someone else's. All that was missing from the Thompson's suite was a roaring fire and a Trivial Pursuit game. Maybe a New Year's ball to drop and Dick Clark's irritatingly saccharine voice wishing them all health and happiness.

"Has anyone seen Wes?" she asked.

Catherine shrugged and looked to her husband for an answer or confirmation.

"I think so," David volunteered. "We spoke with him last

night. We could call the front desk and find out." As he moved toward the phone, Franny started to panic. Since she'd only been in the room for five or ten minutes, it was a gamble leaving so soon. They would probably talk about her once she left, but finding Wes seemed far more important.

"I'm wondering," she said, "if the damage is substantial enough maybe the insurance company would pay for a short-term stay. Perhaps the hotel would give us a group rate depending upon the number of nights we'd be staying and the number of rooms we'd need."

They all looked at her.

"Why don't I speak with someone downstairs to see if that's possible." She really hadn't contributed much. Making a silly cup of coffee in the morning was pittance in comparison to the others.

"I'll be right back." She left her purse on the chair and strode boldly to the door, then waited in the hallway for a moment, ear pressed to the wall, trying to catch some dialogue, but everything sounded muffled.

"Hi. Who can I speak with regarding a short- or long-term stay for a group of people?" she inquired to the pale-looking woman whose name tag read ANNE. She appeared nice enough. Tall, thin, tired. She wondered who stayed here over the holidays and if they get paid time and a half. Maybe this should be her new line of work. She was barely getting by on what she made now. Her days busily empty, her evenings unimportantly filled. It was time for stability. For friendly officemates, a structured environment, and a normal life.

Franny told Anne about her recent plight, leaving out the

information about the sex on her floor, and the list she had made late last night, or early this morning.

"My God, that's terrible," Anne said, and then she seemed momentarily frozen. As if Franny had lost her somewhere in her long-winded story. She thought she saw her lips move slightly, but no sound came out.

"So I was wondering if you had a package or discount program you offer. You know, for people who stay for a week or even a month. Is that kind of thing even available?"

Anne nodded. "Thirty vs. thirty. If you're staying thirty days or more, a thirty percent discount is given along with a lovely welcoming basket. We also offer a packing and unpacking program."

"What's that?"

"We can arrange for housekeeping to unpack for you and then pack when you're ready to leave." She watched the woman's quick and efficient movements as she looked up the information on the computer and then printed it out for her.

"Oh," Franny added nonchalantly, "I was wondering if you could tell me what room Mr. Bater is in. He's part of our group."

"I can call up to the room for you . . ." the woman was in middial when Franny stopped her.

"I think he might be sleeping," she said. "If you'll just tell me his room number."

The woman frowned, pressed her lips together while trying to smile, and tilted her head slightly to the left. "I'm sorry. I can't give that information out. I can only ring the guest for you. It's policy."

"Look, a lot of us might be staying here for a long time. All I'm asking for is some help. He's not going to care if you tell me." Perhaps she should have mentioned the sex part. Hell, she should have said she was his girlfriend or wife. "Mr. Bater is going to be really mad if he misses some important information because"—she looked at the woman's tag again—"Anne, you didn't give me his room number."

She could see the woman's face starting to redden. She bit on her lower lip, and then mumbled something Franny couldn't make out. "Look, none of us have slept much. I don't even know if I've got a home to go back to. Please."

"Room 906." The words fell out so hurriedly and softly she wasn't even sure she'd heard the girl correctly.

"Thank you." Franny smiled to herself. She was taking charge, leaving the subservient, polite, barely noticeable Southern girl behind. The fire had burnt her outer shell and left a new, bolder, smarter creature to emerge.

Back in the elevator, she pressed the ninth floor instead of the Thompson's. She needed to see him.

She knocked on his door, but received no answer. Perhaps he was there and didn't want to see her. Maybe Anne called him after she left and alerted him a visitor might be coming up. She visualized him thanking the nervous girl for the heads up. She bet he was secretly standing by the door staring at her through the peephole snickering.

She waited a moment longer, anger burning a hole inside her belly, and for a brief second thought she heard the sound of a woman giggling coming from inside. Frustrated, she went back to the Thompson's room.

After breakfast, which was done picnic style with one of the hotel's comforters on the floor—just as she had envisioned—

Joy and Franny decided to walk the few blocks back to their apartment building for an update. By now several inches of snow blanketed the sidewalk and cars, while mounds gathered on top of anorexic-looking tree branches. Franny's shoes were unsalvageably wet. Her feet were numb in some spots, felt like ice in others. Her teeth chattered and she was sleep deprived. Joy was pale and tired.

"You know, it's only been about thirty hours since we've been gone, but I swear to God I feel as though I've been through a small war," Franny said.

"Childbirth wasn't this exhausting," Joy added.

They looked at each other and laughed to keep from crying.

"Our first mistake was being sober through all this," she said. "If this had happened back home, we'd be drunk on my cousin's moonshine so we wouldn't have remembered a thing."

Joy laughed, her lips curling up slightly at the sides of her mouth. Franny could tell she'd just scored bonus points for funniness. With or without Wes, the fire, for her, had been good. New friends, possible new job, and a bolder, funnier personality.

They walked hesitantly down their block and were greeted by huge orange and white barbershop cylinders that sprang up from three potholes. At twenty feet high they were more than an eyesore. Plumes of gray steam poured into the air. Their lobby smelled like a bus terminal. The carpets had been removed, and large industrial machines that cleaned the air hissed loudly. The electricity was back on, but there was still no heat or hot water. The elevators were also out of commission.

"There's one on each floor," the super said, turning his head in the direction of the noise. "The apartments are really cold so most people haven't moved back in," he added, handing them each a stapled packet of paper assessing the damages, a letter from the board, emergency procedures, and numbers for the fire department, police, and nearby hospitals.

"This doesn't seem very safe." Joy stated. "Did Con Ed even fix the problem?"

The super shrugged. "They said they'll be back after the holiday to actually fix the electrical system. What they've done now is only temporary."

Joy turned to her. "I have a feeling I'll pack a few more items and sleep at my aunt's again tonight. We've got a car coming to pick us up in the morning, so if you'd like, we can drop your belongings off here before we head up to the country for the weekend."

Her heart sank. She was hoping for another night with Joy. "Sure. That's extremely kind."

The two moved slowly, carefully up the stairs pointing out burnt spots and water leaks. At the eighth floor Franny stood in the doorway of the stairwell not knowing what to do. "Well, call me if you need anything."

"You too," Joy added, her brown eyes big and blinking.

"Seriously. In this situation we're stronger in numbers." She looked at her neighbor, at the sparkling ring on her finger, the diaper tote slung over her shoulder, her Gucci handbag in her grasp, and wondered if she'd ever have her life. Wondered why she didn't already have it. She wanted to kiss her good-bye, almost leaned forward, but the moment passed and all she could think of to say was thanks. "Talk to you tomorrow. You know, about claims or whatever," anything to keep conversations going, keep the chain in motion. Joy nodded and continued to climb the stairs.

From the moment she pushed open her door she was hit with a scorched, sulfur scent. She set her bag down, eyed the plastic mask that lay on her dining room table. She hated her apartment. Wished it had burned down.

Her couch was done in a needlepoint-like stitch and revealed a pattern of swirly flowers of some sort. Her carpet was a depressing nubby brown, her table and chairs were lightwood and glass and belonged in some else's living room rather than her city studio. In her attempt to urbanize herself, she bought black florescent floor lamps and a black coffee table from Pottery Barn. Copies of the *New Yorker*, *New York*, *Vogue*, and *Elle* lay upon it, making it resemble a doctor's office. Fluffy, puffy decorative pillows were stacked neatly on the floor next to the couch, which was pulled out every night to sleep on.

The windows had been left open and the room was dusty and cold. Black and gray specks covered her once-white windowsill, which looked like ants had invaded. Her mirrors were foggy and everything felt damp, like it had rained inside the apartment. The fridge needed emptying, clocks resetting, clothing put back, and items unpacked.

She tried her aunt, got their machine, then checked her own.

"Hi sugar. Shame to have missed you. Hope you're alright." Her aunt always spoke in short choppy sentences, like a telegram. *Shame to have missed you*. Stop. *Hope you're all right*. Stop. "We were at friends' for dinner. Wish we'd have known. Bad timing I guess. Looking forward to seeing you tomorrow. You're in my prayer box tonight. Maybe it's time you think about coming home. Your mother misses you somethin' awful."

Hearing her aunt's accent coated with memory made her suddenly ache for Mississippi. For her mother's cheese mashed potatoes, her friends—who had a habit of swimming naked in the lake, drunk on gin—for the simple, sweet sound of the Southern cricket-infested night air.

She opened a bottle of wine, lit candles, acknowledged how empty the apartment seemed while looking for a place to put herself. It was odd being here alone. She felt as if she'd been with the same people for a month in a confined space and now that it was over, had forgotten how to be by herself. Almost didn't know who she was without them.

Franny looked out the window onto her quiet, snow-covered street, which had been reopened. The commotion was gone. The fire trucks and police cars were also gone, as if it had never happened. In a few hours Thirty-fourth Street would be swarming with adults and children all waiting to catch a glimpse of massive Snoopy, Garfield, and Underdog floats. Across the park at West Eighty-first Street by the Museum of Natural History people were watching the balloons get fatter, sipping hot chocolate and coffee from Starbucks cups, and munching on homemade cookies. It was events and activities like these that broke up the daily monotony, added a level of excitement to life.

Joy's aunt lived on a high floor, which overlooked the park. If they had stayed another night, Franny could have stood out on the terrace and seen the floats getting prepped for their big day. She could have held Simon or one of the twins while pointing to the larger-than-life characters. She could have pretended she was one of the power people who have stood there, smokes in one hand, champagne flute or martini glass in the other. All over the United States people were cooking and setting tables. Guests would be filling themselves with succulent turkey, overcooked stuffing, every traditional, generic Thanksgiving dish one would expect. The train to her relative's seemed like a torture chamber, the dinner a death sentence.

She eyed the area where she and Wes had had sex less than forty hours ago. She took off her clothing and crawled over to the spot, put her face to the nubby carpet and inhaled the lingering, burnt smell that had gotten trapped in the fabric. She breathed in deeply and took another whiff, held it tightly in her chest, like a big hit of pot. She put her ear against her hardwood floor to hear if Wes was home. She did this from time to time, when she was bored, or wanted company for dinner. Usually he'd be on the phone, probably talking to friends or random women who had crushes on him, high-pitched laughs, and talked in questions, never ending a sentence with a single period.

Where was he? Shouldn't he be knocking on her door, asking if she wanted to go out for a bite after each had settled back in and unpacked? Didn't he owe her that?

She was surveying her apartment from this position when a hat caught her eye, lying haphazardly under her console. She remembered being hit by it as they kissed, and as she reached for it with her left hand, her right rubbed the spot on her head. It was still slightly sore. The cap was faded blue from wash and wear, an exclamation point was embroidered on it. She tried it on, wanted to know what it was like to be him. She lay back down—the hat on her head, the carpet scratching at her skin—

and tried to picture his apartment: She saw a bike and minimal but expensive, high-end furniture decorated by some woman from Bloomingdale's while he was at work. She closed her eyes and pretended he was here, resurrected his rich, prep school voice. Suddenly, she heard a door click open, then snap shut. Heard his feet, the sound of keys dropping on a table. She lingered for five minutes waiting for him to come up and see how she was, then ten. Stayed in the same spot, as if she couldn't leave, needed to know what he was doing. She heard him pick up the phone. Waited for hers to ring, and when she caught him mumble something to someone else and hang up, she still gave him another five minutes before pulling herself off the carpet. She walked loudly on the floor to see if that would spur any change. Nothing.

He wasn't coming up to see her.

She missed the hotel. Missed the glossy, luxurious, exciting feeling it offered. It was seductive, like a lover. She wanted to go back. Almost needed to.

When she couldn't stand the silence any longer, she threw her laundry into a basket. She stripped her sheets, removed the pillowcases, collected the towels, and went downstairs. At least she was getting exercise.

She was shocked at how terrible the basement looked. The newly laid blue freckled tile was ruined. The floor was wavy and bubbled, having melted from the heat. Much of the ceiling had caved in and large chunks of dark gray matter covered the floor. All seven machines were turned off. The dryer doors had been left open so dust and God knows what filled the insides. A cockroach, which ran over the rubble, was the breaking point.

She knocked on the super's office door to find out when the

machines would be fixed, and when she received no answer, turned the brass knob and entered.

The place was a mess, smoky and moldy, though Franny got the feeling this was its original state. The only light came from the back room that held supplies and tools. Static poured from a walkie-talkie, which drowned out the Spanish music coming from an old radio. There was a TV, VCR, and a desk piled with papers. As she turned to leave, something silvery caught her eye. She thought of Catherine's earrings as she walked back to the desk. A metal toolbox lay open, a pair of pliers stared at her, as if they had been waiting for her all day. They felt cool on her skin, solid in her grasp. She ran her fingers over the raised, metal ridges. Put her left index finger in the contraption's sharp teeth and pressed. She watched the tip turn red before pulling it free, scraping her skin enough for it to bleed. A feeling of power raced through her. A celebration of her new, savvy self. She turned her attention to the ceiling. Con Ed had carelessly taped several unruly wires to the wall, which ran from the laundry room to the super's office ending at the storage room. Franny followed the messy trail with her eyes, finally settling on a place where the tape was coming apart. Wires hung down imitating week-old sun-dried-tomato-flavored spaghetti. All it would take is one, maybe two tugs on the tape to produce some damage, help push the wires together so that they could touch, then create a charge or spark.

Back in her apartment, she peacefully repacked a bag, as if she were doing a reenactment, and waited for the sounds of sirens, for the hurried voices. She smiled as she thought about the Four Seasons' ultralarge tub, the soft bed, the fluffy carpet. She was calmed knowing it wouldn't be long before there was a knock at her door. She bet Joy was still upstairs, packing and tidying up before heading back to her aunt's apartment. Franny might even see her in the lobby. Or better yet, she could ring her bell. "I hate to be the bearer of bad news," she could say. "Looks like they're evacuating us again. Can you fucking believe that?"

A bottle of champagne was in her hand. Her overnight bag, plastic face mask, and flashlight rested by her feet. Comfort moved through her as the wailing, piercing cry of fire trucks got louder and louder.

Chapter 16

Louise

Suite 2410

Stats

Birth Name: Louise Cantezara.

Occupation: Rock star.

Age: 44.

Bands: Me, Myself & Eye, Horse House, Zsa Zsa, Hit Me Harder.

Solo Albums: Neon Personality, Too Much Is Never Enough, Wish I Was, Unlimited Lou's Greatest Hits.

Top Awards: Grammy—Album of the Year, Record of the Year; two platinum records.

Tattoos: A mini bottle of tequila located at the small of her back, a platinum-colored record the size of a quarter on her left ankle, "love thyself" in French over her right wrist.

Rehab Stays: Three.

Drug of Choice: Coke.

Drink of Choice: Anything but scotch.

Smokes: Camel Lights, a pack a day.

Famous Friends: Other aging rock stars like herself—Mick, Lou, Iggy.

High Points: Fucking Bowie, accepting Grammy, signing record contract with Sony.

Low Points: '82–'89, '04–present.

Years She Can't Recall: '82–'89, '93–'97.

Relationship History: Unsuccessful.

Born: Fort Lee, NJ.

Lived in: Seattle, '77–'94; New York, '95–present.

Instruments: Gibson guitar, drums, lead vocals.

It's 3:00 a.m. at a bar. There's still another line to do, another song to perform, another party to crash, another autograph to sign, another line to do, another drink to swallow, another song to sing, another, another, another . . . It never stops. Not the shaking in her hands, not the coke she puts up her nose or the vodka that slides down her throat or the chords that play monotonously, continuously in her head or the lyrics that fill random bar napkin after random bar napkin, the ones she can never read once she gets home as the sun is coming up to greet her and the drugs are wearing off and the throbbing in her chest is starting and her eyes are heavy. Her cell phone is ringing. Who the fuck is calling so early? Unless it's her drug dealer. He promised to meet her at the apartment, but she's late and can't remember what time she told him to arrive and doesn't know what time it is now or if there are keys in her bag or if there's anything in the refrigerator and wouldn't it be so nice, so very, very nice if someone, anyone, was waiting with a large spicy Bloody Mary. And a joint. She'd gladly offer up any of her platinum records for a big beautiful Mary and some weed. She deserves it. She worked hard. Sang several songs last night. Performed just as the contract stated. She did the tricks they requested and now she's tired. And thirsty. Who the hell are they to tell her what she can and can't have? She's a rock star. She's Unlimited Lou. She's special, even if no one's told her that in a long time. She can still party with the best of them. Her mother told her to leave her mark on this world and goddamn it, she has. She slept with Bowie once for Christ's sake. Was almost married to one of the Eagles. And if she wants a goddamn Bloody Mary, she should fucking have one.

Day 1: Waking

Lou's not exactly sure where she is except that she's not in her apartment on Elizabeth Street. She doesn't know the time or how she ended up here.

Last night is sort of hazy and she slightly remembers her publicist, Honor, going through her bags in another room. She packed bags though. She was brought here? *Yes. Yes she was.* By Trevor and Knox. She needs a drink. She needs a drink and some coffee and a cigarette and a shower. She needs all of this right now.

She lifts her pounding, heavy head off the pillow, feels a pull in her neck. A crack in her lower back. Her mouth is dry and her nose is stuffed and her eyes are having trouble focusing. The bed is soft and warm and someone has drawn the curtains. She flips on the lamp to the right of the bed, the bed with so many fluffy pillows. A sea of them. Lou could lie here all day.

The light is blinding to her and once dimmed, she can see a robe is folded over the chair, slippers are underneath it. The room is decorated in blond, tan, and beige wood and every sedate blah color you can imagine. She searches for a clock and finds it on the other side of her where another lamp resides. A matching pair. The only places that have matching lamps like this with rooms decorated in blah are rehab clinics and hotels.

She stands, which proves to be a mistake because the room is still spinning and causes her head to throb harder. She stumbles to the window and as she pulls back the curtains, which reveal a beautiful New York skyline, she remembers. *Ah, yes. The Four Seasons.* She was brought here by her publicist, Honor Kraus. Brought here to dry out, yet again.

She reaches for the open pack of Camel Lights, her hands shaking. Her breath is offensive, even to her, and her skin feels crispy. Crackly. She can't find any matches or her lighter and she has to pee and stumbles from the bedroom into another room, a living room. Her guitar, keyboard, and sketchbook are leaning up against the couch. A Discman, pile of CDs, packs and packs of gum, bags of Tootsie Pops, a carton of cigarettes, pens, colored pencils, and headphones are scattered on the coffee table. A week or two's worth of clothing is piled on the couch exactly where she left it several hours ago or maybe a day ago. Perhaps she's been asleep for a week. Wouldn't that be fantastic if she's slept through her entire detoxification?

She's still in her purple suede shirt and jeans and the room is eerily quiet and she vaguely remembers a nurse coming in to give her a sedative and take her pulse and check her blood pressure and maybe that's why her mouth is so dry. It could also be the gram of coke, the six drinks, the hit of X.

She does recall packing, Honor going through her bags, Morgan, the hotel manager, stopping by. There was a bottle of vodka, a party, a late-night thing, kissing a sexy drummer—and the rest, like many nights for Lou, is gone. Vanished, like her bottle of vodka, which she'd like right now and thus decides today is not a good day to detox.

She searches through her bag, takes hold of her wallet, and finds her credit cards are gone. Cash, gone. Bank card, gone. Only her driver's license, which expired five years ago, remains. Her cell phone is missing as well. She grabs her guitar where she's hidden extra cash inside, slips her hand into the hole, and nothing. That too has disappeared. Her keys, the gram of coke, the tab of X, the three or four joints, all gone. Fuck Honor. She's tricked her into coming here. Told Lou this is the best place, a relaxing place to help her do this.

She opens the refrigerator, her body already anticipating the lovely, stinging taste of vodka and when she doesn't hear the familiar clicking of mini bottles as the door swings open already knows they've been removed. Inside are plastic bottles of fruit juice, cans of energy drinks, containers of yogurt, bowl of chopped fruit, small boxes of cereal, and a thing of milk. She slams it shut. Reaches for the phone.

"Room service," she spits into the receiver. Her voice is hoarse and she reaches for a bottle of Evian that sits on top of the bar.

"Why don't you tell me what you'd like to order and I'll put the request through for you," a man with a chirpy yet monotone voice replies.

The water instantly lubricates her throat, but leaves her thirsty, unsatisfied. "I'd like a bottle of champagne and vodka sent to my room," she says, realizing she doesn't know her number.

"I'm sorry. I can complete a food request, but that's all."

Panic fills her chest like the smoke from a cigarette, which she has yet to light.

"Look, I know you sell bottles, I've ordered them before so why don't you just connect me to room service . . ."

"I'm sorry. We can't send that up for you. I can fill a food request." His voice is robotic and annoying.

"Why not?"

There's a pause. "My instructions say food only. I'm sorry."

She slams down the phone. Pounds her fist on the desk. She paces. She wants to leave. If she doesn't get something alcoholic into her system she'll lose her fucking mind. Think. Think. Think. And then she remembers, the hotel's bar, a lovely wet bar downstairs.

She finds a lighter, ignites the cigarette, and inhales. She feels her body start to calm down as she shoots a ream of smoke out of her mouth. She searches for a room key and when she can't find one figures she'll just go to the front desk for a replacement. She doesn't need her purse, her cigarettes, sunglasses, or shoes. She doesn't even bother to brush her teeth. She just needs to go.

Her hand is on the door, the lit Camel dangling from her

mouth, anticipation making her jittery when the knob doesn't turn.

She twists the knob again. Pulls. Then pulls harder as she realizes the door is locked from the other side. A scream comes out from her lips, an injured animal, almost inhuman. She kicks the door with her foot. Picks up the phone.

"Yes, how can I help you?" It's the same monotone voice from before.

"My door is locked."

Buzzing is heard on the other end.

"Did you fucking hear me?"

And then the door is opening and a woman dressed in white appears. An angel? She drops the phone as she lunges for the door except as she does something sharp stings her upper arm making her fall.

"How are we doing so far, Louise?" The voice feels far away even though the woman's face is right up against Lou's. And then a cloud passes over her eyes.

"Just take a deep breath with me," the voice says. Something cold is leaking into her arm. "I'm giving you an anti-nausea and a Demerol drip. I'll follow with a flush so you stay hydrated."

Lou thinks the only reason she didn't do heroin was thanks to her fear of needles.

A hand sweeps over her sweaty forehead. She doesn't want to be touched by this stranger, but at the same time it feels so nice. A blissful, hazy state creeps over her. She can't stand but the woman is making her, pulling at her arm. Then she's walking, falling into the soft couch. She thinks of lighting a large joint right before her eyes close.

Day 2: Staring

She wakes on the couch, dizzy and nauseous. Her tongue is stuck to the roof of her mouth. She's so thirsty. She needs a drink. Please God, let her have just one fucking drink.

She reaches for her fags, lights one, watches the smoke escape, pulls herself up, walks into the bedroom and over toward the window, which houses a long, padded leather seat. She tries to stand on it but has trouble. She pulls up a chair, steps on that first, then onto the seat. The window is huge and accommodates her entire five foot nine frame. She presses her body up against the glass. It vibrates in time with the drilling coming from the construction of the building next to the hotel. She looks down at the people passing by, the people in their offices with their day-to-day lives. She watches the demolition crews pushing barrels of chopped-up roof, granite, and cement. She notices how tall all the buildings are. That even at this height something is more than her. The cars whiz by, the people rush off somewhere, the wind whips the flags that hang above their pricey address. Smoke rises from rooftops, from skyscrapers. It all looks so small and large at the same time. She can no longer keep up with the fast pace of the city or the vastness of sky or the people below. Everything is moving on without her.

She misses Seattle. Misses her three-bedroom home where people dropped by with stuff. You'd put on a record, open a bottle of wine, and the next thing you'd know a phone call was made and a bag of coke-a-cha-cha was on the table. *Hey, how'd that get there? What do I have to do tomorrow? Hmmmm, nothing. I'll just take a hit of this, a line of that. . .*

She wasted so much time tooling around Seattle tweaked

and fucked up in a *Dukes of Hazzard* Malibu Chevelle 350 SS, a MadWheels muscle car. She was eighteen when she joined her first band, Me, Myself & Eye, with two other girls. Friends of friends whom she'd met at bars. She had no concept of what she was doing, but she put the guitar between her legs and guys went nuts. That lasted a year.

She was smarter and had learned a few things when she formed Zsa Zsa, named after Zsa Zsa Gabor. All the songs she and her bandmate wrote were about the three Gabor sisters: Zsa Zsa, Magda, and Eva. She smiles, remembering how they would sing with faux Hungarian accents.

If you had a basement, you could have a band. If you had a van, you could be on tour. If you could be on tour, you could make money. Parlay one single into an entire album and get noticed.

Her breathing is fast, her chest hurts, her eyes sting, and if she could only have a hit of something, a little coke, half a line. Why can't they just give her that? Maybe she needs to taper off rather than go cold turkey.

Lou rests her head against the pane. She hears the thud she makes when it hits the glass, which feels cold against her forehead, on her hands. She smacks her head again. Harder. Then again. It stops the throbbing in her temples, stops the ringing in her ears, and replaces it with a sharp pain. One more time for luck. Still nothing. The glass isn't going to break.

She steps down, stumbles back, and falls onto the carpet. The last things she sees are the greasy imprints her hands and forehead have left on the glass. Just another useless mark Lou has made on the world.

Days 3-5: Sleeping, Crying, Jonesing

She itches harshly at the tattoo on her wrist, convinced it's filled with poisonous ink leaking into her skin. The bug sensation paired with the nausea is coming back. She thinks if she were to vomit, which is what she's been doing for the past forty-eight hours, that's what she'd cough up: bugs and roaches and ants and God knows what else that's been living inside her.

Where the hell is the nurse? Why hasn't she come back? She could be dead at this point. Doesn't anyone care?

The vision in her left eye is gone as is her hearing. There's just a buzzing and a rush of blood in her head. Her nose feels raw inside; mucus has been dripping down her throat all day. And she can't stop sweating and scratching, like her skin is on fire.

She's lying on the floor in the bedroom dressed in a T-shirt and underwear that's at least three days old. By her side is her Discman, a trash can filled with puke, an overflowing ashtray, cans and cans of half-drunk Diet Coke and ginger ale. She might have slept in this position but isn't sure. The carpet is too coarse, her skin too irritated, red, and prickly. She pulls off her clothing and decides to lie on the floor in the bathroom instead. She can't get up so she crawls there, dragging her body like someone paralyzed from the waist down.

The bathroom is white and clean. Marble is her friend, cold and hard. No bugs in here. She pushes the fluffy bath mat away and lays down naked on the floor. The cold numbs her skin. She looks up at the ceiling.

She thinks about a bottle of vodka, chilled from the freezer. The unscrewing of the top, the almost sweet sound the vodka makes when it's poured over ice in a frosted glass. She smiles, lulled by the idea of the first sip, the second, the third. How a drink gets better and better as the night disappears and bleeds into darkness. She misses the bitterness on her lips, the stinging on her tongue, the warmth it creates inside her. But mostly she misses the obliteration. The memories it quells, the ones it erases, and the new ones it creates. And the coke. God how she misses the sound cutting coke makes—be it a credit card or MetroCard or business card—mini tap shoes on glass tables, or computer tops, or the backs of guitars.

She loves the way pot fills the cavity of her insides, the peaceful fluffiness valium induces, the caffeine up-all-night jitters speed brings, the out-of-body experience 'shrooms create. She adores them like old lovers who took up space in her bed. They keep her company, she tells her secrets to them, and they make promises, so many promises. And they keep most of them, unlike the people in her life, unlike her parents, or her one-night stands or her friends, or jealous bandmates. They never leave her and are only a phone call away.

The buzzing is replaced by ringing, the sight comes back, and the sweating has stopped. Now her teeth are chattering and her body is shaking and she's not sure, but she thinks she's seeing her skull dancing above her. This is the first stage of lunacy. She's becoming part of the floor.

The last time she was in this position, looking up at the ceiling, was when she'd taken Special K, mistaking it accidentally for coke. But while she was staring at her dancing skull, she got the idea for her ashtray art and her T-shirt designs, her possible new business. *See*, she thinks, *something good can come from almost OD'ing. See, drugs aren't so bad.*

When the shaking is too much, her teeth chattering so loudly in her head that it makes her dizzy, that her jaw is throbbing and her bones are so cold they hurt, she sits on the floor of the swirly marble shower staring at the patches of brown and tan and white as the hot water streams over her. The small space feels confined but safe. She wonders if she can boil the bugs off of her. If only she could wash herself away she'd erase the past two decades. She'd go back to a time when she was happy, though she can't remember when that was. She only has patches of happiness, like the dark marble of the bathroom. She wants to phone her parents but doesn't know their numbers. Or talk to her kid brother but wonders if he'd accept her call.

By the midseventies Lou was in her early teens, Sony had introduced the Walkman, Nixon was asked to resign, the Watergate tapes were still a mystery, and Elvis had OD'd. *Grease* and *Saturday Night Fever* were musical movie sensations, her parents' marriage had fallen apart, and she had developed a passion for punk rock, fashion, and anything alcoholic.

As her family dispersed, as her brother became more distant, as her father seemed to be away on business trips for longer stretches of time, as her mother grew increasingly flirtatious, Lou formed her own family, a handful of musical gods—the Kinks, Blondie, Johnny Thunders, Bowie, who years later she opened for onstage.

During this time, a string of men appeared in her mother's bed. At night she'd stand over these strangers, listening to their hard, deep snores, their erratic breathing. She'd toss aside their dirty underwear, rummage through their trousers or jeans or shorts, take money from their billfolds, pinch a few smokes from their packets of Marlboros, look at the photos in their wallets, drain what was left of their unfinished drinks.

It was in the eighties when she sold her bike for a used guitar, sold herself for whatever she could, and at eighteen, left home to live with friends of friends in Seattle. Diana got married, the space shuttle *Challenger* exploded, Nancy said no, so Lou said yes to everything.

Day 6: Attempting

She stares at her bloated, blotchy face in the bathroom mirror. She's ugly. Old and weathered. When did she become so hard looking? She hates her brows, her lips are too big, her makeup is smeared. She's used up, broken down. A racehorse ready for retirement with one last lap to do around the track. Her hair is dry and if she's going to start over, really start over, why not shave it all off. She's done it before when, after coming off a crystal meth bender, she was convinced she had body lice. She ran around her apartment with a garbage bag tied around her hairless skull. The Lysol she'd sprayed, like self-tanner, dripped off her body.

The nurse has not returned. Housekeeping hasn't come. The room is dirty and smells of vomit and sweat. Honor isn't answering her phone. Even Morgan hasn't visited. What the fuck, why bother?

Rather than shave her head, sliding a razor over her wrists would be much easier. A clean cut. A simple stroke, like fingers over guitar strings.

If she could, she'd throw something at her reflection, but Honor has systematically removed the soap dishes along with anything breakable or sharp edged from the room. The drinking glasses have been replaced with large plastic cups, the kind you'd have gotten at a frat party. Even the glass tops to the tables have been taken away.

And then she sees it.

The remote control belonging to the flat-screen TV in the bathroom.

Flinging that against the beautiful mirrored wall in the beautifully, perfectly marbled bathroom will surely break the glass, and Lou is desperate to get something out of her system. And then it's in her hand, and then it's hurling in the air and into the glass cracking it on impact.

Shattered, Lou thinks she looks decent. Pretty even. The jagged pieces make her appear broken and whole at the same time. Unfortunately, not one shard is removable. It's as if the entire mirror is held together by superglue. The seven years of bad luck doesn't faze her. Her life sucks already, what's another seven.

Hours later—a nap, eight cigarettes, four Tootsie lollipops, three cups of coffee—she sits down and tries to write a song on the Four Seasons' stationery, like in the old days, but the paper is too pretty. She switches to the cocktail napkins she finds by the ice bucket. They feel good in her hand and remind her of the times when she would write long into the wee hours of the night creating brilliant music high on coke and speed alongside Johnny and Blondie and Iggy and a slew of others. But the lyrics don't come as easily as they used to. They aren't as authentic. All music executives are two-beer queers these days anyway.

Her head won't stop with the words and the music and the songs and the ants and the bugs and the names and the liquor, if she could just have one drink. One drink to calm down. One lousy fucking drink. What's wrong with that? And if the drug programs didn't work what the hell makes Honor think this will, and who the fuck is Honor anyway to put her here? She didn't ask for this. She wouldn't be doing this if she didn't think she could make a quick buck off Lou. She doesn't love Lou. She's in it for the money. Everyone is in it for the money. They don't know how hard it is to reinvent yourself. How hard it is to write a song. How hard it's gotten for *her* to write a song. The instruments feel weird in her hands. Her fingers aren't calloused the way they used to be. She's fat and out of shape. The cigarettes make her cough and her teeth are yellow and her hair is dry and falling out and her nails are brittle; the bed's turning a pretty color of light purple. She wheezes and she knows that it's becoming increasingly harder and harder to get to that happy, stoned place. It takes too many drinks to keep her drunk. And deep down she knows this is her last stop. Honor is all she has left and if she can't get through this, she'll be just another faceless rock star who's OD'd and how fucking boring is that?

The napkin is still in her hand. She writes "Fuck You!" in big childlike scribble.

Days 7–10: Shaking. Pacing. Choking. Dying. Itching. Scratching. Smoking. Chewing. Bathing. Breathing. Breaking. Waiting. Waiting. Waiting . . .

———

Day 11: Fixing

Lou is on the couch, jaw sore from grinding her teeth and chewing gum, strumming her Gibson when Honor arrives decked out in Chanel, dripping of perfume and makeup. Her semicropped, eggplant-colored hair brings a rosy glow to her skin. Her lips are full and colored a pale reddish brown. She wears a beautiful tiny-flower-print dress with a black fur collar. She's so pretty, Lou thinks. So put together, a look Lou, no matter how hard she's tried, has never mastered. She watches Honor inspect the room. Picks through the cigarette butts in the ashtray, smells the residue in the plastic cups, sifts through the garbage.

"You're looking better," Honor says, her eyes scanning the open sketchbook.

"No, I'm not."

She sighs. "Have you showered?"

"Not really."

"No matter. Brush your teeth and let's go." She looks at her watch. "You'll feel better after you've had your hair cut and nails done." She stamps out her half-done cigarette. "Louise. Come on."

Honor picks up the phone, her ring clanks against the receiver. "Yes, I'm bringing Mrs. Sands downstairs for her spa treatments. Could you please send housekeeping up immediately so that the room is fresh upon our return. Thank you."

"Who's Mrs. Sands?" she asks, stripping off her sweat pants and Grace Jones tour of '83 T-shirt, throwing on a pair of jeans and velvet shirt in its place.

Honor shrugs. "My maiden name."

She met Honor one night at a bar in New York after she'd

been kicked out of her last band and forced to go solo. Lou wooed her with her funny stories, lulled her into seeing her talent, tricked her into loving her. She was the rocker, Honor the power player. Beauty and the beast. Ten years her senior, Honor was classy, worldly, striking. A warm body, a full wallet, a sharp bite, and a smart mind. The list of important people she knew was endless.

It was Honor who got her an agent. Honor who kicked her ass into gear. Honor who cleaned her up, let her sleep in her guest room when Lou was out of money, out of a home, and out of drugs.

Lou takes a deep breath once they've left the room, another once they enter the elevator, a third upon exiting. The spa smells of fruity shampoo and the lights are bright and the greeting from the staff too cheery. The beige theme permeates the entire hotel, even in here.

She and Honor take seats at the pedicure station. Within minutes a woman is at Lou's feet, another at her fingers. She hasn't shaved her legs for almost two weeks, having a woman do it for her feels luxuriously weird.

Honor places a hand on top of Lou's and pats it three times, winks, and then returns to leafing through *Vogue*. "See, you're doing it."

Lou is about to say something when she sees Morgan appear. Or she thinks it's Morgan. The person standing in front of her is pale and drawn. Painfully thin. Deep circles reside under her eyes and the crisp, healthy person she knew seems to have vanished. Lou turns to Honor for clarification. Perhaps on drugs, everyone looks prettier than they actually are.

"I just wanted to check on you," Morgan says. Her hands grasp a jumbo-size Starbucks cup. Smoke is emanating off of her making Lou ache for a cigarette. "You look great. How are you feeling?"

"Good. I guess. I'm still here."

"We wouldn't have it any other way," Honor says, interjecting.

"Great. That's just great. I'm so pleased. When you're up to it, how about lunch in your room? Or if you prefer, we could do a reenactment of our first lunch in the restaurant."

Lou watches Morgan's gaze switch from hers to Honor's.

"Sure. This is our fist day out, so we're just taking it slow. But I think lunch would be fine. Lou?"

"Ah, you remembered I was here, too. Excellent. Now that's real progress ladies."

She watches Morgan's face drop a little, as if she's disappointed her, which makes Lou want to cry. Her hands are soaking in warm soapy water, and her heels are being rubbed raw, and all she wants to do is get high and go home.

An hour later Lou has moved to the salon part of the spa. Honor and the stylist are standing over her talking.

"Could I get a Coke?" she says, her voice raw. "The liquid kind, not the powder." She watches Honor in the mirror, who lifts an eyebrow and smirks.

"Of course," says the stylist, who isn't in on the joke, but smiles as if she were.

A Coke arrives in a clear tall glass with just the right amount of ice cubes and it tastes so good going down Lou's throat that she almost chokes in her rush to devour it. Immediately, she wants another.

Honor sips her espresso while Lou chews on the ice as inches of dry, dead-looking hair fall in clumps to the floor.

"When was the last time you had a cut?" The stylist asks, judgment gone from her voice.

"A year?"

"Well, we'll get this looking a whole lot better."

The salon part of the spa is full, busy with the buzz of divorced women each trying to fix themselves. Everyone is too self-involved to notice Lou slip the stylist's extra scissor into the sleeve of her sweater. The metal feels cool on her skin and to make sure the end is sharp enough, she presses the tip against the edge of the padded black chair and her wrist. The pain sends a throb to her temples and she smiles, thinking at least there's always a way out.

Lou feels lead by Honor as they stroll up Lexington Avenue. All that's missing is a leash, the kind out-of-town women strap onto children they fear will be snatched up or wander off. Lou could be either. Someone passes by who looks like her dealer. What she wouldn't give for a beer.

Since it's Saturday, the avenue is a mess of people. Each looks juiced up on something as they rush down the street, arms filled with shopping bags. Where's the difference between the Botoxed, diet-pill-popping, coffee-drinking addicts and her? What's the distinction between the painfully thin women rushing around Bloomingdale's and Saks and Bergdorf's with their hands extended, new purchases in one, their credit cards in the other?

When the two enter Lou's hotel room, everything is perfect once again and the room has that freshly vacuumed smell.

Housekeeping has erased any trace of her. The puke-stained trash can, the overflowing ashtrays, the empty soda cans, the wet towels, the stained robe.

Her CDs are in a neat stack, her guitar is leaning up against the wall, the candy and gum and other food-related paraphernalia resides by the bar, the sketchbook is on the table, the "Fuck You!" napkin is gone. Her clothing has disappeared and upon looking in the drawers in the bedroom—the room that now has fresh sheets and new pillowcases—her clothes are neatly folded. It's as if Lou never existed.

She enters the bathroom and her reflection startles her. The person staring back is almost unrecognizable. Her hair is smooth and silky. Three inches shorter, the long layers just touch her shoulders, and it's the first time in four or five years that it's all one color. A real color. Deep brown. Not something purply or reddish or fake. Her nails are clean and perfect and the burgundy color matches her toes. Her brows arch perfectly. Her skin is dewy and blemish-free. Her legs are soft and silky, like her hair. And if she can just hold onto this . . . It's then that she remembers the cracked the mirror. The one she broke, but this one has been fixed. How can they do that so fast? It's like some bizarre *Twilight Zone* episode, so Lou can't tell if she dreamed it or actually broke the mirror. What is real, however, is the pair of scissors, which she quickly slips out from her sleeve and sticks in between two perfectly fresh and fluffy towels.

She pees quickly and flushes, opens the door, and finds Honor standing in front of her.

"I wasn't doing anything."

Honor places a hand on either side of Lou's shoulders, and

at first Lou thinks Honor is going to lean in and kiss her, like in the old days, like when they were both doing X, and Lou is about to pucker up when Honor brings her body into Lou's and tightly embraces her.

"Please, I'm begging you. I don't know what else to do." Honor's breath is hot and perfumey and her grasp is so strong it pushes air out of Lou's lungs. "Please stay clean."

She thinks how good it feels to have Honor here, to have her in this position, being held and momentarily loved. As Lou brings her hands up to return the embrace, she feels Honor release her hold, feels Honor's body start to move away.

"I'll try to come back tomorrow. And if not Sunday, then Monday around fiveish."

No. Lou needs Honor. She needs something.

"I thought we could watch TV?"

"I'd love to, but I've a dinner date and some errands to run beforehand."

"How about a game of cards?"

Honor is moving out of the bathroom hallway and into the living room. Is already extracting a Parliament from her Hermes bag and is casing the room for a lighter or book of matches.

"Come on, one hand of gin," Lou insists.

Honor is still eyeing the room, the cigarette dangling from her lips.

"I'll show you my sketches."

"I can't, Louise."

Lou almost stomps her foot. "Why not?"

"Must you be entertained every second of the day?"

"Is spending a little time with me too much to ask for?"

Lou goes to the fridge but remembers there's nothing of value in there.

"I just spent seven hours with you," Honor states. Frustrated, she sets her bag down on the table and searches for a lighter.

"So? What's another two?"

"Let's not do this. We've had a nice day."

"Who are you having dinner with?"

Honor sighs, takes her coat, and drapes it over her arm.

"See you Monday." She leans in to brush Lou's cheek, but Lou moves away.

"You said Sunday."

"I said I would try for Sunday."

Lou grabs onto her sleeve. "Come on, can't you cancel whoever you're dining with?"

"I can't. It's a new client." The cigarette has yet to be lit, and Honor is holding it now between her fingers, frustrated.

"I thought you weren't taking on new people."

"I wasn't. I'm not, really, but this fell into my lap, and it could be very profitable."

"So you lied?"

"I didn't lie about anything. I didn't expect to . . ." She stops, throws her hands into the air. "Why am I explaining myself? Do you know how much this little stay is costing me?"

"No one asked you to pay for it."

"Well you certainly couldn't have. It's not like the old days when we had money to burn." She takes a deep breath. "There's no need to feel threatened. You're not being replaced."

"How old is she?"

"What does it matter?"

"How old?"

"She's twenty. She's young and talented, and she actually reminds me a little bit of you. But most of all she's a hard worker and as far as I can tell . . ."

"What? Won't shove a quarter of a million dollars up her nose? Won't cause you the trouble I do?"

"Yes. Yes to everything." Honor is yelling now. "Happy?"

"Is she your new project? Is that why you can't meet me tomorrow for brunch?"

Honor's face freezes. Lou watches pity wash over her eyes.

"See you Monday," Honor says through pressed lips.

"Don't go like this. I'm sorry."

Honor is silent. She reaches for her bag, but Lou arrives at it first and holds it way from her grasp.

"I get jealous. You know I get jealous."

"Give me my purse."

Lou is smirking, batting her eyes playfully.

"I'm not kidding. I'm late and I need to go."

Lou doesn't move.

"I need to go!" Honor's voice is loud and harsh. She grabs her bag and is gone seconds later. Only the lingering scent of Chanel perfume remains.

Loneliness fills the cavity of Lou's chest so quickly, so harshly that it knocks her to the ground. Tears bleed from her eyes. She needs to fill the space. She reaches for a Camel Light, finds the lighter in her pocket, and after taking several drags knows it's not enough. She calls downstairs and in a *Groundhog Day* experience has the exact conversation with the monotone voice about putting through a food order when vodka is her request. She begs the voice, sounding like Honor begging Lou to say clean.

"Please, I'm fucking begging you. Just send up one shot. One shot glass filled with whatever you want, okay? You decide."

"I'm sorry. I can't."

He won't be the only one sorry, she thinks, slamming down the receiver.

She walks into the bathroom and extracts the scissors from their hiding place.

What does it matter if you're sober if no one's there to see it? If, at the end of the day, it's still just you, looking at a prettier version of yourself in a five-star hotel mirror.

She strips down naked and waits for the tub to fill with hot water before getting in. The tub is deep and roomy. The scissors are long and sharp. The metal is cool in her grip and she wonders if it will be hard to get the blood off. If Honor will be mad. If this was the mark her mother meant when she told Lou to leave her thumbprint on the world.

At forty-four she's already missed the Jesus years, which is fine because Cass, Joplin, Hendrix, Smith, Morrison, and that Nirvana guy all died too young anyway. Everyone would say they saw it coming. It's right there in her music, in her words that fans are always quoting back to her—or telling her how her songs changed their lives. And she's happy for that. That's what keeps her going. That and the blow. And the speed. And the coffee and the cigarettes and the liquor.

If she were to die now it would be fine. She's lived enough for two people, twenty-eight tours, seven records. Past punk rock, disco, grunge, folk, Dylan's "Tambourine Man."

She can already see her funeral. Hipster bands like the New Pornographers, Franz Ferdinand, and Belle & Sebastian would sing odes to her. Her old bandmates from Horse House, Zsa Zsa, and Me, Myself & Eye coming together once more, performing a rock chronology of tunes that made her popular. She envisions a benefit CD being released. People she doesn't like making money off of her death. The cultural professors would dissect the lyrics, blogsters would speculate what really happened—a conspiracy? Blame the Scientologists for her untimely passing. But in the end, she'd be reduced to nothing more than an hour special on E! or VH1. A cover story for *People* magazine. A rockology for *Rolling Stone*.

She's so tired. Her body aches, like she has the flu. And she's got chills that still won't leave her. The perfectly white ceiling however is skull-less. The room isn't spinning. Her breathing is deep and even. Her eyes feel heavy.

When she wakes, it's to the sound of vacuuming and knocking on her door.

Housekeeping.

It's another day. Another fucking day and Lou has been clean for the past twelve of them.

She's back to freezing, teeth chattering. In the middle of the night the water turned cold and Lou got out of the tub, wrapped herself in towels and robes and slept on the floor. She stands now, dizzy. Hungry nausea passes over her as she catches her reflection in the mirror. Her hair is still styled, though somewhat messy. Her eyeliner is smeared, but in a sexy way. She wets her hands, runs them through her hair. Puts her mouth under the sink, drinks, swishes the last bit, and spits it out. She applies some lipstick, retrieves her guitar, sunglasses, and a cigarette from the other room. She cracks open one of her own CDs, slips in her greatest hits on the stereo, and lets the music fill the empty space.

Returning to the bathroom, she stands on the edge of the tub. Pretending she's back in Seattle, performing in front of a crowd of screaming fans, she strikes a rock pose. She resurrects the smell of cheap beer and sweat as she squints, making the metal lights sparkle. She contorts her face, flashes her signature expression: lips puckered, twisted off to the right, mock surprise on her face.

She's still sexy. Old, tired, and clean, but sexy.

She walks from the bathroom and into the bedroom, toward the window. The knocking has stopped. Housekeeping will come back later. She tries to stand on the padded cushion like she did the second day she was here, but her body is too exhausted, her muscles too sore. Every time she tries to pull herself up, she falls.

It's only after her fifth attempt that she notices her fingerprints are gone. The smudges her greasy head and hands made almost two weeks ago have been erased.

She wants them back. Wants to place herself over something familiar. Something that was hers. But she can't. She's clean now. Like the room. Like the window.

And like the workman on the building across from the hotel, the ones who continue to haul barrel after barrel of debris and broken bricks in the hope of fixing the roof, she too needs to start over.

The guitar is cold and yet feels like a second skin up against her bare chest. Rather than letting it cover her naked front, she swings it onto her back and tries once more to pull herself onto the sill. It takes more effort than she'd like, but on the forth hop off her left foot and with the right one on the padded seat, she is finally triumphant.

She knocks on the window, hoping the men will hear, which of course they don't. Can't. But she stands there until they see her and her crotch and her breasts, which are pushed up against the glass.

She stands there until they point, wave, and make crude gestures.

She places her lips on the pane and ever so carefully, sexily, sweetly, kisses the glass.

When she steps down a bright burgundy pair of perfectly placed puckered lips are staring back at her. And once again, she's left her mark.

Chapter 17

Morgan
The Restaurant

It's the end of December when I acknowledge something is seriously wrong with me. I can feel it. Sharp and biting. I keep finding myself purposely leaning up against others in the subway, letting my body touch theirs, swaying to and fro with the fast movement of the train. I brush up against them. The warmth of their skin, the strong feel of their muscles makes me feel momentarily better, until I step out of the train. Then the emptiness returns, a kind of hollowness as if I haven't eaten all day.

My clothing is too big on me. My hair is limp and flat and I notice in the shower and at night when I brush it that more and more strands fall out. I look skeletal and am constantly cold.

Even my mother's face was one of deep concern the other day when she stopped by the hotel with her bridge group. I'm tired all the time, there are dark circles under my eyes, and when I look in the mirror I see traces of my sister. I stand looking at myself now in the full-length mirror in room 407.

I hate this room. It's small and because it resides over the kitchen, it smells of something fried. Even I have to admit I look terrible. But the more I stare at my reflection, the more I see traces of Dale, and I smile because it's the only time I feel connected to someone and for a moment all is calm and something inside me rests.

This is my third search today. Though the hotel is completely overbooked because of the holidays, hardly anyone is in their room. Rather they're racing about the city: tourists trying to grab a piece of the Big Apple while Manhattan-bound New Yorkers are hoping for a last bit of holiday cheer. Everyone seems to have somewhere to be: a party to attend, a romantic dinner to eat, a relative or old friend to visit, a tree to hang an ornament on.

I shut the closet door and scan the room, making sure I've left it as it was fifteen minutes earlier. The two Flexeril pills I took from Mrs. J. Beere have started to take their relaxing effect. The room is cloudy and my eyes feel heavy.

I exit, make it to the first floor, and find myself a comfy seat in the lobby. Too sedated to move, I sit like a rag doll slumped into one of our leather-bound chairs and watch people move blissfully in and out of the hotel.

Four days later the large clock on our flat screen blinks 11:47 in neon as our guests stare at it, each waiting for the ball to descend over the drunken and uncomfortably squished crowd that presides over Times Square. Dick Clark and Ryan Seacrest are making uninteresting banter as they try to create false excitement for the midnight hour. Snow is falling. The people outside are wearing colorful, silly themed hats, shaking rattles, blowing paper noisemakers into the ears of the unlucky people standing next to them.

The bars inside the hotel aren't much different. Though the group is clearly more upscale, they too don the hats and hold the holiday paraphernalia. In the restaurant part, it's an entirely different scene. The women wear evening gowns. The men are in tuxes. Toasts are being made, champagne filled flutes are lifted, music that's upbeat but not too loud is being piped throughout the lobby. Every person here knows that tonight, at this moment, they're part of an exclusive club—just one of the promises we make. A silent deal is understood when a guest purchases a room for the night or makes a reservation.

The dinner is a five-course prix fixe that costs $450 per plate. In this room the necklaces and rings shine and glisten like the ball that's due to drop any moment. Our other two dining areas, the Thai Lounge and the Garden are also packed with paying people. For many, this is the perfect way to say good-bye to Father Time and hello to Baby New Year. Past and present, old friends and ex-lovers meet for a second at the magical moment when both hands collide on the clock.

I watch waiters remove half-eaten or picked-at plates of duck confit knowing that earlier lobster risotto and mushrooms, baby lamb loin wrapped in a mint chickpea crepe had been ingested. The last course is just being set down: *fromage* and raspberry-infused chocolate soufflé. Fresh fruit and special fortune cookies wishing everyone a Happy New Year are set in the middle of the table.

In the past three weeks Lou has been resurrected, perhaps not her career, but her body is clean and momentarily drug-free. Bernard, I've been told—accidentally by a friend we have in common who thought I knew—is dating someone. My parents are on the first vacation they've taken in over fifteen years, which means they will be flying over the Western Hemisphere when I turn thirty-three next week. My calendar is relatively blank for the month of January with the exception of Trish's gallery opening, which, ironically, falls on the date that Bernard and I were supposed to have moved in together.

Like a reenactment from a month and a half ago I head into the restaurant, smiling warmly at the filled tables. I nod, greet a few guests, ask how their evening is or if they've enough champagne. I then push through the swinging doors that open into the kitchen, which is a mess of plates and food and trash. I mentally greet the moist heat, welcome the familiar banging of the pots, clanking of plates and glassware, nod an inconspicuous hello to the steam from the scorching water and the wet heat from the dishwashers. Our new chef winks as I pass by him. My eyes adjust quickly this time to the light, my body almost instinctively understands how to move to the culinary dance the kitchen is doing.

It only takes a few seconds to find Renaldo. And I'm so relieved, so very relieved to see him standing by the sink area, his white apron on, a black basin in his hands. He is cute and young and still exudes the innocence that drew me to him. He smiles knowingly, almost seems happy to see me.

I slide up to him, whisper into his ear that I need help reaching a jar of jam kept in the dry pantry. Would he lift it down? At this his smile widens. He rests the heavy plastic basin on the counter, then willingly follows me, as if we are old friends, which, by now, we are.

This time there is no flipping on the light, just the dimming of it, and the sealing of the door behind me. This time nothing is hurried. There's no tearing at buttons or the abrupt lifting of shirts over one's head. No pulling at the strings of an apron, no look of confusion or the waiting for understanding to register on one's face. There is, however, the gentle cupping of breasts. Of Renaldo's hands on my ass. Of my fingers running up and down his smooth back. Of his salty-tasting tongue in my mouth. And the comfort of his familiar yet unique smell: olive oil and sweat and a hint of Old Spice. I close my eyes and breathe as if I'm wearing the brace, easily and deeply. He lifts me up onto the elongated cutting board. I have no belt, no pants that need to be unbuttoned since I'm in a black sequined dress. Special for the holiday. I run my hands under his shirt and remember how good he felt up against me. How good he feels now. How much I want to be held and touched. Bernard disappears and Trish, my mother, Lou and Honor, Vicki, Anne, even Dale momentarily say good-bye. It is just me and Renaldo. I undo his belt, undo his pants, push them down, hear them drop to the floor, feel the elastic band of his boxers. And then he's inside me. Our bodies are moving back and forth, slowly. Easily. *Yes*, I think. *Keep going*, I mentally encourage him. I grasp his face, hold his chin, feel for his cheeks and lips to see if he is smiling. He twists his face to the left and kisses my hand on the palm side, just like before. He is so gentle, so kind. All fear is gone. I don't care if I get caught. I don't care if I get fired.

My mantra is different this time, too. *I will be happy. I will get better*, I say under my breath. *I swear to God I will*. He pauses for a moment, tightens his grasp and brings me close to his body. He kisses my cheeks. I know he notices the wetness. I know he can feel my chest heaving up and down, feel me shaking. He tries kissing away the tears. I feel his tongue at my cheek as it rides up my face, as if licking away the salty sadness. He holds me like this, my arms wrapped around his neck, my legs wrapped around his waist, my dress riding up on my ass, my thong on the dirty floor.

For a moment we hear the distant muffled hooting and shouting emanating from our tipsy guests. The sounds of the bustling kitchen, of clapping and hollering coming from outside.

Renaldo rocks me, whispers in Spanish, and I imagine he's sharing the story of his life, or that he's telling me not to cry, or maybe he's wishing me a happy fucking New Year, it doesn't matter. His smell and voice and soft yet firm body up against mine is like a healing balm. It's all I need.

When we exit the pantry I walk past the kitchen staff, who are so busy they don't notice me or that I've tossed my underwear into the trash. And by the time I'm back in the restaurant nodding once again to guests, and smiling like a sly fox, it's already a New Year.

Caterers in crisp white shirts and black pants pass out mini hors d'oeuvres. A bar has been set up by the entrance, which is already being visited by guests. A DJ is spinning electronica remixes of Billie Holiday and Sarah Vaughan off to the side at the reception desk. Trish's gallery is filled with artists, hipsters, and Upper East Siders who mingle with fans anxious to see her famous parents and those who want to meet the artists.

Heads are nodding, people are laughing, their hands holding wineglasses or bits of food on small black plates as they look at the purposefully placed artwork, each aligned perfectly on the white walls.

This is the first post–New Year's event I've been to. It was part of my resolutions/goal list: Meet more people. Get a full physical, put on more weight, cut back on coffee, stop drinking Red Bull, quit smoking—had a cigarette on the way over so I'm still working through that one—become more artistic and educated, and try to put my life together were part of the top ten. I've not spoken to Trish since my uncle died, so I'm feeling a little disconnected from her.

As the invitation promised, three artists are being show-cased at her opening. Their bios and project summaries hang on Styrofoam signs. Price sheets are available by the DJ.

Trish looks elegant in her black dress with silver outlining the edges. Her hair is swooped up and held together with a large silver clasp. She flutters through the space greeting each guest, handshaking and grinning, looking as if she's running for office.

"I'm glad you came," she says, hugging me warmly, quickly. I want to stay in the embrace a moment longer, let my body register what it feels like to he held and I remember why I like her. How sisterly and familiar she looks, even smells.

"Wouldn't miss it," I say, choking back a tear. And I make a note to add "Build stronger relationship with Trish" to my goal list.

A woman asks if she can take my coat while another offers me champagne, wine, and sparkling water.

"You've done a terrific job. The place is amazing." I say as we both reach for a glass of wine.

"Thanks." Her attention is fleeting as she waves to someone over by the bar. "Do you want me to introduce you around or roam on your own?"

"I'll take an introduction."

I follow Trish through the swarm of people, catching bits of dialogue here and there as the music fills the airy, spacious room. Loneliness washes over me as I look at the other guests, all of whom seem to be here with someone. "Is your friend Olive coming?"

"She'll be here later."

I nod. "And your folks?"

"They're being interviewed in the corner." She points to a trendy couple talking to a man scribbling feverishly in a small notebook."

"Hang here for a moment, okay? I'll be right back," she promises, slipping away behind one of the freestanding walls and leaving me to check out the work on my own.

Displayed on the first wall off to my right are black-and-white photos of mannequins—some are dressed, others are naked. Each is faceless and arranged in an array of positions. Some are of tan, faceless busts who sport wigs. Pieces of masking tape with someone's name written on it with a Sharpie are placed over the mouth area.

The second artist has done a collection of people impersonating celebrities, though men are dressed as women, women portray men. Here, a black Britney is masculine and thick. A girly Bill Clinton smiles shyly at the camera, a bunch of wilted daisies in her hand.

The third artist commandeers the most space, consuming the two half walls that have been built specifically for the showcasing of work.

In one of the pieces, a screaming woman's face is in the center of the canvas. A ring, money, a miniature groom, a house made of Legos, all of which have been attached to the painting, surround her. "I want" is spelled out using pennies. I think of Bernard, that today would have found me moving in with him. That we would be leading the life most New Yorkers want: a rent-controlled apartment on the Upper West Side, both of us working at good jobs, weekends spent reading the *Times* in bed or at the kitchen table followed by brunch with other happy New York couples. I think about all the things I want for this year and wonder how I can possibly achieve them.

Another collage is of two boys, perhaps brothers, who are facing one another. Medals from high school sporting events have been placed around their faces along with badges from camp or Boy Scouts, college acceptance letters from Yale and Harvard, a report card or two, and CPR certificates. Underneath, the words "Mother's Favorite?" have been spelled out using stickers in the shape of newborns.

I finish my glass of wine and trade it for a fresh one when I see the caterer pass by. Goals are easier to achieve drunk. While waiting for Trish to return, I read the artist's bio: Gage Paulson uses objects he's found on the street, oil paint, and photographs he's taken along with other material to create disturbing, yet character-like versions of people while making statements on society.

I twist around and find Trish and a broad man dressed in jeans, a T-shirt, and leather jacket standing behind me.

"What do you think?" he says. His face is leathery, like Lou's, and I think perhaps I should have called and invited her to this. Or Anne. She's been on my list of people to reconnect with as well. His hair is thick and wavy. He's got a few days' worth of stubble and he seems to take up a tremendous amount of space.

"Morgan, this is Gage, the artist."

When we shake hands, his grip is forceful and tight. His eyes are dark and there's an inner nastiness about him that penetrates through his artistic persona. He smells of arrogance and narcissism.

"Your work is really dimensional," I say.

"Most people find it disturbing."

"Sure, it's disturbing too."

His smile widens. I glance at Trish, who rolls her eyes.

"I'm going to keep lapping," she says. "Pontificate amongst yourselves."

"So,"—I continue, draining my glass, annoyed that Trish would leave me with him—"how long does it take to complete one of these?"

"A few months. I work on several at a time. The hardest part is finding the right concept, followed by the exact objects that depict the person or situation."

He points to the photo closest to the window. "This one's my favorite."

I step up a notch to champagne, switching glassware once more, as I give my attention to painting number three.

The piece is of a woman screaming. Ghoulish and ghastly, her face is twisted, her dull eyes are exaggerated, her mouth is open, and it looks as if she's screaming. A Sweet'N Low packet and straw, personal e-mail ads, and a bottle top from a beer are stuck to a painted canvas. The leprechaun from the Lucky Charms cereal box and the letters from the word "lucky" cut up in pieces have been glued and the words "A charmed life" are written in green. Pennies and horseshoes and other superstitious items are stuck to the painting as well. And then I see it. Anne's bracelet. The one she feels naked without, the one she lost. I look at Gage. He's smirking, eyes squinty. Then I glance back at the photo, see the words "Anne's Achilles' heel" written underneath. I'm flushed with confusion. My mind races as I try connecting how he knows her. I reel back to the concierges' meeting with Julia, Cecile, and Anne when she told us about the Internet guy. I think about how devastated she was at the loss. Anger seeps through my thick disorientation. Doesn't he know how much she loves that? How dare he take that from her. My head feels as if it might explode with questions. The air has left my mouth and I can feel my heart throbbing. A dizzying effect takes over. The electronica music is pumping in my ears, loud and stifling. I search for Trish, want to physically move away from the man leering at me. Want to leave the party.

I retreat from Gage and head toward the front door with the intention of getting my coat when I see Anne enter the gallery. She's trailing behind a man who's introducing her to a group of people. She's already shaking another guest's hand, her mouth already forming the words, "Nice to meet you, too," when she sees me.

I keep moving toward her while scanning the room, this time faster, desperate to find Trish when another figure catches my eye. Slim with soft features and long hair and I know from the body, from the very cut of her shadow, it's my sister. I swear to God it's Dale. Suddenly, Marty is here, too, standing next to her in a suit and tie. And I can't tell who's real and who's not. I find Trish but she's talking to a group of people who look important. I gaze at the photo of Anne, then back to the woman who entered just to make sure it's the same person. I want to move faster but the room is spinning. I want to run to the real Anne and tell her not to look. I want to save her from the work, the way I wanted to save Lou, the way I wanted to save my sister who, after several glasses of liquor, seems to be following me. And I want my mother. I want my mother like I've never wanted her before. I want to apologize for everything. Everything that was her fault and for the things that weren't. For them not going to every doctor. For not trying every possible medication. For them waiting too long. And I want Bernard here, too. Want to tell him it was me. He wasn't too much man, but perhaps I wasn't enough woman.

I stare at Anne. Recognition starts when she glances my way. But then I see her eyes move from me to the wall. Her eyes grow wide. Her mouth drops open as her face contorts into sheer horror—mirroring herself in the photo. We both look to Gage and it clicks, he's the one she dated from the Internet. The finder of objects.

Gage begins to clap. Loud and sharp. "Well, well. What a surprise. One of my muses has shown. Ain't it a small world."

The room becomes silent. The music stops. People turn their heads toward her, their hands filled with mini plates and champagne glasses. Their eyes swell, their expressions register an array of different emotions: confusion, surprise, fright, pity. Then Anne is screaming, gut-wrenching and injured. "I can't do this anymore. I just can't."

They are the same words Honor used several weeks ago in Lou's room. They are the same words I utter every fucking morning of my life when I hit the alarm and realize another day is ahead of me.

She begins to walk toward Gage, tears streaming down her

cheeks, when something bright reflects off her face. She turns away from him and looks out the window to see where the light is coming from. A loud booming sound of a truck or something whooshes by outside. And then she's moving. Running. And I no longer want to stop her, but join. Want to follow, freefall with Anne. Tell her not to leave without me. I want to beckon Dale to grab hold of my arm and sail out the window with me as well.

I lurch forward, my hand extended, feel all the muscles in my neck and shoulder stretch. I hear the sound of glass breaking. Feel myself falling. Feel a sharp pain as I drop to the freshly glazed floor. Feel my head smack something as my eyes close.

It's a month later when I repeat this entire story to my sister as I sit by her grave site. I fill her in detail by detail because it's the last time I'll be visiting. The last time I can conjure her up. Even the dead need to say good-bye.

Heavy wet flakes of snow clump together, making the cemetery look like a huge quilt. The air is so cold it seems almost thick, and it freezes in my lungs. It's icy and lonely. I watch leaves drop. Watch people pass by. I look at the rows and rows of tombstones— a sea of fading grays and tans, breaking apart and chipping—and think of how many lives are no longer. And how cold my sister's body must be. The grass is brown, the trees thin and barren. Though I'm dressed in thick layers, like someone prepared to go hiking in the Arctic, it does nothing to protect me from the wind, which cuts through the flannel and wool. I feel a small vibration, hear a loud roar from the subway above my head. It collides with the chirping of birds and my own heavy breathing.

The scar above my eye is still red from where the stitches were removed two weeks ago. If Marty were still alive I'd have joked that we now have matching wounds, a family trait.

The man who brought Anne as his date was the first to run down the stairs and see if she was breathing, which she wasn't. A circle of guests stood over me, and I vaguely remember thinking how nice it was not to be the one in charge this time. How nice it was to have someone tell me to lie very still, have someone else hold my hand until the paramedics came. Tell me what happened—that I split my head open when I hit the floor, that bits of glass from the window cut me, that I passed out for a few moments. To ride with me in the ambulance, sit with me while a plastic surgeon Novocained my forehead, then stitched me up.

I stand, brushing snow and leaves and dirt off of me. I lay the lilies against Dale's headstone. Like the rest of the cemetery, it feels cold, the stone solid and bumpy in some spots, smooth like glass in others.

Old habits die hard and I do one last room search.

I use the key to let myself in. No need to knock, I know no one's inside as I enter into familiarity. I strain to smell the faint fragrance of crisp citrus. I see the bouquet of yellow roses, take note of the plant off to the left, another on the window sill.

I walk into the living room. It's modern and sleek with its chrome chairs and coffee table, glass dining room table. The cream suede couch, piped in black, and the cream plush rug, which is fluffy and clean, indicates she's careful with her belongings. Takes pride in her home. Though the room is bright and airy, there's a sadness that lines the cocoa-painted walls, sleeps under the bed, and is stored away in the cabinets. Most who enter this dwelling won't see it. It's odorless. Invisible.

A woman lives here. I know from the smell, from the flowers, from the books, mostly bios and memoirs, which tell me she's interested in people's lives, in their struggle. The music taste is harder to decode. Mostly groups—the Eagles, Fleetwood Mac, Coldplay—or compilations from the eighties and nineties, which tell me she's in her thirties, still holding onto her youth while the New Pornographers and Death Cab for Cutie say she's willing to step out of her comfort zone.

The closet houses white shirts and suits in browns, blacks, navy, and tans. Not a bright color is in the bunch. She's a serious, hardworking New Yorker. Nothing frilly or overly girly. That there are no short skirts or tight spandex dresses implies she's slightly tense, self-conscious, conservative, and tough.

The bedroom mirrors the living room. There are no stuffed animals, no overwhelmingly large pillows that engulf the bed. The walls are a cool minty green. The wooden antique desk and chair look as if they were bought at a flea market.

There are no prescription pills in the bathroom. The makeup and nail polishes are all soft neutral colors. Like the rest of the rooms, everything is neat and organized.

The kitchen is sparse and clean with its faux marble floor and matching countertop. Inside her refrigerator reveals the single woman's dining plan: bottle of white wine, champagne, orange juice, 2 percent milk, Diet Coke, vitamin water, Red Bull, Illy coffee, butter, eggs, a few random bottles of salad dressing, and condiment packets from takeout restaurants. Ice, frozen yogurt, and vodka are found in the freezer.

Satisfied, I look at my watch, take one last look, and walk to the front door where two black LeSportsacs reside. I estimate about six to eight days' worth of clothing are inside. Somewhere warm is on the docket since there are no skis, no sports equipment. There's no passport so the traveler isn't going somewhere exotic. A plastic bag from Toys R Us holds two presents, making one assume the traveler is visiting someone with kids.

The photo of two girls—one dressed as a cat, the other a mouse—hangs above my head. Rather than sadness, there's a slight, almost tiny drop of comfort. A reassurance that these children had love, from each other, even from their parents.

The back brace is in the compactor room, no need for it. The bracelet Lou sent me, a sterling silver link chain with mini silver-and-glass ashtray charms is a permanent fixture on my wrist. A second skin that reminds me I've quit smoking and that I'm connected to someone. The letter she wrote me is on the counter along with the thank-you note I received from Anne's parents after I spoke at her funeral. There's also an article from the *Times* that talks about Trish's gallery opening. The party, the dead girl on the street, and that a manager from the Four Seasons who sliced her forehead open upon hitting it on the floor, thankfully, isn't mentioned. Rather it covers her famous parents, makes generalizations about Trish, her eye for art, and highlights the man who did the portrait of Anne.

I take one last look around the apartment realizing that upon my return, everything will remain exactly as I left it. Things will go undisturbed. Unlike the hotel, no one will be cleaning up after me or erasing my existence. Rather, I'm surrounded by proof I exist.

I lift the bags, turn off the lights, and think of how much better this year will be. How I welcome the chance to start over. I don't need to say good-bye to Dale as I take one last look around my apartment before I get into the car waiting downstairs, which will take me to LaGuardia Airport. I know she won't be coming back.

This time the only one returning will be me.

Acknowledgments

An enormous thanks to:

The amazing, never tiresome team at William Morris Endeavor who always champion my projects and efforts; Lauren Heller Whitney, Anna DeRoy, and especially Andy McNicol, who keeps me grounded and is a constant voice calm and wisdom. I can't thank you enough for that.

The wonderfully enthusiastic team at HarperCollins: Mauro DiPreta, Sharyn Rosenblum, and especially Carrie Kania and Jennifer Schulkind, who understood these characters and embraced this project from the first page. A better duo of women I could not have found.

My writer friends and advisors: Dani, Shari, Darin, and Jen for their kind words and support; Charles Salzberg, for our Sunday-night dinners; Ross Goldberg, for his Web work and eye for detail; Jami Beere, for her never-ending gusto; and Jessica Knight, for being a terrific assistant and friend.

And to my parents and dear friends, who were there from the very beginning to see this all come to fruition.